THE EIGHTH
DEADLY SIN

A Fictional Mystery
By

John S. Richardson

Raven Publishing, Inc., Tampa, Florida

THE EIGHTH DEADLY SIN

This book may be ordered through Raven Publishing, Inc.
at:
P.O. Box 271763, Tampa, Florida 33688
Or by calling 813-469-5626
Or by e-mailing johnillini@tampabay.rr.com

ISBN 0615317685

Cover Art by Anna M. Richardson
Photographs by Heather N. Richardson
Layout by CrunchTimeGraphics.com
Printed in the United States of America

www.ravenbookwatch.com

DEDICATION

To my wife and soul mate Deanna and my wonderful daughters Anna and Heather, who not only encouraged me to continue writing, but also provided much needed technical support and to the many friends who encouraged me to keep writing until the book was finally finished.

Cover Art by Anna M. Richardson

Photographs by
Heather N. Richardson

"The boundaries which divide life from death are at best shadowy and vague. Who shall say where one ends and the other begins."

Edgar Allan Poe

PREFACE

THE FOLLOWING INFORMATION IS PROVIDED AS AN INSIGHT INTO THE REAL LIFE WORLD OF THE SERIAL KILLER. *THE EIGHTH DEADLY SIN* IS A FICTIONAL ACCOUNT OF JUST SUCH A KILLER. ALL OF THE CHARACTERS IN THIS NOVEL ARE FICTIONAL, YET WHO IS TO SAY THAT SOMEWHERE IN THIS WORLD, AS YOU READ THIS NOVEL, IT IS NOT REALLY HAPPENING.

No one knows just how many of these demented souls are presently active and no one knows how many have never been caught. No one can tell you what one looks like, because they blend into society as if to create an invisible facade. According to information derived from articles on the F.B.I Web Site, VICAP (Violent Criminal Apprehension Program), you would look for a Caucasian male ranging from 20- to 40- years old of average build and appearance and in many cases, of somewhat above average intelligence. These people very often work in the same jobs as you and I and in many cases are our neighbors and / or co-workers. They are often consummate generic citizens.

In his book, 'Profiles Of The Criminal Mind', Brian Innes maintains that as much as 85 percent of the world's reported serial murders occur in the United States. Much of the rest are from Europe with England and Germany accounting for the bulk of those cases. These numbers, however, should be tempered by the fact that in the U.S. and Europe, reporting statistics and criminal apprehension programs are infinitely better than much of the rest of the world. In many countries, much of this type of crime goes unreported or is erroneously categorized. More than 90 percent of reported serial killers are male with 84 percent being Caucasian. Eighty-six percent of serial killers are heterosexual. Eighty nine percent of victims are Caucasian with 65 percent being female. The reason that they are able to take so many victims before being caught is that they are for all intents and purposes, invisible. They blend into society.

Utilizing VICAP's extensive data base we are able to look at specific serial killers. Classic examples of these invisible killers start with the charismatic Theodore 'Ted' Bundy, a suave manipulator and former law student with the looks of an All American fellow. Through charm and guile he was able to lure young ladies away from safe places to their ultimate death. Bundy died in the electric chair in Florida after killing what some estimate to be thirty plus young women in Washington State, Colorado, Idaho, Oregon, Utah and finally Florida.

Dennis Rader, the BTK (Bind Torture Kill) killer, in Wichita, Kansas killed at least ten women, men and children including a family of five over a 35-year period. He was a church going man who ultimately rose in the ranks to become the leading deacon and assistant to the preacher at his local church. Rader provided the local press with his self-proclaimed nickname through a series of letters that he had sent to a local television station.

In a two and a half year period in the early 1980's and on the heels of Ted Bundy's crimes in and around Seattle came Gary Ridgeway, a factory worker who murdered at least forty eight women in Washington State. Because he dumped so many of his victims near the Green River, east of Seattle, he was dubbed by the local press as "The Green River Killer."

Ridgeway often went door to door for his Pentecostal church espousing the scripture. It is believed in some circles that his proclaimed goal in life was to rid the world of prostitutes. He was arrested and convicted of forty eight murders on the 18th of December, 2003 and avoided the death penalty by disclosing the locations of his victims.

During the years between 1978 and 1991, the cannibal Jeffery Dahmer, murdered 17 boys and young men mostly in the city of Milwaukee. He dissected many of them keeping some of the remains in jars in his refrigerator. After his arrest and conviction Dahmer was beaten to death by other inmates in prison.

Perhaps the most famous American serial killer of recent times was a fellow who was voted "Man of the Year" by the junior Chamber of Commerce in his home town in Iowa. Named after an American Icon, this monster even dressed as a clown for children's events in the Chicago suburb of Des Plaines. Beginning in 1972, John Wayne Gacey murdered 33 young men burying 14 of them in the crawl space under his home.

Although the list is endless, several other noted American serial killers of recent memory are: Richard Ramirez, "The Night Stalker," in Southern California; Angelo Buono and Kenneth Bianchi, "The Hillside Stranglers," also from Southern California; Edmund Kemper, the 6-foot-9-inch serial killer from Northern California; Anthony De Salvo, "The Boston Strangler"; David Berkowitz, "The Son Of Sam," in New York City; "The Zodiac Killer," in the San Francisco Bay Area who has never been caught; Wayne Williams, who allegedly killed as many as 20 boys and young men in the Atlanta area and Henry Lee Lucas, the good old boy from Georgia who claims over 100 victims, although most of them were never confirmed.

While less common among serial killers, let us not forget the fairer sex. Aileen Wuornos, Florida's famous female serial killer. She preyed on older men who were looking for sex, killing at least eight victims.

Unique in the annals of serial killers was Charles Manson, from Southern California, who as a family man held true to that concept by having his family do his killing for him. Finally, the world's most famous serial killer, London, England's, "Jack the Ripper," name withheld pending further investigation.

Many serial killers have been diagnosed as both, sociopathic and psychopathic. In part, this translates to persons who demonstrate anti-social behavior and show no remorse for what they have done. For some unknown reason, sociopathic individuals do not possess a conscience like most people. Don't be misled by their actions; they are among the best actors and actresses in the world. They learn at a very early age to appear sympathetic when the need arises in order to blend into society. A noted PHD and expert in the field of human behavior, Martha Stout, authored a book called, "The Sociopath Next Door." In her book, she maintains that "one in twenty five ordinary Americans secretly has no conscience". Does that mean that all of these people are serial killers? Not even close. Many sociopaths go through life without ever bothering a soul. Many are captains of industry or petty criminals, but it is those few who go over the edge that ultimately become serial killers.

Why do some sociopathic psychopaths kill, while others do not? There is a theory called nature/nurture. Occasionally, a person, specifically a male, is born with a propensity to commit violence. In theory, according to Brian Innes this is because of an abnormal makeup in their chromosomal structure or in some cases, a trauma to the head in early life.

Each of us has twenty three sets of chromosomes that control and contribute to things such as the color of our hair, the color of our eyes, the shape of our bodies and what sex we ultimately become. Normal females have an XX chromosome makeup while normal males an XY makeup. Occasionally, a male will be born with an XYY makeup and is considered a "super male" in some circles. This "super male" may actually have a marked propensity to commit violence. This phenomenon is seen in the nature side of the nature/nurture equation. If a person with a propensity to commit violence is raised in a volatile environment, typically with an abusive parent (the nurture side of the equation), the mix is often lethal. While this explains in part, the molding of a serial killer's early life, no one can yet say for certain what lies deep inside the mind of a serial killer.

What happens to a serial killer just before they kill is something that happens to all of us at one time or another. We get an urge. Unlike those of a serial killer, however, the urge that a normal person experiences is nowhere near as intense. A normal person, more often than not, can control their urges, a serial killer cannot.

In her book 'The Criminal Mind,' Katherine Ramsland, theorizes that the early signs of a potential problem in a young child include a fascination with starting fires and pleasure in torturing small animals. These symptoms hint at, but don't necessarily equate to what may be a serious problem later in life and have ultimately been associated with many serial killers.

THE CONNECTION: What prompts someone who is not a criminologist, psychiatrist or psychologist to write a fiction novel about a serial killer? On July 14, 1966, Richard Speck snuck into the student nurse's dorm at South Chicago Community Hospital and murdered eight student nurses. One escaped and eventually identified him. My younger sister was born in that hospital.

Before moving to Florida in 1973, I resided with my family near a suburb of Chicago called Des Plains, where we often shopped and frequented restaurants. It was there, in 1972, only a few miles from where we lived, that the aforementioned John Wayne Gacey began killing the first of his 33 young male victims.

The high school I attended in a suburb of Chicago was, among other schools, in the same athletic conference as a high school called Evergreen Park. Years later, when I first saw the high school picture of the Unibomber, Ted Kacznski, in the newspaper, I was stunned. I was certain that I had seen him somewhere before. While I could not pinpoint it, I could only assume that it was either at a sporting event, a shopping center or bowling alley that I frequented quite close to where he was raised. We attended high school at the same time only eight miles apart.

When I moved with my family to Florida, we settled in a suburb of Tampa called Carrollwood. Like many others that resided there, we shopped and went to the movies in a center called Main Street. On November 16th, 1984, police arrested Bobby Joe Long leaving the theater in Main Street shortly after he had killed his ninth Bay Area victim. His fortunate downfall was that he let one victim go. As an ironic side note, that young lady is now a county police deputy.

In 1986, Oscar Ray Bolin kidnapped and later murdered at least two teenage girls, taking one from a busy shopping center at the intersection of Dale Mabry Highway and Ehrlich Road in that same suburb of Carrollwood. The victim was kidnapped within view of many people. My family and I visited, shopped at and passed by this center on a daily basis during that time.

Throughout my life, I have lived in low crime areas yet have crossed paths with numerous serial killers without realizing it. While it is impossible to tell how many others may have crossed my path; the fact is that they are out there hiding in plain sight for all to see, but for only a few unfortunate victims to actually know. The irony of living among some of the most monstrous killers in the world without being aware of it is the inspiration behind this novel. There is no question that many other people, including perhaps you, the reader, have crossed paths with one or more serial killers in your life without knowing it. Do you think you have?

TESTIMONIAL

(Roula's Story)

It was the summer of 1977 in Yonkers and I remember that most of the people in and around New York City were preoccupied with the likes of one of its citizens and it wasn't Reggie Jackson of the New York Yankees. I lived in a multi-storied red brick apartment building on Pine Street just off Broadway with my husband and in-laws. The building had a courtyard in the middle and most of the tenants could see the back of the other apartments from inside the courtyard.

Each day I would walk down the stairs from my fifth floor apartment, get in my car and drive to my job in the nearby town of Mount Vernon. One morning as I made my way down the steps, I noticed that near the bottom there was a somewhat stocky man with dark hair sitting sprawled across the steps. He was a scary looking man and as I approached him, I asked him to move so that I could pass by. He said that I would have to tell him my name before he would move. I refused, saying that I didn't give my name to strangers. I then asked him his name. He said it was David and I eventually told him my name was Roula.

This went on for awhile and so it was that each day I would go down the stairs and say good morning to David who always sat in the same place, then go on my way. One morning after getting into my car to go to work, I found that it wouldn't start. Remembering that David was sitting on the steps again that morning, I went back and asked him if he would help me. He did help me and got my car started.

By then I had known him for awhile, so I thought that it would be the neighborly thing, to offer him a ride, since he was now headed down the street. He thanked me, but said it was only a short distance, so he would walk. I again offered, telling him that it wasn't a problem, and this time he accepted my offer to drop him off at his destination, which I did.

I remember that David lived across from our apartment but on the second floor. I also remember that his dog would often sit on the fire escape, particularly on hot days. My recollection is that most of the tenants did not like David, as his personality was rather offensive and in fact, he was not a very likable person at all. One day, when I came home from work, I saw a bunch of people gathered around his dog which was lying dead on the ground. It was rumored that someone had climbed up the fire escape and thrown his dog off to its death. Some said it was because of a grudge or something like that. When David found out about the dog, he literally went berserk, screaming and yelling obscenities at everyone

It wasn't long after that according to an article in the newspaper, that a woman saw a man tear up a parking ticket that had been placed on his car which was parked close to a fire hydrant. She called the police because she lived in an area where a recent murder of two people had taken place. The police linked that unpaid parking ticket to David and the Yonkers police were sent out to try and contact him thinking that he may have witnessed something connected to the murder. When the officers looked in the back of David's yellow Ford Fairlane, which was parked on Pine Street, according to that same report, they saw a rifle sitting on the seat. This then allowed the police to search his car and ultimately arrest the man that all of New

York had been looking for. The David that I had come to know, was none other than David Berkowitz, the Son of Sam serial killer.

I later read that David had killed at least six people and wounded seven others before being arrested on August 10th 1977. The Yankees went on to win the World Series that year, but no one, not even the Yankees got bigger headlines than the man who once rode in the front seat of my car

****

I want to thank my good friend Roula for sharing her true life experience and agreeing to allow me to include it in *The Eighth Deadly Sin.* Her story points out one of the truisms of life; that you just never know who might be living next door to you.

INTRODUCTION

As early as the fourth century, religious leaders dictated that there were sins inherent to mankind that exceeded the spirit and bounds of the commandments. They called these "The Seven Deadly Sins," also known as "The Cardinal Sins". These were sins of the spirit and of the soul; sins that did not necessarily affect another person directly. First identified by St. John Cassian in the fourth century, they were later listed by Pope Gregory the Great in the sixth century as to their nature, calling them: luxuria (lust), gula (gluttony), avaritia (greed), acedia (sloth), ira (wrath), indivia (envy) and superbia (pride) (Wikipedia.org). Because they were sins of the spirit and of the soul, they were hence, sins of the self, and those that were possessed of these sins were considered undesirables.

When Dante wrote "The Inferno" as part of "The Divine Comedy," during the fourteenth century, much credence was lent to the premise that these seven sins existed and were in fact, a reality of life. By accepting the dictates of this religious doctrine certain actions or inactions became sins because they didn't conform to the teachings of such doctrines; thus forming the basis for what cultures and societies would use as a measure for their citizens throughout history. One became branded as good or bad depending on their acceptance of these standards. These were not necessarily sins for which there were earthly punishments, such as imprisonment or death; for the sins, in and of themselves, did not violate prevailing manmade laws. Rather, these were sins of the mind and of the flesh that were regarded as unacceptable in the realm of religious doctrine.

For almost as many years as "The Seven Deadly Sins" have existed in the minds of mankind; writers, thinkers and scholars have tried, but in vane, to determine the nature of "The Eighth Deadly Sin". Numerous theories and hypotheses have been offered; some with good logic, many ridiculously inane and yet, there has never been a universally accepted definition of "The Eighth Deadly Sin".

Somewhere, in this account, is a latent reference as to yet another suggested definition of, "The Eighth Deadly Sin," through the mind of a demented killer.

CHAPTER ONE

A dense fog had set in, making visibility almost impossible as Lauren made her way through the cool, heavy night air toward her car. Beads of moisture trickled down her face as she fumbled in her purse for her keys. Suddenly she stopped and turned, looking back into the fog. Thinking she had heard a noise, she called out.

"Is anyone there?"

Hearing nothing, she continued toward her car. After several steps, she again heard something and turned quickly, staring curiously into the gray black mist.

"Hello?"

She could hear her voice crack slightly. Then there was only silence. As she turned again in the direction of her car, out of the corner of her eye she caught a glimpse of some sort of movement in the distance. At first she couldn't make out what it was, but as she stood there, unsure of what she had seen, it began moving toward her. She could now see that it was the silhouetted figure of another human being.

Turning again in the direction of her car, her pace instinctively quickened and with each hurried step she glanced back over her shoulder. The clicking of her heels on the concrete surface below was the only sound she could hear as the silent figure moved closer. Despite her quickened pace, she didn't seem to be getting any closer to her car, and she now could hear her heart beating faster from the fear of the unknown. As the figure was almost at her back, she screamed out.

"Help me!"

There was no one there to hear her cry for help, just her and the stranger in the mist. Then she woke.

Sitting in a chair in front of her computer in the middle of her den, perspiration dripping down her face and gasping for breath, Lauren now realized that she had had yet another of her recurring nightmares.

After regaining her composure, she sat in the darkened room, staring intently at the computer screen for what seemed like an hour; yet was only minutes. She consciously blocked out all of the sounds and images of the outside world and the light from the computer screen had symbolically become the center of her universe. So intense was her concentration on the screen that even the sound of someone walking on the wooden floor in the hallway didn't break the trance- like state that had overtaken her. It was only when she heard the door handle turning that she was finally able to come back to reality, quickly pressing the minimize button on her computer to hide what she had been looking at.

"Lauren," her husband called out, "grading papers?"

"No, Brian, just responding to queries to the English Department web site."

While she had, in fact, been answering web site queries, she had stopped momentarily to watch the traffic in a chat room, which is when she must have dozed off.

Her husband leaned into the entrance to the den and shook his head.

"Lauren, you should have been born five hundred years ago so you could have lived that stuff. I have never seen anyone so wrapped up in a job as you are."

English literature was Lauren's first love. Although she was aware that Brian knew little about the subject, she had nevertheless tried to relate to him what life was like at the dawn of that era some five hundred years ago.

"Perhaps I was, Brian."

"Yeah, and maybe I was William Shakespeare," he chuckled.

Lauren sensed that Brian felt he had gotten the best of her. She turned her gaze away from the screen and toward him.

"Surely you jest, my lord, for I have learned over the years that the inability to express one's emotions is a trait necessary for acceptance in the field of law and order. And after all, Shakespeare was a romantic, not a cop."

A broad grin spread across her face as she stared into his eyes.

"Yeah, well when you finally realize that some of us have to take care of the real world out there, maybe you will come to appreciate what I am rather than what I'm not." He turned and left.

From the time Lauren was a young girl, her world had centered on the great works of English literature. She lived to teach and the great romances and tragedies of that period often seemed to mold her life. Perhaps it was this aspect of her personality that put a real strain on her fifteen-year marriage, a marriage that had already defied the normal odds in the world of law enforcement. Or perhaps it was the grim reality of her husband's job as the sergeant in charge of the Homicide Detective Division of the local police force. In any event, the last several years had found them drifting farther apart and for reasons that neither of them fully understood.

Lauren's relationship with her father had been very close. She sensed that Brian felt that his unexpected death two years ago was the trigger that started pulling them apart. Her father had lived out his life in the same small town in upper New England where Lauren was born, eking out a living doing odd jobs after the death of Lauren's mother. There had been times when Lauren would talk long distance with him twice daily and hardly a day would go by when she didn't look at his picture. It was only recently that the depression she felt after his departure seemed to ebb.

While her state of mind had improved, her relationship with Brian hadn't and, in fact, had changed for the worse. Lauren was quick to assure Brian that while she did grieve over her father's death for quite some time, it had not changed the way she felt about him. Nevertheless, she always wondered why the local police and particularly her husband had not delved further into his death. To Lauren, her father had died under unusual circumstances.

According to the police report, her father had hung himself from a rafter in the small cottage where he lived. Since there was no reason to believe otherwise, the local police ruled it a suicide. Lauren was reluctant however to accept the fact that her father had committed suicide. She had just talked to him the day before the incident and he was in the best of spirits. She didn't understand why Brian seemed to readily accept the decision of the local police in her home town.

While they had once talked about going to counseling together, nothing ever came of it, and neither of them had made any special effort to reconcile their differences. Lauren, however, had sought counseling on her own through a psychologist who had been referred to her by a close friend. After talking with her at length, the psychologist told Lauren there was something from her childhood that she wouldn't let surface. He recommended Lauren see a specialist in childhood trauma. Shortly after,

Lauren rationalized that perhaps she didn't want to know what was beneath the surface that she was suppressing. She stopped going to see him and never did go to the specialist.

Despite having been raised in a series of foster homes, Brian St. John had risen above what life dealt him. Each day, he was faced with a dose of real life from the streets and yet somehow maintained a certain degree of tolerance for the world around him. Lately, however, the inner peace which was his best quality seemed to be eroding. He didn't understand what he had done, if anything, to turn their picture- book marriage into its present state of simple coexistence.

Lauren often told him how she disliked the stories of rape and murder that he brought home and of the criminals that went free on technicalities. These things seemed to be at odds with the natural order of her universe and didn't fit into what she perceived life to be. So, she shut them out. For the time being, she let him believe that this was causing them to drift apart. In her mind, while she rationalized this was at the heart of their problems, she knew instinctively that there was something else hidden deep in her subconscious. Something she didn't understand.

She loved the small liberal arts college where she had spent the last five years teaching English literature and on the surface this seemed to be all that was needed in order to sustain her. In her mind, life was orchestrated through the many classic stories that made up her day. These were the age- old tales of heroes and damsels and villains and dragons. Though not unlike life itself, in Lauren's world the hero always slew the dragon and won the fair lady's hand. The villain never got off on a technicality.

Lauren was fully aware that much of the crime Brian talked about had taken place in the many books that made up

English literature. However, unlike the reality of Brian's world, she found herself able to accept these crimes for there was always a final resolution. This had been Lauren's life for as long as she could remember and despite seeking counseling, she never could understand why she lived in these fantasies. She only knew they made her feel good.

She was an attractive woman in her early 40s and blessed with that rare combination of very fine, long flowing auburn hair and expressive green eyes. Her mother's great-grandparents had immigrated to this country from Ireland in the late 1800s and settled in rural Maine. Her father's family, which had been traced back over six hundred years, had immigrated from England and Scotland, making Lauren a true Anglo. Her features tended to lean toward the Irish side of her heritage and the tone of her skin gave the impression of someone who spent a good deal of time outdoors.

While she exercised regularly, it was to stay in shape rather than to keep off excess pounds, for she was also blessed with the kind of metabolism that kept her looking lean, no matter what life style she led. She often wore her hair up, which made her look even taller than her 5-foot-9 height. Despite being on the slim side, she was often told she had a very attractive body and carried herself with an air of sophistication that was the envy of many less confident women in her world.

Ever conscious of her image, Lauren dressed smartly, but in keeping with her conservative nature. Her wardrobe was anchored by numerous ankle length skirts and silk blouses. She had two dozen pairs of dress and casual shoes, as well as running shoes that saw regular use.

Among her closest confidants, Lauren was sometimes called by the nickname Guinevere, after Lady Guinevere, Queen to King Arthur, protector of the mythical kingdom of

Camelot.   While this chapter of history was significantly before the traditional beginning of modern English literature, it nevertheless captured her fancy. She ultimately became completely engrossed in that legendary union of two people and with the place that was considered the center of culture at the time in a land now known as England.

When Lauren and Brian first dated in college, he was a young, idealistic student of criminal justice. Lauren would often refer to him as Arthur, mentally putting him on a white horse riding off to defend her honor and the lives of those dedicated citizens of Camelot.

Professor St. John was truly a portrait in contrasts. On the surface, she had the appearances of a successful career woman with an ideal marriage. She was attractive, intelligent and had a beautiful body.   She exuded a confidence that set her aside from her peers, yet there was another side to her. This side was deeper, more troubled. It was a side Lauren did not understand, and it sometimes haunted her subconscious mind through recurring dreams.

These dreams had begun about two years ago and persisted to this day. Lauren had told her psychologist of seeing a silhouette of a stranger walking in a mist. In her dream, the figure keeps walking toward her, but never reaches her. She keeps walking away, but the figure keeps coming until she wakes, shaking and sweating from the reality of the image she sees and from the terror she feels.

Whatever it was, it was pulling her away from the real world and further into the world of fantasy. It bothered her, but the fear of what it was kept her from returning to counseling, at least for the time being. For now, she was content, finding solace in the words of the great writers and poets of times past. However, while she repressed thinking about it, buried deep in her subconscious thought was the rest of the story of the life of Lauren St. John.

Sergeant Brian St. John looked like a cop. He had short, neatly cropped brown hair and soft blue eyes. While not handsome in a classical sense, he was, as his attractive female partner often said, very easy to look at. Brian was tall enough that Lauren could wear heels when the occasion called for it and still be several inches taller than her. His body was lean, but with good definition, and he had been a better than average athlete in his younger days. His demeanor spoke of a soft confidence and he seldom showed any anger. Years ago, he attempted to find out about his ancestry, but had come up against a dead end. Brian truly did not know anything about his heritage.

Lauren believed that time and the many tragedies he was forced to witness in his job had changed some of Brian's long believed feelings about absolute right and wrong. It seemed to her that he now looked at criminals in terms of degrees of guilt. She, however, remained steadfast in her realm of literary fantasy and the resultant persona that came with it. The firm lines of right and wrong formed the premise on which her strength seemed to build.

Once Brian had asked her to go on a ride along with him while on duty. He thought it might bring her out of what he perceived to be a temporary rut by drawing her more into his world. Department policy prohibited relatives from riding along with officers while on duty, but because of his stature in the department, Brian was able to have the policy waived. He could not have picked a worse day, however. Shortly after the morning roll call, he was summoned to the scene of the brutal ritualistic murder of a beautiful woman about Lauren's age.

Brian was the homicide detective with the most experience and as the sergeant in charge he was assigned to take over the investigation. His department later learned that this was the third of three similar murders over the past two years in north and central Florida, none of which had been solved. The result of Brian's little experiment only served to push Lauren farther away, as the violence in his world was that from which she was trying to escape.

The rigors of his job were sometimes so intense that as time passed Brian found himself withdrawing more and more inward and away from Lauren. As his assignments often required him to be away at night, their paths crossed less and less as time passed. Encounters between the two of them over the past months had been, for the most part, brief with both of them going out of their way to be pleasant.

This night was no different. Brian returned to the den to give Lauren a quick kiss on the cheek on his way to bed. Before leaving, he turned and stood in the doorway just watching her. He almost spoke before catching himself. She was facing the computer again with her back toward him and while there was but a short distance between them, to Brian, she appeared far away, almost surreal. The moment had taken him back to years past. A tear trickled down his cheek as he began thinking about the many good times they shared over those years. He always enjoyed her extremes of enthusiasm and sorrow, and he shared those times with her as best he could.

Something had changed however, and Brian was about to respond to her last comment in hopes of gaining the upper hand. His instinct quickly stopped him, realizing that it wasn't important who won the exchange of words. Although he tried, Brian couldn't bring himself to say what was on his mind. He wanted to kneel in front of her and tell her that he loved her, but for some reason, yet unknown to him, he was unable to. He didn't want to leave this brief encounter on a sour note; so he spoke to her once again.

"Lauren, I'm sorry if I sounded cynical. Maybe someday I'll be able to say something romantic to you again. At least I hope so."

Lauren detected a hint of desperation in his voice and without turning, she responded.

"Thank you, Brian, please don't wait too long."

She instinctively knew that he felt a sense of urgency in her last comment, but said nothing more.

After saying goodnight, Lauren shut the door to the den and again turned her gaze to the computer. For a moment, her mind returned to a night two years ago when the two of them had gotten into the only real argument they had ever had. Lauren had met another English professor at a Shakespeare conference in Chicago and become quite enchanted with him. She had dinner with him and a group of other associates the first night of the convention, then just the two of them on the second night. They had talked well into the evening, and while she felt a bit guilty, she nevertheless felt a special kinship had developed between them. They thought and dreamed about the same things: English history and literature.

About a week after the conference ended, Lauren received an e-mail from him and they agreed to start exchanging ideas and experiences. She corresponded with him for several months before asking him if he would change his Internet name to Lancelot, the knight of the Round Table who had come between Arthur and Guinevere. Lauren found herself so caught up in the euphoria of the moment, that she agreed to fly to Chicago to meet with him again. Before she could mention it to Brian, however, he discovered the plane ticket she had purchased and became upset with what he perceived as a lack of common sense. Lauren knew Brian was right, but for some reason logic had deserted her. In the spirit of keeping the peace, she agreed not to go to Chicago and to cease all correspondence with the professor. This proved very difficult; however, even to the point that Lauren had left the door open between the two of them when she sent him what Brian thought was the last e-mail.

This incident, at least in her mind, had triggered what now seemed to be the force that was driving them apart. She could not understand what seemed to be a paradox in her life, for she had never before indulged in anything like that during their married years. It was as though her emotions were not hers to control. She likened her actions at certain times to that of a marionette, as though some outer force was pulling the strings that controlled the way she acted. She found over time that when these feelings overwhelmed her, they only seemed to last for short periods before subsiding.

The college had provided Lauren with a computer to be used for school business, such as answering web site queries from home. Tonight, there were several queries to answer so after exiting the chat room, she began responding to them one at a time. She turned the lights in the den off and the computer screen now formed a stark contrast in the darkened room as each query seemed to blend into an endless line of words without meaning.

A feeling of isolation began to overtake her and she felt totally alone when suddenly something alerted to her to a change in the energy level in her body and in the air around her. She looked over her shoulder, expecting to find Brian watching her, but he wasn't. Then the screen seemed to almost brighten, drawing her attention back toward something she felt was coming. After swinging her head back quickly and focusing on the screen, she sat up and the nerves in her body tensed, bringing her to a heightened sense of anticipation. She couldn't understand what had prompted this sudden change in the energy she was feeling, but now felt certain that some sort of contact was about to be made.

"What, am I losing it again?" she asked herself, recalling numerous other instances when she had feelings like this, but for no apparent reason. Lauren hoped that this time there would be a plausible explanation, so with her fingers poised to respond, she sat eagerly anticipating something that might explain the feeling. Maybe it was her imagination, but the screen now seemed to be pulsating without explanation. Suddenly a new query appeared.

I am trying to contact a professor in your English Department whom I understand has a unique interest in that period of English history that had to do with Camelot. I was given the name Lauren St. John and informed that she is an expert in this regard. Please have her contact me at the below internet address.

Her intensity escalated as she responded to CAMEO@AVALON.COM. Avalon, she thought to herself, The Isle of the Dead.

"I think I'll see if he knows what Avalon really is," she said aloud, as she chuckled then responded.

This is in response to your recent query regarding Camelot. I am Ms. St. John and I happened to be answering queries tonight so you need look no further. How may I be of assistance and what can I tell you about the college? By the way, are you from Avalon?

To her surprise, Cameo responded almost immediately.

But for one brief shinning moment there was Camelot.

12

Lauren recognized it as a line from the Broadway play "Camelot" and thought to herself, while it wasn't quite as literary as it could be, at least the person knew something about Camelot.

Cameo continued:

Cameo is my name, but in my heart, I am Prince Malagant and I have come on my white horse to rescue you from that which would divide your house. But for now my Lady, I must leave thee as quickly as I have come, for I must go off to fight yet another battle. Before I go, however, the answer to your question: No, I do not live in Avalon. That sacred island paradise is reserved for the spirits of King Arthur and his Knights of the Round Table. The spirit of the rogue Malagant would not be admitted. So until the morrow, I bid thee, Lady Guinevere, sweet night.

"I guess he knows about Avalon," she said to herself, "but how did he know to call me Guinevere?"

Her breathing, which intensified during the brief encounter, subsided somewhat as she sat and pondered what had just happened. Lauren questioned how it was possible to realize a change in the flow of the energy in the air around her while alone with only her computer. She wondered what he meant by going off to fight another battle. Was it truly symbolic of some deed or act that he was about to perform? All these things passed through her mind as she sat in the darkened room.

She could hear the muffled sound of her husband as he rolled over in bed, and it brought to mind the other comment that Cameo had made.

"He said, 'divided,'" she said aloud. "He said that he would rescue me from that which divided my house, and he called me Guinevere. What am I talking about? He doesn't know me, yet nevertheless had my nickname, but from whom?"

These were sobering thoughts that left her feeling quite uneasy, but the most disturbing thing to her was that he said, in his heart, he was Prince Malagant. It was Malagant, she recalled, in one of the many interpretations of the myth of Camelot that kidnapped Guinevere. She paused and thought to herself, with the exception of the heroics of Lancelot, who rescued Guinevere , it was only Malagant who knew what fate was in store for her. Nevertheless, this encounter had brought back a feeling of excitement that she had not experienced since meeting the professor in Chicago two years ago.

CHAPTER TWO

The sun shines nine out of every 10 days in Florida, but many of them are either too hot or too wet to ride around with a convertible top down. Lauren bided her time waiting for that first cool day after the long hot summer and down went the top on her 1966 powder blue Ford Mustang convertible. She could have easily afforded a new car, but opted to keep this one because it reminded her of her father. She received it from her father's estate when he passed away. The Mustang had been kept in a garage during the last years of her father's life, which he spent as a semi-invalid. Lauren had it restored to mint condition. Perhaps she liked the car because it made her feel different or perhaps because it had been her father's, but whatever the reason, she wouldn't part with it.

It was fall, and the air was cool enough for a sweater, so the drive up Interstate 75 to the college was a real pleasure. She made it perfect by putting a CD of old songs by the Platters into the small portable CD player on the seat beside her. She especially loved music from the 40s and 50s, a time when things were easier to understand and deal with than in today's world.

Brookshire College was located about 30 miles north of Tampa and a few miles east of Interstate 75 in a somewhat rural area of Pasco County. After exiting the interstate, she drove through the small nearby town and over several hills until she reached the college. The campus consisted of five Spanish style buildings with red tile roofs spread across the banks of a sizable lake. The lake was surrounded on all sides by hills, including the one on which the school rested, essentially forming a valley around the lake.

The main administrative building, which also housed the English Department, was once a Spanish mission. A huge bell hung on the top and there was an ornate fountain surrounded by a circular driveway in the front. There were only about 1,500 students, and because of the somewhat remote location, all of the students stayed either in dorms or rooming houses in the small nearby town of only 2,000 people.

Lauren's day started as usual with a visit to the faculty lounge for a cup of black coffee, no sugar. She was always one of the first to arrive and only her immediate superior, the head of the English Department, was there ahead of her, reading a magazine called 'Modern Crime'. He didn't bother to look up when Lauren greeted him.

"Morning, Arthur,"

"Morning, Ms. St. John," he responded.

Arthur Holmes was a cranky man in his early 60s who hardly ever smiled. He had lost most of his hair to father time, was slightly overweight and read through a pair of horn- rimmed glasses with bifocals. His suits never seemed to fit properly, and his shirt was almost always partially untucked. Having never married, Arthur still lived alone; thus his personal life remained a mystery to most of the other staff members. One thing, however, that everyone did know about him was that he loved a mystery.

Arthur left his native Scotland as a boy to come to the United States with his family, spending a good part of his earlier years in rural Massachusetts. He alleged to be related in some obscure way to Sir Arthur Conan Doyle and maintained it was his family name that gave the great author the inspiration for Doyle's fictional character, Sherlock Holmes. Hence, Arthur had taken a keen interest in the Sherlock Holmes mysteries very early in life. While no one actually believed him, they nevertheless gave Arthur the benefit of the doubt given his stature in life.

"Did you know, Ms. St. John, that Sir Arthur Conan Doyle was knighted for his work in connection with the Boer War in Africa in the early 1900s?"

"I suppose, sir, that is why they call him, 'Sir,', Sir" she replied in a somewhat patronizing tone. A day did not go by that Arthur didn't tell some member of the staff something about the man he so admired. Lauren just took it in stride and went about her business.

The click of her heels against the tile floor echoed through the empty corridor as Lauren made her way to the small office she called home. Despite the fact that she never seemed in a hurry, she always walked at a quick pace. The style and grace with which she carried herself left little doubt in any man's mind that this was no ordinary woman.

"Mornin', Ms. St. John," a voice called out. She recognized it to be the custodian, Clement Bell. Clement was an aging, somewhat squat man, who had spent the past 15 years of his life here at the college.

"Morning to you, Clement," she responded with a broad grin.

She knew Clement never missed a chance to watch her walk down the hall and felt that he probably waited there for her each morning just to say hello. Her smile never let him down.

Once inside her office, she opened the blinds and breathed in the magnificent view of the lake through a huge picture window. This setting had been a consistent source of inspiration for the many poems and short stories she had authored; though she had yet to have anything of significance published. She wrote more for own gratification than she did for others', as it seemed to bring her closer to the world she loved.

Her office furniture was a testimony to the subject she loved and taught. Book shelves made of dark English cherry lined the entire wall. The book titles on the shelves read like a 'who's who' in English literature: Shakespeare, Keats, Byron, Wordsworth and Scott with a bust of William Shakespeare right in the middle. To Lauren, Shakespeare's writing represented that period of English history when everything seemed to be in flux. During the time of the 'rebirth of learning'; called the Renaissance, the Tudors controlled England. Henry VII and VIII, Mary Queen of Scots and Elizabeth, among others, dictated the times. This era was marked by the English Civil War and Crusades and was more representative of English literature than Camelot which was more myth than reality. Lauren, nevertheless, related more to Camelot despite teaching primarily traditional English literature.

On the wall behind her, hung her diplomas for her graduate and undergraduate degrees from Columbia University along with an assortment of other awards. A picture of her father that sat on her desk seemed conspicuously out of place among all the references to English literature. With the office dimensions only 10 feet square, it was all she could do to fit in a conference table. On the table sat four or five dozen files that contained various assignments and reports turned in by her students. Despite the challenges of space, Lauren still considered it to be her home away from home.

****

"If you haven't already given me your topic for the research papers due at the end of the semester, I need to have them no later than the end of the week."

Lauren had begun her first class of the day, an elective for juniors and seniors, called, "Before the Dawn of English Literature." The course dealt with writings prior to 1476 when the printing press was introduced to England.

"Friday," she reminded the class, "we were talking about the relationship between King Arthur and Lady Guinevere and what impact Lancelot may have had on the moral issues of the day. In other words, are we to believe, based on the rumored affair between Lancelot and Guinevere, that this sort of thing was tolerated by that society? Was it commonplace, or simply accepted because of the stature of the people involved?"

A rather outspoken senior named Josh Martin raised his hand and without waiting to be called on began speaking.

"Professor, first of all, we are talking about the mythical kingdom of Camelot and hence the characters involved are also mythical, correct?"

Lauren appeared slightly annoyed.

"I suppose, Josh, it depends on how much credence one puts in the extensive research done by the scholars of the present and the past. Why do you ask?"

"Well," he said, "I have the impression, based on Friday's class, that you are convinced these people really existed, and based on some of your previous comments, you seem to be defending the alleged affair."

"I'm simply…."

Josh interrupted her.

"What I am trying to say is that if they are real people and subject to the laws and morals of the day, then why should Lancelot and Guinevere be exempt from scrutiny by the subjects of the kingdom?"

In an even tempered, yet firm voice she answered.

"Josh, first off, if you interrupt me again without raising your hand you will be dismissed for the rest of the class, understood?"

He reluctantly nodded his understanding.

"Good," she said. "If I sounded like I was condoning this affair, please understand that I was doing so to relate what unquestioned loyalty Guinevere's subjects had for her. Recall that I was talking about her subjects: the ones that followed her to Camelot after their own land was left in shambles at the hands of Prince Malagant. At least in the interpretation we are studying.".

Josh again raised his hand.

Showing her obvious impatience and annoyance, Lauren pointed toward him.

"Yes, Josh, what is it?"

"Although her subjects condoned it, I wonder if, perhaps Arthur's subjects viewed her as nothing but a slut."

Lauren's face flushed.

"Tell you what, Josh, you haven't yet given me your topic for the research project, so I'll give you one. You can report on just why you think Guinevere was viewed as a slut by King Arthur's subjects. And it damn well better be based on some solid research."

Josh threw his hands in the air. "I didn't think you'd take it personally…."

Without changing the expression on her face she interrupted him.

"Do we understand each other?" Josh nodded his understanding.

After class, Lauren returned to her office and began grading papers. She was reading a report when she was interrupted by a knock at the door. Without looking up, she answered.

"Come in. The door is open."

"Do you have a minute Professor St. John?" Josh Martin - entered and sat in one of the chairs facing Lauren.

"Yes, Josh, but only a minute."

Lauren was normally very receptive to her students and spent as much time as was needed to help them, but now she now seemed abrupt and irritated, tapping her pencil repeatedly on her desk without looking up.

"Professor, you seem to be concentrating. I can come back if it's not convenient."

"Not at all Josh, I just have a lot on my mind. There is something I have to attend to tonight, and I need to finish grading these papers." Her thoughts flashed to last night's encounter on the internet.

"Anyway what can I do for you?" Without waiting for his answer, she returned her attention to the report she was reading and ignored him.

He stared at her for a moment before responding.

"Professor, it's about the assignment you gave me, but you're in another world right now, so why don't I come back later."

"Fine, Josh, any time." She continued reading, so he left the room.

Soon after, Lauren stopped reading and her thoughts went back to last night's encounter with Cameo. These thoughts drifted somewhere between fear and curiosity.

The events of the day which usually kept her beaming with enthusiasm seemed a chore and she kept looking at her watch, wishing she could make time pass quicker. She was hoping to again correspond with this person to see what had prompted the contact in the first place, but without the risk of being interrupted by someone at the college. The e-mail he sent created a mystery in her mind and she wanted to resolve it before it became a problem.

She called Brian from her cell phone on the drive home to make sure that he would again be coming in late and was relieved to hear him say he might not be finished with a stakeout until morning.

Lauren and Brian St. John lived in an upscale lakefront condominium in a suburb of Tampa called Carrollwood. There were eight free standing units of about 2,300 square feet. Each unit contained three bedrooms and two baths. They were built so that each ground floor unit had a patio and each second floor unit had a balcony facing a ski size lake. The complex had a large swimming pool and jacuzzi with a tiki hut nearby. A long dock extended out into the lake with a gazebo at the end where several small boats were tied up. The facility was replete with amenities, and the front of the complex was hidden from outside view by a concrete wall anchored by a huge stately looking iron gate that worked by remote control.

Because Brian had no particular preference, their second floor condominium was a testimony to Lauren's taste. Old English furniture in dark cherry dominated the motif in all rooms except the family room. Early in their relationship, Brian told Lauren he did not care what she did in the rest of the home as long as he had one room where he could prop up his feet and watch football on Sunday. He was a staunch Tampa Bay Buccaneers fan.

In order to make it comfortable for him, Lauren decorated the family room in rattan furniture with brightly colored cushions of a floral design to give it the feeling of being outdoors. This, she often told visitors, was Brian's room.

When at home, Lauren spent much of her time in the den, which was anchored by a huge, natural cherry roll top desk she had inherited from her father. She had limited, but nevertheless fond memories of when, as a young girl, she would pretend to be a grown up working like her father did at this huge desk. Her father was as kind and as gentle a man as she had ever known. She often told people that all he wanted out of life was peace of mind and a small bit of happiness, two things that appeared to have eluded him.

She used the desk as a credenza and created a workspace by placing a huge slab of white marble with ornate edges on two wooden file cabinets. This was placed in front of the roll top desk, which sat against the wall farthest from the door. A swivel chair of deep burgundy sat between the two desks and because her computer sat on the roll top desk, she usually faced away from the den door when working.

Just as in her office, one complete wall was lined with book shelves that matched the cherry desk and contained upwards of 300 books. The floor was done in rich beige Italian tile and the walls were deep plum. The forest green stuffed leather side chair that sat beside her desk was all it took to complete the picture. Lauren had carefully chosen every detail to match a painting she had seen in an art gallery which depicted a traditional English room from the early 1900s.

After scanning the mail, she walked to the small bar near the window of the den that overlooked the lake and poured herself a glass of California Chablis. It was a bottle she had received as a gift from her college roommate and best friend, Robin Bennett. Staring into the clear glass of wine for a moment brought back memories of the several visits she had made to Robin's home in the small city of

Los Gatos in northern California. Lauren retained fond images in her mind of the trip down the peninsula from San Francisco and of the highway that wound its way through the foothills of the Santa Cruz mountain range to the outskirts of the Almaden Valley. There, the valley rose gradually into the San Gabriel Mountains, which seemed to be protecting this place from the outside world. Time appeared to have forgotten the small city where Robin lived and the people who lived there liked it that way.

The bottle was the last of the wine that Robin had sent her, each bottle having come from a different small winery near Los Gatos. The wine had been a gift for her 40th birthday, and it represented good times and friendship to Lauren. She had been saving the last bottle for a special occasion, but tonight, she thought to herself, she didn't need an occasion. She put off trying to contact Cameo for the moment.

With the bottle in one hand and a glass in the other, she went out onto the balcony and sat on a chaise lounge that overlooked the lake. A small sailboat seemed to drift aimlessly in the distance, and the azure sky was without a single cloud.

She poured a glass of wine and slowly drank until the glass was empty. As the late afternoon sun warmed her face, Lauren felt a soft glow overtake her so she poured a second glass. Instead of taking a drink, however, she raised the glass of clear white wine toward the setting sun and stared into the myriad of reflected light beams as if looking for something. The light beams seemed to dance back and forth and as she swirled the wine. An inner peace slowly engulfed her. She couldn't recall ever having felt so good and yet so alone as she did at that moment. It was a rare time when Lauren's mind was so completely at peace.

After relaxing for about an hour, Lauren logged onto the Internet and into a chat room that she occasionally visited. Watching the comments had often been a source of amusement for her, as she would mentally try to convert some of the dialogue into what might have been spoken 500 years ago. She once toyed with the idea of writing a short story that took place in old England, but with today's language.

While she enjoyed the inane nature of the many comments, she had yet to get into an actual conversation with anyone. It was still early in the evening, and there wasn't much activity, though she did recognize the first name that appeared: Jane Eyer. The name, she would later learn, was a play on Charlotte Bronte's character Jane Eyre from the romance novel of the same name. Still feeling a bit unfocused from the effects of the wine and perhaps because this person's name suggested a literary mind, even if misspelled, she succumbed to the temptation and for the first time started a conversation with someone. She used her Internet name: Guinevere.

Hello Jane Eyer, are you a governess?

She waited, and after several other comments, she received a response.

Finally, someone with an appreciation of literature. Should I call you My Lady or will Guinevere suffice? I sometimes think this Internet is an intellectual vacuum. You can't imagine, or perhaps you can, how many people have never heard of Jane Eyre.

Lauren was quick to respond: *Guinevere is fine, and yes I can-only one person in my recent memory figured out who Guinevere was. By the way, why did you misspell the name Eyre?*

Jane Eyer responded: *If noted, as you did, I know you're the real thing. Are you a teacher of some sort, or just like to read the classics?*

At this point the traffic started to get heavier.

Monster: *Hey ladies, I'm here. Anyone wanna do the monster mash?*

Several more senseless comments blipped by before Lauren replied: *I teach English literature at the college level, and I also do read every classic I can get my hands on. By the way, by any stretch of the imagination, has the name Cameo ever popped up in your internet travels?*

Jane Eyer again responded: *Not as I can recall. Why do you ask?*

Just curious, Lauren responded. *It is someone who recently contacted me on my school web site. The thing is that he asked for me by name. He then proceeded to call me Guinevere, my nickname. It was sort of eerie.*

Another comment separated her response.

Babe: *Yeah, monster, I'm ready, where do you live?*

At this point Jane Eyer opted to send an instant message so only Lauren could read it.

I don't know how long you've been doing this, but do be extremely careful. I once told a guy where I lived and from that day on, he harassed me. He found my telephone number and called me at all hours of the day and night. I changed my phone and called the police who tracked him down. They warned him, I think, and that was the end of it. Anyway, from then on I would describe a girlfriend of mine and make up a city just to get them off my back and give them something to do. Once, when I was half looped, I gave a guy my supervisor's name and approximately where she lived.

Why did you do that? Lauren answered.

I couldn't stand the bitch and wanted to get back at her for a lousy review, Jane Eyer wrote.

Did he contact her? Lauren asked.

Yes and I'll be damned if they didn't hit it right off. Jane Eyer responded, then added. *They met and started dating and all, and I think they will end up engaged. Ended up good for me though. She's much easier to live with now.*

Jane Eyer disappeared after that last comment, and Lauren reasoned that she was, embarrassed at what she had disclosed. She watched for another minute or two then got ready to sign off when suddenly, out of nowhere, there came a familiar name.

Cameo. *Guinevere, remember me? I'm the one who went to your school web site. I'm so happy to communicate with you again and to learn that you browse the web.*

The muscles in Lauren's face tightened, wondering if this was some sort of colossal coincidence. Nevertheless, she answered.

Cameo, how did you happen to be on line at the same time as me? And by the way, did you win the battle and slay a dragon?

Dude: *Like I'm fucking delirious for you, let's move on?*

Macho: *Hey, Gwen, ya want a real man, drop the wimp and move up.*

Dude: *Hey, Macho, I was here first, get lost.*

Shantuse: *Hey, Dude, why don't you and Macho both get lost.*

The senseless messages were beginning to irritate Lauren, and she was about to sign off, when Cameo came back.

Cameo: *I always win the battle Lady Guinevere. If I thought there was a chance of losing, I would not go into battle. And as for meeting you once again, here on the*

Internet, it must have been a colossal coincidence.

"Hardly an Arthurian attitude," she said to herself, then signed off without further comment. As she leaned back in her chair, Lauren thought to herself that his choice of words was curious: colossal coincidence. Then she uttered quietly:

"But how do I know that Cameo is a man?"

CHAPTER THREE

The new day brought clouds and cooler weather and Lauren was faced with yet another boring staff meeting. These monthly meetings were attended by department heads and senior staff members and since Lauren was a senior staff member, her attendance was required. She selected one of the many ankle length skirts from her closet, a black one this time and an off- white silk blouse. She dressed quietly so as not to wake Brian who had slipped in while she slept.

The skirt was a wrap around that parted as she walked revealing her legs well above the knee. This was contrary to Lauren's conscious effort to keep her legs covered, particularly in mixed company. She had the legs of a model, but became easily embarrassed if she inadvertently showed too much of them while in public.

After arriving at school, she stopped at the teachers lounge for a cup of coffee before going into the meeting. In her mind, most of the faculty members were pretty boring except for the most recent addition to the history department, a man named Greg Allsop. He was younger than most of the other teachers, perhaps in his mid- thirties and rumored to be single. He stood about six-foot-three and had the build of a young Adonis. His full head of jet black hair was slicked back, somewhat like a 60s greaser, and he was a very handsome man. None of the female staff, all whom admired him, could figure out why he was wasting his time teaching at a small remote college such as Brookshire. Lauren noticed on several occasions that he had been staring at her from a distance but hadn't thought much more about it. But someone else had.

Just before entering the conference room she noticed Clement, the maintenance man, standing off to one side.

"Hello, Clement." She said with a broad grin, knowing full well why he was waiting there.

"Mornin', Ms. St. John. Say, do you have a minute?"

Glancing at her watch, she shrugged while walking toward him.

"Sure, Clement, what is it?"

Clement was uncomfortable around women in general, but particularly around Lauren. Every time she came near, he would fidget with his hands and sway from one side to the other in a rocking motion. His constant motion was a bit irritating, but it wasn't that often that she was around him so she said nothing.

"Well, I just thought you should know that the new teacher, Mr. Allsop," he paused, "well, he sure likes lookin' at you."

"What do you mean, Clement?"

Clement squirmed a bit more then responded.

"Well, I know it's none of my business, but the other day when you was in your office, I saw him lookin' in your window. Stayed there for about five minutes seemed like, just lookin' in."

"Thank you, Clement. I'll keep an eye on him," Lauren responded. "Not at all an unpleasant thought," she murmured under her breath as she started back to toward the meeting room. Before she turned to go in, she couldn't help but notice that Greg Allsop was standing at the head of the stairs about 30 feet from the conference room, looking in her direction.

"Hi there," Lauren said, slowing down to see what his response would be.

"Hi, yourself," he said, as a broad smile captured his face.

Lauren paused, looked at him for a second, then walked in his direction until she was about five or six feet away. She extended her hand.

"I'm Lauren St. John." She could now detect the aroma of a musky after- shave that smelled like the outdoors. It made a statement to Lauren: that Greg Allsop was not afraid to let you know that he was a man.

"I haven't had much time to talk with you. Are you enjoying yourself here?"

He shook her hand.

"Then it would be very nice if you would take the time," he replied, ignoring her question.

The tone of his voice didn't tell her if he was joking or serious, but she didn't have time to find out. Someone called her to come to the meeting.

As she walked away from him, she couldn't resist continuing the little game.

"Maybe, I'll do just that Mr. Allsop."

It was a huge room with cathedral ceilings and windows that looked out onto the staff parking lot. In the center was a mahogany table that was long enough to seat twenty people with two large chandeliers that hung at each end of the table. Deep red stuffed leather arm chairs sat around the table. A large globe sat at one end of the room and a fireplace at the other with a matching deep red leather couch sitting in front of it. Over the fireplace was a picture of the school's founder, Martin Brooks.

Conrad Harrison, the current president of the college, was an overweight and somewhat pompous man of about 50 who didn't have much to do with the faculty. He only ceremoniously attended the staff meetings and often dozed off when one of the staff members was giving a report.

Lauren sat looking out at the parking lot which she found infinitely more interesting than the report on the lawn maintenance schedule that was being given. It was then, out of the corner of her eye, that she noticed Greg Allsop walking toward a black 1960s vintage Jaguar. Lauren knew it to be from that time period because a professor that she had once dated while in college drove one just like it. He was married which had gone against all of her standards, but she had found herself caught up in the romance of the moment, rationalizing that his wife was the cause of all of the professor's problems.

Greg Allsop stopped for a moment and looked around as though trying to see if anyone was watching him then opened the trunk. Removing a small black carrying case that resembled the type used to carry a lap top computer, he again looked around before shutting the trunk. As he made his way back across the parking lot he continued to glance behind himself. Normally, Lauren would not have given it a second thought, but she was curious why he had taken such caution to see if anyone was watching him.

About that time, the chair person signified the end of the meeting. Lauren made for the door before anyone could engage her in boring conversation and just in time to see Greg Allsop walk back by.

"Hello again," she said in an attempt to catch his attention. This time however, he appeared in a bit of a hurry, simply nodding to her as he disappeared down a hall, clutching the case under his arm. Curious, she thought, a bit ago he wanted to get to know me, and now he can't even stop to talk.

Making her way back to her office, Lauren began her morning ritual of grading papers. The students had not yet begun to filter in and as she sat at her desk, she could hear the sound of someone walking in the hall. The sound appeared to stop outside her office. Glancing up, she saw Greg Allsop looking in the small square window in her door.

Motioning him to come in, she swung around in her chair facing him as he entered.

"Hi," she said, a wide smile on her face.

"I'm sorry I didn't stop to talk earlier," he responded. "I had something to attend to. Anyway, I would like to get to know you better. I haven't really taken the time to make any acquaintances yet. How do I go about doing that with you?"

Lauren saw his eyes moving back and forth from her eyes to her legs and it was then she noticed that her skirt had slipped off her crossed legs, exposing much more than her comfort level allowed. She flushed at the thought of this handsome younger man staring at her legs, yet at the same time, she didn't want to make an obvious gesture that would surely embarrass him. She slowly rose, thus solving the problem before talking again.

"Well, why don't you join me in the faculty lunch room, say around 11:30?"

A smile captured his face.

"I'll be there, but don't leave if I'm a few minutes late, I have a class that ends about then."

Throughout the morning, Lauren kept thinking about him and the feeling she had gotten when she realized that he had been staring at her legs. In many similar instances in the past, she would simply cover her legs and offer a blank stare. This time, however, the feeling was different. Despite her embarrassment, she sensed a feeling of excitement.

At lunch five or six other teachers invited themselves to sit with Lauren, allowing her to direct only half her attention to Greg Allsop, who had joined her and whom she now called Greg. The conversation was mostly about classes, students and the like and anything but stimulating. Wanting to apologize for the crowd, she leaned toward him and spoke in a soft voice so that the others could not hear.

"I'm really sorry about the crowd and that we didn't get to talk much. Perhaps it will be less crowded another time."

He followed her lead, leaned forward propping his chin in his right hand, a foot from her face.

"Perhaps it wouldn't be so crowded at dinner."

Lauren was taken aback and it showed on her face as she leaned back in her chair, staring at him. She could feel her face become flushed and was at a loss to answer him when he came to her rescue.

"I know that came as a surprise, so I don't expect an answer, but do me a favor and think about it for awhile. Just an innocent evening, you pick the place."

She didn't bother to respond as he stood, left the table, then glanced back at her and smiled.

With the exception of the professor in Chicago, having dinner alone with another man since she got married never crossed Lauren's mind, in spite of the seeming deterioration of her marriage. Now however, she found herself beginning to rationalize that what Greg was proposing was simply a meeting of two colleagues. What could be wrong with that? After all, Brian had an attractive female partner, and he undoubtedly had dinner with her often.

The afternoon seemed to drag along slowly and by 5 o'clock, she had all but put the dinner offer out of her mind when the door to her office swung open and in walked Greg.

"Hi, given my offer any thought?"

She swung her swivel chair around until she was facing him and sat there as though in thought for a moment.

"To tell you the truth, Greg, I haven't had time to even think about it." Her face flushed at what was an obvious lie, but in fact, she hadn't yet dealt with the thought of having dinner with a good-looking single man without telling her husband. It was then that she again noticed his eyes moving back and forth from her eyes to her legs, which she now realized were again somewhat exposed. Lauren placed her hands on the sides of the chair about to push herself into a standing position when he spoke.

"Don't get up on my account."

She was startled for a moment.

" Whatever do you mean?"

"I mean just that. Don't get up. You needn't stand on my account."

She couldn't tell whether he was just being polite or wanted to continue looking at her legs, but she was quite nervous at the thought of sitting in front of this man with her legs now exposed well above her knees. She squirmed in the chair and didn't know how to handle the uncomfortable feeling so she just sat there, knowing full well that her face revealed her uneasiness.

"Well, what do you think?" he asked, "about dinner, I mean."

"I don't know. I mean, I am married...," she responded.

Greg interrupted her.

"As I said earlier, just an innocent dinner, colleagues getting together. You pick the place."

Lauren felt that she had lost control of the situation, and it took her back to a time in her senior year in college when she had last let her emotions rule her logic, having had an affair with the married professor.

"That's all it could be Greg,." she said, feeling a sense of intimacy overtake her. Her response had all but said that she would go out with him without really saying yes.

"Of course," he said. "Does that mean yes?"

"Let me think about it overnight. I don't often make snap decisions."

He turned toward the door.

"Hey, that's all I can ask. I'll be waiting with bated breath for your answer."

She sat alone without moving for several minutes, staring down at her legs and marveling at the fact that she had let this man look at her the way he did.

"My god," she said to herself, "I was posing for him. If I wasn't, then why didn't I simply cover my legs like I had so many times before?"

A smile captured Lauren's face as she began realizing that she had been in control of the situation. Greg had been captivated by her body, not her mind, which was an experience somewhat foreign to her despite the fact that she was a very attractive woman. Since her marriage to Brian, she hadn't let another man close enough to her to even consider the possibility that she was attractive to the opposite sex. In her mind she rationalized that the Chicago incident was one of intellect and not romance. Her thoughts suddenly focused on the legendary affair between Guinevere and Lancelot that brought about the demise of the union between Guinevere and Arthur. She felt a sense of guilt, but quickly put it out of her mind and went back to work.

After working for awhile more she looked at the clock on her desk and realized that she had lost track of the time. It was 6:30 p.m. and already dark outside. Stopping what she was doing, she listened but couldn't hear a sound from out in the hall. She reasoned that Clement had probably finished with his evening chores and left. Since there probably wouldn't be any teachers or students left in the building, she was most likely the last one to leave.

Gathering up her brief case and some papers that needed grading, she headed to the door, but glanced back at her desk before going out in to the hall. Something seemed out of place. After pondering for a moment, nothing came to mind, so she went out into the hall, closing the door behind her.

As the sound of her heels clicking on the tile floor echoed through the empty halls an eerie feeling came over her; a feeling that she wasn't alone. She stopped and listened. Hearing nothing, she again made her way toward the stairway that led down to the first floor. Again, she thought she heard a sound coming from somewhere in the hall behind her. Stopping and turning quickly, she peered into the darkened hallway, seeing only the shadows created by a dim light coming from the door to a maintenance closet which had been left slightly ajar.

"Clement must have forgotten to turn that light out," she said quietly to herself.

After reaching the head of the stairs, she took several steps down before again hearing another noise. This time the noise was more distinct. She was now at eye level with the second floor and peered through the wrought iron railings toward the dark end of the hall. For the briefest of moments she thought she saw some sort of movement in the shadows.

"Hello? Is anyone there?" She awaited a response, but there was none. Turning again, she made her way down the stairs to the first floor glancing behind her as she reached the bottom. It was then she was sure she heard a door shut on the second floor. She stood for a moment looking up at the stairs above her but wasn't of a mind to go back up to see who it was. As she reached the double doors that served as the main entrance to the building, she could make out what appeared to be the sound of footsteps coming from above her; so she again called out,

"Hello, is anyone there? I'm going to lock the front door." She waited, but no one responded.

Lauren pushed on the brass crossbars to open the doors then cursed aloud.

"Why won't this door open?"

The door moved only a few inches then stopped. She looked down and saw that someone had linked a chain with a lock on it across the bars that opened the doors, making it impossible to open them. Her head snapped back toward the staircase when she again heard the sound of footsteps which were unmistakably coming from the second floor. The sight of the chain on the door and the sound of footsteps coming toward her caused a rush of fear. She wasn't going to wait to see who it was.

Remembering that there was another exit at the end of a hall to the right, she made a hasty retreat toward that door, hoping that there was no chain on it. As she neared the other door, she could see that there was also a chain on it. The footsteps she heard now seemed to be right around the corner from her, so she retreated into the only other door she saw, which turned out to be a broom closet. Standing in the darkened closet, perspiration now dripping from her face, she wondered what had caused her to be so alarmed. After all, she was in her school building. Why should anyone be trying to harm her? She had no enemies. But that logic didn't answer why, if there was someone there, they didn't answer her. Then it crossed her mind that in the five years she had been at the school, she couldn't remember anyone ever putting chains on the door. Maybe Clement had waxed the floors, she thought. She was embarrassed that she had gone into the broom closet but, nevertheless, she felt very uneasy about the whole situation.

Suddenly, her thoughts flashed back to her office, and she could now see in her mind what had perplexed her just before she had gone out of her office into the hall. The picture of her father that sat on the right side of her desk had been turned face down. She gasped, putting her hand to her mouth to quiet the sound. Perhaps the cleaning people had turned the picture face down. That thought however didn't rest well with her since she was in her office until after the cleaning crew left for the day. She needed to deal with the problem at hand so she put it out of her mind for the time being.

After about five minutes of nothing but silence, she slid the door open a crack and peaked out in to the hall. She could see the exit and whoever had put the chain on the door had now removed it.

"Thank goodness," she sighed to herself.

After opening the closet door and going out into the hall, she made her way to the door that led to the side of the building, glancing back as she did. Once outside, she walked back toward and past the double doors to the school glancing back several times before finally reaching her car.

A window between the first and second floor and above the double doors afforded her a view of the landing between the floors and as she opened her car door, she again glanced in that direction. She was sure she saw some sort of movement on the landing, but in the brief second that she saw it, she could not make out what it was.

Perhaps a person coming down the stairs, she thought to herself. However, given her elevated level of fear, she decided going to go back to find out what it was wasn't an option. She got into her car, waited several minutes with the motor running then drove off.

There was no online chat that evening, only a glass of wine on the balcony and a great deal of thought and wondering. The night was an endless sequence of shadows and noises and broken sleep until she was no longer able to keep her eyes open. The incident had left her a bit shaken, wondering what or who might have been in the school and why. Lauren called the school and left a message for the security guard, who was only on duty during the day, to call her in the morning.

CHAPTER FOUR

It was morning, and Brian was coming home from a stakeout as Lauren was about to leave for work. He seemed a bit on edge and when Lauren asked how his night had gone, he snapped back that it wasn't worth talking about. In order to avoid any tension, she didn't push the issue.

"I'm sorry I snapped at you, Lauren."

"That's okay. I know it must be rough out there," she responded without expecting a reply. She got one anyway.

"It's bad enough that I have to put up with the criminal element, but when I have to fight city hall as well," he said, "it makes life pretty difficult."

"Meaning?" Lauren looked perplexed as she faced Brian for the first time during the conversation.

"Meaning," he responded, "I'm on a stakeout and can't find out the real reason why I'm - watching this fool."

"Anything I can do? Like listen?"

"No. Lisa…." He stopped in mid sentence. "That is, my partner, is a good sounding board."

Lauren stood, still staring into Brian's eyes for a moment before turning toward the door. She opened the door to leave for school.

"Well, at least you have someone to listen to your problems."

Daylight and the sight of friendly faces had taken the edge off Lauren's memories of last night as she pulled her Mustang into the faculty parking lot. Looking around, she noticed that Greg Allsop was just getting out of his car.

"Hey there, Mr. Allsop, how are you this morning?"

"Fine, Ms. St. John. And yourself?"

"Good as could be expected…," she replied, but before she could say anything else, he interrupted her.

"Have you given any thought to the dinner thing?"

She paused and looked into his eyes for a moment. The words that Brian had uttered this morning flashed through her mind: "My partner is a good sounding board.".

"Absolutely, Greg." She had dispensed with the formal talk. "I would love to have dinner with you. But only as a colleague."

"Of course, it's a start." He said as they began walking toward the school.

"It's a start?" she repeated. "What does that mean?"

"It means….." he paused, "…the start of a friendship."

"Oh." She looked at him and the corner of her lip started to curl into a half smile.

"Is tonight too soon?" He asked as he moved in front of her and stopped to await her response.

She thought for a moment and then looked into his eyes.

"No, I suppose not. Where would you like to go?"

He couldn't hold back a broad grin.

"Somewhere quiet. I hate noisy restaurants where you can't hear yourself think. Do you know that little Creole place in Ybor City?" He was referring to the old Latin section of Tampa that was once home to dozens of cigar companies. It was now a popular tourist area, sporting a multitude of clubs and restaurants, many of which served Cuban cuisine.

"You mean the one just off 7th Avenue?"

"That's the one," he responded. "How's seven o'clock?"

Not wanting to be committed if the evening didn't

go well, she replied:

"I will meet you there.

"Oh, by the way, Greg, were you at school late yesterday?"

"No, I actually left early. Why do you ask?"

"No reason," she said, hugging her books like a high school freshman as she walked toward the building. She smiled to herself at the sudden turn of events.

Once inside, she hurried to the small first floor office that served as security head quarters and found that the regular guard, Peter Gunn, wasn't there. In his place was a man whom she had never seen before.

"Hi, I'm Lauren St. John, one of the teachers here. Who are you?" The man stood, and as he did, stepped to within a foot of Lauren and looked down at her. She could smell the foul odor of his breath and body, and it appeared that he hadn't shaved in several days. She quickly stepped back and waited for his response. He stood there looking at her, but didn't say a word until she again asked: "Who did you say you were?"

He responded in a very deep and somewhat gruff voice.

"The temporary, ma'am. Mr. Gunn is sick today."

"Well, I wanted to report something to Peter. Will he be back tomorrow?"

"Don't know, ma'am. I'm a temporary. Just do as I'm told." After he finished talking, he went back into the small cubicle, sat down and then looked at Lauren with a grin.

She winced and took another step back when she saw his mouth was full of rotting teeth.

"Forget it. I'll get with Peter tomorrow," she said as she hurried off.

The rest of the day seemed to drag, but the events of

the previous day still lingered in her mind so before leaving for the day she went to the administration office to talk with the office manager.

"Mildred, do you know if there was anyone in the main building after school last night? I mean, after Clement would have left?"

Since Mildred was ready to leave, she joined Lauren and they walked to the parking lot.

"I can't think of anyone that would have been here. Clement usually locks up around six or so. Why do you ask?"

"I guess it's nothing," Lauren responded, "but I was pretty sure I heard someone in the building when I left. Around 6:30."

Mildred stopped and turned toward Lauren with a strange look.

"You know, for the past week or so I have had the feeling that there has been someone in the building that isn't supposed to be. Don't ask me why, because I really can't say; it's just a feeling," Mildred went on to explain.

"I left late once last week and was sure I heard a noise from the second floor. And I think everyone else had left. Left me with a real eerie feeling, you know what I mean? Do you think I should report it?'

"Not just yet." Lauren said. "Let's see if it happens again." She purposely avoided mentioning the chains on the doors, in order to not alarm Mildred anymore than she already had. Before she left, Lauren turned toward Mildred.

"By the way, who is that creep in the security office?"

Mildred's face took on a look of disgust.

"Don't know, but he looks like a Herman Munster who can't afford a dentist. Did you see his teeth?"

"Yuck!" Lauren replied. "He gave me the chills, but what happened to Peter? Is he sick?

"I heard that he got drunk and had an accident, nothing serious, but couldn't get up to come to work today."

"Funny," Lauren said, "I always thought he was a teetotaler. Hope he's okay. Anyway, see you tomorrow."

Once home, Lauren took an inordinate amount of time preparing herself for the evening. She repeated to herself over and over that this was just two colleagues getting together to socialize, yet her hair and makeup had to be perfect. She went through numerous combinations of skirts, blouses and heels before one finally caught her fancy. The decision was a silk lavender blouse and a black ankle length crepe skirt that was slit up the middle. It was the type that would surely show her black pantyhose and black heels when she walked. Staring at her image in the full length mirror in her walk- in closet, Lauren couldn't rid herself of the feeling that she was going on a real date and it made her feel a tinge of guilt. But, she rationalized, not guilty enough to let it ruin what she thought could be a very nice evening.

Lauren turned her Mustang onto 7th Avenue, the main street of Ybor City, driving past old buildings that resembled sections of the New Orleans French Quarter. Many of these turn- of- the- century buildings housed shops and restaurants on the first floor and apartments on the second. She glanced from side to side, looking at the wrought iron railings that adorned much of the architecture as she drove down the avenue behind a bus that resembled an old streetcar.

The numerous red brick buildings that once housed a multitude of migrant workers, whose only job was to roll cigars, had long since been turned into mini shopping malls with an accent toward specialty shops. At its apex, Tampa's cigar industry was the largest in the country.

Despite the city's efforts to make this part of the city a tourist attraction, it remained a high- crime area, being located within the police department's District 3: the worst crime area in the city.

Because of the city's large Latin population, Cinco de Mayo, the 5th of May, and Guavaween, the Latin version of Halloween, had become local celebrations resembling Mardi Gras, but on a smaller scale. These events, however, were overshadowed by a local celebration called Gasparilla, a day that is totally unique to the Tampa Bay area.

Beginning over 100 years ago, each February the locals re-enact an attack by the mythical pirate Jose Gaspar, sailing a replica of a pirate ship from St. Petersburg across the bay to Tampa where the mayor of Tampa ceremoniously surrenders the city to the pirates. After a day parade and a 5k race, the celebration culminates with a night parade near the main street of Ybor City, not far from where Lauren was to meet Greg.

Normal weekends would find throngs of tourists milling about Ybor City, gathering in the flavor of old Tampa, but being a weeknight, it was rather quiet.

After parking on a side street, Lauren walked about two blocks to the restaurant and upon entering noticed Greg waiting at the bar. This was, perhaps, the only Creole restaurant in the area and the decor gave a feeling of actually being in New Orleans. Once part of a house, the main dining room was separated into five or six smaller rooms by wrought iron dividers with grape vines hanging from them. Table cloths of red, white and blue adorned each table with a candle inside a wine bottle in the center. The menus were in French and English and featured numerous crayfish and gumbo dishes to complement the full gamut of other Creole and Cajun items.

Greg offered Lauren his hand as they followed the hostess to a remote corner of the back room where the hostess left them after lighting a candle. Perusing the wine list, Greg peeked over the top and looked at Lauren.

"Do you suppose they would think badly of me if I ordered a California Chablis?"

She looked at him curiously.

"How did you know chablis was my favorite wine?"

"I didn't," he responded, "but I did notice the book in your office on the California Wine Country, and I once read a statistic that more than half of all the women in the country that drink white wine prefer Chablis."

"Oh." Lauren looked a bit perplexed. "That must have been the book I picked up the last time I went to visit a friend of mine in California."

"What part of California?"

"A little town about 50 or 60 miles south of San Francisco called Los Gatos," she answered. "It's a beautiful place with a lot of small wineries near some foothills and not too far from San Jose."

"Do you visit her often?"

"What makes you think it's a woman?" she countered.

"I guess I just assumed it, because a beautiful woman, such as yourself, who is married, doesn't often fly across the country to visit a male friend. I have a bad habit of assuming things when I shouldn't. Hungry?"

"Famished," she said as she opened the menu. She looked at the waiter who had now approached them.

"I guess with white wine I'd better have fish." The blackened grouper was the house specialty and exactly what suited the situation, she thought, and ordered it.

Greg looked at the waiter with a half grin on his face.

"Make it two, and with the lady's, that makes three." He waited for the waiter to crack a smile, but there was none.

"I hope he didn't take me seriously," he chuckled.

"A man with a sense of humor is a rare thing today. What else don't I know about you?"

"I collect things," he said, smiling broadly.

"Really, what sort of things," she asked.

"Beautiful things mostly."

His comment brought about the obvious question.

"What sort of beautiful things?" She again waited for an answer that would tell her more about him.

Greg thought for a moment.

"Old books, weapons and toy soldiers. Oh, and sometimes antique jewelry, sort of like that brooch you have on."

Just then the waiter returned, and they both stopped to watch him as he opened and poured the wine. He commented to them in a sort of uppity way that French wine would have been a better choice.

Dinner was a pleasing experience for both as they talked about a myriad of subjects from school to politics. After they had finished dinner, Greg ordered them each a snifter of brandy and Benedictine and leaned back in his chair.

"Only thing missing is a cigar," Lauren commented.

"While it certainly is a generous thought, ma'am," he responded in an exaggerated southern accent, "I don't indulge in that sort of thing."

"Really, what do you indulge in, Mr. Butler?" She had picked up on his attempt to imitate Rhett Butler and offered her best Scarlett O'Hara. However, in her naiveté she didn't stop to think that a question like that directed to a man could open a hornet's nest. At this point of the evening, however, Lauren was feeling quite loose from the wine and after- dinner drink.

"Ma'am," he continued the game, "that is a question that you should only ask a gentleman. So, I shall answer in that vein." Lauren blushed when she realized what she had said. He continued.

"I mostly indulge in the arts, nature and things that lift the spirit."

"You are truly a gentleman, Mr. Allsop," she said, knowing that he had let her naive comment pass, "and I appreciate that more than you might know." .

Greg insisted on paying the check despite Lauren's efforts to split it two ways.

"I'll walk you to your car," he said. "If that's all right?"

"I would expect nothing less from a gentleman, Mr. Allsop."

As they neared her car, Greg noticed several young Latinos leaning against the building adjacent to where she had parked. His eyes never left the group as he opened the door for Lauren, so he didn't notice that she was staring at him while he continued to watch their every move.

"Lookin' at somethin'?" One shouted to Greg in a tone that seemed less than friendly to Lauren.

"Don't pay any attention to them, Greg," she said, finally looking their way.

"Just making sure all is cool, my friend," he responded and as he spoke, his hand went to the pocket inside his jacket. Lauren looked at him curiously but didn't say anything.

"All is cool." The apparent leader of the group responded, and Greg's hand slid down to his side.

"I've seen my husband react the same way, Greg.

What have you got in that pocket?" A grin captured her face.

"Nothing at all, Lauren," he replied, "and was hoping that they didn't know that. Tell me something: are you all right to drive? I mean, your eyes seem a tad, well, you know what I mean."

"I'm fine, Greg," she said, looking into his eyes. "Thanks for asking."

After she drove away, Greg stood in the street and stared at the group of men. One returned his stare as they sauntered away.

Since Brian wasn't there when Lauren arrived home, she decided to retire early and get a good night's sleep. Before she reached the bedroom, however, she felt a strong urge to go on the Internet. It wasn't nearly as strong as the feeling she had the other day, but nevertheless, a desire to have contact with someone.

After signing on and going into the same chat room as before, she immediately saw that Cameo was already there. Lauren was still feeling lightheaded from the wine and brandy she had consumed and had yet to focus on what was being said, when he wrote:

Nice to see you back, I have been waiting all evening.

Six or eight comments went by before she finally acknowledged him.

I've been to dinner with a colleague.

I missed you last night, at least on this site, he responded.

At this point, she reasoned that Cameo must live on the Internet since he has been on each time she logged on. After a series of senseless comments, she answered him.

Busy, busy, Cameo, but I did think of you.

Enough to meet me? he answered and after several other comments, Lauren responded.

Excuse me! Where did you ever get the idea that I would even consider meeting you? Still feeling the effects of the alcohol she typed*: Besides, I live in a far away place called Camelot and you couldn't possibly find me.*

Lauren's curiosity about this person was increasing with each response and again, just as the other night, she felt as though someone was watching her. She could feel the nerves of her body responding to something unknown and unseen, as though someone or something was trying to influence her actions.

Cameo responded*: I, my Lady, am a citizen of Camelot. Perchance we have encountered each other in another life. But don't be too sure that I could not find you. I think perhaps there is not another like you, so it may not be all that difficult.*

This comment bothered Lauren enough that she wanted to do something to throw Cameo off the track.

Again a series of other remarks passed, but Cameo didn't wait for her response.

Surely you must realize that as a citizen of Camelot I would have only the most noble of intentions. Yes, my Lady, I assure you we shall meet for but one brief, shining moment, just as before.

She leaned back in her chair and thought for moment before answering.

Well then, only if you can find me will you know what I look like. I live in a small city which is located in the foothills of the San Gabriel Mountains. I am a photographer by trade. You find me.

She signed off.

For some reason unknown to her, her first thought had been of her best friend Robin Bennett, but she felt that she hadn't given him enough information to go on, other than her profession. Therefore, she reasoned it shouldn't cause a problem. Nevertheless, it bothered her that she had done something so stupid, but now it was too late to reverse it. Lauren thought that she would at least rectify the situation by letting Robin know about her mental lapse. It was still only six o'clock in California and Robin may not be home yet, but at least she could leave a message. When she called, Robin's answer machine picked up.

"Hey, this is Robin. I'm walking Zorro, my Rottie, so leave a message, and I'll get back to you."

Lauren knew that Robin didn't have a dog anymore and that the message was for safety reasons.

"Robin, this is Lauren. I just wanted to let you know that I did a dumb thing." She went on to tell her about her online chats and the contact she had with someone, then asked Robin to be careful and forgive her.

"By the way," she said, "not that it matters because he won't find you, but if he did, he thinks your name is Guinevere. You know where that name comes from. Ta ta. Oh, and I need some more wine."

Lauren had slipped into some silk pajamas and was dozing off to sleep when she heard a sound like a car door slamming shut. She quickly got up and gazed out the bedroom window which overlooked the parking lot side of the condo. She could see Brian's partner, Lisa Cantrell, talking to him next to a police- issue black Ford.

Lisa was apparently dropping him off, which meant that at some point during the day she must have picked him up. It appeared through her somewhat blurry vision that their hands were touching, but she couldn't be sure. Lauren opened the curtains slightly, and as she peered through the parted curtains, her mouth dropped wide open. She wondered if in fact she was really seeing things right? It appeared to her that Brian had embraced Lisa then kissed her. She opened the curtains a bit farther in order to get a better look, but by that time Lisa had gotten back in the car and Brian was walking toward the door of the building.

Hearing the front door to the condo open, she quickly got back in bed and pretended to be asleep. A single tear slowly made it's way down her cheek and onto her pillow, but she remained quiet, not wanting Brian to know that she had seen him or for that matter, not actually knowing for certain what she had seen.

JOHN S. RICHARDSON

CHAPTER FIVE

It was the weekend and Lauren was still replaying the scene in her mind. How fortunate, she thought to herself, that she had not seen Brian for almost two days now. His latest stakeout meant that she didn't have to face him until she had time to gain her composure, for she would surely have broken down if forced to face him immediately. She knew full well that her marriage was shaky, but she never thought for a moment that Brian might be having an affair.

Lisa was an attractive redhead with the body of an aerobics instructor and had thus far made no attempt to get to know Lauren despite several overtures on Lauren's part. This only served to add to the suspicion in Lauren's mind. She only knew what Brian had told her about Lisa which was that she came here from California where she worked in homicide. She wasn't married and lived alone in a townhouse just off Bayshore Boulevard, one of the more upscale areas of South Tampa.

It was now Saturday and Lauren decided to go shopping close to the area where she thought Lisa lived. Hyde Park Village was an upscale shopping district in South Tampa, located just north of Bayshore Boulevard. This area of the city was a testament to Tampa in the 1920s and 1930s when many of the large old frame houses had been built. The entire area had recently experienced a restoration craze. Many older houses were being restored inside while still maintaining the outward look of the era in which they were built. The result had been to cause skyrocketing increases in real estate values.

Lauren strolled leisurely through the many quaint shops that encircled a small park with a large fountain in the middle. It was the lunch hour and most of the restaurants had outdoor seating that usually filled up quickly on a day like this. Consciously or not, Lauren had chosen to shop in an area that was only a mile or so from where she thought Lisa lived. After browsing for about an hour, she walked leisurely to the area where she thought Lisa lived on the off- chance that she might see her. Brian once told her that Lisa lived in a condo on a side street just off Bayshore and across from one of the oldest restaurants in Tampa.

Bayshore was a true boulevard that hugged Tampa Bay for about four and a half miles. The median that separated north and south bound lanes was filled with rows of trees and oleander bushes. Old mansions and stylish high- rise condominiums lined the boulevard. Some of these grand old structures had since become historic sites.

The view from the boulevard was breathtaking and afforded a panoramic picture of the bay and the downtown area of Tampa across the water. The wide concrete walkway on the bay side of the boulevard remained one of the favorite areas for local joggers and cyclists. Lauren knew she wouldn't be out of place having worn shorts, a short sleeve shirt and running shoes.

The sun was shining and it was 65 degrees so Lauren seized the opportunity to sit on one of the many benches that lined the walk. From here she could watch people going back and forth. She knew generally, but not specifically where Lisa lived but was quite sure it was close to where she chose to sit down.

Just as the warm sun almost lulled her to sleep, out of the corner of her eye, she caught a glimpse of a redhead rollerblading past her. From the back it looked like Lisa, but she couldn't be sure. The woman stopped about 200 feet from her and leaned against the ornate concrete wall that separated the sidewalk from the waters of the bay. She stood there gazing out over the glistening water, occasionally glancing back as though waiting for someone. The woman looked enough like Lisa from the back that Lauren decided to find out for sure.

Putting her sun glasses on, she began walking toward the woman when suddenly she stopped and stood staring in total amazement at what she saw. A tall, dark, good looking man dressed in casual slacks and a golf shirt had stopped next to the woman, who she could now see was definitely Lisa. Trying to look inconspicuous by only half looking in their direction, Lauren could see that the man had engaged Lisa in a conversation. The man she saw was none other than Greg Allsop. Lauren's face flushed, and she quickly turned away, wondering what she would do next.

While she was able to steal an occasional glance, Lauren couldn't hear any of their conversation. Her entire world was shaken as her mind searched for a possible connection between these two people, but to no avail. She didn't want them to know she was there, so when they began walking in the opposite direction, she followed far enough back so as not to be noticed.

After walking several hundred yards, Lisa walked across the boulevard, leaving Greg, who was now leaning against the concrete sea wall railing. Lauren watched Lisa as she walked toward a small, red sports car that was parked on a side street about a block from where he was standing. Removing something from the car, she began walking back across the boulevard toward him. As she got within about 100 feet, Lauren realized that Lisa was carrying a small, black case, like the one she had seen Greg with at her last staff meeting.

After exchanging a few words, Lisa handed Greg the case and rollerbladed away. While he had not spotted Lauren, Greg was careful to make sure that no one else was looking, peering from side to side before crossing back across the boulevard. He got into his Jaguar, which was parked on a side street, and drove off.

Lauren stood there for minute or so, wondering what she had just seen. Her world, which was already in turmoil, had just taken on a new dimension. Nevertheless, her stomach reminded her that she had not eaten all day, so she decided to return to the Hyde Park area and have lunch. She needed time to sit quietly and think about the recent sequence of events. Pausing momentarily, she opted to go a bit out of her way on her return to Hyde Park in order to pass by the red sports car and see if Lisa was still in the area.

After crossing the boulevard, she strolled slowly past the red sports car and as she did, glanced at the license plate, one that she wouldn't soon forget. Lisa, Lauren thought, had quite obviously had it personalized for what she felt was a testimony to herself. The license plate read: *Red Hot*.

Right then, Lauren caught a break. Lisa had just finished taking her rollerblades off and was entering a condo immediately across from where the car was parked. She made a mental note of the number 1194 on the door, then kept walking. At the next corner, she noted the street was called Sago Drive, then took a piece of paper from her purse and wrote down Lisa's name and address.

After arriving back in Hyde Park, she selected a restaurant and the hostess seated her at a small outside table that sat along a wrought iron railing next to the street. The table afforded a full view of the fountain and many of the shops in the area. Knowing that she had to drive home, she opted to order a bottle of sparkling water, then sat for about 10 minutes, staring into the dancing waters of the fountain. Her mind wandered, but rather than thinking about the situation at hand her thoughts returned to her best friend Robin Bennett. The more she thought about what she had done, the more she worried and decided she would call her again. She knew Robin's number by heart, but for some reason she drew a blank. She fumbled through her purse for her small book of phone numbers.

Strange, she thought, it's not in my purse. "Come to think of it," she whispered aloud, "I can't remember seeing it for some time now."

"Oh well," she said quietly, "I guess I'll have to wait until I get home to call."

Lauren knew full well that she would not rest until she found out what all the strange happenings meant and talked to Robin personally to tell her what she had done. She decided against lunch and headed home.

The drive back to Carrollwood took Lauren past the state-of-the-art football stadium which was home to the Tampa Bay Buccaneers. It was named for its sponsor Raymond James but locals call it Ray Jay.

Across the street was one of the most modern and upscale minor league baseball parks in America. Named Legends Field, it was the home of the New York Yankees spring training games. These two temples of sports were testimony to the continued dynamic growth that the Bay area was experiencing. Every time Lauren passed by this part of town her thoughts turned to Brian and his love of football. The drive home in traffic took about 30 minutes and the whole time Robin kept popping into her mind.

Upon returning home, the first thing she did was find Robin's number on the list she kept on the side of the refrigerator and call her from the kitchen phone. The same recording as before echoed through the phone, leaving Lauren with a very empty feeling. After leaving a message, she again looked at the list and called the number for Robin's photographic studio.

"Hello, this is Bennet Studios. We are not in at the moment; however, if you'll leave your name and number, either Zoro or I will get back to you."

"Robin, this is Lauren. I wondered if anything was wrong or if perhaps you didn't get my message. I feel really stupid for what I did. Please call me as soon as you can. Love ya and say hello to Zoro for me."

"Something wrong with Robin?"

Lauren dropped the phone and let out a gasp, not realizing that Brian was home. He had emerged from the den down the hall from the kitchen.

"My God, you startled me. When did you get home?"

"Been home all morning, must have just missed you. Where have you been all morning?" he asked.

"Oh, just shopping in Hyde Park, and no, I don't think anything is wrong with Robin. But I had called the other day and she usually calls me back immediately."

"Maybe she's on vacation or at a seminar or something," he said, "you know she travels quite a bit. Did you call her cell?"

"I know she's gone a lot, and no, I didn't call her cell. She just changed numbers and I can't find the new one," Lauren responded, "but she always checks her messages and calls me after I call her."

"There could be a number of reasons why she hasn't called," Brian said, "but if you don't hear from her in a few days, let me know. I have a colleague in the South Bay, a cop I met in Denver at the last convention. I'll ask him to stop by and see if there is any problem. He wouldn't have any jurisdiction in Los Gatos, but could certainly check things out."

"Oh, that would be wonderful, I really appreciate it and maybe it won't even be necessary. Let's hope so. You're very thoughtful."

Her face felt flush and a warm feeling came over her as she stared briefly into Brian's eyes. Brian had always been a thoughtful man and what he had just offered reminded her of that part of him that she so loved. Years ago, Lauren would have put her arms around him and kissed him to say thank you, but that now proved difficult for her.

Brian turned, heading toward the front door then stopped with a curious look on his face.

"By the way, what did you do to Robin that was so stupid?"

"What?" Lauren responded, pretending she didn't hear in order to buy some of time to think of an excuse.

"You left a message that you felt really stupid about what you had done."

For some strange reason, the wine that Robin had sent to Lauren popped into her mind.

"Oh, I asked Robin to send me a case of the same wine she sent me last year for my birthday. It's all gone."

"That doesn't seem so stupid to me. Anyone would do that for a good friend." Brian said.

Knowing that her excuse seemed lame, she quickly added.

"Yes, but I asked her to express it to me. I must have sounded desperate, and I wanted her to know that that wasn't the case. Or actually, it was the case, of wine that is, but not the case. Well, you know what I'm saying."

Brian shook his head.

"Only because I've known you so long. But if I didn't know you, I would think that you are the case. You know, mental." He laughed so Lauren knew he was kidding.

As he started out the door, Lauren called out.

"Brian, thanks again. It was nice of you to offer to call that other police officer about Robin. I'll let you know if she doesn't call back. By the way, will you be back soon?"

"I was only going to the store for a bit, but I really don't need to go. Why what do you want?" Brian stood at the now opened door, waiting for her answer.

"I just wanted to ask you something." Lauren became visibly nervous, having decided to test Brian's reaction by asking him something about Lisa.

"I can go to the store later. What did you want to ask me?" Brian said and shut the door, taking a seat at the kitchen table.

Lauren knew that she had to pose the next question in a manner that would not create any suspicion in Brian's mind, but would also illicit a definite reaction. The kind of reaction that would tell her if perhaps Lisa was a subject that was off limits. She was now regretting that she had done this on the spur of the moment, thinking that she should have given it more thought. Pausing for moment, she looked at him.

"Does your partner, Lisa, own a small red sports car?"

"Yes. It's a Porsche 968. Not new. I think it's a 1994." His face reflected his curiosity. Lauren couldn't see any other emotion on his face other than that of curiosity and that would be normal with anyone who was asked a question like that.

"Why do you ask?"

Her lips twisted a bit, as she knew that she might be playing with fire.

"Oh, nothing really. I thought I saw her today." She waited for any sort of response that would reveal an emotion on his part.

"If you were down in Hyde Park, it's likely it was her. She lives down that way, and she isn't working today." Lauren studied his face closely for any trace of anger, but saw none.

She was ready to up the ante a bit.

"This car had a license plate that said 'Red Hot' on it. Sounds a bit arrogant, if you ask me." She again studied his face, fully expecting him to react negatively to her last comment.

"Yeah, I agree," he said, "and I don't need to tell you that it causes me a lot of aggravation. You know all the bullshit comments from the other cops."

His face showed no anger whatsoever, which surprised Lauren. She thought that he would ask her where she had been or what she had been doing, but he didn't.

She thought for a moment, then decided to continue her questioning.

"I didn't recognize the man she was talking with, his back was turned to me." Brian's face muscles tightened and for the first time his face showed some emotion.

"Where was she?" he asked.

"On a side street. I had gone down toward Bayshore, because I love the drive along the bay and just as I turned onto the boulevard I saw, or at least I thought I saw, someone that looked like her. I know I saw that license plate. No mistake about that. That is really what made me think it was her more than anything else."

The intensity seemed to be building on Brian's face and it was obvious that this had bothered him.

"Anyway, that was all I wanted to ask you."

He didn't respond for a moment, appearing deep in thought.

"What?" he asked.

"Oh, nothing, I just said that was all I was going to ask you about. I was just curious."

All of a sudden, she sensed her face must be showing what she was feeling. Her face was flush. She realized there must be other, perhaps far more reaching implications to the conversation she was having. If Brian said anything to Lisa about this, she would most assuredly tell Greg Allsop. Then Lauren would probably never be able to learn what was going on between the two of them. She thought for a moment, then spoke again.

"Brian, I didn't want to get Lisa into any trouble, perhaps you shouldn't say anything to her."

"Please don't worry, I won't say a thing. I'll just keep an eye on her."

"Why?" Lauren asked with a curious look on her face.

"I probably shouldn't tell you this. Please don't repeat it, but I have been asked by the higher ups to keep track of her activities. I really have said more than I should." He got up and left.

Lauren was shocked by what Brian told her and for more than an hour after he left for the store she sat trying to piece things together. Had Brian really been asked to watch his partner and if so, why? Or was he perhaps trying to throw suspicion off of their relationship? If in fact he really was watching her activities, what had she done that would cause that kind of action on the part of the police department? How did Greg know Lisa? And what was in the black case? Her efforts to see if, in fact, Brian was involved with Lisa had only added more confusion to the whole situation.

After rehashing the facts in her mind, she finally decided to seek someone's help and who better than a master detective? She decided she would seek the help of Arthur Holmes, but without using the facts or real people involved. Picking up the phone while she looked up his number in the faculty directory, she dialed him and got an answer.

"Hello, Arthur, this is Lauren." She thought he would be surprised at a call on the weekend and he was.

"Why, Ms. St. John, to what do I owe this rare pleasure?"

"Arthur, I have a small problem and was wondering if a master detective like yourself could help me out." She knew the right thing to say as she could feel that Arthur was quite complimented at her having asked for his assistance.

"Yes, Lauren, what are the details?"

"Well, you see," she said, "I have this neighbor that I think is a little weird. He is always watching me, and I feel very uneasy about some of the things he does. I was wondering if you knew of any way that I could check his background. You know, to see if perhaps he has a record or anything like that."

She made up a story, because she didn't want anyone to know what was going on, at least not yet.

"Sure thing, Ms. St. John, if you will come see me on Monday, I will show you some programs that are available to check people out; you know, on the Internet. Or, if you want, I can do it for you."

"I should do it myself Arthur. I wouldn't want to get anyone in trouble needlessly."

"Okay, see you Monday then and don't you worry,

we'll nail this guy if he's a problem for you. Oh, by the way, did you know that Sir Arthur Conan Doyle was a medical student at Edinburgh Royal Infirmary in Scotland?"

"Really?" Lauren responded, trying to act interested.

"Holmes credits his mentor and teacher for the development of the Sherlock Holmes character. His name was Dr. Joseph Bell and he wrote a book called *'Eerie Trick of Spotting Details'*. It has been used time and again by would be criminologists for analyzing clues at a crime scene and the suspects themselves. Doyle even incorporated the 16th century sciences of physiognomy and phrenology, which...."

"Excuse me, Arthur, Physi- what and phreno- what?"

"Oh, Physiognomy was the school of thought that said that you could determine the nature of a person by their external features such as chins, teeth, nose, hair, and so on. It was, of course, determined to be mostly baseless in fact," Arthur continued without so much as a breath. "However, it can help in determining where a chap might come from or lived and so on. Phrenology followed and incorporated psychology. Well, anyway, you're not interested in all that, I'm sure. "

"Thanks, Arthur. I don't know how I got along all these years without that information," she chuckled. "Anyway, I knew you would be able to help me. SAC-D would be proud of you."

"Who? He asked.

"Why, Sir Arthur Conan Doyle of course."

"Oh, must be a generation thing," he responded.

CHAPTER SIX

It was Monday and upon arriving at school Lauren went immediately to the teachers' lounge where she hoped to find Arthur. As usual, he was the first one there and she was relieved that no one else was around to interrupt them. She wasted no time getting to the point.

"Good, morning Arthur. Can we get started?" Lauren seemed a bit abrupt and Arthur let her know about it.

"My goodness, Ms. St. John, you're in a real hurry. What is this guy, a serial killer or something?" Arthur laughed at what he felt was an extreme reference.

"Nothing like that, Arthur. He is just a man that makes me very nervous. By the way, I trust that you won't say anything to anyone about this. I want to be sure that there is really something to this guy before I go shooting my mouth off."

"Not a problem, Ms. St. John. You know there is an unwritten code among us investigators. Sherlock would never reveal any information until the moment was right and it had the most impact."

After speaking, Arthur folded his arms in front of him and leaned back with a satisfied look. Lauren sensed that he liked the fact that she had come to him with a mystery even if he perceived it to be a little one.

"Now if this turns out to be something real, I want you to promise to let me help you," he added, "you know you can't be too careful."

"Absolutely, Arthur, I will probably need all the help you can offer."

Lauren was stroking him, but had no real intention

of telling him anything. After all, it involved her husband and another teacher, and she did not want anyone at school knowing any of her private business.

Arthur rose and instructed Lauren to follow him to his office then locked the door behind them. His office was anything but a testimony to the image of the thorough, meticulous sleuth that he wanted to portray. His desk consisted of a conference table on which numerous books and folders were scattered about. An old brass lamp sat on the table and a floor lamp that looked to be losing its shade sat next to a stuffed couch that had a gaping hole in the middle of the back. Folders were everywhere, stacked waist- high on the floor and against the walls. Many of the stacks had accumulated months of dust. His love of the great detective, however, was evident everywhere. Posters of scenes from the many movies about Sherlock Holmes hung on the walls and a bust of Sir Arthur Conan Doyle sat atop a bookshelf surrounded by many of his works. A bronzed pipe sat on another shelf surrounded by many more articles associated with the legendary detective.

Arthur felt compelled to caution Lauren about sharing any of what they were about to do with anyone else.

"I must ask that you keep this to yourself, but there is a program on our main menu that can be used to look up people's background. It's called 'Tracker.'" He had turned his computer on and was looking at the menu.

"I always wondered what that program was and when I tried to get into it, it asked for a password."

"Right," Arthur added, "and I have the password."

"Because you're a department head, Arthur?" she asked.

Arthur stopped what he was doing and looked at her.

"No, Ms. St. John, because I stole it."

He chuckled at what must have seemed out of character for him.

"The only people who have the password are the head of administration and her staff and of course the old man." Arthur made reference to the head of the school, Conrad Harrison. "They keep it private because it costs a lot to use and they figure everyone would be checking out everyone else without permission."

"So how did you get a hold of the password, Sherlock?" Her voice bore a hint of sarcasm.

"For me to know, my dear, and for you to find out." It was the first time that she had ever heard Arthur refer to her as anything but Ms. St. John. Lauren reasoned that he was excited about the possibility of being involved in a mystery.

"Anyway when it asks for the password, you type in as follows." Arthur typed in the password, '*GERTRUDE*', rather than saying it out loud. "Then when it asks for your identity, you type in..." He typed the word, '*CONRAD*', ...for you know who."

It appeared to Lauren that Arthur was taking every precaution in order to maintain the secrecy connected with the program. She looked at him curiously.

"Aren't you being a bit over- cautious?"

"No, I am not," he whispered softly. "You never know what the walls hear. Someone could be listening as we speak."

She nodded her head and acted as though she agreed with him.

"What's next?"

"Well, as you can see, you have several options available to you," he said. "You can run a credit bureau, do a check of a drivers record, asset check, any professional licenses, and of course, criminal records. These can all be accessed by a choice of the person's name, social security, date of birth, home address, and so on. The more information you have; the more likely you are to find the person you are looking for. This is good for every state, and if there is anything available on the person in question, it will show up."

"This is terrific," she said, "I only hope she...." Lauren stopped in mid- sentence, "that is, the old duffer, is in here."

Arthur twisted his mouth and looked at her questioningly.

"Well, I sure hope you find her," he stopped, "that is the old duffer. Also, be sure you put Conrad in as the identification of the user. It's the old man's code. They never question him and he is half- way senile so he won't remember whether he used it or not. The others who have access to the program have to account for their time on line. By the way, don't order a credit bureau. You need the individual's permission for that. We don't want any law suits, do we?"

"Thanks a million Arthur. You're an angel and I won't forget the favor. By the way, who is Gertrude?" Lauren stood and was walking toward the door as she spoke.

"It's the woman who left the old man standing at the altar, the only one he ever got close to marrying. I'm not supposed to know that, but hell, I am related to Sir Arthur Conan Doyle, am I not? Oh, excuse me, SAC-D." Arthur's voice bore a hint of sarcasm.

"You certainly are, Arthur, and you know who would be very proud of you. It isn't just anyone who can appropriate confidential information like that."

"You're being kind, Ms. St. John. I stole it."

Within moments of returning to her office she was on-line and into the program, *'Tracker.''*   Since she had no data on either Lisa or Greg, she decided to try to identify each of them by a driver's license. Her first option was the state for which she typed in Florida. The next option was to go to the driver's license heading, followed by several options as to how to identify the party, including name, address, social security number and date of birth. Lauren led with the only thing she had and entered in *GREG ALLSOP,* then waited. The screen soon showed a list of three people with that name. Next to each one was their date of birth. She perused the names and oddly, none of them had a birth date remotely close to the age that she presumed Greg to be. It then occurred to her that he had only been in Florida for a short time and may not have gotten his Florida license yet.

She quickly backtracked and found an option entitled *National Search.*   Lauren again entered his name and the list came back with sixteen names. She scanned the birth dates and came up with three in the mid 1970s which would put them in their early to mid- thirties now.

One lived in San Francisco, one in St. Paul, Minnesota and the third in Chicago. She pushed the enter key on the one from California and the screen showed a home address, marital status and physical description as detailed on the drivers license: five-foot-five, red hair, green eyes, 140 pounds. She mentally eliminated him, then entered the second name, the one from Minnesota. The screen printed out a description: six-foot-eight-inches, blonde hair, blue eyes and 275 pounds.

"Must be a Viking," she said to herself. Then finally she entered the third name: six-foot-two, blue eyes, brown hair and 185 pounds.

"Bingo," she said aloud. She copied down the last

four digit's of his Social Security number - the only ones available, 5567; his date of birth, 11/18/73; and a home address of 435 N. Michigan Ave., Chicago, IL. Reading down the screen, it indicated that if you wanted to order any additional reports, press enter. She did.

She was now faced with three options: background report, credit report or criminal report. She opted for background first. Her face showed a look of bewilderment as the program ran its course and the results came on the screen: *NEGATIVE REPORT - NO INFORMATION AVAILABLE.*

She immediately went to the second report, credit bureau. Her face again revealed her apparent concern as the second report came up: *NEGATIVE REPORT - NO INFORMATION AVAILABLE.*

"Oh shit, I wasn't supposed to do that."

With eager anticipation, she entered the third option for the criminal report. Again, there was no report and Lauren couldn't understand why the name and personal data was in the computer, but no report of any kind existed. She immediately picked up her phone and called Arthur.

"Arthur, I found the person I was looking for in the computer and the date of birth and physical description matched. It even showed a home address."

"Yours, Ms. St. John?"

"My what?" she answered back. "Oh, my address, yes, of course, he lives in the same building as me."

She didn't know if her delayed response had confirmed what she felt Arthur already suspected, but didn't care much at this point.

"Right, next to you?" Arthur said with a hint of sarcasm in his voice.

"Oh, all right, so it isn't who I said it is, but that's not important now. What is important is that I accessed all three available reports, you know: background, credit and criminal; all three showed a negative report. No information available. What does that mean?"

"Appears to me, Ms. St. John, that your mysterious person has had his records wiped clean. The chances of a person having absolutely no information in any of the three reports is next to nothing." Arthur pondered for a moment. "The fact that their name and address appears is strange, however. If someone erased all the data in those three reports, why would they even leave the name and address in the data bank? Doesn't make sense. Anyway, let me know when you need some help. That is, when you really want to confide in me. By the way, did you say credit report?"

"Thanks, Arthur, soon perhaps, very soon." Lauren replied, "and yes, I screwed up, but since there was no report, I guess we're okay."

She immediately went back to the same program and entered *LISA CANTRELL.* Twelve names came up and she determined that perhaps four fit the approximate age of Brian's partner. Following the same procedure, she eliminated the first three by description and the fourth showed an address of 1515 El Cajon Blvd., San Diego, CA. She whispered to herself:

"Gotcha now, Red Hot."

She then ran the first report. As she watched the screen, the muscles of her face tightened and her expression took on a blank stare. The screen displayed: *NEGATIVE REPORT - NO INFORMATION AVAILABLE.*

Avoiding the credit report, she went right to the third program, which read the same. Lauren felt a cold chill overtake her and tiny bumps formed on her arms.

"Could I have input the information wrong?" she said aloud.

Not possible, she thought to herself, the names came up right. Was there a logical reason for what appeared to be a colossal coincidence?

"Not a coincidence," Lauren said out loud, "this has been done on purpose. But why?"

Since no answers were forthcoming at this point and classes were about to start, she put it aside for now.

Throughout the day Lauren kept a look out for Greg Allsop, but he was not to be found. She finally decided to go to the administration office and see where his next scheduled class was.

Miss Poindexter was a plump woman in her late 50s who reminded everyone of someone's Aunt Bea. She was equally as nosy, but very protective of any information that emanated from her office. She was a career secretary who had been with the college for most of her working life and knew pretty much everything that went on at the school.

"Hi, Mildred," Lauren smiled as she walked toward her, "can you tell me what classroom Mr. Allsop is in next period?"

"Yes, I could, Ms. St. John, but it wouldn't do you any good. He had to go out of town on an emergency. He'll be back in a few days."

Lauren looked puzzled and waited for Mildred to offer something else, but she didn't. She finally got tired of waiting and addressed her again.

"Do you know where he went?"

"You'll have to get that from him, Ms. St. John." A smug look overtook Mildred's face, which Lauren assumed was because she knew something that someone else wanted to know.

"Why, is it classified information? I just wanted to

talk with him." Lauren was a bit perturbed at this point. "Well, at least you can tell me when he is expected back."

"Not quite sure. He said a few days." Mildred let her know that the conversation was over as she turned and walked into the Dean's office.

Lauren walked back toward her office with her head half pointing in the air as if in thought. Most of the teachers and students were in class and the halls were empty, so the sound of her heels clicking on the tile floor was certain to be heard at a distance. Before she could reach her office a familiar face peaked around a corner and smiled.

"Hello there, Ms. St. John." It was Clement, the janitor.

"Hi to you, Clement." Lauren's face opened into a wide grin, "what are you up to?"

"Heard your footsteps coming down the hall and wanted to say hello." Clement went into his nervous fidgeting routine as Lauren stopped to talk with him.

She looked at him with an inquisitive half smile.

"How did you know it was me, Clement?"

"Oh, Ms. St. John." He blushed a bit. "There's no mistaking your walk. Only a nice lady like yourself sounds like you do."

"I'm curious, Clement, what sound are you talking about?"

Clement began shifting from one side to the other and twisting the fingers of one hand in the other then finally responded.

"Well, I don't know what this might sound like and I hope you will only take it as a compliment, but it's sort a like a thoroughbred horse. You know, they walk with a certain gait that tells ya that they're confident and refined."

"Thanks, Clement; I guess." she said, "I know it's a compliment. I've just never heard it put quite that way." It suddenly occurred to her that Clement, who always seemed to know what was going on in the school, might shed some light on Greg's sudden trip.

"By the way, Clement, did you know that Mr. Allsop was gone for a few days?"

"Yes, I did, Ms. St. John. Talked to him just before he left."

"Do you know where he went?" Lauren sensed that this conversation might lead her somewhere.

"No, only know that he flew somewhere. Somewhere far." Lauren's interest in what Clement had to say suddenly seemed more important.

"How do you know that, Clement?"

"Well, I overheard, by accident mind ya, I wasn't snoopin' or nothin'. But anyway, I overheard him making a plane reservation and I heard him say that it would take five hours to get wherever he was going."

This was the longest that Lauren had ever talked to Clement and it showed as he was now twisting his earlobe and standing on one foot with the other. While she felt sorry for what he must be going through, she nevertheless knew that she could use Clement's attraction for her to her advantage. She didn't want to ask him to do anything that might make him feel uneasy, so she opted to try and make him suggest something. Looking directly at him and with her most innocent face, she took the next step.

"I really need to ask him something about the upcoming semester. I can't imagine how I would go about finding out where he is." She looked away to give it time to sink into Clement's somewhat limited thought process. Finally, he spoke.

"Ms St. John, I think I might know how you can find out."

"How's that Clement?" She waited for his answer, impatiently tapping her foot on the floor.

"Well, I saw, by accident mind you, I was cleaning up his office at the time. Anyway, I saw him writing something on his desk pad when he was talking on the phone. You know, about going away." Lauren continued the ploy.

"Well, that doesn't do me any good, Clement. His office is probably locked, isn't it?' She waited for his response with the most innocent look she could conjure up.

"You must have forgot, Ms. St. John. I have the master key."

Lauren felt that he actually thought he was telling her something she didn't already know.

"You mean, you would let me in to his office?" She was almost ashamed of herself for manipulating this nice man. On the other hand, her mentor, at least in the area of investigation would be very proud of her, so she persisted.

"Course I would for you, Ms. St. John, but you can't say anything to anyone. Promise?"

"I promise and cross my heart." Her hand slid gently across the soft material of her blouse. Clement watched her fingers then moved to unlock the door.

Her heartbeat immediately increased as she entered Greg's office. A feeling of guilt came over her knowing that she was going to look at something she wasn't suppose to see. She had been plagued by a recurring and unpleasant memory since childhood. Each time she felt guilty about something, it would remind her of another time when she felt an unbearable guilt. She was 12 years old and had gone outside in order to peek in to her parent's bedroom after hearing what she thought were strange noises. She remembered seeing her father on top of her mother, both of them wearing no clothes. She never forgot the look on her father's face that day. She had already learned the facts of life and knew that he was trying desperately to please her mother. She remembered to this day, what her mother kept saying.

"Are you done yet, Joseph?" Over and over Lauren could hear her mother saying, "are you done yet Joseph?" She had watched as her father stood and walked away with his head bowed. A lone tear had fallen from his cheek. This had made her very sad, but it made her love for her father intensify from that day on.

"What's the matter, Ms. St. John?" She could feel that Clement had sensed the sadness in her eyes.

"Oh, nothing Clement, I just thought of something. I guess I feel like a voyeur, being here when I shouldn't."

"A what, Ms. St. John?"

"A peeping Tom, Clement."

"Oh, well you better peep in a hurry. Someone is liable to come along any minute, and you can't get caught in here."

She spotted the calendar on his desk and sure enough, it had a telephone number written on it with the comment: 'flight 1120, leaves Tampa at 9:30 A.M. and arrives 11:30 A.M'. It didn't seem like a long flight, she thought, as she jotted the number down. Just about that time, Clement poked his head in the door.

"Someone is coming. You need to get out of there before we both get into trouble." After she left, Clement locked the door and had taken a few steps just as two teachers turned the corner and passed by Greg's office.

Lauren made a hasty retreat to her own office and called a travel agent that she had used in the past. She gave the information to the agent, then waited for a moment before finally asking, where it was going. San Francisco was the agent's answer. Robin Bennett immediately flashed in her mind. Lauren knew that there could be no possible connection between Robin and Greg and that it was just the reference to the city that made her think again of her best friend. But it did prompt her to pick the phone up and call her one more time. The same response came on the other end, so she dialed Brian's number at the station.

"Hello, Brian." He immediately recognized her voice. "Remember you said if Robin didn't call me back soon that you could have someone in South Bay go over to her place and check on her? Well, I think it's time."

"Of course, Lauren, I'll call him today. Don't worry. I'm sure there is a logical explanation for this." Brian's soft, yet confident voice made her feel a bit more at ease, but she knew she would not rest until she knew if Robin was okay.

The station was normally a bedlam of activity in the afternoon and the noise of a dozen different conversations made it difficult for Brian to hear, but after waiting several hours for the time difference, he contacted Detective Manny Suarez in San Jose, California.

"Manny, it's Brian St. John in Tampa. I haven't talked with you since that seminar we took a couple of years ago."

"Como esta amigo, que pasa?"

Manny was a third generation Mexican- American with not even a trace of an accent, but he always greeted people the same way, in Spanish.

"Doing fine, Manny, just fine. How about you?"

"Right as rain, Brian. It's good to hear from you, what prompts the call?"

"I need your help. My wife has a friend named Robin Bennett who lives in Los Gatos…."

Manny interrupted him: "Great little town, I wish I lived there, but I can't afford it. No, San Jose is more on my budget."

Brian continued: "Anyway, this gal and my wife went to college together, and they keep in pretty close contact. I mean like if Lauren, that's my wife, calls her, it's never more than a day before she calls back. Well, she's been trying to reach Robin for several days now and keeps getting her recording."

"Maybe she's just on vacation or at a meeting or something," Manny answered.

"She has never gone anywhere for a long period of time without calling Lauren first. Lauren does the same for her. I guess it's their way of looking out for each other."

"Want me to look in on her?" he asked.

"Man, that would be doing me a big favor and maybe you, too."

"What do you mean, me, too?" Manny asked.

"Meaning, she's a dynamite looker. Long black hair, crystal blue eyes and a body that won't quit. You will definitely enjoy meeting her, I guarantee."

"You realize that I don't have any authority in that jurisdiction? But thanks for the assignment. I'll stop by tomorrow. What's the address?"

Brian thumbed through his address book.

"Here it is, 167 Royal Palm Trace. Her number in Los Gatos is 555-1616. Good luck."

With his work done, Brian put it out of his mind and went back to the report he had been reviewing on a break-in in an area not too far from where he lived. A woman had been surprised by an intruder while in the shower, but was able to set off the alarm in time, sending him scurrying out a window.

CHAPTER SEVEN

Lauren swung the door open and punched the four-digit code that deactivated the alarm to the condo. The red light on the answering machine was lit,. She pushed the button and listened to a message that Brian had left her.

I have to go back on the stakeout for a couple of days, so I won't be able to call you, but wanted to let you know that I talked to the cop in San Jose. He will check on Robin. When he calls, I left word for the station to call me. Be good and lock the doors.

"Lock the doors," she said quietly, "he's never said that before. Oh well, I do anyway." Still holding her briefcase and the mail, she checked the second message.

"Hi, Brian, this is Lisa. Sorry I missed you before you left. I hope your friend is okay. Anyway, have a good trip and don't worry about the stakeout, I'll handle it."

Click. The message was over and Lauren stood staring at the phone in disbelief, her face wretched in confusion as she tried to figure out what Brian was doing.

"Whatever it was," she murmured, "he apparently wasn't doing it with Lisa. But what could he possibly be up to that made him lie to her."

Since one message remained she played it. She could hear music in the background, but no voice. The music played for five or ten seconds then the caller hung up. It seemed strange to Lauren, but nothing to worry about. She shrugged her shoulders then placed her briefcase, cellular phone and the mail on the table next to the phone.

She had planned on grading some papers, but set them aside, picking up a yellow pad of paper, a bottle of

Chablis and a glass, then went out on to the balcony and sat on the chaise lounge.

For the next half hour she let the events of the past several weeks unfold in her mind, drinking two glasses of wine in the course. Finally, she began jotting down some of the pertinent facts as she knew them, saying each one out loud as she wrote them down.

"Lets see, first I am approached by the young Adonis, Greg Allsop and he asks me out to dinner." She cocked her head to one side as though in thought. "Amazingly, I accept and feel very good in the process. We are confronted by some sleazy punks after leaving the restaurant and he intimates that he has a gun in his jacket.

"What was next?" She tapped the pencil against her forehead. "Oh. I think I see the slut kissing my husband." She was feeling rather good now, and her last comment made her chuckle. "Then, I follow the slut on a Saturday morning. Oh, I forgot Greg and the small black case in the parking lot. Anyway, the slut meets, of all people, my Mr. Allsop."

She stopped for a moment and stared out at the lake.

"Did I say 'my Mr. Allsop'? What the hell is the matter with me?" The effects of the wine had distorted her normally formal speech and she blurted out, "Oh shit, I forgot about Cameo. Yes, I tell him about myself, no, about Robin." She laughed at herself with each mistake.

"Then I check out Greg and the slut, find them in the computer, but with no apparent backgrounds, like they had been erased on purpose." She giggled again.

Her laughing suddenly came to an abrupt end and her self- directed conversation stopped short as she heard what she thought was a noise coming from inside the condo. She quickly rose, spinning around.

"Is anyone there?"

There was no answer. The empty bottle of wine had taken the edge off her nerves so she shrugged and said sat down again

"Must be my imagination. Let's see, where was I? Oh, then I find out that Greg is gone for a couple of days and to of all places, San Francisco." Writing as she talked, she continued.

"Then my husband tells me that he's going on a stakeout, and he is really going off somewhere, using the excuse that a friend had whatever, died maybe. If anyone could hear me talking to myself, they'd think I was nuts. They'd probably be right." Glancing in the direction of the empty wine bottle next to her, she thought it might be a good time to get another bottle.

"Yes. I'll need it to solve this mystery."

Lauren had consumed more wine that she was used to drinking and as she rose to go into the condo, she stumbled and knocked over the empty bottle. Just as the bottle hit the concrete floor of the patio, she again thought she heard a noise coming from inside. The sound resembled a chair sliding across the floor. She cursed herself silently for drinking so much wine and not being in control of her faculties. While she had never been a regular drinker in the past, she noticed that lately she had been consuming more wine than she normally did. It seemed to make her problems go away, at least temporarily.

"I know," she said nervously, "I'll go on the internet."

She discarded the notion that she needed more wine and was content with the idea that it would settle her nerves if she could have contact with someone.

"Perhaps that Cameo person," she said quietly.

It was now dusk as she made her way down the hallway toward the den, leaning against the wall several times in order to catch her balance. Once inside, she flicked the light on and positioned herself in front of the computer screen, facing away from the door.

After getting on-line, her attention was again directed to another indistinct noise that made her spin around in the direction of the open den door behind her. Rising and peering into the darkened hall, she again asked if anyone was there. There was no response. She shook her head vigorously; trying to shake off the effects of the wine and clear her mind, then listened again. Hearing a noise this time had a more sobering effect on her as she peered down the empty hall half expecting to see someone; but there was no one there.

After sitting down and listening for several minutes, she again turned her attention to the screen, then announced her arrival into the familiar chat room.

"Ah," she said to herself, observing an endless line of meaningless comments, "the usual group of castoffs and perverts. Oh well, I guess I have to take the good with the bad." She tried to contact Cameo.

Cameo, are you there? I would like to talk to you.

A series of other comments passed by but there was no response from Cameo. She again entered her request.

Cameo, are you there? This is important.

Again there was no response. After waiting for about five minutes, she turned the computer off and sat motionless in front of the blank screen. It was then that she noticed the blank screen had captured a somewhat hazy image of the darkened hallway behind her. As she stared intently at the screen, a terrible thought came into her mind. Had she locked the door as Brian had suggested? She couldn't remember actually locking the door. However, since it was something that she did routinely, perhaps she did and it simply didn't remember.

Just as she began rising, her eyes caught what appeared to be some sort of movement on the blank screen of the computer. Spinning her head around, she looked at the dark hall, but there was nothing there.

"This must be the wine doing this ,"she whispered to herself. "I am not afraid. I am not afraid."

Standing, then moving slowly to the door, she turned the den lights off so that she wouldn't be seen if her worse suspicions were true and there was someone else in the condo. Leaning forward and easing her head out the doorway, she peered down the hallway. Night had set in and Lauren now realized she had not turned on any other lights in the rest of the condo. The dim moonlight shining through the balcony door at the other end of the hall was the only thing between her and total darkness. Gathering up every ounce of courage, she took a step out into the hall.

She could hear the beat of her heart with each step she took down the hallway. The images created by the light from the moon seemed to be swaying through the balcony window and ever so slightly against the wall at the end of the hall. The adrenaline in her system was now working overtime, bringing her to a heightened sense of the sounds and smells around her, things that she normally didn't notice. With the palms of her hands flat against the wall, she took a deep breath and continued the short, yet arduous trip to the family room. She inhaled and exhaled with each step in order to get better control of her rising fear, and all the muscles of her body became tight in anticipation of what she might encounter. The distance from the den to the family room was only about 35 feet, but to Lauren it seemed an endless trek. She labored with each step, her body now aching from the strain and tension of every muscle until she finally reached the end.

Once inside the family room, she was able to see a bit better from the effects of the moonlight shining in from the balcony. Her first inclination was to turn the light on, but she thought better of the idea, reasoning that if there was someone in the condo, they would then know her whereabouts.

Again moving slowly, so as not to make any noise, she was soon within a foot of the front door. She slid her hand methodically up the door frame to the knob. Her fingers slid across the smooth cold surface of the brass handle to the center where she was able to feel the position of the lock. It was all she could do to keep herself from screaming out, realizing that she had not locked the door. Just as she was ready to fling the door open and run, the silence was broken by the ringing of the phone. Lauren stood there frozen from the fear that gripped her body. Then she remembered that the people that occupied both of the units on the second floor of her building were on vacation. The tenants had a crime watch and always let others know when they would be gone. Because of this, she reasoned that running might not be a wise choice of actions.

The phone rang a second time, but she resisted the temptation to answer it, knowing full well that it would be a dead giveaway to anyone who might be in the condo. She held her breath momentarily so that the sound of her breathing didn't interfere with her hearing. The only other noise she could hear was the swaying of the trees in the gentle breeze outside. She knew that the answering machine was programmed to pick up after the sixth ring, so she waited, staring into the dim light coming from the open balcony door, half expecting to see someone. The machine finally clicked on and her voice answered.

Hi this is the St. John residence. We are unable to come to the phone right now, so please leave a message, and we will get back to you.

After the beep, there was nothing but silence on the other end until the tape ran it's course and the machine went dead. She stood by the door for several minutes waiting and expecting the worst, but there were no further noises. If she opened the door, the lights from the hallway would reveal her position. Even with the light from the moon, it was so dark in the far corners of the room that if, in fact, there was someone else there, she wouldn't know. She didn't dare lock the balcony door for fear that she might lock herself in with anyone who might be there. So, after standing in the dark for what seemed like an hour, yet in fact was only minutes, she was able to gather up enough courage to face the situation rather than run from it.

Several beads of perspiration made their way down her face, falling silently between her breasts. She began moving very slowly, very carefully toward the kitchen, just off the family room. A set of kitchen knives sat in a wooden block on the counter and with her hand shaking; she quietly removed the largest one. Now armed and feeling a little more secure she made her way back to the front door and locked it.

For a moment she toyed with the idea of calling 911, but held back, thinking that if there was someone in the condo, the sound of her voice would give her position away. On the other hand, she thought to herself, maybe whoever it was had left. It would have been easy for someone to have gone out the balcony door and crossed over to an adjoining balcony then scaled down some trellised vines, or for that matter gone out the unlocked front door.

With each passing minute, Lauren was gaining more confidence. The glow that she had from the wine had all but left her, bringing her ability to reason back to near normal. Perhaps the movement on the computer screen had been created by her distorted perception from the wine. Perhaps the noises were the same old readily explainable things that she had heard in the past, but had intensified in her mind from the fear she was experiencing. Perhaps Brian's insistence that she lock the door had made her a bit more paranoid than normal. All of these rationalizations seemed logical, but weren't enough to totally ease her nerves; the movement on the darkened computer screen was all too real to her.

Gathering up every ounce of courage she could and never taking her eyes off the darkened hall, Lauren slowly made her way to the darkest corner of the family room farthest from the hall. With her back to the wall and the knife clutched in both hands in front of her, she slid down into a sitting position. She peered into the darkness over the top of a coffee table that sat in front of her, propping her knees up in front of her, forming a sort of shield and rested her hands on them. With the knife still held firmly in both hands, the blade pointing upward, she sat waiting and watching.

Sitting in the darkness, she remembered what Brian had told her about a rash of recent break-ins in the area, and it was those thoughts that kept her on edge until she could no longer keep her eyelids open. Finally, sleep soothed her mind and the fear left like a bad dream.

CHAPTER EIGHT

The sound of seagulls in the distance woke Lauren to the bright sunshine of a new day. She sat for several minutes, looking at the knife that was still in her hands and at the open balcony door. My God, she thought to herself, she would have been easy prey if someone had been there last night. It suddenly dawned on her that this was a school day and when she normally got up, at least at this time of the year, it was still dark, so she must be late. Scurrying to her feet, she glanced at the digital clock in the kitchen, which read 7:00 a.m., then went down the hall.

She searched each room diligently for any trace of an intruder and could find nothing until she entered the master bedroom. Nothing seemed out of place, except her jewelry box. She was always careful to close it and yet it was open. Looking through the box, she saw that several valuable rings were still there, along with a diamond necklace worth about $4,000. To her, this meant that there had been no thief in the condo or these items would be missing. She noticed the brooch her mother had given her was not in the box. It was a family heirloom and while Lauren didn't think it was very valuable monetarily, it did have a lot of sentimental value, having been passed down through the family over generations.

A feeling of desperation overtook her at the thought of losing it, as the brooch and a few pictures were the only links to her mother she still had. Sitting on the bed for a moment, she began to retrace her steps of the past few days. It didn't make sense to her that someone would take the brooch and leave the more valuable items, so she reasoned that she must have left it somewhere. It suddenly occurred to her that she may not have taken it off the blouse she wore when she had dinner with Greg.

She went to the closet and quickly located the blouse she had worn that night and to her relief, it was there.

"Strange," she said softly to herself, "I usually wear it on the left side." After removing it from the blouse, she held the brooch in the palm of her hand and stared down at it.

She again spoke softly to herself:

"If only you could tell me what really happened. Why did daddy leave you after all those years? Why wouldn't he talk about it?" A tear rolled down her cheek as she recalled her early childhood when things were better.

After a hurried shower, she put her makeup on and put her hair up, though several strands fell loosely down each cheek, causing her to look a bit disheveled. She put on a full- length olive green skirt and a white silk blouse and stood in front of the full- length mirror which was mounted on the back of the closet door. While she wasn't quite happy with the way she looked, it would have to do. She was late.

Before leaving, she checked all the windows to ensure they were locked and then locked the balcony door. For some unexplained reason, she suddenly became a bit nervous and wanted to get out of the condo as fast as she could. After picking up her briefcase she set the alarm, then walked at a hurried pace down the hall. Glancing nervously as she passed the closed doors of the other condos, she finally reached the front door.

"I'm being ridiculous," she said to herself. "If there had been someone there, they would have done whatever it was they were going to do and left."

As she made her way through the morning traffic, it occurred to her that she should call school to let them know

THE EIGHTH DEADLY SIN

that she might be a bit late. By now she was merging onto Interstate 75 while looking for her cell phone. She opened her briefcase only to find that it wasn't there. She then recalled that she had laid it on the small table next the house phone when she came home the day before.

"Damn," she said out loud, realizing that she must not have noticed it sitting there when she picked up her briefcase before she left for school.

"Oh well," she murmured, "they'll have to wait."

All the way up the interstate, the events of the past evening kept racing through her mind. Had she really heard the noises and seen a movement on the screen or was it the effects of the alcohol?

"Nothing was missing, and I am safe and sound," she said out loud. Lauren had effectively convinced herself that last night was just her imagination and she was never in any real danger. As she turned into the driveway to the school, she remembered the phone call that had come in while she was standing at the door in the dark. She then realized that she had not stopped to check caller I.D. in order to see who had called. After coming to a stop in her assigned parking place, she made a note in her folio to check it when she got home.

Things went relatively normally during the day and an inquiry with the office let her know that Greg Allsop was still not back. As the day wore on, however, Lauren again became concerned about the strange sequence of events that had taken place over the past several weeks. She realized that perhaps she wasn't capable of dealing with them by herself.

She couldn't confide in her husband, because he was obviously lying to her about something. She couldn't reach Robin so that pretty much left one person. That person was someone she had known for over five years and who had never asked anything of her. In her mind, Arthur Holmes was beyond reproach and completely trustworthy. He was probably the only one she knew who might make some sense of the whole thing. She had now made her mind up to ask for his help.

She wasn't quite sure how he would respond, knowing that there was another teacher involved and possibly the reputation of the school. Further, Lauren's own husband, who Arthur thought the world of, was involved. Nevertheless, he was her only possible answer, so she stopped in his office before going home for the day.

"Arthur?" Lauren had quietly slipped the door to his office open.

"Yes, Ms. St. John?" He peered over the top of his glasses. "What can I do for you?"

"Well, remember how you helped me the other day, you know with the problem neighbor?" She felt a tinge of embarrassment, sensing that Arthur knew she had lied to him.

"Yes, of course, the old man."

"Well, Arthur, my problem goes much deeper than what I told you."

"And it doesn't involve your neighbor, does it?" He awaited her response.

"No, but I sensed that you already knew that. No, Arthur, this could involve several people and you know two of them. Frankly, Arthur, I don't know what to do about it. For that matter, I'm not quite sure that I even have a problem."

At this point Arthur's curiosity had been aroused. He stood facing her.

"Whatever do you mean?"

Lauren thought for a moment then looked directly into Arthur's eyes.

"I don't know if I have the right to involve you in this or whether you will even want to be, but I have no one else to turn to."

She knew that Arthur seldom got excited, but sensed that the smell of a mystery had started his blood flowing. He became visibly excited.

"It would appear that you have a mystery in your life, and yes, you have every right, Ms. St. John. I am your friend and colleague and for that matter who better than I to help solve your mystery?"

Her face broke into a broad grin and she put her arms around his neck and kissed him on the cheek. He blushed and touched the spot where she had kissed him with the tips of his fingers.

"I knew I could count on you, Arthur. You are a friend and you're right, there is no one else that I would rather turn to. This, however, isn't something that I feel like talking about at school. Can we meet somewhere?"

"Of course, Ms. St. John, name it."

"First of all, if we are going to be working together on this caper, you have to start calling me Lauren. Agreed?"

"Agreed, Ms. St...." He stopped in mid- sentence, "...Lauren, of course. Let, get on this caper." He smiled broadly.

"Good, let me call you at home tonight so that we can set something up. That will give me chance to put the details down on paper."

"Can't wait, Lauren, can't wait."

The day had gone by quickly and Lauren left the building, slipped into her car and started the engine, all the time wondering if she had done the right thing. During the ride home, she sketched out what she would tell Arthur when they met.

After opening the door to the condo and disarming the alarm, she put her briefcase down and noticed that her cell phone was not on the small table where she had left it. Noting that there were no messages, other than the hang up call from last night, she went to the bedroom looking for the phone, but it wasn't there. As she walked past the den, she saw that it was sitting on the chair in front of the computer. Puzzled, she picked it up then went back to the family room and pushed the retrieve button on her answer machine to find out what number had called last night. The number came up: 469-5626. Her face squinted a bit as the number seemed familiar, and then her expression turned to one of terror.

"My God, that's my cell phone number," she said aloud. Her breathing rapidly escalated, and she spun around as though expecting to see someone. "Someone made that call from inside the condo last night."

Fumbling through her briefcase, she found the faculty directory and nervously dialed Arthur's home number.

"Arthur, please help me. I need to meet with you now."

"Slow down, Lauren, what happened?"

"Can you meet me as soon as possible?"

"Of course, tell me where."

"There is a little Italian restaurant in Carrollwood called Savino's. It is near the intersection of…."

"I know where it is." Arthur had stopped her in mid-sentence, "I'll be there in an hour."

Savino's was adorned with traditional red and white table cloths and offered a wide range of Italian dishes in an intimate setting of only a dozen tables. Each table was separated by a lattice divider with interwoven vines and authentic looking artificial grapes giving each table a feeling of privacy. A small fountain bubbled in the middle of the main dining room, and the dim lights seemed to add the necessary touch that created the overall feeling of an Italian piazza.

Lauren fidgeted with the hardened wax on the Chianti bottle that served as a candle holder while staring nervously at the door. Finally, Arthur entered and immediately saw her sitting at a table farthest away from the entrance, the one that afforded the most privacy.

"Thank you for coming, Arthur. I know this was such short notice, but I guess I sort of panicked and needed to be near someone I could trust."

"I wouldn't have missed it for the world." Arthur responded. "I'm as curious as the Cheshire cat and was about to call you when you called me. How can I help?"

Without asking, Lauren poured him a glass of the Chablis from the bottle she had ordered before his arrival

"Where do I start?" She sat staring at Arthur for a moment, and then began talking again.

"First off, Arthur, I must ask you to keep all of this completely confidential. It is of the utmost importance that you don't reveal any of this to anyone, at least not now. Do we agree?"

"Yes, of course, Lauren." He smiled. She grinned and reached across the table, placing her hand on his.

"Arthur, you are a good friend and I shall never forget that you were there when I needed one. It means the world to me. Frankly, Arthur, I didn't know where to turn. I only hope that I am not wasting your time, for I truly don't know if I really have a problem or if the past several weeks have been a series of colossal coincidences. Anyway, here goes. I think someone broke into my condo last night, but that's getting ahead of myself."

For the next hour, Lauren described in detail everything that had happened from the initial contact with Cameo and the door being locked at school right up to the discovery of her cell phone being used to call her while she was in her condo. Arthur had taken a yellow pad out of the portfolio case he was carrying and took notes. Finally, her story told, she sat looking at him, not knowing what to expect.

He returned her gaze. "There are far too many coincidences for this to be nothing but your imagination. The incident with your cell phone is what makes this a truly dangerous situation. I believe there is something very sinister underlying this whole series of events and what we need is a plan of action in order to find out what it is. You can rest assured, Ms. St. John, I mean Lauren, we will get to the bottom of this."

Lauren could sense a feeling of pride in his voice. She had always thought that he lived a rather mundane life, but it now appeared to her that this whole episode seemed to be making him feel important again.

Arthur couldn't hide his enthusiasm. A grin spread across his face as he rose from the chair and tucked the yellow pad in his portfolio and offered her his hand.

"Come with me. I have something in my car that I think you should have." She dropped a twenty- dollar bill on the table and they walked out into the cool night.

Arthur drove a 1964 Austin- Healey sedan, a car that was very popular in the British Isles at one time. While it looked to be in good shape no one could figure how he kept the old thing running. Those close to him knew that he would drive it until it fell apart. It was, Lauren thought, his last remaining link with that part of his past.

"What do you have for me, Arthur?"

He opened the door and reached inside the glove box, removing a small leather valise and handed it to Lauren.

"Here, don't give me any argument, just keep it for any real emergency." She unzipped the valise and took out a small .32 caliber, five- shot chrome revolver. At first, she tried to give it back to him, but he made it a condition of him helping her.

"Lauren, I don't want to scare you, but I can only help you if you're still alive. I don't know if you know how to use it, but if not, go get some lessons and keep it with you. We have no idea what this situation is all about and you could be in danger." Lauren finally gave in and put it in her purse, hugging him goodbye before leaving.

"You are a true friend and don't worry, my husband is a cop and while I don't particularly like guns, I do know how to use one. Brian made sure of that years ago."

After starting his car, Arthur rolled his window down and offered some parting words of assurance.

"Don't worry, Lauren, I will be putting a plan together starting tonight, but by all means don't let your suspicions be known to anyone else. Act completely normal and give some consideration to having dinner with that Mr. Allsop again. We need to extract some more information from him."

As he drove off she felt a tear come to her eye, knowing that she had a friend as gallant as Arthur. Their meeting had made her feel much better than she had when she called him earlier in the evening.

"Give some thought to Mr. Allsop," she murmured to herself. "That's not going to be difficult."

JOHN S. RICHARDSON

CHAPTER NINE

Brian sat on the edge of the bed staring at a picture of Robin Bennett and his wife Lauren. It had been taken on Robin's last birthday when Lauren had spent some time here in California. Seeing the picture started him thinking back to when the three of them were in college together. Brian had always thought that Robin was the most beautiful woman he had ever seen and her glistening black hair and crystal blue eyes were still vivid in his memory. Just as his mind started to drift off, a voice from the other room brought him back to reality.

"Brian, make sure you don't touch anything. I don't want to have to explain another set of prints."

"Not a problem, Manny. I know the drill." Out of habit, Brian had already slipped on a pair of thin rubber gloves.

"You know, I'm taking a chance being in here with you even though your wife has a key. By the way, amigo, it seems a bit of an over reaction for you to come all the way out to California just because your wife hasn't heard from this gal. But I guess it must mean a hell of a lot to you, so what the hell?" Manny stopped next to Brian and looked at the picture he was holding.

"Thanks, Manny, I know that, but if you knew the relationship between Robin and my wife you'd agree that it wasn't overkill, especially since you weren't able to locate Robin. And I owe you one, Manny." He paused. "Do you see anything that might shed any light on this?"

"If you feel like you owe me one, Brian, a box of Cuban cigars might be a nice touch, but no, I don't see anything yet. Man, those are two beautiful women," Manny said as he looked over Brian's shoulder at the picture. "Which one is the Bennett woman?"

"The brunette," Brian responded, "and I'm sure you know that Cuban cigars are illegal in this country."

"Who's the other one?" Manny asked.

"My wife."

"You're a lucky guy, Brian."

Brian turned and looked at Manny with a solemn look on his face.

"Yeah, but luck has a way of ditching you when you least expect it."

"I won't even go there, amigo."

Brian walked slowly through the Spanish- style bungalow that Robin Bennett called home, glancing back and forth, searching for anything out of the ordinary, but nothing seemed out of place. In fact, it appeared that Robin had not changed over the years. Everything was meticulously in its place. She had impeccable taste when it came to dressing and furnishing her home and Brian had always called her a neatnik. The living room was furnished much like his condo in dark cherry wood. It was about 1,800 square feet with three bedrooms and a small den which, in this part of the country, made it worth at least three- quarters of a million dollars.

Toward the rear of the house, off a small laundry room, was a door with a sign marked "darkroom." Brian reasoned that this was where Robin did her developing work, knowing that she had run her photography business out of her home. After entering the small room, he pulled the string at the end of a light bulb that hung from the ceiling and a red light came on.

Glancing back and forth, his eyes suddenly stopped on a shiny object that was sitting on top of a large manila envelope atop a three- drawer file cabinet. Using a pencil, he carefully picked up what appeared to be a piece of jewelry. The red light didn't offer much illumination, but he was able to see that it was a brooch or pin of some type. As he continued staring at it, he soon came to realize that it was quite like the brooch that Lauren prized so much, one which had been given to Lauren by her mother.

As curiosity got the best of him, he laid the brooch back down then picked up the envelope and opened it. Inside was a group of 8" X 10" glossy color photos. The first one was of Robin sitting on the side of a bed, giving the appearance of posing. She was wearing a tight- fitting, black after- five dress that was open in the front, revealing her more- than- ample cleavage. Her long, flowing jet black hair, which fell well below the top of her shoulders, was draped in front of her, forming a sort of frame in which her face seemed to rest. Around her neck was a diamond studded black collar and she was wearing dark hose and black heels. Brian's first impression was that the pictures were rather out of character for Robin who normally dressed on the conservative side, though he knew first hand that she had posed for some pictures during college.

As he looked at the next picture, he noticed it appeared a bit more sexual in nature than the previous one. There was more cleavage showing and her dress was higher on her thighs. As he flipped through the photos, he noticed that the look on Robin's face in each of the photos was very solemn, giving him the impression that she was perhaps uncomfortable having her picture taken. After looking at the next few pictures, he noticed that she was wearing a brooch like the one that had been sitting on top of the envelope. Before looking at the rest of the photos, he went back to the first one and sure enough she was wearing the brooch pinned - above her left breast in every picture. He quickly returned to the last picture he had looked at and continued.

In the next picture, Robin was standing and had slid the hem of her dress above the top of her nylons, displaying a full view of her shapely legs and a hint of her thighs. Wiping a bead of sweat off his forehead he went on. A gasp escaped his mouth as he looked at the next picture. She had taken her dress off completely and was sitting on the bed in her bra, panties, nylons, heels and the collar. Her full breasts seemed to be pushing out of the flimsy translucent material of her bra, causing him to feel a tinge of guilt. Looking at this picture made him feel like a voyeur, likely because of the strong feelings he had for Robin, feelings that he had never told either Robin or his wife about. What bothered him most now was that the look on her face had become more intense with each picture, making him think that perhaps Robin had not posed for the pictures willingly.

Despite being alone in the room, Brian blushed when he looked at the next to last picture. Robin had taken off all but her stockings, the collar around her neck and heels and had turned her back to the camera in a standing position. The thought of seeing this beautiful woman, his wife's best friend, totally naked, was almost more than he could stand. It took him back to the time in college when he had once before seen her like this. He stood staring at the picture of her magnificent body for several minutes before putting it down to look at the last picture.

Brian was a seasoned cop who had seen it all, but he wasn't prepared for what he was about to see next. His face reacted with a look of sheer terror before his knees buckled and he sank to the floor gasping.

"My God, no!"

As he screamed out, his stomach wrenched with a feeling of nausea. He covered his eyes and began sobbing openly when Manny finally came into the room.

"What the hell's the matter?" Manny screamed.

Brian was gasping to catch his breath when Manny grabbed the picture out of his hand.

"Jesus Christ," Manny said loudly, "who would do a thing like this?"

He held in his hand, a picture of Robin Bennett lying on a bed in a pool of blood with her head completely severed from her body. Her head had been placed above her torso, and it appeared that the brooch that Brian found had been placed on her stomach. Her head had been arranged with the hair pulled over her face so that it was not clearly visible.

Putting his arm on Brian's shoulder, Manny led him out of the darkroom so he could regain his composure.

"Man, you must have some strong feelings for this lady. I'm really sorry that this is the way that it ended up, but let's find the bastard that did this and fuck him up."

After a half hour or so, Brian regained control of his emotions and took the picture of Robin's dead body into her bedroom. Holding it up to the light that was coming from between the drapes of the bedroom window, he studied it and then looked at the bed. After several glances back and forth he looked at Manny who was now entering the bedroom.

"I know where she was killed." He handed Manny the picture and walked toward the bathroom.

"Have you been in here yet?" Brian asked.

"No, not yet." Manny answered.

"Shit." Brian blurted out.

"Look at this." Across the mirror someone had written, in what appeared to be blood, the word 'ELECTRA'.

"What the hell is that?" Manny asked.

"Haven't a clue, Manny, but I have a hunch we'll find out." Before returning to the bedroom, Brian did a thorough check of the closet which was off the bathroom, then sat on the edge of the bed where Robin had been murdered. After a bit, he began shaking his head then looked at Manny.

"What the hell am I going to tell Lauren?" Brian had slumped over and was holding his head in his hands.

Manny looked at him before answering.

"Nothing, amigo."

"What the hell do you mean?" Brian shot back.

"You have no actual body, only a picture of a body with a face you can't make out clearly. Other than the writing on the mirror in the bathroom, what we're looking at here doesn't look like a crime scene. There is no blood on the bed and nothing else is out of place. Wait until we can be sure it's her."

"Why would anyone go to all the trouble of killing someone then purposely make it difficult to identify her?" Brian asked.

"Who knows why people do the things they do, but at this point we don't have a body and can't be sure that this picture is Robin Bennett, so lets cool it until we are sure. Hell, we don't even know if someone has been murdered."

"Meaning?" Brian said, looking at Manny.

"Meaning, Brian, I've seen some very strange

things done with a camera. Give me 48 hours to see what I can find out and then tell your wife about it."

"Makes sense to me, Manny. But I just had a terrible thought."

"What's that, Brian?" Brian looked through the closet before answering.

"Nothing, Manny, just something I gotta check out. I'll let you know if it means anything. By the way, find a guy with a black after- five dress slit down the middle in a size six and you've got the killer. The dress she was wearing in the picture isn't in her closet. Let's hope it isn't some sicko's souvenir."

Manny nodded his head.

"Let's leave this scene just like it is then if our worse case suspicions are true, we'll explain it later. If she's still alive, she'll never know we were in here." Brian nodded in agreement.

"Brian, let's get back to the station and look on the computer for some ideas. But first, let me take a picture of the mirror and get a sample of whatever was used to write on the mirror." After taking a picture, he scraped off a small bit of the substance from the mirror.

"Brian, this seems to be more like lipstick than blood. I guess that's one in our favor. Oh, and let's bring those pictures with us."

Back at the station Manny had given the sample from the mirror to someone in the lab and asked that he look at it as a favor since he didn't have a case to reference it to. Returning to his office, he brought Brian a cup of coffee and signed on the internet. Manny Googled on an FBI computer program called VICAP which was an acronym for Violent Criminal Apprehension Program. By using the program, he was able to home in on recent murders in the area. He looked at Brian.

"You know this definitely screams out serial killer with the way the body was displayed and all, at least in the pictures. But come to think of it, I can't recall anything like this since I've been here in the last ten years, at least not in that sleepy little city. I know I'd remember something that bizarre."

A perplexed look came to Brian's face as he sank back in the chair across from Manny's desk. Manny continued:

"Let me expand the geography on this search and see if there's anything in L.A. or..." Manny stopped short as he looked up at Brian.

"What's the matter, amigo? You got a strange look on your face."

Brian was silent for a moment before responding.

"Do your search Manny, but include Florida."

"What the hell you talkin' about?" Manny said, with a shocked look on his face.

Brian sat up straight and then leaned forward, propping his elbows on his knees and resting his face in his hands. He took several deep breaths and looked at Manny.

"Several years ago, there were three cases with some similarities to this in Florida. One was just outside Tampa."

"You mean the victims had their heads cut off, amigo?"

"No, Manny, I mean beautiful women about Robin's age, they all lived alone, etc. I helped in the investigation, but we never got close to solving it because we didn't really have anyone experienced in that type of case. The FBI took the case over because they had other cases like it in other parts of the country."

"You figure the connection here is Robin and you?"

"No." He paused. "Robin and my wife. Don't ask me what I mean, because I don't know yet, but remember that small pin, the brooch that Robin was wearing in those pictures?"

Manny nodded silently.

"My wife has one just like it."

Manny reached for the pictures of Robin they had taken from her home and glanced at several.

"Yeah, I see it. So your wife has a brooch just like this one. You aren't suggesting that she…?"

Brian stopped him in mid- sentence. "Of course, she had nothing to do with it, but the likelihood there's no connection seems too remote to be a coincidence. Robin always admired the pin, even though it was a cheap imitation of a real one."

"Maybe the Bennett woman liked it so much that your wife had one made for her, for a birthday or something?" Manny waited for a response.

"No, I think I would have remembered something like that, Manny, but I'll find out for certain. Man, I don't know how I am going to keep this from her for even 48 hours."

While still staring at his computer screen, he interrupted Brian.

"Here are your cases in Florida. What were some of the similarities?"

Brian's face took on a look of intensity as he spoke.

"First off, the women were very attractive and in their late 30s or early 40s. From a distance, they looked a lot like Lauren. I chalked it off to coincidence. One was a professional woman who worked for a local university. I, of course, had no reason to connect that to Lauren in any way. In fact, I remember asking Lauren if she had ever crossed paths with the victim since she was in the same field, and she said hadn't."

" Neither of these appears to be near Tampa, so if only one was in your area, why did you suspect that it was a serial killer?" Manny asked.

"I ran the same program you are using and found one with similarities in Chicago and another somewhere in the Northeast. It was in a small city in western Maine," Brian said. "There were a lot of similarities with the victims, including age, build and profession. That's why I suspected a serial killer. Other than that, none of the other aspects were the same, at least not that I remember. And then I thought that the murders were so far apart geographically that they probably weren't linked."

"Don't let that influence your thinking, Brian. "I've heard it said by a number of authorities on the subject that many serial killers travel significant distances in the course of a year. One book I read said that while it isn't necessarily normal, some serial killers travel extensively in pursuit of the right victim. But let me ask an obvious question." He paused. "Were there any brooches or pins left behind as part of the evidence?"

Brian thought for a minute then answered.

"You know, there may have been, but none had been placed on any of the victims as in the case here, at least that I remember. I wasn't very experienced in serial killer cases and may not have made that connection. I'll look at the personal property when I get back to see if maybe there could have been one in the purse of any of the victims. I could have overlooked something like that, depending on how their property was listed in the report."

"How were they murdered?" Manny asked.

"I think one was strangled, one was stabbed repeatedly and the third was beaten to death with a blunt object, but I had better look at the files before I go any further. Also, we never found any of the weapons, and DNA was extremely limited. In any case, we would need a suspect for DNA to mean anything, unless he was in the Florida Department of Law Enforcement DNA Bank, which we couldn't determine."

"Sure, but it could tell you if it was the same killer," Manny said then asked, "Where were the bodies found?"

"Again, Manny, I don't remember all that much about them. It seemed like they got taken away from me so quickly that I really never had a chance to digest everything. If you're looking for an M.O., we couldn't make a connection. All three were dissimilar. Dissimilar enough, in fact, that we thought that they may be the work of three different killers."

"No, amigo." Manny responded, "I'm not looking for an M.O., I'm looking for a signature."

"I've heard about signature killers, Manny, but never actually got deep enough into this type of case to be able to establish one. Tell me more."

He leaned back in is chair and propped his hands behind his head as Manny began talking.

"I went to a lecture series by a noted cop who talked about signature killers. He specifically talked about several killers: Bundy, in Washington, Colorado and Idaho and then Florida; The Night Stalker, Ramirez, in Southern California; The Green River Killer, Gary Ridgeway, up in Washington and Edmund Kemper, a local guy up in Berkeley who stood six-foot-nine. Anyway, he maintains that M.O.'s change according to the circumstances that are taking place in the killer's life. A signature never changes;

it's like a finger print."

I'm listening, go on." Brian said.

"Well." Manny said as he sat back in his swivel chair, spinning around to face Brian. "A modus operandi in the case of a serial killer can be where the killer goes to find victims, at bars as an example. It could also be where they dump the body or what geographic area he or she operates in. The killer may prefer to frequent bars or shopping malls to try and pick up women or simply break into the victim's house. He may then take them to a certain area, like a park. He may dump the bodies in plain sight or bury them or even take the victim homealive, like Gacey in the Chicago area, or Dahmer in Milwaukee and kill them there.. This is the killer's M.O.," Manny continued.

"Okay, I get it. What else?" Brian asked.

"Now if you know much about serial killers, you know that every so often an uncontrollable urge comes over them and they literally have to kill. They are not in control and are unable to stop themselves."

"Right." Brian nodded his understanding.

"The reason isn't important at this point. You know the scenario of punishing the mother etc., although some have double motives. Ramirez down in L.A. always robbed his victims, and he left with any cash or jewelry that was lying around. Your gal in Florida, Aileen Wuornos, used prostitution as a ruse, but always left with a payday. They all take souvenirs to remind them of the kill."

"Really?"

"Yeah, man," Manny said excitedly. "When Gacey was caught they found a dresser drawer full of watches, necklaces, rings and such in his house. What is important, however, is that if the killer can't find a victim at the usual haunts and the urge has taken control of him or her, the

M.O. will change to suit the urge. Many killers have been known to change M.O.'s simply because they couldn't find a victim the usual way. Remember that Bundy usually met his victims in public places like parks and beaches, until he got desperate."

"Oh yeah, that's right," Brian said and shook his head.

"That is until he was on the run and went to Florida where he broke into a coed dorm at a university and killed two young ladies. It is assumed that couldn't find a victim in the usual haunts or that he was being cautious because he was on the run.

"I remember that." Brian said.

"The signature, on the other hand, doesn't change. This could be how the body is arranged when the crime is committed, for example. It could be something like how the pain is inflicted on the victim. Like in one case that the speaker cited, the killer took an inordinate amount of time torturing the victim nearly to death. He allowed the victim time to recover then repeated the process."

"That's fucking sick," Brian interjected.

"I know, right?" Manny continued. "One killer that the guy talked about arranged the body of his victims so that they had to watch him as he killed them. He got off on it."

"Jesus," Brian said. Manny continued.

"I think it's about sexual gratification and control in a high percentage of serial killings, although on the surface it didn't appear to be in the case of the Green River Killer. He claimed to be cleansing the world of prostitutes. But when you get right down to it, there was probably a control motivation there also. I think his mother was a slut who brought her boyfriends home with her."

"Nice," Brian scoffed.

"It's a pretty complex job finding out what the

signature is as opposed to the M.O., and sometimes takes several victims before a trend is established. This doesn't necessarily solve your crime, but it can tell you if a series of murders is the work of one serial killer. Often a copy-cat killer doesn't know the signature of the real serial killer and it would only look like the serial killing on the surface.

"Please explain," Brian said.

"Well," Manny continued, "as an example, I remember one case where a guy wanted to get rid of his wife. He killed her in the same fashion as an active serial killer at the time. He had read everything he could about the murders so that the serial killer would get blamed, but he didn't have a clue about the signature. Anyway, he didn't do his homework I guess; the killer had already been arrested on a totally unrelated crime and was in jail when he killed his wife. Knowing the killer's signature, they figured it was an attempt by a copy cat and they caught the husband."

"Thanks for the education, buddy. Maybe I'll re-open the cases when I get back to Tampa."

Brian rose to leave for the airport as he shook Manny's hand.

"I'll peruse our files and if I can establish the signature for the three murders in Florida. I'll give you a call. Maybe we can find the connection."

"Before you re-open those cases, amigo, be sure you check with the FBI." No tellin' what they may have found out. By the way, Brian, you got one thing in your favor."

"What's that, Manny?"

"You said that the other victims in Florida looked like your wife, I mean physically. Don't get me wrong amigo, she is a real looker, but she doesn't look anything like the Bennett woman."

As the red eye made its final approach to Tampa International Airport , Brian gulped down the remains of a martini he had been nursing and anguished over what he was going to have to do within the next day or so. He loved his wife with every fiber of his mind and body and couldn't stand to think about how devastated she would be when she found out. He knew, however, that he had to tell her very soon despite the fact that there was no body.

It was early Saturday morning by the time he got back to Tampa. When he opened the door to their condominium he found Lauren sitting on the couch with a glass of wine in her hand. After dropping his overnight bag on the floor, he walked over in front of her and with an inquisitive look on his face.

"Isn't it a bit early for that?"

Lauren swirled the white wine around the glass and took a sip.

"Not when you haven't gone to bed from the night before."

Brian sat on the edge of the coffee table in front of her and stared into her eyes.

"It would appear that something is bothering you, want to talk about it?"

After taking another sip, Lauren responded: "Where have you been?"

"I left you a message that I had to go on a stakeout. Didn't you get it?"

She swallowed the last bit of wine and placed the glass on the side table next to the sofa.

"Sure I got it, but you got a message from your partner, what's her name, 'Red Hot'? She said she wanted to talk to you before you left town and hoped that your friend was all right. 'Red Hot' said she would take care of the stakeout. Well, at least you weren't with her, I guess."

Brian's face took on a look of desperation as he moved to sit on the couch next to her. He couldn't bring himself to tell her about the events in California, hoping beyond hope that Robin wasn't really dead.

"Can you just trust me for a couple of days on this? I'll tell you what's going on very soon."

Lauren had it all planned out. She was going to tell him all about her suspected intruder and how she had to look for help from a colleague rather than from her cop husband. She was going to make him feel really bad, in hopes of punishing him for not being there when she needed him, but she stopped herself short.

"I guess we'll have to trust each other, because I have something to tell you, too. I guess you'll have to wait a couple of days also. By the way, do you plan on being home for the next couple of days?"

"Yes," Brian responded, "unless an emergency comes up."

He picked up his overnight bag and walked down the hall to the master bedroom. After dropping the bag on the bed, he glanced out the door to make sure Lauren was still sitting on the couch. He searched the jewelry box on the top of the dresser and couldn't find the brooch. He quietly looked through every drawer, but found nothing. He didn't dare ask her about it yet, since it would certainly arouse her suspicion, but he knew he couldn't rest until he found it.

CHAPTER TEN

Brian was not on duty Sunday and after recovering from jet lag, he remembered that he had promised one of the other cops that he would play golf with him. He asked Lauren if she minded if he was gone again.

"Not at all Brian, it will give me a chance to get some shopping done." Her first thought was that it gave her a chance to call Arthur in hopes of going over his plan.

"Okay, then I'll be back about four." Brian turned and was out the door before she had a chance to say anything further.

She quickly telephoned Arthur and found him at home.

"Arthur, I don't want to be a pest, but I was wondering if you had laid out our plan yet?"

"You bet, Lauren, when can we meet?" Arthur's tone was very upbeat.

"Is an hour too soon?" she replied with equal enthusiasm.

"Just tell me where and I'll be there," he responded.

"There's a park near the Hillsborough River right off Fletcher Avenue on the east side of town near the University." Lauren had referred to The University of South Florida, Florida's second largest school. Do you know it?"

"Yes," he said, "I think it's called Lettuce Lake Park or something like that. I have been there before. Excellent idea."

"Good," Lauren replied, "See you there in an hour."

Going to her closet, she surprised herself by

selecting a pair of tight fitting white jeans that she had not worn in over a year, a red silk blouse and white heels, and for some reason she decided to wear her hair down.

She knew Arthur had only seen her with her hair up and probably didn't know her hair actually fell well below her shoulders. Glancing in the mirror, she realized how different she looked and for some reason, she couldn't tear herself away from looking at the image she saw.

"I'm a totally different person," she said to herself, "more exciting, more daring and perhaps more mysterious." Swinging her head from side to side to free her long auburn hair, she put on a pair of sunglasses and again spoke softly to herself.

"If Mr. Allsop could only see me now. Of course, why not let him see me this way? After all, my mentor and personal detective told me I had to have dinner with him again." Her first thought had been Greg Allsop and not her husband.

The Hillsborough River flowed in a snake-like path from the northern part of the county through the city of Tampa and was, in fact, one of the sources of fresh water for the area. It eventually flowed into Tampa Bay where the water became brackish not far from the Bayshore area where Lauren had seen Greg Allsop and Red Hot together. The park was replete with grandfather oaks and winding paths that led off into dense woods scattered with pine and palm trees. Picnic benches dotted the park which was known for its wild life and scenic views.

Lauren pulled in the entrance and drove about 300 yards up the winding road until she saw Arthur's car. She spotted him sitting at a picnic bench with papers spread out in from of him. As she walked toward him she saw him do a double take then stare at her. Lauren was anything but conceited, but she knew that today she looked like dynamite; it made her feel good that the very stoic Arthur Holmes couldn't keep his eyes off her.

"What's the matter, Arthur, you're staring?"

"At my age I don't say this often, but wow!"

"Does that mean that you approve, Mr. Holmes?"

"Lets put it this way, come to school that way and Mr. Allsop will be begging to take you to dinner."

"I was hoping for your approval, Arthur, it means a lot to me. However, I won't have any trouble getting him to go to dinner with me, so I think I'll hold the look in abeyance until the night when we actually meet. Maybe that way I'll get the psychological edge on him. And besides, I don't think I'd have the nerve to come to school looking like this. I'm too conservative." Lauren paused, then said, "What if Greg doesn't come back?"

"Oh, he will." Arthur said with a wide grin.

"Sounds like you've found something out Detective Holmes."

"Yes," Arthur said, handing her a piece paper and awaiting her response.

"Pardon the expression, Arthur, but holy shit." Lauren's mouth fell wide open, "a Federal Agent?"

"This comes from a very reliable source of mine in Washington." Arthur smiled with a look of satisfaction. "And that's not all. Look at this." Arthur handed her a second piece of paper.

After reading for a moment, she again looked at him.

"This is depressing. You mean that Red Hot is an agent too? I was hoping that she was just a tramp or something."

"It would appear so. Not that she's a tramp, I mean,

but that she's an agent as well. But Lauren, this comes from a different source, and I am not quite as confident of this one."

"Well, my world has just turned upside down. What else you got?" she asked.

"Only the plan, but first I need some additional information from you. Have a seat across from me." Arthur picked up his pen and started to ask questions and make notes on a yellow pad.

"Lauren, where were you born?"

"A small town in western Maine called Portersville. I think it was named after its founder. He was some sort of religious type, the head of the local church I think. It's located on a lake, and there probably weren't more than 1,000 people in the whole place."

"When were you born?"

"June 22nd, 1963"

Arthur looked up at her. "That makes you a…?"

"A what?" She asked, "oh, you mean astrologically; a Cancer, but only by a few minutes. I was born at two minutes past midnight. Is that pertinent?"

"I don't know. I just want to gather all the facts I can. Brothers or sisters?"

"No, an only child," Lauren answered, brushing the hair off her face. Putting her elbows on the table and face between her hands, she leaned forward with a somewhat uncharacteristic smile.

"Just how personal are you going to get, Mr. Holmes?"

The look on her face made Arthur blush a bit. She sensed he could see a subtle change in her personality.

"You don't have to tell me anything that you don't want to, Lauren, but the more information I have, the better able I am to solve your mystery."

Lauren sensed that he had taken her comment a bit defensively and hurried to correct it.

"I don't know what came over me, Arthur. Of course, I'll tell you anything you need to know."

"Parents' names?"

"My mother was named Angela."

Arthur interrupted her, "What was her maiden name?"

"Borden."

Arthur smiled.

"Not the Massachusetts Bordens?"

"Huh?" Lauren stammered, "Oh ,no, not the Lizzie Bordens. Anyway my father," she paused, "well, I called him different things, but his given name was Joseph."

"Different things?" Arthur peered over the top of his spectacles.

"You know, pet names. I sometimes called him my hero."

"Any pet names for your mother?"

"No, Arthur, I don't recall any, just 'mother.' "

Arthur again stared over his glasses at Lauren.

"Just 'mother'; not 'mommy' or 'mom'?"

"Come to think of it, it was always just 'mother'." Lauren began twisting the hair that had fallen in front of her face in a circular motion. She sensed that Arthur noticed she was a bit on edge.

"Enough of that for now," he said. "Let's talk about school."

"I was very shy in high school, never dated much. As I remember, I looked forward to going away to college, except that I missed my dad."

Arthur noted the use of the term dad on his pad.

"Okay, you get to college and your life changes.

How?"

"Definitely, as you know, I went to Columbia on a scholarship and majored in English. I loved everything that went along with the subject. I guess I am sort of old fashioned that way. I often wish that I could have lived hundreds of years ago. Things seemed so much simpler then. You know what I mean?"

Arthur nodded.

"I do know, Lauren, and I have often wished the same myself. Only problem is, they didn't have the modern crime solving techniques that they have now. Don't know how effective I would be as the detective I always wanted to be. I want you to know how much this means to me. I mean that you would trust me to help you in your time of crisis. And don't be too sure that you didn't live hundreds of years ago."

Lauren put her hand on his.

"I know, Arthur. I feel like it has brought us so much closer and I trust you implicitly, so you can ask anything you want."

"Even if it is embarrassing?"

"Anything, Arthur, anything."

Arthur paused, then removed his glasses and stared into her eyes.

"Are you and your husband having problems?"

Lauren didn't hesitate.

"Yes, we are, and I don't know if it is anything we can solve."

"Do you want to solve the problems?" Arthur awaited her response.

"I'm not sure. There are times when I think we would both be better off without each other and as I told you, I think he might be having an affair."

"Yes, you mentioned Red Hot?" Lauren nodded yes.

"How do you feel about Mr. Allsop?"

"Frankly, Arthur, he is a very good looking man, and I need to watch myself around him. Isn't it ironic? We suspect the two people that my husband and I appear to be attracted to. And it seems that they are federal agents. And perhaps investigating us or at least Brian? I can't imagine why they would be investigating me."

"Have you heard from your friend in California?"

She sensed his strain when he asked the question.

"No, I haven't and I become increasingly worried as each day goes by. Brian said he was having a friend look in on Robin, but he hasn't heard anything back yet. Or, at least he hasn't said anything. This is what is so coincidental about the whole thing. I can't get a hold of Robin for over a week now, my husband goes on a stakeout without his partner, Greg Allsop leaves for a few days to San Francisco…what does it all mean, Arthur?"

"I don't know just yet, but I can promise you that I will get to the bottom of it. Let's review the plan.

Arthur had laid out a plan that included checking the background of Brian and Robin and having Lauren spend some time with Greg Allsop, in hopes of finding out why he went to California. His plan included checking out Lauren's background and finally, trying to find out more about Cameo, even if it meant having Lauren meet him in person. As long as Arthur was nearby. She listened intently and agreed with everything he wanted to do, but as she swung her legs over the bench to leave, Arthur grabbed her hand.

"What is it, Arthur?"

"This is a bit delicate, and I don't want you to take it the wrong way, but how did Brian feel about Robin?"

Lauren bit her lower lip gently and a solemn look captured her face. She paused for a moment before speaking.

"Well, Brian doesn't think I suspect it, but I have always felt that he has been in love with her since college. To his dismay, she always thought of him as the brother she never had, but I truly feel that if she had the same feelings for him, that he would have asked her to marry him rather than me."

"What makes you think that, Lauren?"

"I've always felt that he wanted someone who was more spontaneous and assertive than I am. Don't ask why I think that, I just feel it."

Arthur removed his glasses and looked at her.

"Perhaps if he could see the way you look today, he would change his mind."

"Why, do I look that much different to you?" she asked.

"Not only do you look different with your hair down, but I sense a different personality. You're just lucky that I'm not 20 years younger and 50 pounds lighter."

A broad smile swept across Lauren's face. She leaned over and kissed him on the cheek.

"Perhaps it's my bad luck that you're not, Mr. Holmes." She rose, then turned and looked at him and said, "Tell me something, Arthur. Why did you never marry?"

"I guess someone like you never came along in time, Lauren."

She smiled and took his hand in hers. "Thanks for that, Arthur. By the way, there is something I wanted to ask you, and while it may seem a bit off the subject, I would nevertheless like your advice."

"What's that, Lauren?"

Well, a couple of years ago I went to a fortune teller and she told me some things that seemed to come true, at least in the sense of the big picture. Do you think they have anything to offer? I mean, do you think it's stupid to go to one?"

Arthur rested his chin on his hand and thought for a moment. "I've gone to several over the years, but like anything else in life, some are good, some aren't. Some are legit and others are simply scams," he offered. Lauren nodded her agreement.

"I do believe," Arthur said, "that certain people have special powers that most of us don't have, such as pre-cognition, clairvoyance, premonition and such. It's been theorized by some very significant thinkers that people once had much more of these powers. They think that religion is the culprit that has diminished those abilities over the years,"

"I suppose that's right," Lauren responded.

"Think about it, Lauren, why do you suppose that there were so many witches burned at the stake in places like Salem or even in old England for that matter? Do you think they were all real witches or just people with a God-given gift that the people of the times didn't understand?"

None of this was news to Lauren, who had extensive knowledge in the area of English history, but she knew that Arthur was feeling good about passing on his own knowledge to her; so she let him talk. She wanted him to feel like he was helping, so she prodded him,

"Why do you think that those people did what they did?"

"Well, I suppose that through intimidation and even persecutions of the masses, a small minority of people were better able to dictate their thinking and philosophies to those people and hence gain control of them. It's commonly known that scientists, as an example, were among the most persecuted people in history. Scientists tried to answer the many unanswered questions that the religions of civilizations throughout history could not. They were persecuted in an attempt to keep them quiet. As long as religious leaders had the general population believing that the answers to all questions should come from the church, they controlled their thinking."

"Hmm," Lauren murmured.

"It was actually quite hypocritical," Arthur said, "in that many of these religious zealots demanded that people accept, without question, the teachings of the Bible and other doctrines when in fact they were persecuting any dissenters. As I recall, the Bible attempts to teach us to forgive those who trespass against us. But don't let me get off on a tangent, or we'll be here all day."

"Do you know of one that you would consider both honest and gifted? A seer, I mean?"

"As a matter of fact, I do, Lauren. Here, let me write the name and number down for you." Arthur reached in his back pocket and pulled out a small address book. "Yes, here she is. Her name is Fatima."

"Fatima? Wasn't that the daughter of Mohammed?" Lauren asked.

"Yes, but don't let the exotic name fool you. She's actually Bonnie Clark from the north side of Chicago. And don't forget, go after Allsop. Oh, and one thing I forgot to mention to you: pay for anything you buy with cash, no credit cards. I'm sure you understand that."

"Don't worry, Arthur, Mr. Allsop won't stand a chance. And thanks for the name, I'll call her." Lauren knew that she was a different person today and sensed that

Arthur thought the same.

Once in her car she wasted no time in calling Fatima. After the sixth ring someone answered.

"This is The Terrestrial Plane, how can I help you?"

"Hello, my name is Lauren St. John, and I was referred to Fatima by a friend of mine named Arthur Holmes."

"This is Fatima speaking. Yes, I remember Arthur. How is he doing?"

"He's doing fine, but I'm not doing so fine. I'd like to come in and see you," Lauren said with a sense of urgency.

"I have an opening the end of next week…."

Lauren interrupted her, "I can't wait until next week. My problem is quite serious. But if you can't help me…."

Fatima stopped her, "I can tell by the vibrations I'm getting that you may be in danger. Of course, I will make some special arrangements for you. My normal hours are nine to six but if you wish, I will stay late today if you can get here."

"I can. What's your address?"

After noting the address, she drove toward a suburb just east of Tampa called Brandon. From the park where she met Arthur, she was able to get quickly on I-75 heading south. After driving about 10 miles, she got off at the first Brandon exit, heading east until she was at a street called Parsons. She drove about two miles south where she came to an oak lined street with a row of small single-story bungalows set back from the main road about 50 yards. At the far end, she saw a small, somewhat inconspicuous wooden sign that indicated she had arrived.

The building, which was typical of the surrounding area, was a small frame house of about 1,200 square feet that had been converted to a business. There weren't many zoning restrictions in this part of the county; hence several of the other houses on the block had also been converted into small businesses. There was a large grandfather oak with a birdbath under it off to the left side of a cobblestone walkway that led to the house. Lauren made her way up the path to the house, and as she did, she noticed that there was a small white dove sitting on the ledge of a window off to the right of the front door. As she grew closer to it, she half expected it to fly away, but it didn't. The small bird just sat there, its tiny black eyes staring at Lauren. She stopped and looked back at it. She then stooped and extended her hand. Much to her amazement, the bird flew off the ledge and landed at her feet, all the time looking at her.

"Are you trying to tell me something, little dove?"

The bird cooed, then as though in a panic, spread its wings and flew off behind the house. Lauren stood and quickly looked behind herself. She gasped at the sight of a large black raven sitting on a branch of a nearby oak tree with its wings extended. It was staring directly at her.

"My, God," she said to herself, "this isn't a good start."

Upon entering the front door, she saw the usual display of trinkets and paraphernalia scattered on the many shelves that lined the store. There was a small glass counter off the right with several dishes containing multi-colored stones and an assortment of incense, one of which was burning. The aroma, along with the soft sounds of the environmental music that was playing, made Lauren feel quite at ease. As she stood there, however, one thing stood out and seemed a bit out of place. A voice came from behind her.

"You think that the Voodoo doll is out of place, don't you?" Lauren turned and saw a woman standing at a door off to her right. "I am Fatima and you must be Ms. St. John."

Fatima was a slender woman about 50 years of age with an attractive face in a mystic sort of way. She was dressed in an ankle-length, black crepe skirt and contrasting off-white blouse. Her hair, which was very fine, reached down almost to her waist, and she had several gold bracelets and rings on her wrists and fingers.

"Please, call me Lauren. It's a pleasure, and yes, I was a bit surprised by the Voodoo doll. What is the significance of it?"

"It was a gift from a High Priest in Haiti. A Voodoo High Priest is often referred to as a 'Papa' and a priestess as a 'Mama'. The priest that gave me that figure was called Papa Devereaux. You see over there?" She pointed to a far corner of the room. "That is the serpent that the High Priest manifests. Those who believe, gather under the auspice of the serpent to worship. It's such a shame that the Voodoo religion is so often viewed as being evil and demonic. The ritual dances and ceremonies that they perform are for the purpose of driving away evil spirits. Isn't it strange that a religion that had it origins over 10,000 years ago and still survives can be looked on as an evil thing?"

"Why, yes, I suppose so, but to tell the truth I never gave it much thought. But you say it is over 10,000 years old, how can that be? I mean, isn't it associated with the country of Haiti, which has only been in existence since some time after the discovery of the New World? Isn't that correct?"

Fatima locked the front door then took Lauren's hand leading her into a back room which had a no chairs, but cushions everywhere and incense burning on a small foot-high table in the middle of the room. In the middle of the back wall was a plaque made of some sort of teak wood with the words 'The Seven Deadly Sins' burned into the wood. Lauren stared at it for a moment. Under those words was the numbers one through eight with something written after all but the eighth number. They read:

1) Luxuria (Lust)
2) Gula (Gluttony)
3) Avaritia (Greed)
4) Acedia (Sloth)
5) Ira (Wrath)
6) Indivia ((Envy)
7) Superbia (Pride)

As Lauren read the list, Fatima answered her question.

"You are partially correct. You see, when the slave trade began in the New World, slaves brought with them their own forms of Pagan religion. When slave owners purchased slaves from the traders, they separated them from the standpoint of tribes and villages so that they didn't speak a common language with each other." Lauren listened intently.

"This was done to prevent them from offering any resistance to their owners and to try and get them to accept Christianity. But eventually some of the different aspects of the various native religions came together to become what we know today as Voodoo. Since the authorities in the slave trader days would often beat and even hang anyone that practiced Voodoo, those that did eventually had to go into hiding to practice Voodoo; thus making it even more mystical. It's a very sad testimonial to our civilization."

Lauren smiled...

"You find this amusing?" Fatima looked at her with a frown.

"No, not at all." Lauren said, "It's just that before I came here, Arthur was giving me a history lesson about how other religions including Christianity, Islam and Judaism persecuted people who didn't believe in their religion and even stifled scientific investigation for fear that some of their beliefs would be found to be hypocritical. Then to hear it from you again, well, I'm sorry if you misunderstand my smile, but it was only because of the irony of it."

"Enough said, Lauren, Arthur must be a very perceptive man. And he's on the right track. Please sit anywhere you would like," Fatima offered.

After sitting on a group of pillows, Lauren leaned toward Fatima.

"Why is it that you know so much about Voodoo?"

"In my profession, I feel that it is important to study all religions," Fatima responded. "They often affect the way we think and the way we perceive the world around us. It helps me to understand people and their needs. More importantly, it seems to open up mental blocks that people may have so that I am better able to see their future. You see, Lauren, my gift is precognition. It isn't always present; but if I am able to penetrate your subconscious thought, I am able to see where your life may take you. My images are often vague, but with details that only apply to you. Then there are times that the images are so real that they frighten me."

Lauren nodded as Fatima continued talking.

"It has been theorized in some intellectual circles that many more people were given the gifts of precognition, clairvoyance and other metaphysical abilities in times past. It is further thought that those who professed to be religious leaders did in fact stifle free thought and ultimately drove many of those gifts away. You see, if we don't believe in those gifts because of the way we are raised, we might never realize that we have them. So, the stifling of thought by whatever means and by whatever powers, led to a gradual erosion of those abilities among people over long periods of time. In people that had those powers, that is."

"Interesting concept," Lauren said, as .Fatima continued talking.

"It's like any other part of the body; if we don't exercise it, it doesn't grow to maturity. If I had lived a few hundred years ago, I would have been branded a witch and perhaps burned at the stake. Today, most people just consider me eccentric or a kook. I thank my higher power every day for the gift I have and for people like Arthur and yourself, people who aren't afraid to believe in things that seem abnormal to others."

Lauren looked at her curiously.

"You said higher power, are you perchance ...." Fatima stopped her before she could finish.

"A recovering alcoholic? Actually, my drug of choice was prescription drugs. But 'a rose by any other name,' you know."

"Yes, I know. My father was a recovering alcoholic when he passed away. He hadn't taken a drink for 14 years. I'm sure that it's a very difficult thing. Recovery, I mean."

"I already sense you had a close relationship with your father." Fatima said.

"Yes, I did," Lauren responded. Lauren found herself being drawn in by the magnetism of this woman. Her soft voice and confident manner seemed to add to what appeared to be some sort of mystical knowledge about life, the depth of which Lauren had yet to explore. Fatima dimmed the lights and sat beside her, taking Lauren's hand in her own.

"Before we start, Fatima, I was curious about the plaque on the back wall. While I have seen 'The Seven Deadly Sins' written many times, I have never seen an eighth. Why is it blank?"

"Because it exists in the mind of the beholder. For centuries, thinkers and scholars have offered their versions of the eighth deadly sin, but there has never been a universal acceptance of any one of them. Some are ridiculous, and some offer some real insight, but none seem to answer the unanswered question. You are at liberty to form your own definition of the eighth deadly sin. You might also take note of the plaque on the other wall." Fatima pointed behind herself. "It's the Seven Holy Virtues. Each offers a counter to one of the sins. Funny, but I have never seen anything written about an eighth virtue. I guess no one is interested," she laughed. "Now let us journey into your future."

After sitting quietly for several moments, Fatima suddenly jerked her hand back and looked at Lauren.

"Oh," she paused, "you've seen a raven."

"You mean the one outside? Yes, but first I saw a white dove. Then the raven scared it away."

Fatima took her hand again.

"Was the white dove safe?"

Lauren looked at her with concern.

"As far as I could tell, it just flew in back of the building. Why? What does it mean?"

"The white dove can mean that you came here with an open mind and with pure thoughts. These types of thoughts normally create a smooth path, one that would help me see your future. But there is another force at work here. Something evil and that is what brought the raven," Fatima explained.

Lauren's face bore an obvious concern.

"Does it mean that you won't be able to see my future?"

"I can't tell yet," Fatima said. "Sometimes, it means that whatever the evil force is must be ejected before I can help you. All I can tell you now is that it is trying to stop me. When I tried to look at your life line all I could see was the raven. First, I must determine why the force is here and why it chooses to block your thoughts or perhaps change them. One thing I can tell, however, is that something or someone has been watching you. Did you know that?"

"Yes, but I can't tell who it is. I had a break-in where I live. The person didn't harm me, but certainly did terrify me. Actually, it's a sequence of events that lead me to believe that I am in danger. That is why I asked Arthur for help. I don't have any enemies that I know of, but there is this person on the internet." Fatima squeezed Lauren's hand tightly and leaned her head back.

"This force that is blocking me from communicating with your subconscious is coming to me in the form of a dense fog."

Lauren gasped, putting her free hand to her heart, before she could respond, Fatima began shaking.

"I see a figure in the mist," she stammered. "It's the silhouette of a person. It's the force that is blocking my visions. I can't see through the mist. I have to stop now. It is too powerful."

Fatima was visibly shaken from the brief encounter breathing heavy sighs until she finally came back to normal.

"Lauren, this is an evil force that is watching you, and I feel that you are in danger. I can't seem to determine what it is yet. Give me some time to consult a colleague of mine, and I will meet with you again. Whatever it is must be stopped."

Lauren looked at her questioningly.

"Fatima, you used the term 'force'. What exactly does that mean?"

"I can't say for certain right now, but I've seen people with psychic abilities who use mind control to manipulate other people. A person that would do such a thing may have sociopathic tendencies, free of any conscience and hence of infinite danger to others."

Lauren rose to leave then turned toward Fatima.

"That's a very scary thought, I hope you're wrong. One final thing, when we talked about the white dove, you expressed a real concern as to whether it was hurt. Why was that?"

Fatima stood, looked her in the face.

"There is a superstition in some Indian cultures that says the death of a white dove signifies that the person that is closest to it at the time of its death will also die."

The drive back to Carrollwood was an endless stream of thoughts and visions in Lauren's mind, and by the time she got home, she was physically and mentally exhausted. Before going to bed, she took two sleeping pills.

CHAPTER ELEVEN

A good nights sleep had put Lauren in a much better mood and she dressed like most days with a long wrap-around skirt that went down to her ankles. She chose red with heels to match, an expression of power and confidence. The top two buttons of her white silk blouse were purposely left undone, revealing a slight hint of the rise of her breasts. There was, however, one thing different about her ensemble today and only she would know what it was until the moment was right.

Lauren was early to school in hopes of catching Greg by himself and was pleased to see him sitting alone in the teacher's lounge, reading the newspaper. Her biggest challenge was coming up with a way to entice him into asking her to go to dinner without seeming to be the aggressor. She knew however, that she had to carry out her part of the plan no matter what.

"Hey, Greg, nice to see you again. Where have you been?"

Greg peered over the top of the paper and smiled.

"Does that mean you missed me or just curious about where I've been?"

"Both," Lauren answered, "but mostly I missed you." Lauren felt that if she pushed the other issue too much, he might back off. She waited patiently for him to make a move, but he offered only small talk for a few minutes before two other professors entered the room. Knowing that the opportunity had passed, she quickly came up with another approach.

"I have to run for now, but stop by and see me later."

Lauren felt her face become slightly flushed. "I want to ask you something." She had committed herself and now had to come up with some legitimate reason, other than asking him to dinner, in order to maintain the role of the pursued prey, while at the same time giving him an opening to ask her out.

It was 4p.m.. and all her classes had ended for the day when she finally came up with a solution to the problem at hand.

"I have it," she mumbled to herself. "He is a history professor, and I am looking for a subject for a theme paper assignment for my class in 'the History of English Literature'."

She had no sooner come up with the idea when she heard a gentle rapping at her door and Greg's smiling face appeared through the small rectangular window.

"Come in," she said, rising to greet him.

"How's your day, English Lady?" She sensed his mood was upbeat.

"Good, History Man. What about yours?"

He nodded, indicating that all was well.

"What's this important question you have to ask me?" he said as he sat in the side chair about five feet away from Lauren's desk.

She had purposely placed the chair there, knowing that he would stare at her legs when she sat down again, but she didn't sit quite yet.

"I hate to be all business," she said, "but I am assigning a theme paper in my 'English Literature History' class and hoped that you might help me in developing it. It should tie into what was going on in England and the British Isles in the 18th century. You know, what impact the times had on the literature of the period." She was trying her best to remain aloof while at the same time providing an opening for Greg to ask her to dinner.

Greg broke the silence.

"Damn, English Lady, I thought you were going to suggest that we have dinner again."

She didn't respond, wanting to keep the upper hand. Getting ready to give him her best shot, she raised her hand up as she put her index finger to her lips. Then with a questioning look on her face she moved toward a stack of books on the floor next to where Greg was sitting.

"I know, I have a book here that might give us some ideas."

She knelt down beside Greg's chair only a few feet from him, but facing sideways. The wrap-around skirt fell back, revealing a glimpse of her leg all the way up to her right thigh, showing the darker part of the top of her hose and a hint of bare skin. For the first time in her life Lauren was wearing nylons that were held up by a lace garter belt and not just panty hose to school.

Greg rose up in his chair, peering intently at her beautiful exposed leg. It was all she could do to keep from returning his glance, but the electricity in the air told her that he was hooked. Rising, she looked at Greg and could see full well that he had taken the bait. Lauren raised the palms of her hands up and shrugged, as if to indicate that she couldn't find the book.

"I guess I must have left it at home. Well, I have nothing else to do tonight, so I'll look for it."

That was all the opening he needed, but she wasn't through as she returned to her desk and sat in her swivel chair allowing the skirt to once again slide back, revealing the top portion of her stockings.

After watching her cross her legs, he finally let his gaze meet her eyes.

"Since we're on the subject of English history, let me ask you a question." He leaned forward in his chair while Lauren sat motionless, waiting for his question. "Why don't we have dinner again?"

While she knew what the answer was going to be, Lauren wanted to again keep the upper hand.

"What does one have to do with the other?"

"Well," Greg said, "we can talk about your theme."

"Oh," Lauren twisted her face a bit in order to make him think that she was pondering his question. "I guess it wouldn't hurt, and it would help me with the theme. Okay, let's."

With that, Greg rose and took a step toward her, all the time glancing back and forth at her legs.

"Lauren, I don't want you to think this is anything but on the up and up, but how about letting me cook dinner for you at my place? It would be a better atmosphere to discuss the theme, you know, a bit more relaxed."

Without realizing it, he was playing right into Lauren's hands. Playing it right up to the end, she allowed the intentional frown on her face to gradually change to a smile.

"I guess that would be okay." She paused. "What time? And, oh, where do you live? And can I bring anything?" She tried not to show how excited she was at his suggestion, but her questions sounded almost breathless.

"Just your lovely self. Here's my address." He handed her a card with his name, address and telephone number on it. "How about 7o'clock?"

After he left, Lauren stayed in her swivel chair, staring at her still exposed legs and still smiling.

"It was easier than I thought," she murmured to herself. This was the first time that she could remember using her sexuality so blatantly in order to gain something, but she mused, "It is for a good cause. After all, I am not going to do anything wrong. Well, at least I certainly don't intend to."

When Lauren arrived home, she was greeted by Brian who was sitting in the family room on the couch reading the newspaper. She immediately became tense, realizing that his presence may create a problem for her plans for the evening. She tried to act casual.

"Hey there, I thought you were supposed to be on stakeout tonight."

"I am, but I've got some time to kill and thought I'd do it here. What are you up to tonight?"

Before answering, she picked the mail up from the end table next to where Brian was sitting and began thumbing through it.

"Grading papers, Brian." She responded to his last question. "When do you have to leave?"

Brian stood up and started for the door.

"Right now. I guess we'll have that talk another time."

Before he reached the door, Lauren stopped him in his tracks, holding a postcard in her hand.

"My God, Brian, haven't you looked at the mail? It's a post card from Robin. She has been shooting in the mountains for a magazine layout, and we are not to worry about her."

Brian spun around in his tracks, took the card from Lauren and read it. Trying to hold back his emotions and the disbelief he was feeling.

"I don't get it," he murmured.

"What, Brian?" She heard him but didn't understand his comment.

"What I mean, Lauren, is that I don't get how she

could go off like this without telling you. She knows you'd worry your head off if she didn't call about something like this." Handing the post card back to Lauren he added, "It doesn't say where she is, I mean, what mountains."

The broad grin on Lauren's face was almost more than Brian could bare and he couldn't bring himself to destroy her happy mood with what he thought he knew. Trying his best to mask his surprise and feelings, he again headed for the door.

"That's great, Lauren. I know you're relieved."

As Brian made his way to the stakeout location, he attempted in vain to contact Manny in San Jose to see if he had learned anything further. He spoke to himself in a voice that half trembled.

"If only this were true." But in his heart he knew that there was something much more sinister going on in California.

The apparent knowledge of Robin's whereabouts only added to the feeling of euphoria and anticipation that had captured Lauren. She was going to have dinner with an attractive man at his apartment and hopefully learn something about what was going on between her husband and Red Hot. And hopefully learn something about the strange string of events that had recently upset her life. Then, to top it off, her dearest friend was okay. Or so she thought.

As Lauren showered, she could feel her mood gradually change. It was a feeling that she had experienced a few times before, but only during the past couple of years and one she didn't understand. This feeling was more intense than the other day when she met Arthur. Her normal nature was not at all aggressive and she hardly ever attempted to intimidate anyone. In fact, she most often avoided situations where she was the center of attention.

By definition, Lauren was laid back, but not tonight. Tonight she felt a sense of being in control and of power.

Rummaging through the deep recesses of her large walk- in closet, she found a box which bore the logo of a local shop that specialized in exotic ladies apparel. She took out a black leather mini skirt, white silk blouse and black mesh nylons with an accompanying garter belt and sheer lace white bra and panties. She stood for a moment, trying to remember the last time she had worn the ensemble.

"Yes," she said aloud, "I wore it six years ago for our anniversary." She felt a tinge of sadness as she remembered that Brian had been called away on that occasion, too, spoiling her surprise. Brian never did see the outfit she had intended to wear. She quickly put that incident out of her mind and her mood shifted back.

Standing completely nude in front of her full length mirror, she began slowly sliding the panties up her legs, all the time watching herself. She then slipped the strap that held the nylons up around her waist. Next, she cupped her breasts in the bra and hooked the clip in front. Her perfectly formed, firm breasts pushed against the translucent material giving the impression that the bra was too small.

Pausing for a moment, she looked at her image in the mirror then said quietly, "Hmm, not bad for 40-something years old."

The leather mini-skirt slid easily up her thighs to her waist and rested a good ten inches above her knees, fitting as perfectly as it did six years ago. She ran the soft material of the white silk blouse across her cheek before putting it on, all the time admiring the more than ample cleavage of her breasts. For a moment, she left the blouse unbuttoned and simply stared at herself. Slipping the buttons in place, she tucked the blouse in before sliding each nylon hose up her legs. With the nylons in place, she slid her skirt up in order to hook the nylons to the belt, stopping to comment aloud.

"My, wouldn't Greg like to see me now." Then she hooked the nylons to the strap and slid the skirt back down.

After selecting a pair of black heels she sat on the bed and put them on. Once again re-examining herself in the mirror, she realized that something was missing. Applying some perfume to her neck and arms, she went to a drawer in the back of her closet and took out a thin, black velvet collar that was adorned with zircon stones and slipped it around her neck. Returning to the mirror, she took a brush in one hand and with the other hand, removed the clip that held her hair up. Her long, flowing auburn hair dropped freely below her shoulders as she brushed it. She grinned...

"Mr. Allsop, you haven't got a chance,." she said aloud.

Selecting a small leather hand bag, she then set the alarm, locked the front door and went down the stairs to the foyer. When Lauren walked through the foyer of the lobby and out the front door, she saw a middle-aged man standing there whom she recognized as a neighbor. As the clicking of her heels against the tiled front steps of the condo entrance caught his attention, she began putting on a show. Swinging her long flowing hair as she passed him, she offered a broad smile and acknowledged him.

"Hey, Mr. Baker, how are you tonight?

The man stood staring in awe with his mouth wide open as Lauren whisked by him.

"Lauren, is that you? Jesus, you're fucking gorgeous."

Lauren was a bit shocked at the language, but took it to be a supreme compliment which only added to her confidence.

"Thank you, Mr. Baker." She turned and smiled. "I'm fucking pleased that you approve."

She couldn't believe what she had said, but continued on to her Mustang all the time smiling. As she slipped into the driver's seat, her skirt slid up to her bare thighs and she couldn't help but notice that Mr. Baker was straining to take in the view. She was thoroughly enjoying the attention in an almost exhibitionist manner, but still didn't understand why she was acting like this. It was totally out of character for her.

Being a bit early, she decided to take a longer, but more scenic route to Greg's apartment. She went through the downtown area and picked up Bayshore Boulevard, driving leisurely down the route that hugged Tampa Bay. By the time she reached the boulevard, dusk had set in and the night was refreshingly cool by Florida standards. She pulled off a side street, parked and began walking across the boulevard toward the concrete retaining wall along the bay.

As she reached the other side, she watched a car full of teenage boys drive by.

"Woman, are you ever hot,." one remarked. Lauren turned her head, smiled and winked at the boy who was now leaning out the window. After they drove off, she thought about the comment and it reminded her of Brian's partner, Red Hot. With that thought, she suddenly realized that she had, in fact, pulled onto the street where Red Hot lived. Curious, she thought to herself, I wonder if it means anything. Looking at her watch, she realized she still had 45 minutes to kill. She walked over to the only restaurant along the boulevard, one that had been there for over 50 years and went into the bar area.

Despite the fact that Lauren hardly ever went into a bar alone, she felt quite comfortable tonight. Her senses were sharp, her mood upbeat and she felt more in control with each passing minute. Instinctively, she knew that one of the men sitting at the bar would hit on her, but it didn't bother her. The half round bar was situated so that it afforded a panoramic view of the bay from one side. She chose a stool that allowed her to take in the view then glanced quickly at the men sitting at the bar. Lauren ran her hand across the smooth hardwood bar in a very sensual manner, enjoying the richness and deep color of the mahogany finish.

She glanced at the men sitting at each side of her then the bartender who was a husky Latin man with a goatee.

"What'll you have?" he asked.

"A glass of Chablis please, make it a California wine." She smiled at him. The man stood staring at her as though in a trance until she brought him back to reality.

"Is there a problem?"

"Oh, no ma'am, I apologize for staring, I, well, you are just so very pretty that I, well, I'll bring your wine."

Lauren had never encountered such a rash of compliments in such a short time and under normal conditions she would be embarrassed, but not tonight. Tonight she was a different Lauren.

After taking a sip of the wine, she glanced toward the man sitting to her left. He was a small man perhaps in his 40's and seemed on edge after the smile Lauren afforded him. He didn't speak, but nervously returned her smile. Before she had a chance to turn her head toward the man to her right, the man spoke.

"I'd ask ya if y'all come here often, but I already

know the answer since I come here every day. Besides, a man would not forget a woman that looks like you."

Lauren turned her head toward him. He was an overweight man, probably in his 50s and partially bald. He was dressed in a cheap looking light blue suit made of some sort of crepe material and white shirt that was halfway untucked. His trousers were forced well below his waist by his protruding stomach, and he wore large horn-rimmed glasses that were propped up on the end of his nose.

She looked directly at him and responded to his comment.

"Then what's your backup line?"

The man half grunted and laughed.

"I got no reason to believe any line would work on you lady, so I guess I don't have one."

"You're certainly right about that," she said as she turned away. Lauren noticed that a third man had entered the bar and was sitting on the other side opposite her. He was halfway turned away so that she couldn't make out his face, nor could she clearly tell much about his build or age. After ordering another glass of wine, she watched him pick up a napkin and write something on it thinking he must be making a note to himself. But rather than putting it in a pocket as she might expect, he simply pushed it away from himself and finished his drink. She glanced away for the briefest of moments and when she looked back in his direction again, she was only able to see his back as he left the bar.

The bartender pocketed a dollar tip that the man had left and began wiping the bar in front of where the man had been sitting. He glanced at the napkin and after reading it turned toward her and the other two men.

"What do you make of this?" he said.

"What's that?" the man to her right asked.

"The guy who just left here, he wrote something on this napkin and just left it."

"Well." the man added, "are you going to share it with us or keep us guessing?"

"Oh," the bartender said, "he wrote the word Camelot. It doesn't make any sense."

Lauren spun around on the stool then slid off and walked rapidly toward the door, but was too late to catch the man as he had driven off in a small green compact car. She went back to the bar and the two men and bartender were staring at her.

"Man, what got in to you?" the bartender asked.

"Nothing." She responded, "can I have that napkin?"

"Here, lady, hope it helps you."

Lauren left the bar and got in her car, all the while staring at the writing on the napkin. It can't be, she thought to herself. It must just be a coincidence. After starting her car she drove in the direction of Greg's apartment.

Greg lived on the upper floor of a small two- story brick apartment complex that, by Lauren's best guess, had only six units. It was nestled amongst some very large grandfather oaks and had ivy vines growing up the side of the building. Each unit had either a patio or balcony with wrought iron railings. The grounds were in excellent shape, as was the entire upscale area where the apartments were located. This was the old area of Tampa and most of the houses reflected the architecture of the times. Large two- and three- story wood frame homes, many of which had been restored, were in abundance, and the streets which were paved with bricks many years ago were very narrow. His apartment was on the back side of the complex facing toward the bay.

Before ringing the bell, she took out a brush and ran it through her long hair. She adjusted her blouse to insure that it gave an ample view of her cleavage and smoothed her mini skirt. After three rings, the door swung open and Greg just stood there with his mouth open staring at her. About 30 seconds passed before she finally spoke.

"Aren't you going to ask me in?"

"Huh? Oh, of course. What the hell? I mean you were an attractive lady before, but, lady, tonight you're lethal. Why have you hid this person from me for all this time?"

Greg was wearing slacks and a golf shirt with a vee down the front and as she moved past him and into the living room she could smell the aroma of the musk he was wearing, which she recognized as one of her favorite scents. He followed her, all the time watching the gentle swaying motion of her hips.

The apartment was not much bigger than a studio with a small kitchen off of the living room and what she ascertained was one bedroom. Despite being small, it didn't seem congested. There were double sliding glass doors that led out to the balcony, giving the impression of openness and a fireplace that sat on the wall immediately adjacent to the doors. The small kitchen was separated from the living room by a counter and the cabinets in the kitchen hung down over the counter, but allowed for a gap that was large enough to allow a conversation between people in each room. The furniture was dark wood and covered with a light, flowered cloth pattern.

She stopped and turned toward him then stared directly into his eyes.

"I hate your furniture," she said.

"Don't blame me," he responded, "it came with the apartment, and you know on a teacher's salary, well, expensive furniture just isn't in my plans. But never mind that, tell me what's happened with you?"

"What ever do you mean, Greg?" She said in her most innocent voice.

"You know what I mean. You went from being a very attractive, but very conservative, sophisticated woman to probably the sexiest, hottest woman I've seen in quite some time."

She almost blurted out; "Hotter than Red Hot?" but thought better of it.

"Anyway, I just felt like I needed a change. Don't let the appearance sway your memory. I'm still a married woman, and we are here to discuss my English assignment." Her face broke into a wide grin as she spoke.

"Right, Lauren, but I hope you'll allow me the latitude of an occasional stare." His eyes moved to her blouse and exposed cleavage.

"I guess that wouldn't hurt anything, only just looking. Now, what about my assignment? Any ideas?" She grinned.

He walked over to a small desk that was just outside a door that appeared to lead to the bedroom, picked up a piece of paper and handed it to her.

"Here, I've made a list of events that shaped the world back then and even suggested what books may have been inspired by them."

She glanced at the list then looked at him.

"My word, it appears that you've completed all my work. I guess there is no reason for me to stay any longer." She smiled at him, knowing that she wasn't going anywhere, but trying to keep him on the defensive.

"The deal was dinner came with the ideas. I thought that if I finished the work, we would have more time for dinner and such."

"What constitutes such?" she said in a playful manner.

"Such means, you know, getting to know you better and so on, but it's going to take a bit longer now."

"Why is that?" she asked.

"Well, now I have to get to know the two of you. I mean, this new Lauren St. John takes my breath away. I gotta know more about her."

"What makes you think I will let you get to know her?"

"Well, you went to the trouble of dressing like this, you must...." She interrupted him.

"Well, I got what I wanted, the information." She twirled some strands of hair and cocked her head to one side, all the time smiling.

"Ms. St. John, I know you are playing with my mind. Don't get me wrong, I like it, but please don't even think of leaving for quite some time to come. Sit down and I'll pour you a glass of Chablis. From California, right?"

"Good memory, Mr. Allsop. Where should I sit?"

"Where I can see you while I am getting the wine, of course."

Lauren moved over to a stuffed chair in the corner of the living room within full view of Greg in the kitchen. She wanted to make sure that he watched her sit down.

"Is this okay?" She slowly eased into the chair, allowing her skirt to slide up her legs revealing the dark part of her nylons. She crossed her legs, then crossed them again, all the time looking at Greg's eyes, which were focused on her legs. At this point Lauren felt that she could safely take the next step.

"So tell me, where did you disappear to last week?"

"Oh, I had some business to take care of, nothing important." The cork popped as he spoke. He poured two glasses of wine then went back into the living room.

"It's none of my business what you did," she said, "I was just curious where you went. You know, to give us something to talk about." While she already knew he had gone to California, she thought she would start there to see if he would actually tell her the truth.

"California, the Bay Area, you know, San Francisco," he said as he approached her and handed her one of the glasses of wine.

"Thank you. I love the Bay Area," she said, "as a matter of fact, I have a dear friend that lives in South Bay. I roomed with her in college, but not in California. She was raised there and wanted to move back after school. I visit her at least once every two years or so. You may remember we talked about it the last time we had dinner."

"I remember you mentioning her. Is she as good looking as you?" Greg sat in a chair directly across from her where he had a good view of her legs. His eyes danced back and forth from her eyes to her legs as she talked.

"I always thought she was better looking than I am, but completely different. She has long jet black hair, a dynamite body and is very Anglo looking." He interrupted her.

"And crystal blue eyes?"

She was taken aback.

"How did you know that, Greg?"

"Oh, I don't, just took a wild stab based on your description of her."

She wasn't quite satisfied with the answer, but dropped it for the time being, continuing her probing.

"Do you have family out there, Greg?"

"No, Lauren, this was just business."

She pressed on.

"For the College?"

"No, something from another life." He replied. Lauren picked up on the comment immediately.

"Oh, so you have another life as well. Earlier you wanted to know about my other person, maybe we can swap stories." She crossed her legs again, hoping to keep the intensity of the moment.

Greg leaned forward in his chair, which put him within a few feet of Lauren.

"Tell you what, you keep crossing your legs like that and I'm liable to tell you anything you want to know."

She felt her face flush and she became a bit flustered, fidgeting in her chair. She pondered his comment for a moment then responded.

"Interesting comment, Mr. Allsop. Let me give it some consideration." She was trying her best to keep the upper hand and not to appear anxious.

By this time, they had both finished their wine. Greg went to the kitchen and filled the glasses again. She had not eaten since breakfast, having worked through her lunch, so the wine began to affect her almost immediately. By the time they had finished the second glass, a warm glow had engulfed her, and she was feeling a bit looser. The conversation continued to revolve around California, and since he continued to skirt around her questions effectively, she became a little more direct.

"Mr. Allsop, you are not giving me direct answers to my questions. How do you think I am going to get to know you better?"

He responded the instant she stopped talking. "You have stopped crossing your legs, Ms. St. John. How do you expect me to get to know you better?"

She looked him straight in the eyes.

"Hmm, it would seem that we are negotiating something here."

After finishing her third glass of wine, she leaned forward and handed Greg her glass. As he went to the kitchen to refill her glass, she thought to herself that this type behavior was not ladylike and she should probably get up and go before she lost any more control. But, she could not bring herself to leave, for in her mind, her mission was not accomplished.

"Isn't it a bit warm in here, Greg? Would you mind opening the balcony doors?" She said, fanning her face with her hand. She then moved back the silken material of her blouse until a third button popped open, exposing a bit of the top of her lace bra.

After opening the double doors, Greg returned to his chair and his eyes went immediately to her breasts.

"Want to go out on the balcony?" she asked as she rose from the chair.

"Sure," Greg replied, following her out on to the balcony.

Lauren was tying to sort out in her mind just how direct she should be, since it appeared she wasn't getting any straight answers.

"Lauren, exactly what is going on here?" he said. "First, and I am simply making an observation here, you make up some seemingly weak reason that gives us a chance to be together. Then you do a complete makeover and look like one of the sexiest woman I have ever seen. Don't get me wrong, you were sexy before, but now, well you get the point." She looked at him questioningly. He continued. "Then, you persist in asking me some very direct questions about my whereabouts over the past few days. Well, I just don't know where this is going. Mind you, if you are here simply because I've swept you off your feet, then I'm thrilled to death, but I don't think that's the reason."

She turned away from his glance and stood against the railing of the balcony, looking out at the lights along the boulevard. She felt him slip his hands around her waist. She remained completely still, not yet responding to the last question.

Without turning, she answered.

"Well, Mr. Allsop, I sort of feel like you are not who you say you are, and I'm kind of curious as to who or what you really are."

He thought for a moment.

"What makes you think that? I really haven't done anything to lead you to believe that, have I?" As he spoke, his right hand moved ever so slightly up the side of her ribs.

The combination of the wine, the cool night and the man gave her a feeling of excitement. She nevertheless, felt quite uneasy. She thought that if she let him know anything, she would lose any strategic advantage she had gained. She didn't want to do that, so she opted to remain aloof for the time being.

Lauren knew that if she did nothing about the movement of his hand that he would probably continue to test her response and he did. For within a moment, his left hand began to move very slowly down the side of her hip to the upper part of her thigh. She could hear the sound of each breath she took and hoped that he hadn't noticed that her breathing was now coming faster.

Perhaps he would be a little more willing to answer her questions now, she thought to herself. A soft sigh escaped her throat, and she knew instinctively that he would take this as a sign that she wasn't objecting to his advances. Suddenly, he slid his right hand up just under the rise in her right breast stopping just before touching it.

"It's a very beautiful view from here," she said, trying to hide her nervousness. He didn't answer, but let his left hand slide another six inches farther down the side of her leg to where it was within an inch or two of the hem of her skirt. She felt one of the fingers on his right hand slide up to the rise of her breast and his left hand slide an inch or so under the hem of her skirt. She knew she should stop him now, before it got out of control. This was the time to start the negotiating.

"So, Greg, where did you say you went the other day?"

"I told you, San Francisco."

"And I forgot, what was the purpose of the trip?" she asked. By this time, he had slid two more fingers to the slope of her breast and had slipped the thumb of his other hand under her skirt, raising it ever so slightly. The encounter was at the point where it could be stopped, but if it went any further she wasn't sure that she would have the resolve to stop him. With that, in a single motion, she turned around. Facing him, she held her glass out and said, "Look, my glass is empty." She felt this gave her the advantage since she didn't actually tell him to stop, but successfully halted the encounter, leaving it open for him to perhaps try again.

He returned with her glass of wine and found her leaning against the railing of the balcony, again looking out toward the bay. Greg stood directly behind her and within moments, his hand had returned to her waist. He wasted no time before letting it slip slowly down until it was on her thigh just above her the hem of her skirt. She made no attempt to stop him. He moved his hand to the hem of the skirt and lifted it several inches, caressing the soft materials of her stockings as he did. Lauren remained perfectly still knowing that there was a major decision to be made in the next several moments, one way or the other. While she had every intention of stopping him at the appropriate time, she wondered to herself if, in fact, she would have the strength of conviction to do just that.

As she stood there in the cool evening, feeling the touch of a strange man's hands, an image of Lady Guinevere flashed in her mind and she thought of the reality of Guinevere's union with Arthur: that she did not really want to marry Arthur as the story goes. In fact, it was a marriage of convenience in order to secure the safety of her people through the strength of Arthur's legions. And when faced with the supreme temptation in the person of Lancelot, she succumbed to her inner passions.

He continued moving his hand under her skirt and up her leg until she could feel his touch at the top part of her nylon. Her heart was beating so loud that she wondered if he could hear it; she did not stop him. He slid his other hand to her blouse and cupped her left breast in his hand. She let her head lean back on his shoulder and a small groan came from her throat. She knew he would take this as a sign of approval and that he would continue his advances.

He did, sliding his hand up her leg until he could feel her bare skin at the top of her nylon while at the same time continuing to fondle her breast. By now, he could feel the line of her panties and he let his thumb slide underneath the silk material. His other hand slid inside her blouse then inside her bra to her erect nipple, gently massaging it between two fingers. She knew that she was almost to the point of submission, when suddenly the mood and the moment was interrupted by the ringing of the telephone.

"Aren't you going to answer it?" she asked breathlessly.

"Not a chance. Let the machine get it," he responded. This proved to be his fatal mistake, as she recognized the voice on the other end of the line.

"Greg, it's me Lisa. Just got some new info on the California case and I need to talk to you as soon as possible." It was Brian's partner, Red Hot.

With that, Lauren grabbed both of his hands and moved them off of her, making a hasty retreat to the living room where she picked up her purse. Then she turned and looked at him.

"It was a mistake to come here and a mistake to let you, well you know what I mean."

He came to her and put his hands on her shoulder.

"She is just a business associate, that's all."

"Really, what kind of business, Greg?" Lauren stared into his eyes with an intensity that gave him a chill.

"I really can't say. It's confidential information, but please don't go."

She briefly toyed with the idea of telling him what she knew about him, but quickly discarded the thought, as it would probably put an end to any chance she had of gaining what she wanted. She made her way to the door and opened it, but before leaving she stopped and turned toward him.

"You were so close Greg, and that hasn't happened since before I got married. It's too bad that you don't want to share…." She paused, clearing her throat, "well it might have been very nice."

With that, she fled into the cool night. All the way

home, she kept wondering if her reaction was more as a result of the fact that she wasn't able to get any information out of him or because she was jealous of Red Hot.

By the time she arrived home a dense fog had set in and she couldn't see the entrance to the condominium until she was several feet away. After punching in her code, the large wrought iron gate squeaked open, and she slowly drove in, parking under her carport. As she slid out of the car, she instinctively felt the presence of someone or something, but was unable to focus on anything specific because of the lack of visibility.

The main entrance to the building was about 150 feet from her car port, which was located on the far side of the parking area away from the building. She waited for a moment and listened, then turned her head around, and stared intently into mist that surrounded her.

"Is anyone there?" There was no answer.

All of a sudden in the distance, she saw the darkened image of something. It appeared to be the silhouette of a person and in a split second it began walking toward her. She slid her hand into her purse and found the cold handle of the pistol Arthur had given her. Gripping it tightly, she began walking rapidly toward the condo entrance, all the time peering back to see if the figure was getting any closer. Her pace quickened, yet she didn't seem to be getting any closer to the door. Despite the coolness of the evening, she could feel beads of perspiration sliding down her neck and cheeks. Every muscle in her body strained, but she couldn't move, standing there as the figure came ever so closer. She removed the pistol from her purse, now breathless from the terror that had overtaken her, pointed it in the direction of the silhouette in the mist and screamed.

"Someone help me!"

The scream was enough to wake her, as she found herself sitting up in the middle of her bed, sweating and shaking. This was a nightmare like so many before it: so intense, so terrifying, so real and yet only in her mind. She glanced at the digital clock on her nightstand which read 4:10, and she was still alone in her bed. No Brian to comfort her; alone in her world. The encounter with Greg Allsop now seemed distant and not real, but the dream seemed almost too real to be a dream. It would live vivid in her memory just as the others had.

CHAPTER TWELVE

"Brian, line one, someone from California. A voice called from across the room. He looked through the glass window of his office at one of his fellow cops who was pointing at him before letting his eyes find the blinking light on the phone on his desk.

Picking it up, he was greeted by Manny.

"Hey, amigo." Manny said, "que pasa?"

Brian answered with one of the few phrases he knew in Spanish.

"Nada, amigo, que pasa contigo? You must be up early, Manny. I'm still drinking my morning coffee."

"Not early, Brian, haven't been to bed yet. Anyway, got something for ya, but I'm not sure what it means." Manny replied.

"What is it, Manny?" he replied.

"Well, you know the word that was written on the mirror in what we thought was blood?"

"Yeah I remember'. Electra'." He said, awaiting Manny's response.

"I did a little research and it seems that in Greek mythology, Electra was the daughter of some dude named Agamemnon who was a hot shot general in the army in ancient Greece. The story goes like this: He was off fighting some enemy and while he was gone, his wife Clytemnestra had an affair with a guy named Aegis... Man, these names are killing me. Anyway, she plots with her lover to kill Agamemnon when he comes back from the war or whatever."

"Aga-what?" Brian asked.

"Agamemnon," Manny laughed, "so, she and her lover kill the husband. The dead husband's son, Orestes and daughter Electra, get wind of it and plot revenge. Only problem is, Orestes is too young to really kill anyone, but his mother is worried that when he grows up, he may be a problem. So she wants to have him bumped off, too."

"Jesus, it's like a soap opera," Brian responded, scratching his head.

"No doubt," Manny said. "So anyway, Electra gets wind of it and sends Orestes off to some uncle or whatever for safe keeping. She puts the revenge on ice until Orestes can grow up. When he grows up, he comes back and kills the mother and the lover. The motivation here on the part of Electra is that she has a thing for her father. You know the reverse of Oedipus, who had a thing for his mother. Remember, he unwittingly killed his father and married his mother."

"Okay, Manny, we know who Electra is, but how does that fit in with Robin or Lauren, for that matter?"

"I got a professor from the university out here working on it. He's a profiler or something. You do what you can on your end and maybe we'll come up with something...."

Brian interrupted him. "There's another development, Manny."

"What's that, Brian?"

"My wife got a post card from Robin Bennet. It said that she was off in the mountains shooting for a magazine. Didn't say which mountains."

"You think it's a forgery?" Manny asked.

"Given the circumstances, I think there is a good chance that it is," Brian responded. "I'm going to go through Lauren's closet when she's not at home and see if I can find some old correspondence from Robin, then take it to our local handwriting expert." He paused, "the thing that perplexes me is that if, in fact, it is a forgery, then how would the killer know to send a postcard to Lauren?"

"Good question," Manny answered, "let me know if you figure it out, amigo, and I'll keep a vigil on this end."

ฅฅฅฅฅฅฅฅฅฅฅฅ

When Lauren got to school that morning, she found a note on her door from Arthur, asking her to come to his office.

"Morning, Arthur, what's up?" she said, walking into his office.

"Well, Lauren, I just got an invitation to a seminar on English Mystery Writers given by one of the foremost authorities in the field."

"How does that affect me?" Lauren asked.

"Well, the seminar is being held next week in Bangor, Maine, about a two-hour drive from where you were raised. Thought I might go over there and snoop around a bit, if it's okay with you."

"I think it's terrific. Let me give you a few names of people who may or may not be alive. You might also pay a visit to our church. Mother was always very close to the pastor. He is, no doubt, retired but may still be alive. He wasn't all that old when I was born." She pulled out a small pad and wrote a few names on it.

"What about relatives, Lauren?"

"To my knowledge, there aren't any left alive and I was an only child. I don't even have siblings. My parents moved away from grandma's house when she committed suicide, but they were still in the general area. She hung herself shortly after I was born, and I have no memory of my grandfather, but from all of the accounts my dad told me, my grandfather was a very nasty man. He even went to the extent of calling him evil."

"Goodness," Arthur replied.

"Yeah, I guess he sort of disappeared a year or so after I was born. When I was old enough to understand, my mother told me that he never forgave her for having a daughter and not a son. Still don't understand that."

"Hmm, interesting," Arthur pondered, as Lauren changed the subject.

"By the way, I went over to Greg's apartment last night. I told him I needed help with a school project."

"Did you learn anything, Lauren?" Arthur asked.

"Yes, I did, that he is a real hound dog," she said.

"Come on to you, did he?" Arthur chuckled.

"California wine and all. It was a very difficult situation. He is a very good looking man."

"But you held your ground!"

"Is that a statement or a question? Never mind, the answer is yes, thanks to a phone call." Lauren smiled.

"I won't touch that one, but remember, we need to stay level-headed."

"Of course," she responded, "but you'll never guess who the call was from."

"Well, I'm waiting," he said impatiently.

"Red Hot. You remember? Brian's partner," she responded.

"What the hell can the two of them be working on?" he asked as he rose, putting his hand under his chin and resting his elbow on his protruding stomach, as if to be pondering the situation.

"I haven't a clue," she responded, "but I have a feeling that this thing is a whole lot deeper than I first thought." She stood as she talked, looking at Arthur, who had turned and picked up a small folio where he kept notes on everything of importance.

He flipped to a page marked "Lauren's Case."

"It fits, Lauren. Remember that you couldn't find anything about either of them on the Internet. Maybe they are connected professionally and perhaps not personally. Think about it. Your husband is a cop, you have had strange goings on, and Greg Allsop has been pursuing you romantically…"

Lauren shot Arthur a look as Arthur continued.

"Well, that's what I gathered from your comment. Please understand, I don't mean to understate your beauty and desirability. Hell, if I was a younger man…. Well, never mind that, but it does seem to be a colossal coincidence that all these people seem to be connected in some way. And then there is your friend in California." He paused.

"Oh my God, Arthur, I forgot to tell you that I got a post card from Robin. She's in the mountains, shooting for a magazine."

"Great news, Lauren, I am happy for you and I know you are relieved."

"When do you leave, Arthur?" she asked.

"I thought I would go up a few days early to start snooping around. I think I'll leave next Monday. By the way, Lauren, did you know that when Sir Arthur Conan Doyle found out that his consumptive wife had but months to live he built her a brick house in a place called Hindhead, south of London so that she could live out her remaining days; called it Undershaw."

"Really?" Lauren inquired, knowing how much Arthur liked to talk about the author.

"Yes," Arthur went on, excited that Lauren was

interested. "It must have suited her; she lived another thirteen years. It saddens me to see what a developer wanted to do." He paused, "He wanted to remodel it and turn it into apartments. I guess it's a sign of the times, although I hear that the good folks of the city council rejected the idea unanimously."

"Good thing," she smiled and turned to leave, knowing that it was so important to this very gracious man to tell yet another story about his beloved author. "That's really interesting, Arthur, you'll have to tell me more later."

When Lauren opened the door of her office, she saw a note on the floor and picked it up.

Dear Lauren, I felt terrible about last night, and wanted to talk to you about it. Could you spare me some time today?

It was signed by Greg Allsop. She pondered whether to play hard to get or make another try at him, knowing that he was showing some weakness and might possibly be more vulnerable now. Deciding to play a waiting game would probably give her a bigger advantage, she reasoned, so she didn't answer the note.

As the day wore on, Lauren continued thinking about the way she felt before going to Greg's apartment, in control and with a feeling of power. She tried, but in vain, to understand what had come over her, knowing that she was a completely different person that night. The incident in the bar should have sent her into a panic, but it didn't. It seemed to her that she wasn't the hunted, but perhaps the hunter. Then it all changed once she drank some wine and Greg touched her. It was then that she seemed to lose the feeling of being in control.

As Lauren approached her car to start the drive home, she was interrupted by a voice from someone behind her. She immediately recognized it to be that of Greg Allsop.

"Did you get my note?"

She turned and faced him.

"Don't even talk to me unless you are ready to tell me what is going on. You know that bitch is my husband's partner, and the only way that she would know you is if you're some kind of a cop." As she turned to leave she added. "And what's in the little black briefcase that's so important?"

Before she could leave, Greg grabbed her arm and spun her around to face him, then said.

"You figured out that I am in law enforcement and as for the little box, it's surveillance equipment, but that's all I can tell you for now. I will reveal it all to you when the time is right, Lauren. Just have a little more patience. But last night had nothing to do with any of it; you just looked so damn hot that I guess you might say we were both saved by the bell."

She interrupted him.

"In any event, you may find that I am going to be getting in your way, because I am going to get to the bottom of the strange events of the past month - whatever it takes."

"Just be very careful, Lauren. There is much more here than meets the eye, and if there is ever anything I can do for you, please don't hesitate to call on me. That includes...."

Lauren again interrupted him. "Don't even bring it up. You got as close as you're going to get."

"That's not what I was going to say," he said, "but I guess..." He stopped short as she got in her car and slammed the door shut.

She turned the key, revved the engine and rolled the window down.

"When you're ready to talk to me about what's

going on here, call, but not before." She sped away.

Once home, she went into the den and turned her computer on to check her personal e-mails. She had six and five were solicitations. The other was from Cameo. At first it didn't register with her how it was that Cameo had her personal e-mail address but as she read the message from him she gasped.

Where has my fair Guinevere been? I have been trying desperately to contact you but to no avail. Have you forgotten your best friend and comrade? I will be on line each night at 8:00 p.m.,. except when I must go off to slay a dragon, and I expect you to contact me.

A sense of alarm overtook her as she read what appeared to be some sort of demand. The fact that he had her e-mail address alarmed her further. Remembering the recent incident in the condo, she immediately got up and checked the balcony and front doors, then returned to the computer. By the time she got back, there was another e-mail from Cameo.

I see you got my last e-mail, so you know that I have been diligent. Now it is up to you to continue the dialogue. Since we last communicated, I did some traveling. I went to California. Ever been there?

She felt the pores of her body tingle. "My God," she blurted out loud, "who the hell is this person?" Her first reaction was to call Arthur. But before she did, she responded to Cameo with a question.

Cameo, I was wondering who you got my personal e-mail from?"

His response was immediate.

Why, YOU KNEW -- I THOUGHT.

Searching her data base, she found Arthur's cell phone and dialed it.

"Arthur, its Lauren, have you got a minute?"

"Always for you, Miss, oops, Lauren. Damn, it is hard to break old habits. What have you got, you sound upset?"

"I went on-line and found an e-mail from Cameo on my personal e-mail. The tone of his text was rather demanding, suggesting that he expected me to keep responding to his contacts. He then responded immediately after I opened his e-mail. I fear that if he knew where I lived, he might be the stalker type."

"Based on the events of the past several weeks," Arthur paused, "what makes you think he doesn't already know? After all, don't you think there was someone in your apartment that night?" he asked.

"Yes, Arthur, but Brian had told me about some break-ins in our area recently and I was trying to rationalize that was all it was. I guess I didn't think that it could have been him, at least not until you just mentioned it. If that's the case, I am in more danger than I thought," she said, as her voice cracked.

"Be sure you save the e-mail, Lauren, and heed what I am about to say. You have the pistol I gave you. Go to a shooting range and get familiar with it."

"Okay," Lauren responded.

"Then practice in your mind," he said, "what you would do in different situations. As an example, what if you left school late and yours was the only car in the parking lot and you see a strange man coming toward you. Reach in your purse and put your hand on the gun. You are carrying it, I hope?" Arthur asked.

"Of course," Lauren replied.

"Or perhaps you're opening the door to your condominium late at night, and Brian is not at home; you sense that someone is near you, put your hand on the gun in your purse. See what I mean? Be ready, be alert, and don't be afraid to use it."

"Okay," she said, as Arthur continued.

"I, along with about 100,000 other people in Florida, have a permit to carry a concealed weapon. I have never had to use it to this point, but I think it might be a good idea for you to get a permit. It may save you a lot of problems down the road. By the way, any idea how he got your personal e-mail? Although, I don't suppose it would be all that difficult since you correspond with a lot of people."

"No," she said, "but when I asked him, he responded that he thought I knew. It was strange, all in upper case letters and separated in the middle by two dashes."

Lauren didn't like guns and the thought of owning one did not sit well with her, but these were special circumstances, she thought.

"Arthur, it's always been against my beliefs to own a gun, despite Brian's occupation and all, but perhaps you are right in this case. How do I go about getting a permit to carry one?"

Arthur cleared his throat.

"It really isn't all that difficult in Florida; you first go to an authorized gun range that offers the necessary class. It takes eight hours and during the last hour of the class you shoot your weapon. While you are supposed to attain a certain accuracy score, I have yet to hear of anyone failing. They give you a certificate. You then get a set of finger prints done. The police will do it for free. Then, you send in an application with a check for, I don't know, maybe a $140 to Tallahassee. In about three to four weeks you have your permit. There is only one thing that could stand in your way at that point. The finger prints go to the FBI's data base, so if you have a record, they will reject your application. I don't think that's a problem for you, however."

"Thanks, Arthur. I'll get on it immediately and no, it isn't a problem."

CHAPTER THIRTEEN

The next day Lauren made plans to enroll in the class required to obtain a permit to carry a concealed weapon. Because of her schedule at school she had to take a weekend class. It was Saturday. The sky was without a cloud and the temperature was about 70 degrees. She put the top down on her Mustang, and after putting on a CD of the Platters, she began the short drive to the shooting range which was located near Carrollwood. The combination of the sun, the air and the music put her in an upbeat mood despite the events of the past weeks. She had a problem, but she was addressing it and she had a close ally in Arthur.

The class had about a dozen people in it, half of whom were females.

"Interesting," she said under her breath. "I wonder how many other women are here because they think they are in danger." She looked at the group of people in the small classroom and noticed a woman about her age sitting by herself in the back of the room. Lauren smiled at her as she walked her way, then sat beside her.

She was quite attractive and on the thin side with shoulder-length, straight brown hair and hazel green eyes. She was wearing tight-fitting, black slacks with short heels and a white turtle neck sweater. A translucent amber stone that had some sort of symbol etched into the surface hung around her neck on a gilded rope chain. For a brief moment, Lauren eyes were fixed in a sort of trance like stare at the stone until she saw the woman smiling at her.

"I don't mean to be nosey," Lauren said, "but may I ask why you are taking this class?"

"I don't mind," the woman responded. "There is this man, I went out with him once and now he won't leave me alone. He constantly calls me after I told him that I wasn't interested in him anymore. I see him at a distance every time I go out. Frankly, it is scaring me and I want to be ready if he becomes a real problem. I see so many newspaper articles about men who stalk and while I don't know if it is a life-threatening situation, I don't want to take any chances.

"Do you own a gun?" Lauren asked.

"Not now," she said, "but I am thinking about getting one very soon. How about you?"

"Yes, I do," Lauren said. "W,ell a friend of mine let me use his, and by the way my name is Lauren."

"I'm Mandy," the woman said. "So why are you taking this course?"

"Actually, my husband is a police detective and he wanted me to take the class." Her face flushed a bit because of the obvious lie she had just told. "By the way, where did you meet the stalker?" she asked.

Mandy's mouth twisted and she looked away from Lauren's stare.

"I'm ashamed to say, but on the Internet. I know that it was a stupid thing to do, but we all do stupid things at times."

"Amen to that, Mandy. I recently did a stupid thing, myself."

About that time the instructor walked in, he was a man in his 50s and quite attractive, Lauren thought to herself. He stood about six-foot-three and had a very lean body. He introduced himself as Scott Allen and added that he was a former police detective with the local department. Lauren's face took on a questioning look, not being able to recall his name or face. She thought she had met all of the detectives on the force since Brian became a cop.

The class content included aspects of the law relating to where you are allowed to carry a concealed weapon, what you had to do in the event you were faced with a possible life-and-death situation and other aspects of your rights to use force.

"Before the recent law change, your first responsibility was to try to retreat if possible," the instructor said. "The new law is somewhat controversial, in that the governor supported a person's right to not have to run away from a potential death threat. You can now stand your ground."

At about noon, the group broke for lunch and Lauren and Mandy opted to walk across the street to a fast food place, each ordering a salad and bottled water. They talked at length and a kinship seemed to be forming in Lauren's mind.

Upon resuming, the instructor went on to explain in more detail when the law allows you to carry your concealed weapon.

"As an example," he said, "you can't bring your weapon into any sporting event, government building, school, airport or any bar or club. That includes the bar section of a restaurant, but not the food section of the restaurant."

During the afternoon break, Lauren and Mandy again talked and Lauren felt a new friendship was forming. When it came time to shoot their weapons in the last hour of the class, both of the women had to rent ear phones, a requirement of the range due to the hearing damage close-range firing can cause. Mandy rented a .38 caliber Smith and Wesson revolver; Lauren used the revolver that Arthur had given her. They were instructed to enter the shooting range with unloaded weapons, lay them on the platform of the booth they were shooting from and never to pass a weapon from booth to booth. They could, however, switch booths while leaving the gun where it was, thereby being able to use each other's weapon.

After the students loaded their weapons, the targets were mounted on a pulley that allowed the shooter to move the target anywhere from five feet to 60 feet away. The student's targets were placed at 21 feet. Lauren surprised herself on the first shot by hitting the target, although it was nowhere near the center. As both women continued shooting, they both got closer to a bulls eye and on the last two shots Lauren finally shot in the bulls eye. Both ladies passed the course and did a high five before hugging each other.

As they left the shooting range, Mandy turned and looked at Lauren.

"Lauren, it's as though I have known you forever. Perhaps we can get together some time. I sense that we both could use a friend."

"Why do you say that? Is it that obvious?" Lauren asked.

"I guess I just sensed it by the look on your face when I was talking about the guy who may or may not be stalking me," Mandy said.

"Well, you are correct, Mandy. I don't have time to talk about it now, but let's exchange cell phone numbers and plan to get together."

Once home, Lauren scanned the mail and opened the patio door to let the cool afternoon air in. She quickly returned to the front door to make sure it was locked before sitting down on the patio. Once on the balcony, she sat down and gazed out at the setting sun. She remembered the day she had finished the last bottle of the wine that Robin sent her and wondered what she might be doing now, maybe I'll call her later, she thought to herself.

Realizing that she had not checked the answer machine, Lauren rose and went into the family room. The red light was pulsating. It was from Arthur.

"Lauren, it's Arthur, I'm leaving a day or two early and wanted to let you know. I'll be staying at the Bangor Inn in for the seminar, but will call you when I go to your home town." She dialed his cell, but got no answer and figured that he must already be on the plane.

Lauren hadn't heard from Brian in two days, which was not unusual with his schedule, so after getting no answer on his cell phone, she called the homicide division at the station. A familiar voice answered.

"Hi, Tony." She recognized the voice of Corporal Tony Vasco.

"Is this my favorite redhead?" he asked.

"I don't know, Tony; don't you have another redhead down there?"

"Yeah, but frankly, Lauren, she don't hold a candle to you. You know you're our pinup lady down here."

"Thanks, Tony, do you know if Brian is around?"

"Haven't seen him in a couple of days. I know he's still on a stakeout, but don't know how long it will last," Tony answered.

"Do me a favor and ask him to call me when he calls in," she added.

"And I always thought he was a smart guy," Tony said as he chuckled.

"Whatever do you mean Tony?"

"If I had a woman that looked like you at home, I'd probably call her every ten minutes and certainly wouldn't go on stakeout."

"Thanks, Tony, gotta go. Give my best to your lovely wife."

"I hear ya, but I can dream, can't I?"

Lauren chuckled as she hung up the phone. Tony had always made a special effort to let Lauren know that he liked her. Since she had finished the wine that Robin sent, she decided to go out and get another bottle for the evening. She changed into a pair of red shorts and a black top and headed for the local liquor store in Carrollwood, which only took about ten minutes.

"Hey Byron, what's going on?" Lauren inquired.

Byron was the owner of The Winery and knew Lauren from her occasional visits to his establishment.

"Not much, Ms. St. John, it sure is great to see you again." Byron was in his 60s and appreciated fine wine and fine women. He was particularly attracted to Lauren.

"I'd like a bottle, no make it two, of that wine from California that my friend sent me. You know the one I told you about. And please call me Lauren."

"Sure thing, Lauren, it's right back here. Come on, I'll show you where it is so the next time you'll know."

In the back of the store was a section labeled California Wines, which was even sorted by county. The bulk of the wines came from the three counties just north of the San Francisco Bay Area: Napa, Sonoma and Mendocino. After gazing at the multitude of bottles, he looked at Lauren and asked, "Do you remember what county it was from, seems like it's either Napa or Sonoma, as I recall."

"Napa," she responded. "I remember that because it was written on the box she sent me in big black letters."

"Here it is. Did you say two bottles?"

"Yes, Byron, thanks," Lauren said as she walked to

the front of the store with Byron following. She felt sure he was watching her every step, which made her feel a bit uneasy.

"If you'd like, Lauren, I can deliver to you the next time you run out."

"No, that's all right, Byron. I'll just stop by." Then as she reached in her purse for her credit card, she stopped; opting to pay cash so he didn't have her personal information. She wasn't quite sure why she was being so cautious, but there was something about the man that made her nervous.

After doing a couple of errands, Lauren returned home. As she approached the door to her condo, she noticed a small basket sitting in front of the door. She picked it up and looked inside. Curiosity quickly turned to anger for in the basket were two bottles of the very same wine she had just purchased. Once inside she immediately called the liquor store and asked for Byron.

"Hello, this is Byron, how can I help you?"

"Byron, this is Lauren St. John. You recall that I just purchased two bottles of wine from you."

"Yes, Lauren, of course I recall. What's the problem? You sound angry."

"I am angry. When I was in your store you offered to deliver any future wine purchases to my home. Well you didn't wait very long, did you?"

"What do you mean, Lauren?"

"When I arrived home, there were two bottles of the same wine that I bought sitting in front of my door in a small wicker basket."

"Wait a minute," he interrupted her. "I did not deliver any wine to your home. I have been here at the store ever since you left. Feel free to ask any of my clerks.

Was there a note or something with the wine?" he asked.

"No, there was not," she responded angrily. "You expect me to believe that this is a colossal coincidence? I mean, you offering to deliver the wine, and the same wine appears on my front door only an hour later?"

He cleared his throat then responded. "I can't imagine what happened, but I know that it wasn't me. Oh, wait a second. Right after you left someone bought two bottles of the same wine. It seemed odd to me, but I didn't think that much about it. Hold on, I'll ask the clerk who waited on the party."

In the background Lauren could hear Byron asking someone where Linda was. The response was that she had left for lunch. He came back and advised Lauren that the best he could do was to question the clerk when she returned from lunch.

"Byron, this is extremely important. I must know who that person is."

"I understand, Ms. St. John; I will call you as soon as she is back from lunch. Although as we have been talking, I've been going through the receipts, and it appears that whoever it was paid cash for the wine."

"Then I can expect to hear from you shortly?" she half asked, half demanded.

"I will absolutely call you when she comes back, and please believe me; I had nothing to do with the delivery."

After hanging up the phone, Lauren glanced at the door and realized that she had not locked it. She quickly moved to the door and turned the deadbolt. Then, as she turned back toward the balcony, her mouth fell open and she gasped out loud.

"My god, did I forget to lock the balcony door when I left?"

She could not recall and now wasn't sure if she was alone. This time she reached in her handbag and felt the cool steel surface of the hand gun in her bag. Moving slowly down the hall with the pistol in her hand, she first searched the den and found nothing. She then moved to the master bedroom and carefully searched the room and the closet again finding nothing, except that the skirt that she had worn to Greg's apartment was hanging by itself on a peg next to the full-length mirror. She stood there looking at it, but for the life of her couldn't remember if she had left it there. It would not be consistent with her normal habit of putting things back where they belonged, but on the other hand, these weren't normal times.

Three hours had passed, and she had not heard from Byron, so she called him.

"Byron, you promised to call me back and as yet have not."

"I'm sorry, Ms. St. John, but the clerk hasn't returned from lunch. This is very unusual. She has a half hour for lunch. I even tried to get her on her cell and didn't get an answer. She's only been here a few days and works part time, so I don't really know her all that well."

Lauren paused for a moment then responded.

"Byron, I hate to be redundant and I can't explain now, but it is extremely important that I talk to this woman. Can you give me her phone number?"

"Ms. St. John, I can't give you that information. I'm sure you can appreciate that. I could get in a heap of trouble if this turned out to be nothing."

"Well let me tell you, Byron, at this point, someone has given out my home address and quite mysteriously someone has delivered some wine that I did not order to my front door. If it wasn't you, then it must have been your elusive clerk. My husband is a police detective, and if need be I will get him involved and we'll get to the bottom of this. Are we clear on that, Byron?"

After clearing his throat he responded, "Ms. St. John, I don't take well to threats. Perhaps we have a case of some admirer sending you a gift which I don't think constitutes a felony or even a misdemeanor, for that matter. So why are you so paranoid about this?"

"I'm sorry, Byron," she said, "but there has been this person that has been, well I wouldn't exactly call it stalking, but I feel very uncomfortable. When this happened, well, I guess I overreacted."

"Not a problem, Lauren." He had returned to calling her by her first name. "I understand, and we will get to the bottom of this, if and when the clerk returns."

"By the way, Byron, inside the basket was a small piece of what looks like nautical rope, about a foot long. Any idea what that's about?"

"Not a clue, Lauren, not a clue."

Lauren poured herself a glass of wine and went out on to the balcony with her cell phone and handbag with the revolver in it. She sifted over the events of the past weeks, again trying to make some sense of it. She remembered she was going to call Robin, so she went into the family room and dialed the number. After several rings, she heard a voice on the other end.

"Hello, this is Robin and who might this be?"

"Woman, you had me worried sick. I've been calling you for the past two weeks and had no idea where you were."

"Lauren, you won't believe this, but this very moment I was just thinking about you. And by the way, I did send you a post card, so don't be scolding me, my best friend."

"I know, but I was so worried that I asked Brian to check on you. You know, as a cop. And by the way, I drank all the wine you sent me since my last birthday and had to go out and buy some. Some friend you are," she chuckled. "imagine me without the wine my best friend sends me every time I have a birthday. So, you've been in the mountains shooting for what, a magazine?"

"Lauren, you won't believe it but I have been engaged by a publication that I've never heard of to do a series of nature shots. They offered me twice what I normally get for some reason, but who cares, as long as they pay me."

"Terrific, Robin, but you know what? I really would like to see you. Things here aren't so great, and I could really use your advice on something. And some moral support. It's something I would rather not talk about on the phone."

After a short pause, Robin responded, "Can you come out here?"

"The problem is that I am in the middle of a semester and can't break away. Is there any way you could come here?"

"Well, if you can give me a day or so, perhaps I can. I just need to get this shoot wrapped up and put to bed. Let's play it by ear and see when I can finish. I'll call you in a few days, and yes, I would love to come and see my best friend. Count on it," Robin said.

Lauren was flushed with excitement about the possibility of seeing Robin again, not having the slightest idea what Brian had seen in California.

She sat on the couch and laid her head back to relax and as she was about to doze off, she heard the front door open and Brian walked in. He went to the kitchen for a beer.

"Hey, stranger, nice to see you again. I understand

you've been on stakeout and by the way, I just got off the phone with Robin, she's going to be coming here in a short while."

The next thing she heard was a beer can hit the floor. "What did you say?" Brian said in a rather loud voice.

"I said I talked to Robin and since when are you so clumsy?"

"Lauren, tell me what you just said." His voice was intense.

"What are you, deaf?" she responded. "I said I just talked to Robin and she will be coming here soon."

Brian tried his best to keep his composure but after hearing Lauren's comments, he was on the verge of near shock given that he thought Robin was dead. He came over to where she was sitting and sat next to her. His face was flush, and he was visibly upset.

"Lauren, this is of the utmost importance. Did you say you talked to Robin and she is okay? Could you tell it was really her?"

"What? Yeah, I guess I can tell my best friend after all these years," she snapped back. "What kind of question is that anyway?"

Brian stammered a bit then responded nervously, "I guess after you didn't hear from her for so long, I assumed the worst. Anyway, that's great news. I look forward to seeing her again."

I bet you will, she thought to herself. He went back into to the kitchen just as the phone rang. It was Arthur calling.

"Lauren, I'm in your home town, and I'll poke around here."

"Oh, hello, Arthur," she responded. "How's the convention?"

Arthur caught on immediately and asked, "Is Brian there with you?"

"Yes, I'll take care of it a bit later, perhaps you can call later tonight," She hung up, knowing that Brian would be gone later.

Brian came out of the kitchen and looked in Lauren's direction.

"Was that Arthur from the college?"

"Yes, he had asked me to complete a little project for him while he's at a seminar."

"I was going to stay home tonight, but something came up at the station that I really have to attend to," Brian said, "and I should call the guy in San Jose and let him know that Robin is okay."

Lauren suspected that Brian wasn't telling her the real reason he was going to the station but didn't care, as it would allow her to talk to Arthur alone later.

Brian made his way through the heavy city traffic all the time trying to figure out what had happened and came up with nothing but blanks. When he got to the station, he immediately called Manny.

"This is Manny, how can I help you?"

Brian knew that Manny often spent 12 hours a day at the station; so odds were that he could connect with him.

"Manny, Brian. You are not going to believe what just happened."

"What is it, amigo?"

"My wife just got a call from Robin Bennet."

'Remember what I said when we both looked at the pictures? Manny said, "that pictures can be doctored? She's sure it was her?"

"Positive and, in fact, she said she is coming here to visit soon."

"Well, for starters Brian, you're a lucky guy. I saw the pictures. But what do you want me to do?" Manny asked.

"Well, in anticipation of her visit, I was wondering if you might call on her. Don't tell her the real reason, but just to verify that she's alive and it was her calling. Make something up as to why you're there. I don't think she would know that we were in her place."

"Not a problem, amigo." Manny responded, in fact, it would be a pleasure. Any thoughts on what I tell her as to why I am visiting?" Manny asked.

"Why don't you tell her that your friends in Florida wanted you to look in on her, because they hadn't heard from her for quite awhile and were concerned. If she says that she already talked to Lauren, just say that you got the request a few days ago and only now got a chance to come by. But whatever you do, don't tell her about the pictures. I gotta assume that she didn't know about them since the last one would have probably sent her running to the cops. Oh, and by the way, could you possibly overnight me copies of the pictures to the station?"

"Brian, this is going to be one assignment I'll be glad to accept. I'll get over there tomorrow and be back to you ASAP. Photos will be on their way."

As Brian hung up the phone, another officer came into his office and dropped off several manila folders.

"Hey Brian, here's the files on those murders that you wanted. Anything going on?" the officer asked.

"No, Ron, just routine follow up on cold cases. Thanks for your help."

Brian had requested the files on the three murders that took place a few years ago in Florida. Now, however, they didn't seem to have the same sense of importance, so he pushed them to one corner of his desk and started to think about how he was going to approach Robin about the photos. Or, he thought to himself, should he discuss them with Lauren first? Leaning back, he propped his feet on desk and closed his eyes. With his hands behind his head, he let his mind drift in hopes of thinking of a solution.

He reasoned that if he told Lauren about the photos, he risked alienating her even more because he had not told her about them in the first place. Further, he had lied to her about where he had gone. Then there was the dire circumstances surrounding the whole situation. On the other hand, if he withheld that information and could not talk with Robin privately, he may never be able to solve what had appeared to be a crime of the worst kind.

Lauren spent most of the early evening grading papers and about the time she finished, the phone rang.

"Lauren, Arthur. Are you alone?"

"Yes, Arthur, you sounded pretty excited about something earlier, what is it?"

"Well, I snooped around the entire town. Not much of a town by the way. Anyway, after talking to about a dozen people, I finally saw this very old lady sitting in a little park in the town square. You know the one?"

"The old lady?" she asked.

"No," Arthur responded sarcastically, "the park."

"Yes, I used to play there as little girl," Lauren sighed as Arthur continued.

"After much small talk, I brought up your family and she remembered all of you. Said you were a little angel, at that point I should have corrected her, just kidding," he laughed at his own joke. "I eventually got to the situation with your grandmother hanging herself and all."

"And what did she say, Arthur?"

"Well, she sat there for what seemed like five

minutes then finally said that it was a terrible tragedy that could have been avoided. I asked her what she meant and she looked at me as though I was an idiot; so I asked her again. She said that if you had been born a boy instead of a girl, all would have turned out well."

"Huh?" Lauren wrinkled her face.

"Yeah, I asked what she meant, and she said that she'd been told that your grandfather was so vehement in his want of a grandson that he took it out on your grandmother and your mother. Evidently your grandmother could never give him the son he wanted so badly, so he took it out on your grandmother when you were born. Your grandmother tried to take the guilt off your mother, then your grandmother hung herself, leaving a note that said she was to blame and not your mother for never bringing a boy into the family. Frankly, Lauren, I can't fathom someone being as intolerant as your grandfather appeared to be, but then I wasn't there."

"Did you find out where the note ended up or anything else?" Lauren asked.

"No, but then I asked her if she knew where the pastor that ran the church back then ended up. She said that the last time she had heard about him, he had built a small log cabin in the woods outside a small town about an hour's ride north of here."

"Arthur, did she tell you how to get there"?

"No, Lauren, but she did say that it was on the banks of a very large lake from what she was told and that the town was called something like Sanity or something like that. From the looks of everything around here, it should have been called insanity, but it shouldn't be hard to find. Anyway, she then excused herself and left."

Lauren was still puzzled about his comment but

Arthur continued, "Lauren, it's the Thanksgiving break next week and I have a few vacation days coming, so I'm going to try and find the pastor or the cabin. There is a good chance that he has passed away by now, but even if he has, maybe he left some clues behind."

"Arthur, I don't want you to use your vacation for me, and even more I don't want you to be in any danger." Lauren's voice gave her concern away.

"Don't worry, Lauren. I'll be careful and as for the vacation, what better way to spend it than trying to solve a mystery?"

As usual, Arthur hung up without saying goodbye. You knew he was finished by the click at the other end of the phone.

CHAPTER FOURTEEN

A cold gray sky hung overhead and the mist from the clouds made the air damp and penetrating. Arthur was pretty sure that he had located the town the old lady had talked about. It was located on the south end of a rather large lake about 100 miles west-northwest of Bangor.

This was not the typical small town built around a town square with a statue of some local hero in the middle. It had no local courthouse, drug store, barbershop, cafe or small department store around the square like so many small towns across America. The entire town was built along the side of a lake surrounded by large hills in the background as though to form a valley in which the lake sat. Because of the topography, the town was elongated with only a few streets stretching back into the foothills. The buildings were mostly red brick and everything seemed quite dismal to Arthur when compared to Florida's eternal sunshine.

By the time he got there, it was evening, so he checked into the only motel in town which reminded him of the Bates Motel in the movie Psycho. The motel room was dingy and small, and the rug, which reeked of smoke, was visibly dirty and worn. The bed creaked when he sat on it and bowed in the middle from years of wear. After buying a hamburger, fries and a vanilla shake at the Dairy Queen next to the motel, he settled in to watch an old movie on TV while making notes on a yellow pad.

Arthur was one of the last of his generation to succumb to the computer age and insisted on keeping all his personal memoirs on a series of yellow pads that he called his internet. Over the years, he had accumulated at least a hundred such pads filled with scratchings about anything and everything that was going on in his life. As the night wore on, he found himself tossing and turning and listening to sounds that were not familiar to him.

Arthur faced the new day about as tired as the end of the day before and with an aching back, compliments of the motel bed. After a shower and shave, as he did every day of his adult life, he dressed and put on his khaki raincoat and a scarf.

Armed with a map of the local area, he began the arduous trip around the lake, driving his Ford Taurus rental about 20 miles an hour to take in all the area had to offer. There was a mixture of large, old, frame houses and small cabins located on both sides of the road, most spaced hundreds of feet apart and fenced. He had chosen to drive along the west side of the lake first for no particular reason, and it seemed that the further north he drove, the sparser the area became. Soon, he could only see an occasional small cabin nestled up on a hill or down close to the lake. With several stops along the way, the drive around the lake took over an hour, ending up back where he had started. He spent another hour in a small general store, talking to some of the locals, but learned nothing that would help him. He didn't want to leave the town without getting some important information, so having skipped breakfast he opted to have an early lunch at a local pub.

At the edge of town, on the shore of the lake was a large log cabin-type bar that advertised that they served lunch and dinner. In front of the bar were three large faded beer signs that showed the effects of numerous bitter winters. There were about a half dozen older model cars and pickups sitting on the gravel parking area in front. The place was appropriately named the Shore Nuff Lounge. He could hear a crunching sound made by his feet with every step on the gravel.. He stopped short before going in the front door and looked at the vehicles in the parking lot. He noted that not one of them was foreign. I guess folks here probably don't take well to strangers, he thought. Anyway, good thing I'm driving a Ford.

Arthur entered the restaurant to a haze of smoke and about five or six men sitting at a worn wooden bar flanked on both sides by groupings of 1960s style tables and chairs with formica tops and chrome legs. There were four booths at the far end of the bar that sat behind three pool tables. The stuffed head of a large deer was mounted above the bar and behind the bar was a heavy set woman who appeared to be in her 50s, laughing and joking with the men. Arthur figured that these were the good ole boys that probably spent some time out of every day of their lives sitting at the bar and talking about the good old days.

Glancing from side to side, he noticed an old woman sitting in one of the four booths back in the corner, drinking a beer. He decided, however, that by sitting at the bar he could more easily talk to someone. He situated himself between two of the men who had been talking with one another and drinking draught beer.

He ordered a beer and tried to begin a conversation with them.

"Wouldn't you know it, the one day I pick to come to this lovely little town and the weather is horrible."

Without looking at him, one of the men responded in a thick brogue unique to the area.

"Don't no one come here for the weathah. It's like this most of the winter, cept when there's snow."

The other man added what Arthur determined to be either a yup or a belch, he wasn't sure. He then faced the man who had answered him.

"Well, I was just passing through."

The man interrupted him, "Didn't think anyone just passed through here. Why would they?"

"Well the truth is," Arthur added, "that I was looking for an old friend. He was a pastor at a church east of here, and I had heard that he had retired in this area."

Almost simultaneously both men spoke up.

"Don't know nothing 'bout no pastor."

The other added "Might wanna talk to the old lady ovah there. She knows everybody's business here bouts." He pointed to the booth farthest from the bar and in the corner, where an old lady was sitting. The one he had first noticed.

"Thanks a bunch, guys. I appreciate it."

Arthur ordered another beer and picked up the one he was drinking, leaving his change on the bar and headed for the booth.

As he approached, without looking his way, the old lady spoke to him.

"No need to sit here, sonny, got nothin' to say to anyone."

"Well," Arthur responded, "then I guess you won't want the beer I bought you, but thanks for calling me sonny. It's been a long time since anyone has called me that."

She looked up and without any expression responded. "Hell, I guess you can sit here for a bit."

Arthur sat across from her and stared at her expressionless face that bore the wrinkles of time and a hard life. He guessed her to be in her 70s.

She finally spoke again, "Guess you want to ask me somethin' or ya wouldn't be buyin' me a beer."

"The guys at the bar said that you were the leading authority on the history of the area."

She chuckled. "Guess you must be a city sort. Whatcha mean is that I'm the local busy body here 'bouts, and you figure I can give ya the answer to yer questions."

In his typically formal way of speaking Arthur responded.

"Actually, there is something that you may be of some assistance with. You see, I am looking for an old friend…." He stopped. "That is, an old acquaintance. He was a minister in this area or perhaps Portersville many years ago and as I heard it, he retired some years ago."

"What's his name?" She asked.

"Well, I'm not quite sure." Arthur cleared his throat at what must have sounded like a rather stupid comment.

"Tell me somethin 'bout this friend," she chuckled, " 'scuse me, 'quaintance."

Arthur's face turned a bit flush and he fidgeted with his hands, and then responded, "I know this sounds a bit odd, but I have never met the man I am looking for. He was a pastor at a Baptist Church down in Portersville during the late 1950s or early 1960s, and he was helping a woman who ended up hanging herself."

The old lady's face grimaced, and her eyes took on a steely look. Clearing her throat, she responded.

"Oh, you must mean the Reverend O'Brian, Sean O'Brian. Yeah, I still think he drove that poor woman to her death."

With his brow wrinkled, Arthur asked, "what ever do you mean?"

The old lady took a gulp of her beer and belched.

"Well my friend, this is a two-beer answer, so you better ante up."

Arthur motioned to the bartender to bring them each another round. She continued talking between gulps. "Ya see, 'cordin' to the story, the pastor was filling this lady's head fullah all kinda nonsense 'bout her husband. Said that he thought her husband would disown her or maybe hurt her if their daughter didn't have a son to carry on the family name."

Arthur interrupted her.

"You mean someone would actually do that?"

"Yep," she responded, "If it was true, that man musta bin pure evil."

Arthur leaned forward and asked in a quiet voice

"What do you think made the pastor think that her husband would actually disown her or hurt her for something like that?"

"Don't know all the details," she said, "but it's told that she thought that if her daughter had a girl, they'd both be in deep trouble, maybe get hurt. And from what I hear, she was a nice lady."

"Do you think she believed the pastor; that her husband would really do something to hurt her? I mean, she had no control over the birth of the baby."

"Don't know that, or much else. Maybe she had a diary or somethin' that might help."

Arthur gulped his beer.

"If she had one, where do you think it might be?"

"Don't quite know that eitha." She said, "but rumor has it that he, the reverend that is, took a place in the woods north of here. I think it might be up off Dundee Circle. It's a bit off the main highway. But I heard that he died a few years ago. The story is that she, the lady that hung herself that is, was 'livin at the pastors church house just before she died; so maybe he took her belongins with him. Lest I'm mistakin', there's a little store on Dundee, 'bout where I think he mighta lived, maybe a few miles after ya turn on Dundee."

"How is it that you know so much about a pastor and a lady from Portersville? It's a long way from here," Arthur asked.

"The pastor stayed with the local judge here while they was buildin' his cabin. Everyone round here knows the story." She belched.

Arthur looked toward the men at the bar.

"The men at the bar said they didn't know anything about it, I wonder why?"

The old lady stood with her beer glass in her hand and shook her head. "

Did ya offer to buy 'em a beer?"

As the old woman finished her beer and was walking away from him, Arthur called to her, "Tell me about the judge."

"He's dead, too." she said, "hell, everbody's dyin." She disappeared out the front door.

It had started to rain rather hard and Arthur didn't relish the thought of driving on unknown roads in these conditions, but he knew he had to forge on. He sat for a while making notes about his recent conversations then began driving toward Dundee Circle.

At this point, he knew that his best chance of getting to the bottom of things, at least here in Maine, was to be able to find the cabin and perhaps something that might be a link to what was happening in Lauren's life in Tampa.

The rain continued a relentless assault on the windshield of the car, making it extremely difficult for Arthur to see, so he pulled over and dialed Lauren's cell phone. Through the static caused by a poor connection, he was able to leave her a message.

"Lauren, it's Arthur. I've been talking to one of the locals and have some good leads. I'm headed to what might be the cabin in the woods where the pastor that knew your grandmother lived out his final days. At least, I think so. I think he passed away a few years ago. I'll call you when I get something more."

The drive up to Dundee Road took about twenty minutes. The road curved with the contour of the lake, then left it, heading up a gradual slope away from it. As he turned west on Dundee, he thought to himself how depressing it must have been to have to live your life in this godforsaken land. On each side of the road sat an occasional small rundown shack or mobile home, mostly in total disrepair. A junk car here and there rusted from time and neglect and a hand painted sign in front of a house saying, "vegables for sale." The English professor in him wanted to stop and correct the spelling, but he went on.

After about fifteen minutes, he spotted a small grocery store that was probably once a house and most likely the place he had been told about. In front were two old gas pumps and a faded Esso Gas sign that seemed to be right out the 1950s.

As he pulled onto the gravel driveway, he noted that both pumps had signs on them, indicating that there was no gas available. Pulling his raincoat over his head, he made his way to the door of the store. Once inside, he could smell the musty air. Most of the shelves were half empty and coated with dust and an old woman sat on a stool behind the counter, looking away from Arthur.

"Hello there," Arthur said. "I was wondering if you might assist me?"

He paused expecting her to look his way, but she continued to stare at what appeared to be an open Bible sitting on the counter. "I am looking for a reverend who may have lived near here awhile back. I believe he may have passed away, but I'm not quite sure."

The old lady interrupted him.

"You'd be talkin' 'bout the reverend that lived up the hill in the log cabin. Hung himself 'bout four years ago and had no kin, so the state came and took his body away. Dirt road right outside the store, it's the only way up there."

Arthur felt obligated to at least buy something, so he took a bottle of soda and put $3.00 on the counter and turned to leave.

The old lady looked at him.

"Only costs one dollah. Don't need no charity, take ya two dollahs with ya."

The dirt road, which was slippery from the rain, wound past numerous trees and a small pond, and as his car reached the top of a slight rise, he could see the cabin in the distance. It was a very small log cabin with a rusted bucket hanging from a well in front. There was no driveway, but the needles from the many surrounding pine trees served to form an open area in front of the cabin where he stopped the car.

Before getting out of the car, he paused to look at the area surrounding the cabin then made some notes in a small pad that he kept by his side. The front porch was weather-beaten and the wood was faded and rotting. The floor boards creaked as he made his way to the front door, pushing aside several cob webs only to find that the door was locked. He peered in one of the two windows on each side of the door, but could only see darkness. After walking around the cabin, he decided to force the lock.

"After all," he said quietly to himself, "what's the difference." Grabbing the handle, he gave it a tug and to his surprise, the door handle broke off in his hand. He pushed the door open and gazed in at the stark interior of the cabin. To the right was a small table and two chairs and to the left, a cot.

There was no refrigerator, and he could see no source of electricity, only a half- burned candle on the table and a small iron potbelly stove . The three windows, two in front and one in back, were covered with burlap bags and as he yanked the bag off one of the front windows, a large cloud of dust spread through the air, causing him to sneeze. A large wooden cross was mounted on the wall ahead of him, and there was a wicker mat on the floor in front of it, which he reasoned had been used to kneel on to pray. His mind wandered to a movie he had seen about the Great Depression and how the sparse and seemingly hopeless life portrayed in the movie had caused him so much sadness at the time. Off in a far corner, he spotted a small brown box which he picked up and took to the chair by the desk that creaked as he sat down.

Peering into the box, he saw several manila folders. After spreading them out on the table, he began to look in them one at a time, pausing occasionally to ponder on the contents of each one. He took out a pen and a small black note book, writing in it as he read, then laid them on the table beside him. Many of the folders contained newsletters with information on parishioners and schedules of the various activities of the church from years past. The last folder contained a newsletter with an article entitled, *Our Friend Needs Help*. It went on to ask for donations for Angela Bordon who had taken sick and was living in the cabin in back of the church. It read that she could no longer afford to pay for her doctor bills and that the church had run out of funds for the needy.

Toward the bottom of the stack was a hand written note that read: *I can no longer bear the weight of my sin. May God forgive me for my part in her death. Just as she took her own life on this day so many years ago, I too shall now go to be with the Lord.*

"My God," Arthur blurted out, "a suicide note that no one has ever seen. How sad." He sat back in the chair, a puzzled look on his face; but before picking up the last thing in the box, he noticed that the handwriting on the suicide note seemed to be different from several other notes that the pastor apparently made. The last thing in the box appeared to be a diary. He settled back in the chair and he read each dated entry, still wondering what all of it meant.

The entries stopped, and Arthur sat back in the chair and sighed at the tragic life depicted in the diary, although it raised more questions than it answered. Nevertheless, he beamed at what he had found and wanted to tell Lauren. After flipping open his cell phone, he realized that he had no service; so he grabbed the box of files, put his notebook in his pocket and went back down the hill, headed back toward Bangor. He couldn't wait to tell Lauren about the information he had found, but wanted to be sure she was alone.

Before starting back to Bangor, he stopped at the county seat, which was located in a small city not far from the town where Lauren had been born and visited the department of records. Searching the listing of births, which to his amazement was still on microfilm and not computerized, he came to the record of Lauren's birth.

"No surprises here," he said to himself, then obtained a copy of the birth certificate and went on his way.

CHAPTER FIFTEEN

Lauren had not yet talked to Arthur and was hoping that Brian would have some reason to go out for the evening so that if he did call, she could talk to him candidly. Brian had already taken a beer from the refrigerator and came over to the sofa where Lauren was sitting. Lauren smiled and spoke.

"I hope you don't mind if Robin comes for a visit. It might be a bit crowded for a few days." She knew full well that he was probably salivating at the thought of having her around for awhile.

"Not at all Lauren, I know you two have a lot to catch up on, and I'll try to not get in your way." She knew that he was dying to see Robin again, but wouldn't show it. Just then, as though by fate, Robin called.

"Hey Robin, it's so good to hear your voice. Are you still coming?" Lauren asked.

Lauren sensed that Robin could hear the stress in her voice.

"If you'll have me, I'll be there soon. I sense tension in your voice, is everything all right?"

Lauren paused to clear her throat. Trying her best to disguise her real emotions, she ignored Robin's question.

"Actually, Robin, I can't wait, it's been too, too long since we've seen each other, and I know we have a lot to catch up on."

"Lauren, if you'd rather I didn't come…."

Lauren interrupted her, "Of course, I want you to come. What's your flight number and when do you land?"

"Surprise, surprise, I'm at the San Francisco airport

right now and catching the red eye on Northeast. It arrives at 11:20. Is that too late?"

Lauren gasped.

"Not at all, but I can't meet you at the gate because of regulations. I have to wait until you get off the tram that takes you to the main terminal. I'll be waiting there. Would you like to say hi to Brian?"

"Of course I would, put him on."

Lauren handed Brian the phone. "Hey, Brian, it's been so long since I've seen you, I can't wait."

"Hello, Robin, coming to visit, I hear. Can't wait to see you again." He paused and thought for a second, "Why don't you bring some pictures of yourself, you know, for our photo album?"

"Actually Brian, I'm already at the airport." Her voice cracked slightly. By the way, will you be meeting me at the gate with Lauren?"

"No," he responded. "I'm on duty tonight, but I'll see you sometime tomorrow."

Brian left for work, and Lauren spent the rest of the day sorting things out and making more notes about all that had happened. After drinking a glass of wine on the balcony, she went to her closet, selected the same mini-skirt, blouse and black patent leather heels she wore to Greg Allsop's apartment and got ready to go to the airport. Down deep she wanted to impress Robin. While their lives had taken opposite directions and they lived a world apart, there was still a tinge of envy on Lauren's part because she always suspected that Brian had strong feelings for Robin.

The drive to Tampa International Airport, which the locals called 'TIA', took about 30 minutes down the Veterans Expressway. By all accounts, TIA was considered to be one of the most user friendly and modern airports in the country. The airport was located just east of the sprawling waters of Tampa Bay and the Courtney Campbell Causeway which led across the bay to Clearwater. The Causeway, which could be seen from the air on incoming flights, offered numerous restaurants, hotels and office buildings as well as a beach called Ben T. Davis. Just south of the Causeway was the Howard Frankland Bridge, which locals often referred to as "The Frankenstein" because of the major rush hour traffic.

Lauren went to short term parking and took the elevator to the third floor where all arriving and departing flights come and go. It was only ten o'clock so she decided to go into the bar in T.G.I. Friday's and have a drink. As she walked from the elevator across the main section toward the bar, she noticed a man standing near the escalators that led to the first floor baggage area. He appeared to be staring at her, but he wasn't close enough that she could make out his face. She didn't want to return his stare to get a better look at him, so she kept walking and looked straight ahead. Normally, she wouldn't think much of it, but because of recent events she had become somewhat paranoid.

She sat at the bar facing the door and watched to see if the man had followed her, but she could no longer see him. Thinking that she might be overreacting, she tried to relax and ordered a glass of Chablis. Just as she crossed her legs she suddenly came face to face with another man four stools down who had turned in her direction. She made him out to be about forty something of average build and rather good looking.

"Flying out tonight?" he asked.

"No, just waiting for a friend," she responded. The man introduced himself as Kevin and said that he was flying to Chicago and came to Tampa frequently.

"I pity you. It gets very cold up there." She purposely avoided telling him even her first name.

"Can I buy you a drink?" the man asked.

"No, thank you," she replied. She had no sooner said that, when she noticed the man that had been watching her had come in the door and sat across the bar from her. While he was somewhat obscured by a row of hanging glasses she thought that he might be close enough to hear her so to the surprise of the man named Kevin, she once again engaged him in conversation.

"What do you do, Kevin?" She was talking a bit louder than normal to ensure that the other man could hear her.

"I own a small company that manufactures bullet-proof vests and other accessories," he said. "How about you?"

As she answered, she halfway looked in the direction of the man across the bar.

"Then you must deal with police departments. We have something in common; my husband is a police detective. I teach college-level English." She glanced to see if the other man had any reaction, but couldn't see enough of his face to tell.

"Lucky man," he said before she interrupted him.

"Well it's time for me to meet my friend. Nice talking to you." She took out a credit card and started to hand it to the bartender to pay for the wine, but quickly jerked it back.

"Let me pay cash for that," she said, handing him a five-dollar bill. As she walked toward the gate, she glanced back several times and could see the man walking slowly behind her at a distance. Just as she arrived at the gate, she could see the tram stop and about 30 people got off, but no

Robin. She figured that the first tram - would be first-class passengers, and she assumed that Robin would have taken coach. Minutes later another car came and in her anticipation to see Robin, she had forgotten about the man.

"She's as beautiful as you are. Is that your friend?" a voice said from behind her.

Without turning she said, "Yes, it is," then snapped her head back quickly enough to see that it was Kevin from the bar.

Robin was wearing a leather skirt and white blouse and her long black hair swayed from side to side as she walked. She spotted Lauren immediately and made her way through the crowd with arms open, dropping her carry-on as she embraced Lauren. They stood there for several minutes before holding hands and walking to the escalator that took them to the first floor where the baggage claim was located.

All the way down the escalator they couldn't stop talking about how good it was to see each other and how good the other looked. After retrieving Robin's baggage, they walked toward the elevators that led to the parking garage. Lauren looked behind her several times, remembering the man in the airport.

"Lauren, why do you keep glancing behind us?" Robin asked.

"There was some creep that kept staring at me," she said. "He followed me into the bar, then back out when I came to meet you. It's probably nothing, but there are some things that I want to talk to you about which have gotten me a bit paranoid. Let's not let it bother us tonight. Let's just go home and drink some wine."

"Sounds good to me, Lauren. Oh by the way, I brought some more California Chablis from those little wineries in Los Gatos. You know, the same ones I got you for your birthday."

"I knew there was a reason I liked you Robin." They both chuckled and got in the car.

After paying for parking, Lauren got back on the Veterans toll road going north toward Carrollwood. About a mile up the toll road, Robin noticed the man in the car next to them kept looking back and forth at them.

"Lauren, do you know the man in the car next to us?"

"My God, I think it's the man in the airport. Try to remember what he looks like, Robin." With that, she put the on the brakes and swerved into the lane behind the man's car.

"Robin, write his plate number down. There's a pen in the console."

The other car sped away, but Robin was able to write down the first four digits of a six digit plate.

"Drat," she said, "I only got four numbers. That gives us a lot of possibilities. Lauren, are you sure he wasn't just ogling you because you're so damn beautiful?"

"All the way from the airport? she asked. "I don't know Robin, but I sure hope you're right. With all that's gone on I have to assume the worst. Ogling is one thing; following me in a car is entirely something else. Anyway, thanks for the compliment."

At home, Lauren took Robin's luggage into the spare bedroom and gave her time to shower and change into something more comfortable. Robin put on a short, white silk robe that extended about six inches above her knees. She was comfortable wearing it because Lauren told her that Brian wouldn't be home until the morning. It was now after one in the morning and both of them were too pent up to go to sleep, so Lauren grabbed a bottle of wine that Robin brought and they both went out onto the balcony. The moon was full and glistened across the still waters of the lake, forming a light that captivated the attention of both of them as they sat staring at it as though in a trance. A gentle breeze was blowing across the lake, making it somewhat cool, but still pleasant.

"Lauren, what is it you were talking about? You know, when you told me that there was something you wanted me to do to help you cope?"

Taking a deep breath, Lauren paused.

"Robin, this is like something out of a mystery novel, but here goes." She related the entire sequence of events including her confiding in Arthur up to the point where he had called her from Maine but that they hadn't yet connected.

Robin sat listening intently until Lauren finished.

"Why haven't you told Brian?"

"I don't know if I can trust him," Lauren responded, "you know, the thing about his partner and all. I just feel like I am so alone now with Arthur being gone and all. I feel like you're the only one in the world that I can trust." As she spoke a tear slid slowly down her face.

Robin leaned over, took Lauren's hand.

"Best friend of mine, I am here for you, and I know we can work this out together. I don't care how long it takes. I'll stay as long as you need me." Robin paused and took a deep breath, then said, "Lauren, I know I shouldn't be laying this on you know, but I've done something I couldn't imagine doing in my worst nightmare, so perhaps you can help me, too."

Lauren looked at her bewildered.

"What is it,Robin? I will do anything I can. We are and will always be the best friends that have ever been.

Tell me what it is, I want to help." Lauren's mood had made an about face. She had put aside her own problems in anticipation of hearing about Robin's problem.

Robin poured herself another glass of wine and leaned back in her chair.

"It all happened about two months ago. I had lost my two biggest customers within a week of each other, which I didn't understand, because I thought I had a great relationship with both of them. At that point, my photography business was all but dead. I had reached the end. My mortgage and car payments were past due, and I had gotten a notice from my lender that they were going to start foreclosure proceedings. I didn't know what I was going to do."

Lauren interrupted her.

"Why didn't you call me? I have some money put away and you know that what's mine is yours."

"I didn't want to burden you, Lauren, and besides, I was so embarrassed that I couldn't have called you if I wanted to. Anyway, as though by fate and out of the blue, a man called me and asked if I could meet with him about some shots he wanted to have done. He seemed a bit odd, but at that point I couldn't be choosy. We met at a local café. You remember the outdoor one I took you to the last time you visited me?"

Lauren nodded.

"Anyway, we talked at length about several shots that he would like me to take, and then he asked me if I had ever done any modeling. I said I had done some in college, but not since then. He then asked me if I had ever posed nude. At that point I was beginning to worry, although I was in no danger since we were in a public place. I told him yes, one time in college."

Lauren interrupted her. "I never knew you did that, how did it feel?"

"At first it was embarrassing," Robin replied, "but I was a bit tipsy and after a bit I didn't feel too bad. It was for a friend. Anyway, my first reaction was to blow this guy off, but when he said what he was willing to pay, I said let me think it over."

"What was he willing to pay?" Lauren asked.

"Ten thousand dollars for about an hour shoot," she said. "He said it was for his own personal use and that he wouldn't show them to anyone else. I thought about losing my house and my car. A day or so later I called his cell and agreed to pose."

"My God, Robin, didn't you think there was some danger involved? I mean this guy could have been a nut case."

Before replying, Robin took Lauren's hand.

"Of course it occurred to me, but I was desperate. I only hope that you don't think badly of me."

"How could I think badly of my lifelong, best friend?" Lauren watched, as a tear slid down Robin's cheek.

"That's not all Lauren. He…," she stammered, "the man I posed for has been calling me relentlessly ever since. He wanted me to pose again, and I refused. I saw him outside my house twice, sitting in his car. I didn't want to call the police because I didn't want anyone to know what I had done. I couldn't prove anything anyway. I get e-mails from him every day. He won't stop. The e-mails aren't incriminating, so I couldn't even prove he is stalking me."

Lauren interrupted her. "Tell me about the shoot, I mean, how did you pose?"

Robin thought for a moment. "Well, he asked me to wear a black, after-five cocktail dress. It was low cut and very tight fitting with virtually no back. He asked me to sit on the bed and then took a picture. Then he asked me to slide the hem of my dress up to my thighs. It was all I could do to keep from running, but I thought of the money."

"I understand, go on," Lauren prompted.

"Then he asked me to take my dress off. You can't imagine how my heart was beating. I was sitting there in my bra and panties with a total stranger taking my picture. He paused to look at me and commented on how beautiful I was, although it didn't mean anything to me. Finally he asked me to take off all but a diamond studded necklace I was wearing and was very specific about leaving my hose and heels on. I said that I wouldn't pose totally nude; but I could see him become visibly upset, and I didn't want any problems. I told him that if I did, it would be the final shot and he said okay and that he would be out of my way as soon as he took the picture. He wanted me to lie on the bed."

She stopped to take a deep breath. Lauren comforted her.

"Take your time."

"After I did, he came over and sat on the edge of the bed and put his hand in front of himself as though lining up a shot. I could only guess, but it seemed that he was blocking out my face with his hand and looking only at my body. I started to sit up when he gently pushed me back then took his last shot. He left, and I didn't see him until three days later when he parked across the street from my house. By the way, I insisted on getting the money up front, and then I put it in my safe before starting. I also had that little hand gun that Brian had given me under the pillow, you remember the gun?"

"Yes, of course I do," she answered, "but it was still very dangerous, what can you do now, I mean about the stalker?" Lauren poured each of them another glass of wine and waited for her response.

"As though by some stroke of fate a San Jose City police officer showed up and asked to talk to me, but I guess you already know about that. He identified himself and said that Brian had asked him to stop in on me because you had not heard from me for awhile."

Yes," Lauren responded, "I asked him to. By the way, when did he stop by?"

"Just before I was leaving for the airport to come here, why?"

Lauren's face wore a frown. "Well, Robin, it was several days ago when Brian called the guy in San Jose. I would have thought that he would have gone to your place sooner."

"I believe, Lauren, that it was not in his jurisdiction and he had to do it on his own time. Anyway, he said that he would drive by from time to time and call me to let me know when he was coming. He said he would do that as a favor to Brian and because, well, he said he liked the way I looked. Something funny though; I couldn't believe the look on his face when I answered the door. It was as though he had seen a ghost or something."

"You did have your clothes on, didn't you Robin?"

"Lauren!"

"I'm kidding." Lauren responded, "but at the same time we must be very cautious about telling anyone anything, even Brian. We can't trust anyone. Think about it, we are both involved in some sort of thing that most people don't experience in a lifetime. The good thing, however, is that it has brought us together again, even though it's under these circumstances. By the way, your post card said that you were shooting in the mountains."

"Yes," Robin said, "it came on the heels of the offer to pose for that man. I think that if it had it come before, I would have tried to struggle through without posing. The money wasn't near as good, but it would have kept me going for a short time. At least it got me out of the house and away from that jerk for a while."

"Tell me, Robin, where did that shoot come from?"

Robin looked questioningly at Lauren then said, "From a small magazine that I had never heard of called Avalon Publications. Why do you ask and why are you looking like that?"

A curious look had come over Lauren's face, but before she could answer, Robin spoke again. "Can I ask you something, even though I have no business asking it?"

"Yes, of course Robin, what is it?"

"You mentioned this teacher Greg Allsop and described the night at his apartment. If the phone hadn't rung, what do you think would have happened?"

"Frankly, Robin, I was totally in his control. I can only imagine or perhaps fantasize what might have happened. Why do you ask?" Lauren waited.

Lauren noticed that Robin's entire body had became tense and her facial expression changed as though she was about to say something, but was afraid to.

"Lauren, I feel like I have deceived you for all these years, but I can no longer keep it to myself. Mind you, I am not trying to cause you any more grief." She paused, "but do you remember during our senior year when you had left to go back home for an emergency?"

Lauren's face looked questioningly then she said, "Yes? What about it?"

"Do you also remember what I said a bit ago about posing for a friend?"

Lauren nodded her head.

"It was Brian that I posed for. He had called me and asked if I wanted to go down to the Tavern on the Green for a beer."

Lauren sat motionless.

"We both got pretty drunk and after a while ended back at my dorm." A tear slid down her cheek as she looked at Lauren's now saddened face. "Lauren, I didn't say anything because I knew how happy you and Brian were, and I didn't want to destroy what you had."

"So why tell me now?" Lauren waited her face now emotionless.

"I guess because of what you told me about what is going on, you know with Brian and you and perhaps his partner. I know you probably hate me now, but I just couldn't hold it in anymore, and it seemed that if I was ever going to tell you, now was the time."

"I don't hate you, Robin, it was up to Brian to tell me, but of course he never did. Did you have sex?

"No, Lauren, I swear. I passed out, and barely remember any details. I don't even remember where the pictures ended up."

Lauren took a deep breath then looked at Robin.

"You know, I have always had the thought in the back of my head that Brian was in love with you."

"No, Lauren, I wouldn't..." Lauren placed her hand on Robin's mouth as though to quiet her.

"Robin, I know you would never do anything to hurt me and what ever happened is in the past. We are and will always be best friends. We need each other now more than ever. Let's just concentrate on what is going on so we can both get our lives back to normal."

Robin embraced her as her tears flowed freely.

"What can we do Lauren?"

"We can start by comparing all of our notes about our experiences and such, agreed? That's how Arthur would do it." Robin nodded her approval.

Lauren went into the family room and picked up a pad of legal sized yellow paper and a pen then went back to the patio all the time looking at Robin.

"Okay, your stalker, what was his name?"

"He said it was Lance something, but I don't remember the last name."

Lauren's face took on a questioning look. "Strange, do you think it could have been Lancelot?"

Robin cocked her head to one side as though in thought.

"It's very possible. Yes, I think it was, like in the Knights of the Round Table."

Lauren put her hand on Robin's hand.

"Robin, my next question is very important, so be sure you think about it. Do you remember the name he used when he e-mailed you?" As she asked the question, she sat erect and stared into Robin's eyes.

Robin pondered for a moment then said, "Yes, I think it was Cameo."

Lauren dropped the glass she was holding causing wine and broken glass to cascade across the concrete floor of the balcony. Her hand went to her breast as she took in a deep breath then exhaled.

"Are you sure, Robin?" Her hand was shaking, and her face flushed.

"What's the matter, Lauren? What is it?"

Lauren gradually regained her composure and then stared into Robin's questioning eyes.

"Robin, when I told you about the sequence of

events earlier, I neglected to tell you what the person on the Internet called him or herself; you know the one that has been contacting me?"

Robin nodded.

She paused, her lip twisted slightly and her eyes squinted.

"It was Cameo. And Avalon, like in Avalon Publishing, is the legendary place called 'The Isle Of The Dead.' It's where the spirits of Arthur and Lancelot and the other Knights of the Round Table went after they died."

Robin gasped, but before she could say anything further, they heard the door opening and Brian walked in. He immediately went to the patio and embraced Robin. The embrace lasted uncomfortably longer and tighter than Robin was ready for and the fact that she had on a brief, tight-fitting robe added to her uneasy feeling.

"Robin, it's so great to see you again," Brian beamed. Robin smiled, but to Lauren it seemed to be forced, thinking she must be embarrassed at what Robin had told her. Lauren did not smile?. In fact, her mood seemed to change and she became somber as she stared intently at Brian.

He laid his brief case on the table by the phone.

"I know you must be tired with the time difference and all, but how about we all go out to dinner tomorrow night? I have to go to the station in the morning for a few hours, but I have no problems with tomorrow night."

There was no immediate response from either Robin or Lauren. Feeling the tension of the moment, Lauren responded.

"Sure, Brian, but what happened. I thought you had to work tonight."

"It was slow, so I just took off early."

"How convenient," Lauren said under her breath.

"Where would you like to go?" he asked.

"How about the place in Carrollwood," Lauren responded, "you know where we went for our last anniversary?"

Robin glanced at Lauren, realizing that she was perhaps laying a bit of a guilt trip on him.

"Sure, Lauren, maybe we should call for reservations."

Brian left for the bedroom to shower and get ready for bed. Robin looked at Lauren.

"If I am a fifth wheel here, I can beg off going to dinner."

"No, Robin," she responded, "that would be two's company and three is a crowd. You need five people for a fifth wheel." Lauren took her hand and grinned. "Anyway, we're going to dinner because you're here. I really want you to come and perhaps we can find something out during our dinner conversation. Wear something sexy and I will, too."

"Okay, so three's company," Robin said as she looked at her curiously then smiled, "but you know Lauren, no one likes a smart ass." She giggled, "and by the way, when we have some time alone, let's go on the Internet and see if we can't find out something about Avalon."

CHAPTER SIXTEEN

When Robin finally woke up it was already ten o'clock and Lauren was sitting in the den working at her computer. Robin poked her head in the den and said, "Hey, roomie, what does someone have to do to get some breakfast around this place?"

Lauren spun around and without answering the question said, "Look at this. I think I may have located our mysterious publisher."

Robin walked up behind her and bent over to look at the computer.

"That's the right name all right, but it's located in Chicago. What do you make of that?" Lauren said, pointing to lower right hand corner of the screen as she turned her head toward Robin. "Look at the date of incorporation."

Robin's mouth twisted as though in thought and then gasped, "Lauren, if I'm not mistaken, that's one day before I was first contacted by Cameo. I remember the date because I had written his name down on my calendar with the time of our appointment and noticed that right next to it I had written your name and telephone number to remind me to call you since we hadn't talked in awhile.

"I wish you had Robin. You might have saved yourself some real problems."

"Not really. At that point I didn't know what this guy wanted," Robin responded. "Anyway, does that program tell who the officers are or any other information besides the date of incorporation?"

"There is a spot where the names are supposed to be," Lauren said. "See, it says president, secretary and so on, but there aren't any names in the designated spots. Why isn't that any big surprise? Wait, there is a name on the bottom where it says registered agent. I guess that's who formed the corporation in the first place. Do you believe this? The registered agents name is Lance Allot. There's a P.O. box number in Chicago, but that doesn't do us any good."

"Don't be too sure of that, Lauren. The post office may tell us which station it is by the zip code, and if it's one of those mail type stores, they may give us a street address."

Lauren looked at her questioningly then said, "And which one of us is going to Chicago to stake out the location?" She paused, then snapped her fingers and said, "Wait, I have a friend in Chicago. Someone I met at a convention."

Robin stared at her and a smile spread across her face, "Lauren, I don't suppose that your friend is a man is it?"

"Robin, what if it is? He's only a colleague, and Brian knows about him. Well, found out about him."

"Lauren!"

"It was nothing; I met him at a Shakespeare Convention. We had dinner a couple of times and got to be friends."

"And then what, Lauren?" Robin said, her grin resembling that of the Cheshire Cat.

"Then, I was going to fly to Chicago to see him, only as friends mind you."

Robin folded her arms in front of her, looked up toward the sky and twisted her mouth as though in deep thought.

"Let me get this straight. You meet this guy, have dinner with him a half dozen times and probably correspond on the Internet for awhile then agree to fly to Chicago to meet with Prince Charming. To do what Guinevere? Go over your notes on Shakespeare? What else don't I know about my best friend?"

Neither of them could keep from giggling.

"Twice, we had dinner twice, and the first time it was with a group of people. Besides, Robin, a lot has been going on in my life over the past couple of years. And by the way, who are you to talk, Miss Centerfold?" They both laughed.

"Lauren, I haven't felt this good in a long time and yet here we are being stalked by some weirdo named Cameo and who knows how much danger we are in."

"Likewise," Lauren responded, "and I think this thing has drawn us even closer than before. Anyway, I'll contact my friend in Chicago and start the ball rolling." Lauren still remembered his e-mail address by heart: LancelotChiTown@aol.com.

Lancelot, it's Guinevere, I know we haven't corresponded for quite some time and you know the reason for that. However, I have a situation here, involving myself and my best friend and could use your help. Seems as though there is an individual with the e-mail name of Cameo who has come into both of our lives in a very negative and dangerous way and we are trying to find out more about him or her. (We aren't sure of the gender, but think it's a man). My friend did some modeling for him through a company named Avalon Publishing. The national corporation records show a P.O. Box in Chicago as the only address for the company and the name of the registered agent is, believe it or not, Lance Allot. There are no other officers listed. I know you know a lot of people in Chicago and if you could help us in any way it would be greatly appreciated. By the way, how have you been doing? Okay, I hope, and I do miss our e-mails back and forth. Hope to see you again some day, Lauren.

"Lauren, you called him Lancelot?" Robin had been reading over her shoulder. "There couldn't possibly be any connection here could there?"

"Not a chance, Robin, this whole thing was a couple of years ago, and I've had no contact with him since then. Besides, I was the one who asked him to use the name Lancelot. His real name isn't remotely close to that."

"What is his name, Lauren?"

"Damien Porter," she responded.

"My God, Lauren, isn't Damien the son of Satan in that movie we saw years ago? Creepy." Robin wrinkled her brow in thought. "Hey, by the way, weren't you born in Portersville, Maine?"

"Yes to both questions, but it's just a coincidence for heaven's sake. Besides, I'm sure he had the name Damien long before the movie ever came out."

The day had worn on and as evening approached, Robin excused herself in order to shower and get ready for dinner. Robin was in better condition than when she was 20. Her firm breasts and long athletic legs were the envy of most women she knew. Her running and exercise regimen assured that there wasn't an ounce of fat on her. Her long flowing black hair which she wore down most of the time shimmered as she swung her head from side to side when she walked. Being of German descent, her crystal clear blue eyes completed the picture. Lauren had once told her that she was the image of the perfect Aryan; a super race of people that the Nazi movement of the 1930s and 1940s in Germany had fancied themselves. As if that weren't enough for one person, Robin also had a Mensa-level I.Q. of 140. Lauren always marveled at how down to earth Robin stayed throughout all the years she had known her. Robin attributed it to her small town mentality, having been raised in the little coastal town of Bodega Bay, 60 miles north of San Francisco.

After showering, Robin put on black mesh hose and a black translucent bra and black lace panties. She had brought along a tight-fitting after-five dress that sat well above her knees. When she looked at herself in the mirror, she realized that she had subconsciously put on the same dress she wore while posing for the nude photos. Stopping for a moment, she pondered what would have made her dress this way, or for that matter, why would she have even brought the dress with her. Nevertheless she continued to put on the diamond-studded black choker collar she had worn in the photos. It perplexed her for a moment, but remembering what they wanted to accomplish, she smiled at her reflection in the mirror and made her way to the family room where Brian was waiting.

Brian rose with his mouth wide open as he saw that Robin was wearing the same ensemble she was wearing in the photos that depicted her as dead. He quickly regained his composure and said, "My god, Robin, you are as beautiful as you were in college, if not more."

She smiled, but didn't respond.

Lauren had not yet arrived, so they made small talk until the sound of the bedroom door announced her arrival. She was dressed the same as she was when she went to Greg Allsop's apartment, knowing that Brian had never seen her quite like this. He was overwhelmed at how she looked and actually had to catch his breath.

"Lauren, I can't remember ever seeing you like this

before; I think I've died and gone to heaven. The two most beautiful women I have ever seen and I am their escort."

ꙩꙩꙩꙩꙩꙩꙩꙩꙩꙩꙩꙩꙩ

The restaurant, which was one of the hottest spots in north Tampa, was called Carmine's. The booths in the back of the restaurant were arranged so as to afford more privacy for an intimate dinner and the open area accommodated large parties. The waiting area was abuzz with people and the typical waiting period was at least an hour, but because Brian was well known to the owners, the hostess always put them ahead of the other people who had been waiting. The bar was two deep and it was all that the three bartenders could do to keep up with the drink orders. Steaks, seafood and pasta dishes were the main entrees and their Caesar salad was known as the best in the Tampa Bay area. The motif was dark oak tables and booths topped by lattice dividers. It had been a favorite of locals for years and none of the regulars were ever surprised to see one of the many local sports celebrities that frequented the restaurant.

Brian took the lead, letting the longtime hostess, Judy, know that they had arrived.

"It will only be a moment, Brian. Just let me see what's available," Judy said. As she looked over the tables, she noticed that the owner, Carmine, had come in from the bar. She motioned to him and he came over.

He embraced Lauren, shook Brian's hand, then looked at Robin. "My lord, Brian, where does this goddess come from?" Carmine always greeted the regulars personally and went out of his way to make them feel at home.

Brian responded, "This is our dearest friend, Robin Bennet, who lives in Northern California and whom both

Lauren and I went to college with many years ago."

Carmine clutched Lauren's hand while still staring at Robin and said, "Lauren, let me show you to our best table."

They were seated at a table in the rear of the main dining room and a waitress known as Liz approached them. "Hi, Mr. St. John, nice to see you again so soon."

Lauren noticed Brian squirm a bit in his seat as he responded, "Nice to see you Liz, can we order some drinks please?" Robin and Lauren ordered a California Chablis and Brian ordered a scotch on the rocks.

"I'll get that for you right away," she said, "and, oh, by the way, Mr. St. John, that partner of yours is sitting in the bar."

By this time, Brian appeared to be very uncomfortable and asked to be excused to go to the restroom.

Lauren looked at Robin and said, "I guess we know where Brian and Red Hot have lunch, or perhaps dinner. I think I'll go to the restroom also, you have to pass by the bar to get there."

As she passed by the bar, several men swung their heads and watched as she slowed momentarily in order to try and get a glimpse of Lisa. Sure enough, she was sitting at the bar and to Lauren's surprise she was sitting with none other than Greg Allsop. Stopping in her tracks, she saw Greg glancing her way, so she used the opportunity to let him know that she knew he was there with Lisa Cantrell by waving to him. Lisa's head swung around to see who he was waving to. Her eyes then met Lauren's.

Seizing on the opportunity, Lauren walked toward them. Greg stood up and gave her a hug, whispering in her ear as he did, "Like déjà vu, Lauren." Then he spoke aloud, "Lauren, I didn't know you knew about this place," he said, pausing. "I think you know Lisa Cantrell."

"Actually, Greg, it's our favorite place and Brian is with me, if you haven't had dinner yet, why don't you join us?" Lauren had taken a bold step but reasoned that it may bring some things to light if they all dined together.

"I don't know, Lauren," Greg said, but before he could finish Lisa interrupted him.

"We'd love to, Lauren. We just don't see enough of each other, so let's take advantage of the opportunity to get together. We'll be over in a minute."

Lauren feigned a smile. "Good, I'll tell the waitress to set two extra places."

By the time Lauren returned to the table, Brian had already come back.

"Brian, you'll never guess who Lisa has with her." Brian shrugged his shoulders as Lauren continued. "One of the professors from the college."

With that, Lisa and Greg approached the table. Lauren watched closely at Lisa and Brian to see if there was any tension between them, and saw that there was.

"Greg, Lisa, this is my best friend Robin Bennet from California; Brian, Robin, this is Greg Allsop, a history professor from the college. Lisa Cantrell is Brian's partner in crime, or stopping crime, I should say."

They all sat down and Greg was the first to speak.

"Robin, what do you do in California?"

"I have a small photography studio specializing in nature shots," she said. "I often go out into the wild and do a shoot for magazines that feature that sort of thing."

What's the wildest thing you've ever shot, Robin?" Greg asked.

They all awaited an answer from Robin and in an attempt to break the tension that had engulfed the group she answered.

"Well, that would be a shot of Lauren and Brian trying to do the twist on a table top at our local college hangout after several beers."

It worked-- the group all laughed.

"Brian, I didn't know you had this other side to you," Lisa said. "You always seem so reserved and, Lauren, I can't imagine you on a table top doing the twist."

Lauren stared at Lisa for a moment before responding.

"Well, I guess there's a lot we don't know about each other, isn't there, Lisa? Care to tell us something about your past?" Her mind flashed to that night when she thought she saw her kiss Brian. The momentary silence was broken as the waitress returned with a round of drinks, but there was no response from Lisa. At that point, Lauren thought she would see if she could cause someone to squirm a bit.

"Greg, how is it that you and Lisa know each other?"

"Yes, Greg, Lisa," Brian responded, "I was wondering myself how a professor from a small college gets to know a cop." His voice bore a hint of irritation.

Without hesitation and almost as though rehearsed Lisa nodded to Greg, who responded,

"We both live in South Tampa and both jog along Bayshore several times a week. We saw each other so often that we finally started to talk one day. One thing led to another and here we are."

The irony of the situation was almost more than Lauren could keep in. She pondered what forces could have been working to bring them all together like this. She felt a tinge of jealousy over seeing Lisa with Greg. Based on his expression, she felt that Brian probably felt the same. Brian suddenly raised his glass and looked at Lauren.

"Here's to a good man who had a dramatic effect on Lauren's life and whose life was taken prematurely. May he still watch over you, Lauren,, and be there if you need him. Here's to Lauren's father, whom I didn't get to know well enough when he was still with us."

Although she didn't know what prompted Brian's toast, she nevertheless felt warm inside and felt a tear trickle down her cheek as she raised her glass.

"Thank you, Brian, that was very thoughtful of you." The others raised their glasses in a toast to a man they had never met and the gesture seemed to take the edge off the moment.

After a bit, another round of drinks was ordered and the conversation changed to small talk. Suddenly Robin looked at Lauren strangely. Lauren sensed that something was wrong.

"Robin, I have to go to the ladies room, want to join me?"

Lauren waited until another lady left the washroom then looked at Robin and said, "Robin, I saw the look on your face and know something is bothering you, what is it?"

"You are right. Remember when I told you about the nude shots, the black dress and all?" Robin asked, then paused. "Well, it just hit me when we were sitting out there. When I posed for Brian, it was in a tight-fitting black cocktail dress, a lot like the one I have on now. Also, it was exactly like the one I wore for the senior prom."

Lauren's face took on a solemn look.

"Do you think it could be a coincidence?"

"Normally I would say, yes, but Lauren, the sequence of the shots was the same as the shots I did for the creep. What does it mean?"

"I don't know, Robin, but let's get back to the

others, we can both think about it for awhile. By the way, where are the pictures?"

"I don't know," Robin responded. "Brian took them. He said he would destroy them." When they returned to the table, they saw that Brian had excused himself and gone outside to take a call on his cell phone.

"Brian, Manny in San Jose. I just got off the phone with a detective in Chicago. He saw my inquiry on the FBI Web site about the serial killings in Florida and the others and asked if I knew anything about them. When I told him that I was checking for another cop in Florida, he told me that I may want to tell you that they just discovered another body. This one was on what he called the near north side of Chicago. It's evidently an upscale area for swinging singles."

"What did he say about the victim?" Brian asked.

"You might want to sit down, amigo. He said that it was a woman in her early 40s, very attractive and get this; her I.D. showed that she was a teacher. Brian cleared his throat.

"How did she die?"

"The bastard cut her head off," Manny responded. "The cop says she was probably alive when he did it. They found her sitting in her car in a park near the lake front with her head propped on top of her torso. He called the place where they found her the Lincoln Park area."

"Did you get his number, Manny, and what's his name?" Brian asked.

"Yes, it's 312-555-2636. Shit, you know I asked him his name and he told me, but I didn't write it down and for the life of me I can't recall what he said. I'm sure I'll think of it, but he said the number was his direct line and only he'll answer it, so you'll get him in any case."

"Thanks, Manny, I'm going to give him a call right now." After hanging up, Brian dialed the number and after the sixth ring a recording came on, indicating that the number he dialed was not a working number. He tried again and got the same recording, then called Manny back. "Manny, did I write the number down right; was it 312-555-2636?"

"That's right, Brian, why?"

"Well, I called it twice and it evidently isn't a working number," he responded.

"Strange, Brian, I asked him twice and repeated it to him. I think I got it right. Why don't you call the Chicago P.D. and ask for homicide. Where was it? Oh yeah, the Lincoln Park area?"

"Will do, Manny, and thanks." After getting the number from information he was automatically connected to main switchboard for the Chicago Police Department and asked for homicide in the Lincoln Park area. After a half dozen rings someone answered. "Lincoln Park Sub Station, how can I direct your call?"

"My name is Detective Brian St. John, and I am calling from Florida about a homicide that was just reported in your district." The voice on the other end indicated that he would be connected to Detective Randy Kowalski.

"This is Detective Kowalski, how can I help you?"

"Detective, this is Detective Brian St. John in Tampa, Florida. I just got a report from an officer in San Jose, a friend of mine, that there has been a homicide in the Lincoln Park area, which I understand you cover. A woman in her early 40s who was found in her car near the lakefront? I'm not entirely sure, but I have a suspicion that it may be connected to some serial killings that took place in Florida over the past couple of years. Can you tell me anything about it?"

The phone was silent for a moment then Kowalski spoke.

"I'm looking at the reports for the last three days and don't see anything. I know there wasn't anything before that or I would be investigating it. Are you sure you got the details right?"

"I got it from my friend in California," Brian responded, "who received a call from a Chicago Detective whose name he unfortunately can't recall. He gave me the number for the guy, but I got a recording saying that the number isn't in service."

"What's the number, Brian? Okay if I call you Brian? And call me Randy."

"Yes, of course." Brian then repeated the number to him twice.

"I'm looking at the front of our book that shows telephone prefixes and zip codes and I can't tell you what's going on, but that prefix, 462 in the 312 area doesn't exist. I am also checking the reports for the rest of the city and don't see anything even close to the homicide that you're talking about. Give me your number and I'll keep an eye out and call you back if I can find out anything else."

Thanks, Randy, I owe you one, here's my number." After repeating his cell phone number to the other officer he disconnected and scratched his head questioningly, then rejoined the others.

As he sat down, Lauren could see that the look on his face was one of concern.

"Anything wrong, Brian?"

He took a sip of his drink, all the time ignoring Lauren's question and staring upward as though in thought.

"Hello, Lauren to Brian, are you there?"

"I'm sorry, Lauren, what did you say? I had something else on my mind. Just police work, nothing to be concerned about." His assurance that there was no problem wasn't the least bit comforting to Lauren who turned toward Robin with a questioning look on her face. Brian's partner Lisa then spoke.

"Brian, is there anything I can do?"

"No Lisa, this is something that I am looking into on my own, nothing that concerns you."

From the look on Lisa's face his answer didn't appear to sit well with her. Lauren smiled inside.

All through dinner the conversation revolved around school, the police force and a myriad other subjects. Lauren noticed that the entire time, Greg had a difficult time keeping his eyes off of Robin. Brian was still distant and appeared to be in deep thought when his cell phone rang.

"Detective St. John, how can I help you?" The voice on the other end identified himself as Randy Kowalski when Brian cut him short.

"Can you hold a minute; I need to go outside so I can hear you better." Once outside, Brian apologized for the delay then said questioningly, "Randy, what's going on?"

"Maybe you can tell me, Brian. I just got a call from a beat officer who not five minutes ago discovered the dead body of a woman that appeared to be in her early 40s. We haven't identified her yet, but she was found in her car near the lake in the Lincoln Park area. Sound familiar?"

Brian felt the blood rush to his head, then responded with a question.

"Randy, how was she killed?"

"Well, I'm not sure," he responded, "but I can tell you this: her head was severed from her body and placed on top of the torso, which was placed behind the steering wheel of her car. What the hell is going on, Detective? How in the hell did you know about this before we discovered her?"

"I can't answer that, Randy, but tell me, do they know how long she has been dead?"

"It appears like she was murdered within the past hour or so and it seems as though the killer wanted us to know that, because he smashed her watch against something, maybe the steering wheel and it stopped an hour ago. Anyway, I checked the log and the time that it was stopped was right around the time that you called me. I think you got some explaining to do," Randy said.

Brian held his forehead and sighed before responding.

"Randy, you are absolutely right and while I can't be sure, I have a theory as to what is happening. Not why, mind you, but what."

"Can't wait," Randy said with a hint of sarcasm in his voice.

"Unfortunately, my friend, you are going to have to wait a bit," Brian responded. "I am at dinner with my wife and some friends, and I need to get back to them. I want to take the time to run my theory by you and help in any way I can, so I will call you back when I can get to the station. If you feel like you want to check me out, call the central station in Tampa. Everyone knows me there. I'll get there after I drop my wife off at home. It'll probably be an hour or so. Hope that's okay with you?"

"I guess it will have to be, Brian, but if you don't call tonight, I'll be calling you."

Brian returned to the table as Greg was picking up the check and took it out of his hand.

"Here, let me pay for that, we invited you to our table and besides, I know about teachers' salaries. The only ones lower than cops when you consider the hours we all put in. Present company excluded Robin, I haven't a clue what photographers make."

All eyes focused on Robin as she smiled.

"All depends on what kind of pictures you're talking about." Lauren's mind immediately went to the pictures Robin posed for and she assumed that Brian's did as well, but neither was about to say anything and neither knew that the other knew about them. Lauren, knowing what Robin had made for the nude photos, couldn't help but let a brief smirk cross her face.

After the waitress brought the check back, Brian signed the credit card slip then rose.

"Lauren, I need to get to the station for a bit after I drop you off, so...." Greg interrupted him.

"Brian, I can take the ladies home if you need to get to the station. Lisa and I came separately; so it won't inconvenience her."

The look on Lisa's face showed her disapproval, but she said nothing.

"Well, if you don't mind, Greg, it would be a big help to me."

Neither Robin nor Lauren said anything, but as they walked toward the door out of earshot of the others, Lauren, who had let the inherent humor of the moment catch her fancy, whispered to Robin.

"Maybe we can get something out of him. Sit in front and let the hem of your dress slide up."

Robin looked at her with a shocked look on her face.

"Lauren, what do you think I am a slut or something?"

Lauren couldn't resist the chance to give her a good natured razzing and said.

"You're right, Robin, too bad we don't have the pictures of you. We could just show them to him and you wouldn't have to lift your dress up," she giggled.

Robin smiled and without looking at her responded.

"Hey, you didn't see Mr. Allsop's hand up my dress, did you?"

Not to be outdone, Lauren replied.

"Well, Robin, it's early."

"Cute, Lauren, cute!"

JOHN S. RICHARDSON

CHAPTER SEVENTEEN

The station was near empty at this hour of the night and when Brian arrived there was already a message to call Randy Kowalski in Chicago. After pouring a cup of coffee from a pot that had been sitting on a burner for a couple of hours he called Chicago.

"Ugh." He coughed, "this is like drinking lye."

"What's that Brian?" Kowalski had picked up the phone.

"Randy, oh nothing. I see you couldn't wait to hear from me. Let me fill you in. My wife has a friend in California. Well she's my friend, too. Anyway, this friend would always call my wife if she was going to be gone for any length of time so she wouldn't worry. My wife that is."

"Uh-huh?" Randy waited.

"Awhile back my wife tried to get a hold of her and couldn't for a couple of weeks so she became concerned. I offered to get hold of a guy I knew in California, a cop, who happened to live near where our friend lives. You know, to stop in on her, which he did."

At this point Brian began to wonder if he was giving away to much information to a total stranger even if he was a cop. He thought for a moment.

"Well anyway, to make a long story short, when we couldn't contact her for awhile we suspected foul play and my friend started to look at crimes on the Internet."

Randy interrupted, "How did he know what kind of crimes to look for?"

Brian struggled for an answer.

"I don't quite know. We had been talking about some

suspected serial killings in Florida and around the country and maybe he jumped to conclusions. In fact, if it hadn't been for our friend being gone for awhile I wouldn't have called the other cop in the first place or even be thinking about serial killers. Got enough to worry about as it is."

Brian wasn't ready to tell anyone else about the photographs they found in Robin's home.

"Anyway, let me finish. He went on the FBI Web site. You know the one I'm talking about?"

"Yes, I do."

"It tracks inquiries and somehow, someone, I don't know who, got that information and called my friend, pretending to be a police officer from Chicago. He gave him the story that I related to you and when my friend in California heard it, he called me. It seemed similar to some of the murders he had seen on the site so he figured I should know. And I, of course, called you." Brian waited for a response.

"Well, I think there's a lot more to the story that you're not telling me, but anyway what's your theory?" Randy asked.

"Randy, you gotta have a little patience on this one. I'll keep you in the loop, but for now I can't reveal all of the details. Suffice it to say that somehow, somewhere, someone is watching and listening. He, hell I don't even know if it is a man or woman, but for now I'm assuming it's a man. It sounds a bit remote, but he made a connection between my friend, the cop in California and myself and wanted me to know about a woman who had been murdered or was about to be murdered in Chicago. I have to assume that he killed your victim up there. But, and this is the bizarre twist, it appears that he called him, my friend the cop, before he killed the victim. He knew that we would both react immediately so that, in essence, he wanted to be murdering her about the same time I was on the phone with you."

Randy's response posed yet another mystery.

"Brian, if your theory is correct, how could the killer be sure that your friend in California would get ahold of you right away? Even if he figured that you would call here immediately? He couldn't be watching him or you for that matter, if he was here in Chicago, killing this woman. Unless he had an accomplice or two which is highly unlikely given the nature of the crime. That is, if it really is the work of a serial killer."

"I don't know," Brian said.

"Brian, the last thing I need here is to have the press think that there's a serial killer on the loose. I was a rookie cop in the western suburbs when John Gacy was killing all those young men and it was hell. I couldn't look those poor parents in the eye. Every time another kid would disappear there would be another mom or dad to look at. "

"Randy," Brian responded, "I haven't got an answer for that one, but do me a favor, when you get the inventory of the victim's belongings look and see if, by chance, there is a small brooch with the silhouette of a woman's face made out of ivory."

"Ya know, Brian, I checked you out. I know you're legit, but if I hadn't, I'd think you were some sort of wack job. By the way before you hang up, do you know what the letters VODU mean? They were scrawled on the driver's side window in what appeared to be blood. Maybe the victim's blood, in capital letters."

"No I don't, Randy, but I'll certainly find out. And thanks, amigo." Brian hung up. "My God, I'm talking like Manny now," he added to himself.

Brian sat thinking for a moment when he remembered what Manny had said to him in California about how many serial killers travel significant miles every year.

"Hell, Chicago's only a two-hour flight from here," he mumbled.

Brian immediately picked up the files that he had requested a few days ago, the files that he had left on his desk. They contained the details relating to the prior murders in Florida. He hadn't looked at them yet because Robin was no longer missing and in the excitement of the moment he had forgotten about them. Now however, he realized that Robin could be in extreme danger.

He thought to himself that whoever had taken the pictures that were left in her home had somehow gotten into her house and placed the pictures in her darkroom, probably when she was off shooting in the mountains. After all, he thought to himself, it wasn't logical that she would have a picture in which her own head had been cut off and not go to the police with it. Therefore, he reasoned, she didn't know the pictures had been put there. That didn't answer how or why she let someone take pictures of her in her lingerie and then in the nude. But then his thoughts returned to the time when he had taken pictures of her and of the excitement he had felt watching her slowly remove her clothes. A frown captured Brian's face as he thought quietly to himself. If Robin had come home and found the writing on her mirror, she would most assuredly said something to the police, or even Manny for that matter. That means that whoever was in her house, must have come back."

"I guess I don't know enough about her private life to know what she may have done or why," he said quietly to himself.

After a moment, his thoughts again turned to the files in front of him. Thumbing through them, he examined each list of inventory items and found no mention of a brooch or pin of any sort. He did notice however, that the files indicated the method of disposal of the bodies was different in each case. He also noted that there didn't seem to be any connection as to where they were suspected to have been picked up.

After again staring at the files sitting on his desk for several minutes, he opted to go on-line to try and find out what VODU meant. He Googled on Wikipedia and the answer came back in a matter of seconds: VODU was another spelling of the word VOODOO. He read on.

VODU is the primitive religion that is based on a belief in sorcery, the power of charms, curses and black magic. Practiced in Africa, it was brought to the West Indies during the slave trading days and is principally found on the island of Haiti. The religion took hold to some degree in the USA in the city of New Orleans because a large population of Voodoo worshipers had settled in that area after slavery was abolished.

"Fine," he said to himself, "now I know what it is, but haven't a clue how it fits in here."

Again looking at the top file while making notes to himself, he saw that it contained a sheet of paper on which the alphabet was written. It was lined paper and the letters were all in upper case. It was printed with different colored crayons and done on a poor quality off-white paper like the kind he used when he was in kindergarten.

The victim was a 41-year-old female, quite attractive, with reddish-brown hair and brown eyes. She had lived in a small city in north Florida and taught elementary school. She disappeared after leaving school late one day about two years ago and her body was discovered a week later in a log cabin in the woods by a couple of hunters.

Brian shook his head and read on.

Her naked body bore no signs of being sexually assaulted, but the killer had written about a dozen indistinct markings on her torso with what turned out to be crayon. They appeared to be letters of the alphabet. Cause of death was heart failure; perhaps, the coroner had theorized, from extreme fright. The file indicated that she had no next of kin to notify as her mother had died when she was a teenager; her father had died about two years before she was murdered, and she was an only child. Records reflected that she had been born in Florida.

He leaned back in his chair and propped his feet up on the desk while staring at the piece of paper that had the alphabet written on it. Something didn't seem right about it, but for the life of him he couldn't see what it was. Finally, he let his feet drop to the floor still staring at the paper.

"Odd," he muttered quietly. "I wonder what it means?" He read each letter out loud, touching each lightly with the tip of the pencil he was holding:

A,B,C,D,E,F,G,H,I,J,K,L,M,N,O,P,Q,R,S,T,U,V,W,X,Y,Y,Z

He whispered so as not to be heard through the open door to his office.

"It appears that someone has duplicated the letter Y. Could it be just a mistake or does it mean something?"

He made a note on his pad to check out whether the letter Y bore any relationship to the other files. Before going on to the next file, he noted that the name Pollux had been written on the victim's forehead in crayon.

After picking up the next file, he again leaned back in his chair, propped his feet up on the desk and began to read. This was the case of a 44-year-old woman, similar in build and coloration to the first one who had been murdered two and one half years ago in a small city in the Florida Panhandle. She was found with numerous cuts and stab wounds in the stomach with what could have been a surgeon's knife. The coroner had noted this,   based on the precision of the cuts.

According to the coroner, the incisions appeared to be made for the purpose of removing the victims naval. As though, the coroner noted, *someone was performing a surgical operation.*   The victim was found in back of a nursing home within a few miles of her home.

There was no brooch or pin among the inventory, but a piece of white nautical rope about a foot in length had been draped across the body near the stomach. The coroner reasoned that the rope had been used to tie the victim's hands or feet at some point, but then also noted that the victim's hands and wrists bore no evidence of being tied. Again, while it was undetermined whether or not there were any next of kin, the police had been unable to locate any. He read on. *The victim worked for the local board of education and had taught school before moving to Florida from her birth place, which was a small town in coastal Maine.*

"My god," he said out loud, "this is getting close to home."   He immediately went back to the first file he had looked at and searched for any reference as to where the victim was born. The records indicated that the victim had been born in Florida, but her parents were in fact from the upper east coast. An inconspicuous written comment on the last sheet under other information indicated that the date that the woman was born was within a few months of the date that the parents had moved to Florida.

"Based on this," he said quietly, "there is every chance that this victim was conceived before the parents moved to Florida and that makes it either an incredible coincidence, or I've hit on at least one of the things that's tying these cases together."

The third file was the one from the Bay Area that he had worked on, but he didn't recall anything about the victim's birthplace, perhaps because it wasn't pertinent to him at the time. Looking back through that file, he noted that the victim was born in the Midwest. No connection there, he thought to himself.

"But look at this," he said out loud as he rose out of his chair. "She was a graduate of a small college in New Hampshire, close to the Maine state line." The body had been discovered in bushes next to a small church on the outskirts of the city.

The information was leading him directly toward a pattern, one that he had hoped he wouldn't have to go to? Despite the fact that the victims were found in three different and apparently unconnected locations, there were nevertheless some undeniable similarities, he thought. First, all three victims were in their early 40s. Second, they were all associated with the field of education, remembering that the one in the Bay Area had also been a teacher. And finally, they all had connections to the upper east coast and in particular the state of Maine.

As all the pertinent facts passed through his mind, he lowered his head resting it in his hand and sighed. He then said aloud.

"This isn't about Robin. It's about Lauren." He couldn't for the life of him, however, figure out why his wife of 15 years would be the possible target of a serial killer. Since he had no idea what had happened to Lauren in the past weeks, he didn't perceive just how imminent the danger really was.

He said in a whisper, he said: "If it's not about Robin, then why did someone go to all the trouble of trying to make it look like she had been murdered? Is he trying to taunt Lauren? Were those pictures meant for Robin to find? Or better yet, were they meant for me?"

That seems a bit remote, he thought to himself, since I live a nation apart from her, but on the other hand whoever it is might figure that I would somehow end up seeing them and that would lead back to Lauren.

Placing his hand under his chin, he leaned back in his chair and mused on the worst-case scenario, thinking to himself that perhaps this is a statement of what is yet to come. As he sat thinking about what he now knew, it suddenly dawned on him that he needed to go to the next step and determine if there were murders in other states that had the same similarities.

Signing on to the FBI's Web site, VICAP, he input 'unsolved murders.' A series of topics were listed, including one titled 'Unsolved Serial Murders.' This category contained high-profile cases of murder that were either still being investigated or cold cases that had been closed because of a lack of information. Most of the latter category consisted of very old cases which were not likely to be of particular interest to Brian so he eliminated them. Those that were under the heading of suspected domestic murder cases were also eliminated along with any unsolved mass murders.

When the program asked for particular parameters for the search, he input: women from 35 to 45, working in the field of education and from the northeast coast of the

U.S. The text contained a caveat that while these cases are classified as serial murders, since they have not been solved, there is no certainty that they are in fact murders of the serial type.

To his surprise, given the limits of his search, 48 cases came up. The first list he looked at gave name, place of birth, profession and the location of the murder. Locations of the various murders ranged from Maine to Maryland. There were murders in cities large and small and in rural areas so he ruled out any connection in that regard. He reasoned that while this information was available, perhaps no one had ever homed in on the parameters that he had just input, particularly as related to victims who were originally from Maine. He narrowed the search to Maine and the states that bordered of Maine and narrowed the count to 16.

The various murders had been committed from as far back as 22 years ago until very recently. He didn't know where the Chicago victim was from originally, but suspected there would be some sort of connection. Under normal circumstances, he wouldn't think that there would be that many victims from the state of Maine and this, coupled with the fact that these were unsolved cases, convinced Brian that these murders, or at least some of them, were the work of one killer.

As he read intently about the various aspects of each case, making notes as he did, it occurred to him that he had written down that another body had been found in an abandoned log cabin in the woods, much like in one of the Florida cases.

He went back over his list and found two more. He remembered that he had already written down three more that were dumped in or behind a church and two that were left near a nursing home. When he finished his notes, he had five victims left in or around log cabins, seven in or around churches and four near nursing homes.

"My God," he said to himself, "that's another connection between these cases and the first three in Florida, but what does it mean? And what about the one in Chicago tonight?" That victim, he thought to himself, was found in her car near the lakefront. That doesn't make any sense. Perhaps the killer was scared off by someone and didn't have a chance to take the body to another location.

By this time he could hardly keep his eyes open, so he leaned back in his chair, again propped his feet up on the desk and closed his eyes. He wondered how he would approach Robin and Lauren about the pictures, or if he should even approach them. He knew they could be in a good amount of danger, but wanted to find out all he could about the murders before confronting them.

প্রপ্রপ্রপ্রপ্রপ্রপ্রপ্রপ্রপ্রপ্রপ্র

"See, I told you he couldn't keep his eyes off your legs," Lauren said.

When they left the restaurant, Lauren had beat Robin to the back seat so Robin had to sit up front with Greg on the ride home. After hugging him good bye and thanking him for the ride home, the ladies made their way up the stairs, giggling the whole way at Lauren's observation. When Lauren opened the front door to the condo, she could see the red light on the answer machine blinking. She pressed the button.

"Lauren, this is Mandy. I hope you remember me from the gun class. I hate to ask you for help since we only just met, but I think I have a real problem. The guy,

remember the one I told you about, well he's back. Somehow he found out that I took that course, and he is very angry with me. When he called, I told him it was none of his business. He told me that if I bought a gun, he was going to use it on me. I would call the police, but I can't prove anything and since I've complained before without any real evidence, they probably think I'm a nut or something. And besides, I don't even know where he lives. Anyway, I hate to involve you in this, but I need a friend and you seemed so nice. You have my number, so if you could call me, I would be forever grateful."

Robin frowned.

"Lauren, I don't know what that's about, but you need to be very careful about getting in the middle of something like that."

"It's pretty much about what she said on the recording, Robin. I didn't elaborate on it when I told you everything, because I frankly didn't expect to hear from her again. I guess I should at least acknowledge her call. I can relate to her problem, since I, we that is, seem to have problems, too. Anyway, maybe we can all help each other. I'll call her in the morning."

CHAPTER EIGHTEEN

Brian had slipped in quietly during the night and was still sleeping when Lauren woke. After putting on a pot of coffee, she went to the den to check her e-mails. There was one from her friend in Chicago.

Guinevere, it was great to hear from you after all this time. I am sorry to hear about your problem and will of course do anything I can to help. I have a friend of mine looking into the address and the corporation. He's a private investigator that I play golf with and he won't charge me anything. I'll contact you one way or the other when I hear back from him and by the way, any plans of coming to Chicago in the near future, I'd love to see you again. Bye for now, and oh, how's your husband doing? Still watching you? - Gemini.

"Looks like he hasn't forgotten those intimate dinners Lauren, but what's with the Gemini?"

Robin had slipped in the den unnoticed and was reading over her shoulder. Lauren immediately spun around almost knocking her over before saying, "Damn it, Robin, you scared the devil out of me. That's the way he always signs his e-mails."

"It would take more than that to get the devil out of you," Robin said. "You'd better be careful how you answer that e-mail, it's loaded."

Lauren turned her attention back to the computer screen then said, "I'll handle it. You want some coffee?"

Robin nodded.

"Good, get me some, too. Black, no sugar." A grin crossed her face. "I think I'll wait until Brian leaves before

I call Mandy. Hey want to go out for breakfast? There's a great little place on a lake not far from here."

By the time they had finished a cup of coffee out on the balcony; Brian had risen and was on his way out the door.

"Lauren, Robin, I have to go the station for a bit, but I'll be back by mid-afternoon if nothing else comes up."

Lauren retrieved the card that Mandy had given her with her phone number on it and dialed. Someone picked up the receiver on the other end, but said nothing.

"It's Lauren. Are you there?"

"Lauren, thank God it's you," Mandy responded. "I didn't say anything in case it was him. How are you?"

"As good as could be expected under the circumstances. Mandy, I got your message and wanted to find out what's wrong. What are you doing right now?"

"Actually, Lauren, I was just sitting here in the dark. I have all my curtains closed, wondering what I am going to do."

"My best friend is visiting here from California, Mandy and it appears that she is also involved in the problem that I am experiencing. Remember when we took that class, I told you that I had done something stupid? Well, it involves her as well and so I thought that if you weren't busy right now, you could meet us for breakfast?"

Lauren nodded silently looking at Robin as if to ask her if that was okay with her and she nodded back.

"That would be terrific, Lauren, where and when?"

"There's a little place off Highway 41 about a mile and a half north of State Road 54 in a place called Land O' Lakes. I can't remember what the name is, but it's on the west side of the street and situated on a lake. We can eat outside and enjoy the beautiful morning. Do you know where it is?"

"No," Mandy responded, "but I will find it. How about in an hour or so? That will give me time to shower."

"See you then, Mandy." Lauren hung the phone up and in the same motion stood and took Robin's hand. "I don't know this woman very well, but I know she has a problem and may be in danger, so I think it's the right thing to do. Hope you agree. Anyway, maybe this will be just what we all needed. After all, three heads are better than one."

"Lauren," Robin responded, "we already have two heads, so lets get it straight, three heads are better than two." Robin giggled, remembering Lauren's fifth wheel analogy.

"Oh," she replied, as she whisked past Robin. "I'm going to take a shower."

Both women opted to wear shorts, a blouse and sandals wanting to take advantage of the glorious weather. Before starting the car, Lauren put the top down on her Mustang. The sight of two sunglass-clad beautiful women, riding in a classic 1964 powder blue Mustang convertible with the top down was enough to cause a stir and a near accident for one 60ish man who sideswiped a plastic barricade while staring at them.

"I guess we still got it, kid," Lauren said as she waived to the old man who had just pulled to a stop.

"Yeah, if you count the Social Security set," Robin said.

The restaurant had been a wood-frame house at one time and by all estimates appeared to have been built in the 1950s. What it lacked in looks, however, it made up by the openness of the inside serving rooms and the open-air deck overlooking the lake where they opted to sit. After ordering coffee, they waited and within minutes Lauren saw Mandy walking toward them. She rose to greet her, but Mandy embraced her before she could extend her hand.

Mandy looked at the two of them then said, "I guess I'm a bit overdressed for this place, hope you don't mind." She was wearing a light gray, pinstriped business suit with a white turtle neck knit sweater and high heels and the same necklace that had attracted Lauren the first time they met.

"Not at all, Mandy, are you on the way to work or church or something?" Lauren asked.

"No, Lauren, I had just come back from an appointment when you returned my call and haven't had time to change yet."

Robin's face bore a slight frown as though in thought.

"Mandy, this is Robin Bennett, the friend I told you about from California. She's here because I asked her to come to help me out with my problem, but as it turns out, we appear to have a mutual problem. But let's deal with your situation, why don't start from the beginning and tell us what has happened. Don't leave out any details."

After ordering breakfast, Mandy began her story. "This whole thing started about a year ago when I was really depressed and very lonely. I know better than to start up with someone on the Internet, but you have to understand, I have no real friends. The only family I have is somewhere in Florida, and I haven't a clue where. So when this person started up a dialogue with me, it sounded so real and so romantic that I guess I got taken in and agreed to meet him. Well, it turned out to be a man," she smiled sheepishly then said, "which is what I expected and, of course, wanted."

Lauren sensed her embarrassment. "Go on."

"Anyway, we met and I was really taken in. He was handsome, appeared to have money and was quite the gentleman. He treated me like a queen. That is until I slept with him, then he started to get very demanding. He kept telling me that he owned me, that it was his birth right. How weird is that? So I told him that I didn't want to see him anymore and that's when he beat me, then raped me. The black eye he gave me went away, but the scars on my neck didn't. That's why I wear turtle necks all the time. I was in a hospital for a week recovering. That was about six months ago when I lived in California. The police couldn't find even a trace of him. He had lied about everything he told me, I think."

"Where did you live in California, Mandy?" Robin asked.

"The Bay Area," she responded.

Robin's face beamed. "That's where I live, south of the city about 50 miles in a town called Los Gatos."

"I know where it is, Robin, but I lived up in the city. So in order to get away from him I moved here to Florida."

Lauren leaned forward and asked, "What made you come here to Tampa, Mandy?

"Well as I said, I had heard that my only family, my sister, lived somewhere in Florida and I have been looking for her for awhile. Then, Lauren, the week before you and I took that gun course, he found me and started to threaten me again. I told you what he said in my message to you-that if I bought a gun, he would kill me with it. Now, I don't know what to do. I'm afraid for my life."

Tears began to slowly slide down Mandy's cheeks and she began to shake when Lauren reached over and put her arm around her.

"Mandy," Lauren said, "we will work this out somehow. I have someone who is helping me a great deal, a real friend. I know he would be delighted to help you, too." Arthur flashed into her mind and a smile came to her face.

"I'm supposed to be talking with him later today, so please have faith. While we're here let me get some more information. My friend is a very thorough detective type and he would ask you some of this anyway. That is if you don't mind?"

"Not at all Lauren, ask away," Mandy sniffled.

"First of all, I never did get your last name."

"It's Romulus. That's my maiden name. I've never been married.

"Is that spelled like the Romulus in Romulus and Remus?"

"Like in what?"

"Ah, never mind, I think I know how it's spelled. When's your birthday?"

"June 21, 1963."

"Does that make you a Cancer?" Robin asked.

"No, Robin, I'm a Gemini," Mandy corrected her.

Lauren glanced at Robin with a look of impatience on her face then said, "I thought we were all about the same age, I'm 44 and Robin is 43. What's your address?"

"I don't actually have a regular residence anymore," Mandy answered. "I moved out of my apartment when he called me, and I'm staying in a motel. It's the one at Fowler and 30th Street near the University."

"Where were you born?" Lauren asked.

"I was born somewhere in Maine, but I don't remember the town. I left when I was just a baby."

A smile spread across Lauren's face and she responded, "that's where I was born. Maybe this is a sign of good luck. And now the most important question," Lauren took a deep breath, looked directly into Mandy's eyes.

"What is your stalker's name?"

Mandy's face took on a solemn look and she sighed softly before saying, "It's Lance."

Before Mandy could say his last name, both Robin and Lauren gasped, each of them putting their hand to their chest and said, "What?"

Mandy was taken aback by their response to the name Lance. Raising her hand to her breast and with a hint of fear in her voice she asked, "What's the matter? What is it?"

Lauren calmed down and explained. "Robin had some business dealings." she looked at Robin then cleared her throat, "in California, mind you, with a man who gave his name as Lance and who later began stalking her. I have had an encounter in a round- about way with a person who has mentioned the name Lancelot. This seems to be connected too closely to be a coincidence. Do either of you think we could be dealing with the same person?"

Robin directed her next comment at Mandy.

"There is an obvious connection between Lauren and myself, but you and Lauren have only just met, at that gun class. It doesn't make any sense."

Mandy took Lauren's hand and looked into her eyes, their faces but a short distance apart and said in a half whisper, "Lauren, I don't want to die. Please help me?" A tear trickled down her cheek.

"Please, rest assured, Mandy," Lauren replied, "we'll get to the bottom of this and you won't die. Keep out of sight and if you can, stay in your room until you hear from me. By the way, are you sure that you weren't followed?'

"Lauren, a horrible thought just occurred to me," Mandy said. "If by chance the man who is stalking me and one who stalked Robin and your Lancelot for that matter, are the same person, then he may be following you Lauren. Maybe that's how he found me, quite by accident.

Remember, we met at the gun range."

Lauren and Robin looked at each other with mouths wide open before Lauren said, "You're absolutely right, Mandy. I never thought of that." All three women began looking around them, glancing at the other customers, but none appeared very suspicious to any one of them.

"I have an idea," Lauren continued. "When we all leave you go first and we'll see if there are any cars that might appear to follow you. If there is, we'll immediately follow that car and get a license number. If not, just continue going where ever you were going. I'll call you on your cell if we notice anything. My detective friend and I have missed each other several times, but he should be getting back soon so I'll be able tell him about your situation and see if he agrees with us and thinks that they all fit in together. Then we'll see what he suggests. No matter what, Mandy, keep a watchful eye out everywhere you go and try to not be in any secluded area by yourself. Oh, by the way, you never said whether you actually bought a gun or not."

Mandy hesitated, cleared her throat then responded.

"Why, no, I didn't. Do you think I should?"

Lauren shook her head and said, "My husband, the cop, has always told me that anyone who is not mentally ready to use a gun should not own one. So I guess only you can answer that one." As Mandy rose to leave, Lauren couldn't help but comment on the necklace she was wearing. "Mandy, that is such a beautiful necklace you're wearing, I meant to ask you about it the first time we met. What kind of stone is it and what is the little symbol etched in the surface?"

"You can't believe how many people ask me about it. It's an amber stone, which is actually a fossil resin. It's found along some seacoasts and made into jewelry. As for the symbol, I don't know what it means. I shouldn't even be wearing it, Lance gave it to me, but it's so beautiful that I hate to take it off. And, oh, it's called an Intaglio."

Lauren watched as Mandy slid into the front seat of a generic-looking compact car and drove onto Highway 41. When Lauren guided her car to where she could see the oncoming traffic, a host of cars sped by her until she could no longer see Mandy's car.

"Shit," she blurted out. "Robin, did you see anything suspicious?"

"Why, yes, Lauren, I saw about 24 very suspicious-looking cars go after Mandy."

"Okay, so I blew it," she said while pulling out onto the highway. "Here, take my cell phone and call her. I put her in my memory under Mandy."

"Hmm, that was rather clever of you," Robin said, chuckling.

"Of course it was, after all I'm the English Professor. Is it ringing?"

"Mandy, it's Robin. We couldn't follow you because a lot of cars came past before we could turn on to the highway so we don't know where you are."

"Actually Robin you just passed me on the side of the road,." Mandy replied, "I saw the cars and pulled over to wait for you."

"Oh," Robin said.

"What did she say, Robin?"

"She said we remind her of the Keystone Kops."

"Huh? What are the Keystone Kops?"

"I thought you were the learned English Professor; they were a bunch of inept silent picture cops who kept running into each other whenever they would chase a criminal."

"She didn't say that."

"No, Lauren, I did." As she giggled, she again directed her attention to Mandy, "Mandy, we'll pull over and let you pass us then follow you for awhile just in case."

Taking her lead, Lauren pulled the car to the side of the road and waited until they could see a small compact car pass by. Lauren looked at Robin.

"Was that her?"

"Must have been, there are no other cars for about 15 miles." Lauren's tires spewed dirt and gravel and a cloud of dust as the car squealed out onto the highway.

Robin smirked. "At least no one can accuse us of being inconspicuous."

Lauren finally accepted the spirit of their inept attempt to be detectives.

"You know, Robin; there is an area just outside the city called Keystone. Perhaps I should move there."

After following Mandy for a few miles, Robin again called her on Lauren's cell phone. "Mandy, it looks as though no one has followed you, so we're going to leave you now. Remember the plan. Lauren will contact her friend and tell him about you, and then will call you as to where we go from there." She disconnected and Lauren headed the car back toward home.

As they walked back into the condominium, Lauren noticed that the red light on the phone was blinking.

"Lauren, it's Arthur, I am staying over another day to follow up with the local newspaper I have a hunch that it may be a good source of information. I'll call again after that meeting.

Lauren clicked it off then signed on the Internet to check messages finding that she had one from Damien Porter in Chicago.

Lauren, I did some checking on that corporation and address for you. First, the address is one of those stores that offer mail services including the box. It gives one the appearance of having an actual street address. A lot of people who work out of the home use it for appearance's sake. Having a street address gives more credibility. Avalon Publishing evidently only just got their P.O. Box there a few weeks ago. They picked a nice area however. The store is in a part of Chicago called the Lincoln Park area. Up scale, artsy with a lot of ethnic restaurants. It's also near the lake, Michigan that is, and Wrigley Field where the Cubs play. The company was originally incorporated in the state of Maine under another name then moved to Illinois. It only just filed under the new name, Avalon. It also recently filed as an out- of-state corporation doing business in the state of Florida, and just recently filed the same thing in California. We checked out the web site for the National Publishing Association and found no record of the company as a member. That doesn't necessarily mean anything since not all small publishers belong to it.

However, and get this, my friend checked the state tax records for sales tax information and there is no record of the original corporation in any of the three states of the company filing sales tax returns or even having a sales tax number. This would indicate that they either have no sales or are not charging sales tax on any sales. It has all the appearances of being a façade.

Lauren, I'm worried about you and I am thinking of perhaps making a trip to Florida. Do you think you could arrange to meet with me?

Robin was again peering over her shoulder and couldn't help but offer her opinion. "Are you serious?

Either this guy is hot to trot for you or he has another deeper motive."

"What on earth does that mean, Robin?"

"I'm not sure, Lauren, but his e-mail seems a bit of an over reaction given that he hasn't seen you in what, a couple of years? He doesn't know exactly what's going on and now he's going to fly to Florida just because he's what, worried about you?"

"Well, I can't imagine what other motive he might have." Lauren said. "Can you?"

Robin put her hand on Lauren's shoulder, raised her eyebrows and responded, "Tell me what your Chicago professor looks like."

Lauren's face twisted a bit from curiosity then she said. "He's about five-foot-ten, perhaps in his early forties, has sandy brown hair and is on the slight side. Perhaps 160 or 170 pounds and has hazel or green eyes. I don't quite recall."

"Let's see Lauren, I'm being stalked, you have been stalked and now Mandy, and a man that fits the description of the man I posed for," Robins face turned red as she spoke, "is willing to fly from Chicago to Florida because he is worried about you?"

"Oh, my God, Robin, I can't believe you would even think that. If you were right, and I am not saying you are, then why hasn't he done something since the last time I saw him two years ago?"

Robin's face stiffened, and she said, "How do you know he hasn't?"

Lauren sighed as she took Robin's hand. "I guess I don't know Robin, but I have to go to school tomorrow, so I think I'll go to bed. Will you be all right by yourself?"

"Don't worry about me. I'm going to stick around

here. I'm going to spend the day on your computer. Maybe I can come up with some ideas. Anyway, good night, I'm going to sleep as well. "One final thing." Robin bit her lower lip with her teeth and wrinkled her nose before she spoke, "this thing is getting quite serious, Lauren. Do you think we should confront Brian with all that we know? I know you have your suspicions about him and that Red Pepper partner of his, but he may be a great deal of help."

"I don't know, Robin, let me sleep on it and it's Red Hot, not Red Pepper."

"Oh," Robin responded, "whatever."

Robin pulled back the covers of the bed in the guest room then reached in her overnight carry on and took out a men's size XL pullover shirt that she often slept in. Embroidered on the front of the shirt was the word 'Zorro' for her Rottweiler that she had loved so dearly before his untimely death two years ago. Zorro had foiled an attempted break-in of Robin's home when the intruder shot him but not before Zorro had bit him. Police determined this from a blood- soaked piece of a plaid shirt that had remained in Zorro's mouth. The police never did find out who committed the crime, but a picture of Zorro still hangs in the local police hall of fame as a tribute to his sacrifice for his owner.

After brushing her teeth, she walked over to the window that overlooks the lake side of the condo and opened it, gazing at the reflected moonlight on the water and enjoying the cool breeze that blew in. The palm trees swayed slightly in the breeze as her eyes fixed on the silhouette of what appeared to be a statue standing under an oak tree, which was the only thing between the condo and the lake. After drifting into an almost trance-like state, she let her mind go back to her college days and the enjoyment of the times she shared with Lauren and Brian. Then her mind drifted to thoughts of the antics that she once enjoyed with her beloved Zorro, and it brought a smile to her face giving her a sense of peace.

Her feeling of euphoria was short-lived, however, as she heard a sound that appeared to be coming from the area of the balcony. Because the den was between the guest room and the patio, the sound was somewhat muffled so she couldn't determine what it was. Moving to the far end of the window and with her head pressed against the screen, she could see the railing on the near end of the balcony but couldn't make out anything else. She swung her head around in a half circle to take in the entire view and as she did, her eyes widened and stopped at the base of the large oak tree.

"My God," she said out loud, "there's no statue there." Slamming the window shut, she hurried to the master bedroom, expecting to find Lauren sleeping, but she wasn't there. Easing her way down the hall in the darkness, she finally reached the family room and let out a loud gasp as she bumped into Lauren who was standing there with a pistol in her hand, staring at the patio door.

Lauren put her hand on Robin's mouth and whispered, "I guess you heard it, too."

"Yes and I also saw the statue, then it was gone."

"Robin, what the hell are you talking about?"

Robin whispered a response, "I was looking out the window and saw what I thought was a statue under that big oak tree. Then after I heard the noise I looked back and there was no statue there."

Lauren whispered back, "I can only guess that you saw the person that made the noise by the patio. I wasn't sleeping either and when I heard it, I grabbed my gun and came here, but I didn't see anyone."

"Lauren, do you think there was someone actually on the patio trying to get in?"

"I don't know, Robin, but let's go look."

"Right, you go first, you have the gun." As they both moved slowly toward the patio door and peered into the darkness, the door to the condo suddenly swung open and they both screamed.

"What the hell are you doing?" Brian yelled out and as he did, Lauren quickly swung her arm behind her to conceal the pistol and hit Robin's arm who was standing next to her. She couldn't tell if he had seen it, and since she was wearing only a night shirt, she had nowhere to put it; so she slipped it into Robin's hand.

Robin tried her best not to be conspicuous, stammering, "Uh, I mean, that is, we heard a noise and came running out here. I have to go to the bathroom, excuse me." She backed halfway down the hall in order to conceal the pistol, while looking at Brian who was looking back at her with a questioning look on his face.

After she disappeared down the hall, Brian turned his attention to Lauren and, after staring at her for a moment, finally spoke. "What was that you put behind your back?

"Who, me, oh nothing, see," she said, holding her empty hands in front of her.

Brian glanced down the hall, but Robin had disappeared into the spare room only to return just as quickly.

"I was looking out the window and saw a statue under that big oak tree. Then I heard a noise and looked back at the statue, and it was gone."

Lauren interrupted, saying, "We both heard a noise

near the balcony. Brian, was that you by the oak tree and you that made the noise?"

Brian looked first at Lauren then at Robin.

"After I parked the car, I thought I saw someone go past the side of the building. So I went around and looked, but I didn't see anyone; I guess there wasn't anyone there. Maybe you heard me make some noise."

"Well, did you stand under the oak tree?" Robin asked.

Brian was now visibly nervous, shifting his weight from one foot to the other before he answered.

"Er, ah, I guess I must have gone back there. Anyway, nothing to worry about now, I'm home." He made his way past the ladies and to the bedroom.

"Robin, are you buying that story?"

"I don't think so, Lauren, if there was someone there, he doesn't want us to know about it. Or worse, if it was only just him, then he's lying to us about why he was out there."

Lauren looked straight at Robin. "Do you still think we should confide in him? Or should we keep prying?"

Even with Brian in the bed next to her, going to sleep was a struggle as she had not yet come down from the tension caused by the night's occurrences. Sleep this night was not sound, as the movement of the trees in the breeze near the bedroom window seemed to lie just below her subconscious, often waking her from a light sleep. Her last recollection was that of Brian getting out of bed to go to the bathroom. She had glanced at the digital clock which read 2:20.

For some unknown reason she woke again and saw that Brian was not in the bed next to her. She rose and went out into the hall peeking in the guest bedroom where she saw Robin sleeping soundly. Curious about Brian's whereabouts, she went to the family room and glanced out the balcony door.

Once again, a dense fog had set in and visibility was very poor, nevertheless she thought she saw some sort of movement in the distance down near the lake. Thinking that perhaps Brian was out there searching for whatever it was they thought they saw earlier, prompted her to go to the bedroom, put on her kimono and sandals and slip out the front door.

Wrapping her arms around herself to keep out the cool damp air, she made her way around the side of the building toward the lake. Halfway down, near the large oak tree, she could see a figure in the distance near the shore of the lake.

"Brian?" she called out.

There was no answer, so she called again. "Brian, is that you?"

There was still no answer, but at that very moment she noticed that the silhouette in the fog had begun to move and in an instant was coming in her direction. Her voice now cracked as she took several steps back toward the condominium while still glancing behind herself and calling Brian.

"This isn't funny, Brian, tell me if it's you."

The figure in the mist began moving faster toward her and she instinctively reached in the pocket of her robe, but the pistol that she had intended to bring with her wasn't there. Then she remembered giving it to Robin earlier. Her pace quickened until she was running all the while looking back at the figure that was coming still closer to her. Just as she reached the corner of the building, she stumbled and fell and her face hit the soft dampened ground. Pushing herself up into a sitting position, she could now see the figure and hear it breathing. It reached out toward her.

Screaming and sobbing, she sat in the middle of the bed, drenched from her own perspiration and struggling to catch a breath from her trembling body. Suddenly the door swung open and Robin came running in, immediately embracing her trembling friend, there in the darkness, until Lauren's breathing slowed and the trembling stopped.

"What on earth happened, Lauren, and where's Brian?"

"I don't know, but I've had another of my terrible nightmares. The ones I told you about. They seem so real, Robin, I don't know how much more of this I can stand. I'm so fortunate that you're here with me since it appears that I can't count on my own husband. He's never here when I need him. I don't want to sound like a whimpering child, but would you mind staying here with me, at least for tonight?"

"Of course, Lauren, but let's hope that Brian doesn't come back. That could be a bit awkward."

CHAPTER NINETEEN

The next morning Lauren got up and as she passed the open door of the guest room she saw that Robin was already out of bed. When she reached the end of the hall she found Robin standing near the kitchen, staring at an area of the floor near the front door.

"Robin, what's the matter?"

Robin turned toward her and had a strange look on her face.

"Take a look at the floor near the front door."

Lauren eased past her and stared before turning to Robin. "What is that on the floor?"

Robin took her hand, "Unless I miss my guess, Lauren, it's several pieces of grass and a bit of mud."

Lauren gasped. "My God, Robin, maybe Brian was out there again last night."

Robin turned and looked at Lauren's eyes, then stepped back with her mouth wide open still staring at her. She gently put her hand toward Lauren's face and brushed it across her cheek, before showing Lauren her hand.

"I don't need to guess about this one. It's mud, mud on your face. I couldn't see it last night in the dark. Do I think Brian was out there last night? Yes, and so were you."

"My God, Robin, I remember falling on the ground in my dream when I was chased. But what you're saying is that it wasn't a nightmare? But how could I get back in the house and into my bed without remembering it?"

"I haven't a clue, Lauren, but why don't you try to get ahold of Brian and find out where he went and if he was out there last night. That is, if he'll tell you the truth."

****

Lauren got to school early that morning and after leaving a message for Brian, spent some time in her office grading papers. Just as she prepared to leave for her first class, she heard the click of heels on the floor outside her office and what sounded like someone sobbing. She hurried out to see one of the other teachers turn down the hall toward the office and she followed. In the office, the entire staff was in tears, sobbing and holding each other.

"What on God's earth is going on?" she asked.

One of the secretaries finally composed herself.

"It's Arthur. He's been in a car crash up in Maine. He's in a coma, and they don't know if he's going to live."

"My God, I don't believe it. Are you sure?" As Lauren spoke she felt a rush of blood to her face and couldn't control the tears that started to trickle down both cheeks. "Who told you what happened?"

The secretary answered, "We got a call from the police in Maine. For some reason he was in a small town in northern Maine and had stayed at a motel. Apparently he had stayed over another day or so and was on his way back to Bangor this morning when he went off the road into a steep ravine."

Lauren felt nausea overtake her and she began to tremble, soon uncontrollably. After going into the hall she leaned with her back against the wall, slid down onto the floor, sitting alone with her face in her hands and wept until her whole body ached. She kept repeating in her mind that she was the reason that Arthur had been in that small town in northern Maine, and she alone was responsible for his accident. If he dies, she thought, she would be responsible for his death.

Her thoughts turned to when Arthur would proudly tell her yet another story about his beloved author Sherlock Holmes and of the way Arthur had gone out of his way to help her in her moment of need. She wiped the tears from her eyes and went back to her office and just sat there in solitude.

Classes were cancelled for the remainder of the day and the Dean of the college was arranging to go to Maine in hopes that Arthur might soon come out of the coma or in the worst case scenario to handle the details of his death. Before leaving, Lauren went back to the main office and got the name of the hospital in Bangor where Arthur was being treated and as she left the office, she noticed the Dean was standing in the hall.

"Oh, hello Lauren, terrible thing that's happened. I guess I have to go up there, but it's not an opportune time for me to be leaving, I have some medical tests scheduled."

Seizing on the opportunity, Lauren interrupted him.

"Dean Harrison, if you have other obligations, I would be happy to go to Bangor to attend to anything that needs to be done. I am much closer to Arthur than anyone at the college, and it wouldn't be an imposition at all. I know they have a substitute on call and I could leave immediately."

She held her breath as he mulled over her suggestion.

"Maybe that wouldn't be such a bad idea, Lauren, in fact, let's do it. You can get all the details from the office. Take a cash advance and the office will make your reservations. I'll tell them to give you whatever you need. And thanks, it takes a lot of pressure off me." In her mind Lauren felt that he didn't want to go anyway and that in fact she was his excuse not to go.

During the drive home, she couldn't stop her tears as she tried desperately to come to terms with herself and her grief. She truly loved Arthur in her own way and had relied on him in so many ways. Lauren thought of the quiet times when he would console her, and how he stepped forward to help her when she needed a friend.

Brian had just come back from a stakeout and saw Robin and Lauren sitting on the couch. Lauren had a look of despair on her face.

"Lauren, why aren't you at school."

"Arthur was almost killed in an automobile accident up in Maine," she said. "He was attending a seminar. They found him in a ravine unconscious in his rental car. He's in a coma, and they don't know if he'll live."

"Oh my God, Lauren, that's terrible. I know how close you are to him. Is there anything I can do?"

Lauren thought for a moment about telling him everything, but then decided that she needed more time to sort things out.

"Perhaps you could talk with the police in Maine, Brian, and get some more details as to what happened. I want to understand exactly what caused the accident."

She handed him a slip of paper with the number for the police on it. In the anguish of the moment, both Robin and Lauren had forgotten about the events of last night, now only concerned with Arthur.

"I'll get on it right away, Lauren."

He went into the den and called the Maine state police in Bangor and after being transferred three times, he finally got to talk to the officer who was first on the scene, Martin Crenshaw.

The officer listened to Brian identify himself and ask a few pertinent questions then responded.

"First off, the roads up there are very curvy and it's not uncommon for a car to go off a road when it's wet and we've had some rain lately"," Crenshaw said.

But this seems a little different. You see, the hose carrying the brake fluid was ripped off. Not cut mind you, but literally ripped. There was a piece of a tree branch up under the hood. This time of year there are often branches on the road, and we surmised that he picked one up somehow and it flew up into the engine, ripping the hose."

Brian thought for a brief second. "Any chance that it was foul play?"

"There's always a chance," the officer answered. "Do you know if he had any enemies up here?"

"No, I honestly don't know." Brian responded. "But can you tell me what kind of car he was driving?"

"Yes, it was a 2006 Ford Taurus. Why?"

"I thought I'd have someone take a look at the configuration of the engine," Brian responded. "You know, to see what the odds might be that a tree branch could cause the rupture of the hose."

Brian paused and the officer spoke.

"Good thought. We had no knowledge of the man or if there was any chance of foul play, so it wasn't an issue with us."

"Before hanging up, Martin, I have one other thing. It is my understanding that he was attending a seminar in Bangor. Where and how far from Bangor was the accident and which way was he headed?"

"Brian, he was headed south on the road back to Bangor, and was about 40 miles northwest of the city. It's not an area that tourists normally go, especially this time of year. Perhaps he had some other business up there. Oh, by the way, the closest town to where the accident occurred is

Portersville."

Brian gasped. "Did you say Portersville?"

"Yes, why?"

Brian thanked him and hung up the phone without answering. He sat for a moment, perplexed by the location of the accident, recalling that Portersville was the town where Lauren was born. Speaking to himself he muttered, "Could this be a colossal coincidence, or was he up there doing something for Lauren? The town is totally out of the way for someone going to Bangor."

Brian picked the phone up again and dialed police headquarters, asking for the garage.

"Hey, Dennis, Brian St. John in homicide, how ya doing?"

"Good," he replied.

"Listen, could you do me a favor and research something for me? I've come across a case of a traffic accident where it appears that the hose that carries the brake fluid was ripped off, not sliced, and there was a piece of a tree branch lodged up in the engine. It was 2006 Ford Taurus. I'm trying to see if it could have really happened that way, because if it couldn't, it may be an attempted homicide."

"Okay," Randy replied.

"Thanks a bunch, Randy. I'll check back with you in a day or two."

Before talking to Lauren, he stopped and thought to himself, with the way Lauren has been acting lately, and now with the somewhat strange accident that Arthur was involved in, maybe I had better hold off telling her about Portersville and the branch in the engine. He paused with his hand on the doorknob to the den and posed a question to himself aloud. "Do you suppose she knows anything about the suspected serial murders and the other strange things that have been happening?" No, how could she, he thought to himself.

"Lauren," he called as he entered the family room. "I talked to one of the troopers in Bangor who said that they were in the process of a routine investigation and would get back to me at the station in a couple of days. I'll let you know what he says."

"Thanks, Brian and by the way, I will be going up to Bangor in order to see Arthur and to attend to any details that need be done. I only pray that it doesn't include a wake and burial."

Both Robin and Brian looked at her in a surprised manner then Brian said. "Is this on behalf of the school or on your own?"

"Both actually," she said. "Dean Harrison is scheduled to have a medical procedure done, so he asked me. Well, I actually volunteered, you know how close I am to Arthur and all. I'll be leaving in the morning."

"Lauren, I can't tell you how important it is to be sure you watch where you're going and what you're doing. There may be more to this than you think, so don't trust anyone."

Brian had let his concerns slip a bit and Lauren was quick to pick up on it.

"Since when has my safety been so important to you?" she asked, thinking about the recent incidents where she was alone and needed his help. She could see by the look on his face that she had hurt him.

"I can't believe you said that," he replied. "Your safety has always been my number one priority."

He turned to leave when Robin stood, facing Brian.

"Wait a second, Brian, maybe I'm the odd one out in this group, but we're all involved in what's happening here. And if what you said is true, then perhaps you can explain last night."

Brian's face turned red, but he nevertheless feigned innocence.

"What are you talking about, Robin, and what do you mean what's happening here?"

"I'm pretty sure you know," she responded. "But for the sake of argument...."

Lauren stepped in front of Robin with her back to Brian and put her hand on Robin's mouth, shaking her head and quietly whispered, "Not yet." She turned to Brian. "I'm sorry for what I said. I will of course be careful. Please don't worry about me."

He turned and left without another word.

As soon as the door closed, Robin shrugged her shoulders.

"Okay, okay, but I hope you know what you're doing. Don't you think I should go with you? Remember how shook up you were last night? And heaven knows, I can't stay here alone with Brian."

"Robin, I can't expose you to anymore danger. Why don't you go back to California and wait until I get back from Maine and then we'll figure this whole thing out?"

"Expose me to any more danger?" she said. "Hello? I've got a stalker back in California and besides there is safety in numbers. No, my mind is made up- I'm going with you."

"Okay, I guess you're right," Lauren said. "But you know I have to believe that Arthur learned something when he went to my home town. Otherwise why would someone try to kill him?"

Robin looked at her curiously and asked, "Why are you so sure that someone tried to kill him?"

"Because, my dear friend, I know him. He is thorough, cautious and pays attention to everything around him. Besides, I don't think he's ever driven over 35 or 40 miles an hour in his life. I've been in his car with him and he drives slowly to the point of being irritating. Let's face it, he was up there investigating what we think is a dangerous stalker or perhaps worse. Then when he's coming back from where I was born all of a sudden he drives off the road. And look at this." She reached in her briefcase and held up a printout of a weather forecast for the entire New England area. "It shows that the weather front that was in the area had cleared up, and there was nothing but clear skies yesterday and for the next two days."

"Where the hell did you get that?" Robin asked.

"Did it before I left school. I guess some of Arthur has rubbed off on me. Anyway, Arthur wasn't in an accident, my dear. Someone tried to murder him. When we're up there, I am hoping to find something that he might have found. Some sort of documents or other information that would shed some light on this whole thing. Robin, would you mind going on line to see what flights are available? We should leave as soon as possible."

Robin went to the den and turned on the computer when she heard Lauren call out:

"Oh, and by the way why don't you see if I have any e-mail? You don't need a password."

Robin scanned the flight schedules and found one that left late in the day stopping at Logan International in Boston then going on to Bangor International. She booked two seats using her credit card. As she scanned Lauren's e-mails, she called out to Lauren who was now in the bedroom across from the den, "What about Mandy? What should we tell her?"

As she waited for a response, she opened the first e-mail.

"My Lord," she whispered to herself. "It's from Cameo." As she read to herself, her mouth fell open and she stared at the words in front of her.

"Lauren," she yelled. "You had better come and read this e-mail."

"What's the matter, you sound like you've seen a ghost," Lauren said as she entered the den, then bent over Robin's shoulder and peered at the words in front of her.

I will meet you at the airport.

Lauren stood erect and put her hand over her mouth, gasping.

"My God, Robin, he knows we are going, but how?"

"I just made our reservations," Robin responded, "but the e-mail was there before that. Look, it was sent about five minutes before I confirmed them."

Lauren put her hand on Robin's shoulder and said. "You want to know what I think?" She paused. "I think he knew all along, that when I found out that Arthur was injured and in the hospital, I would go up there. The timing can only be a coincidence."

Robin turned and looked up at her.

"It damn well better be or this person has some sort of psychic abilities." Her eyes widened and her mouth dropped open. "God, you don't suppose...."

Lauren stopped her in mid-sentence. "Don't be an ass, Robin. It's just a coincidence. Why don't you call Mandy and tell her we're going." Lauren smirked, "I guess she will be in no danger if he's meeting us at the airport."

"Lauren, that's not funny and by the way, he didn't say which airport. Doesn't this scare the living daylights out of you?"

"Of course it does," Lauren responded, "but it's something we have to do, at least if we want to get to the bottom of this. I'll make reservations at the hotel where Arthur was going to stay. I can do it on the computer. It was where the conference was held. You're going to love this, it's a place called Stratford upon Penobscot, which is also known as The Bangor Inn."

"What's a Penobscot?

"It's the river that separates Bangor from the city of Brewer. I guess that's their version of Stratford upon Avon. How fitting. Why don't you call Mandy on my cell? Oh, we're going to need a car. We can do that on line, as well."

While Lauren was on the computer, Robin dialed Mandy's number and got her voice mail. She left a message:

"Mandy, this is Robin. Lauren and I are going to Bangor. The friend that Lauren mentioned to you was in a serious accident, and we're going to try and see what happened. We will both have our cell phones on, so call if you need us, and remember to be extremely careful."

She hung up the phone and thought for a moment before turning toward Lauren. "What about the pistol? Can we take it with us?"

"Duh! Not unless we want to get arrested at the airport," Lauren said, then thought for a moment. "Truthfully, I would feel a lot safer if we had it with us, Robin, and we would only really need it when we went to my home town or where ever Arthur went. I would think we would be pretty safe in Bangor and certainly on the plane. Hmm, what would Arthur do?"

"Fed Ex," Robin said, snapping her fingers.

"What?"

"We Fed Ex it to ourselves in care of the hotel with

instructions to hold it until we arrive. Then when we come back, we Fed Ex it to your address."

"Brilliant, Robin, why didn't I think of that?"

"I guess because you're an English teacher."

"Oh, and I suppose being a photographer makes you some sort of intellect?"

"Well, I did think of it."

CHAPTER TWENTY

After checking one bag each, Lauren and Robin walked briskly toward the tram that would take them to the airside terminal.

"You know, Lauren, I have only been here a couple of times, but I still think Tampa International is the most user-friendly airport in the country, and I've traveled all over the U.S."

"You've been here three times," Lauren said. "Don't forget when I first came here to look around when we were just out of college. Remember?"

"I forgot about that. You know if you had moved here right then, you may not have married Brian. I seem to remember you still had a thing for that professor."

"Stop right there," Lauren replied. "That's a chapter in my life that I have put to bed forever."

"Hmm, Lauren, strange choice of words. You know I never could figure why an English major would take economics if she didn't have to. And get an A besides."

"My Lord, woman, are you ever going to forget that? I never even slept with him," Lauren said. "Well, maybe once."

"Don't tell me, the night before the final exam?"

Lauren slapped her free hand against Robin's forehead and said, "Would you concentrate on the situation at hand. We are in some deep trouble here and all you can do is talk about my escapades in college."

"You're absolutely right, Lauren, and I'm sorry. I'm sure you didn't sleep with him the night before the final exam. No, I distinctly remember it was the night before the mid-term."

There were only a couple of dozen passengers on the 9:40 red-eye to Boston, and both Lauren and Robin had thoroughly studied the faces of all those on board via several trips to the lavatory. After finishing the crossword puzzle in the in-flight magazine, she stuffed the magazine in the storage pocket in front of her and laid back and dozed off. The flight got into Boston's Logan Airport around midnight, and after they deplaned they carefully searched the faces of the people that were standing near the gate, but saw no one suspicious looking.

"Remember, Robin, don't leave my side. As long as we are together we should be all right."

"Consider me glue, Lauren."

After checking their connecting flight on a nearby board they saw that it was on time and leaving from the same concourse, so they had some time to kill.

"Lauren, we've got an hour before we board the flight to Bangor. Let's go in that bar." Robin pointed to an airside bar next to their gate. "And are you sure that the Fed Ex guy got the package in time for a tomorrow delivery?"

"Positive," Lauren replied, "it should be at the desk of our hotel by 10:30 in the morning."

"And did you remember to put some bullets in the package?"

"Robin, you put them in yourself. Why are you asking me?"

"I guess I'm just nervous," Robin replied, as they both sat on barstools that afforded them a view of the people passing by. "What are you going to have?"

"Silly question, Robin, what do I always have?" Robin looked at the bartender.

"Two glasses of the house Chablis please. By the way, Lauren, you did get us one room I hope?"

"Why, can't get enough of me," Lauren chuckled.

"Safety of course. It would be dangerous to be in separate rooms." Robin ignored her chuckle.

"I did, but you have to promise to let me go to the bathroom alone."

"Lauren, really. Here's to finding out what the hell is going on here." Robin raised her glass in a toast.

Lauren tapped her glass against Robin's glass and as she did, she caught a glimpse of a man walking quickly past the front of the bar. "Robin, don't look now."

Robin swung her head around, but didn't see anyone.

"I told you not to look, but you missed him anyway. I know my nerves are on edge, but remember when I picked you up at the airport? Well I didn't see that guy's face very well, but the guy that just walked past was built just like the guy sitting in the bar in Tampa, you know, when I was waiting for your plane to get in. You remember the one that passed us in the car?"

Robin had jumped off her bar stool while listening to Lauren and hurried toward the entrance to the bar and peered out. Looking back at Lauren, she shook her head.

"Either he was a sprinter or a figment of your imagination, there's no one in sight." She came back and sat on the bar stool. "Are you sure you saw someone?"

"Maybe there's a men's room or another store or something that he walked into," Lauren said as she slipped off her stool and walked toward the front of the bar, looking both ways. As she returned to the bar stool she shook her head then looked at the bartender and asked, "Are there any doorways that someone could go in as you go back toward the main terminal? I mean like within 20 or 30 feet?"

The bartender shook his head, indicating that there wasn't.

"Robin, maybe I'm losing it. I could swear I saw someone walk by and yet you got up as soon as I said to look, I mean not to look, you know what I mean. And yet you saw nothing. I don't understand it."

Robin looked at Lauren with a puzzled look on her face. "Lauren, do you realize that your cell phone is beeping?"

"What? Oh, I'm sorry. I just had a strange feeling. Like the ones I've had before, you know, the ones I told you about?"

"No, Lauren, you never told me about the strange feelings. What do you mean?"

Lauren paused for a moment as though searching her mind for something.

"I thought I told you," she replied. "Anyway, I sometimes have the feeling that I am being manipulated. Like someone has some sort of control over me and can make me perhaps do things that I don't want to do. Remember what I told you about that night at Greg Allsop's apartment and how I acted and how I felt?"

"Yes, but what does that have to do with now?" Robin asked.

"It's the same feeling as when I dressed the way I did that night and acted the way I did. That wasn't me. It was totally out of character for me, and yet it was me acting like that. I remember feeling strange, like something was in control of me."

"Why didn't you tell me about this before? And what do you think it means?"

Lauren thought for a moment then replied. "I don't have any idea. Robin, do you think I'm going crazy?"

Robin took her hand and squeezed it, "Don't be ridiculous, you can't go somewhere if you're already there."

"What?" Lauren asked.

"Never mind, but there is something here that is not readily apparent. Perhaps we can find some answers in your home town that might help us or maybe Arthur can show us something that he found."

Lauren's face saddened. "You mean if he lives. You know, Robin, you just made me think of something. Remember what I told you about my last visit with Arthur and what he was telling me about?"

"Yes," Robin replied, "that some people have gifts like precognition and telekinetics and such."

"Right, and here I am talking about having the feeling of being controlled. Like someone is making me do things that I wouldn't normally do. You don't suppose...." She stopped in mid-sentence, "my God, Robin, remember what you told me just this morning?"

Robin looked at her curiously. "What?" she asked.

"When we woke up this morning, you found grass by the door and mud on my face and said that I was actually outside, when I thought I had a dream. Do you suppose someone or something made me go outside and made me think it was a dream? What about all those horrible nightmares in the past? Were they nightmares or real?" Lauren began shaking. "And what if no one just walked past the bar and it was just something controlling my mind?"

Robin took hold of her shoulders and shook her.

"Get control of yourself. Calm down, I'm here with you and no one can hurt you." Lauren finally stopped shaking.

"Are you okay, lady?" the bartender asked, noticing

her odd behavior.

"I'm all right, but did you just see a man walk past the front of the bar? I mean a few minutes ago?"

"Sorry, ma'am, I haven't seen anyone since you came in here."

"Lauren, your cell phone is beeping again. Are you going to check it?"

She flipped the phone open and read that there was a missed call. She looked at the number for a moment then realized who it was.

"It's Fatima, you know the fortune teller." She listened to the message.

Lauren, this is Fatima. I have consulted with a colleague about your situation and really need to talk with you as soon as possible. If for some reason you can't get in touch with me, I must caution you to be extremely careful. We both feel, I mean my colleague and myself, that the strange circumstances around your visit with me indicate that perhaps someone or something intends you a great deal of harm. I can't tell you why; just that there is a force out there somewhere that perhaps wants your soul. Lauren, listen well to what I am about to tell you. This morning I went outside to get my newspaper and found the white dove. It was dead. Be sure and go to the place where your father died. His spirit needs to pass.

Click, the message ended.

"Lauren, please tell me what the message said. I don't like the look on your face."

"Fatima told me that she thinks someone or something wants my soul. And the white dove is dead."

"What is the significance of the white dove?" Robin asked.

"As Fatima tells it, there is a belief in some Indian

cultures that if a white dove dies, the person that saw it last is in danger of dying as well."

'Lauren, when did you last see the white dove?"

"When I first went to see Fatima. Then it flew away and there was a black raven in the oak tree behind me. I have to assume that the raven scared the dove away. That's when she told me about the legend of the white dove."

"Hasn't that been a while since you saw her?" Robin asked, "and if so, how do you know someone else didn't see it since then?"

"I guess I don't, Robin, I just want to go home. I don't know if I can go through with this."

"If someone or something wants you dead, woman, it doesn't matter where you are. On the other hand, if we don't get to the bottom of this... Well, let me put it this way: we save your life if we find out who it is and maybe mine as well." Robin added.

"You mean who or what and remember what Fatima said, Robin. She said that someone or something wants my soul. What the hell does that mean?"

"No one can take your soul, Lauren. I know you believe in a lot of what this Fatima is telling you, but let's be realistic. It's someone, not something. Is that all she said?"

"No, Robin, there is one other thing." She paused then said, "Fatima said that I should go to the place where my father died, that his spirit was trying to contact me. It needs to pass."

"We'll make time when we get to your hometown," Robin said.

In an attempt to relieve some of the intensity of the moment, Lauren looked at Robin and grinned.

"Yes, we'll do that and it's okay if you stay with me in the bathroom, too, when we get to the hotel that is."

Robin shook her head as she looked at her watch, and then motioned Lauren to drink up, as it was time to go to their gate.

"Remind me to call Fatima tomorrow morning," Lauren said.

The connecting flight to Bangor left on time and both of the women seemed a bit more at ease. They had determined by searching the faces of the nine or ten other passengers on board that there was no one suspicious looking enough for them to be concerned about so they were able to relax for a short time.

As the plane went into it's final approach, Robin looked at Lauren.

"You know what this means don't you, Lauren?"

"No, Robin, what does it mean?"

"Well, Cameo's message said he would meet us at the airport and since he wasn't in Tampa or Boston, then we can expect to be greeted at the Bangor airport."

"You know, Robin, I was thinking the very same thing, but think about this. What if he already met us? I mean the man I think I saw go past the bar. I know you didn't see him, but the message wasn't meant for you, it was meant for me. And who is to say that he couldn't meet me in my mind, so no one else could see him?"

Robin thought for a moment then replied. "That's the scariest thing I've ever heard."

The landing was without incident and both women studied the faces of each person they passed as they made their way to the luggage pickup area. There were only a half dozen people waiting for baggage and Robin's suitcase came out almost immediately. After about 10 minutes, the other people had left and all the bags had been claimed, except Lauren's, which had yet to emerge.

"What do you suppose is going on, Robin?" She bent over and peered into the slot where the baggage came out on to the conveyer belt, but saw nothing.

"Excuse me," Robin had intercepted an airport employee. "All the baggage from our flight has already come out except hers." She pointed to Lauren, "can you go back and see if it's stuck or something?"

Lauren joined in. "It's a beige bag with wheels and a bright orange tag on it. Thanks for your help."

The man got on the conveyor and disappeared into the luggage opening. They waited another 10 minutes when the man came out of the door next to the luggage conveyer and began walking past the two women. After looking at each other with a curious look on their faces, Lauren said. "Excuse me, but did you find my suitcase?"

The man turned and looked questioningly at her then said. "What suitcase?"

"Oh, pardon me," Lauren replied, "I thought you were the man that was looking for my suitcase." She saw that he wasn't the same man.

The man turned toward Lauren and said. "Ma'am, I was the only one back there, and I didn't see any suitcase."

Lauren and Robin stared at each other each with a look of fear on their face and as they did, a beige suitcase with a bright orange tag on it came out of the luggage opening with such force that it flew off the conveyer belt, landing on its side only a short distance from Lauren's feet. The man made a bee line toward the door to the back of the luggage room and opened the door.

After disappearing for a moment, he came back out the main luggage area and had a look of shock on his face,

"Ma'am, there's not a soul in the back room. I can't imagine what made that luggage come flyin' out of

that chute like it did. I ain't never seen anything like it."
As he stood there shaking his head and staring into the back
room, Lauren grabbed the suitcase and Robin's hand and
started toward the exit.

"It's him, Robin. Let's get out of here." After
renting a car and receiving directions to the hotel from the
clerk, they made the short trip to the motel, ever cautious to
make sure that they weren't being followed.

As her eyes searched for the motel, Lauren
commented to Robin on how beautiful Bangor is, then in an
instant she said, "look, Robin, there's the Penobscot River.
Follow that road south it should be less than a half mile.
Wait, is that it?"

The motel was a testimony to its name, done in
English Tudor architecture and hugging the banks of the
river. As they drove up to the circular driveway, they were
greeted by a bell hop who was dressed the part of an
English soldier of the Tudor era. The bell boy, who was a
lanky somewhat bumpkin-like young man, opened the
driver's door for Lauren and as she slid out she looked at
him. Thinking that she would add to the spirit of the
moment, she asked. "Are you a Tudor?"

In an 'aw shucks' like manner, he responded. "No,
ma'am, I never even graduated high school."

She looked at him with her mouth wide open then
responded. "Oh, well I guess that would explain a lot of
things."

Robin glanced through the door of the inn which
was decorated much like Lauren's home and office, with
paintings of the English countryside and various other
paintings of the masters of English literature. A large bust
of William Shakespeare flanked by two large lamps sat on
a long wooden table against the wall, and the reception

desk, which was small in size, was made of dark cherry wood. At the end of the lobby opposite the desk was a small restaurant called, 'The Bard's Place,' in honor of Shakespeare, the bard of Avon.

"Robin, why don't you check in while I park the car."

"Don't you think we should park the car together?" she asked.

"It's only 40 feet away and all lit up. I think I will be safe, but if it makes you feel better, I'll have Tudor boy watch me." After parking the car in the adjacent lot, Lauren walked the short distance to the front door, glancing behind herself from time to time, still in full view of the bellboy. As she neared the front door, the bellboy opened it and then looked at her with an odd expression on his face.

She returned his gaze with a similar look.

"Something the matter?" she asked.

"No, not really, but I think you might have left something on your car."

She swung around quickly and looked in the direction of the car noticing what he had pointed to but couldn't make out what it was.

"Would you mind getting it for me?" she asked.

"Not at all, ma'am. Be right back."

He went to the car and picked up what appeared to be a newspaper or magazine and returned to where Lauren was standing. "Oh it's just a magazine; guess you just forgot you put it on the roof of your car."

Lauren was almost positive that she hadn't brought any magazines with her, but when she took it from the bellboy; she realized that it was an in-flight magazine. She immediately flipped to the page that contained the crossword puzzle and saw the completed crossword; she gasped. "My god, it's the one I did on the plane." She thanked him and handed him a dollar then quickly walked to Robin's side. Robin had just finished checking in.

"Robin, look at this." She held up the magazine. "It's the one I read on the plane. Look, the crossword is finished, and it's my printing and even the little stars I draw on things."

Robin took it from her and looked at it. "So, you must have brought it with you."

"I swear I left it in the storage compartment in the seat in front of me," she replied, "but that's not all. It was sitting on the hood of the car when I got to the front door after parking the car. I didn't put it there. He's here. He followed us. Think about it, Robin, first there was the man I thought I saw in Boston, then the baggage incident at the airport here, then this. The mood of the two women had made a total about face as they now suspected that, Cameo knew where they were.

Lauren turned to the desk clerk. "Does the Inn have a security guard on duty?"

'Why, no, ma'am," he responded, "but this is a very low crime area. We never have any problems here."

"By the way, what time does Federal Express normally get here in the morning?" Lauren asked.

"About ten or so," the clerk responded. "Would you like a wake up call, ma'am?"

Lauren sighed. "Something tells me that we won't need one."

After checking to ensure that the windows in the room and sliding glass door that led to the pool area were locked Robin, propped a chair up against the door.

Lauren checked the view from the windows then stopped and looked at Robin.

"Robin, let's think about the people on the flight up

here.   There were only about a dozen other people on board. I know we didn't see anyone suspicious, but then I don't suppose he would try to look suspicious would he?"

"I don't suppose so, but let's take them one at a time." Robin said.   "First, there was the pair of robust ladies that wouldn't stop laughing. I think we can rule them out, agreed?"

Lauren nodded. "Agreed," and added, "then there was the older man with the cane. He looked sort of feeble so I guess we can rule him out also."

Robin nodded her approval. Lauren continued.

"I also can't begin to suspect the lady with the two children, or the two ladies from the Middle East. Remember the ones with their faces covered. Agreed?"

"Yes, and I think we can rule out the lady on crutches, right?" Robin said.

"Agreed, Robin, who does that leave? Oh, yes, the father. Rule him out."

Robin nodded then said, "What about the guy that was sleeping in the back? He had his hat over his face so I couldn't see what he looked like."

Lauren's face appeared puzzled, "I don't remember a man in the back. I wonder why I wouldn't have noticed him?"

Robin put her hand to her mouth and gasped, "Lauren, I noticed him and you didn't. We both noticed everyone else, think about it."

"Yeah, but what are you saying?"

"Maybe there's a reason that you didn't notice him." Robin said.

"Like?" Lauren asked.

"Like he didn't want you to notice him," Robin responded.

"What on earth?" she paused. "Oh my God Robin, you mean he was controlling my mind again?"

"You were the one that gave birth to that theory," Robin said, "but if we follow that logic, why not?"

The rest of the night was a series of interrupted naps as each of them woke numerous times. Any sound that seemed unusual roused them out of bed to look out the window.

The morning sun beaming through a slightly open curtain told them it was time to get up. Neither of them had gotten much sleep, but they were both nevertheless keyed up. After showering, each of them put on a skirt, silk blouse and low heels. They ate a light breakfast in The Bard and got a map from the front desk.

"Have the Federal Express packages arrived yet?" Lauren waited as the clerk went through five or six envelopes.

"Yes, ma'am, this is yours."

Once in the car, Lauren opened the package and took out the pistol and ammunition and gave it to Robin and said, "Here, you load it while I drive."

To Lauren's amazement, Robin held the pistol grip with one hand, pressed her thumb on the button that released the spindle that held the bullets and snapped it open with a flick of her wrist.

"Damn, Annie Oakley, where did you learn to do that?"

"Hell, that's the easy part. Pulling the trigger is the hard part. Let's go to the hospital."

After driving west on Interstate 395 then back past the airport, they ended up on State Road 222 which headed toward the western part of Maine. The hospital where Arthur had been taken was located there. By the time they got to the exit of the hospital, Lauren's face had become flush and tears were trickling down her face.

"I know what you're going through, Lauren, and you must understand that anything that has happened is not your fault. Arthur is a friend and was on a mission for you. He wouldn't want you to take this on your shoulders. And I know he's going to be all right."

After parking the car, they went in the main entrance and stopped at the information desk.

"We're looking for the room for Arthur Holmes. He was admitted the day before yesterday," Lauren said.

The lady at the desk directed them to the second floor room 222 and asked that they check in with the nurse on duty before going to his room. Exiting the elevator, Lauren approached the desk and as she began to ask the way to his room, her voice cracked and she bowed her head trying to hold back a new rush of tears. Robin stepped in front of her.

"We're looking for the room for Arthur Holmes, and would like to talk to the doctor or nurse on duty as to his condition.

The desk nurse looked at them and shook her head.

"I agree. You should talk with the doctor. That's him standing in front of Mr. Holmes room." She pointed to a distinguished man in his 50s who was talking to a nurse.

Lauren frowned and asked, "What's the matter?"

"Nothing," the nurse replied, "just talk to the doctor."

Lauren spun around and walked quickly toward the doctor with Robin right behind her. She didn't wait to be recognized, interrupting his conversation with the nurse.

"Excuse me, doctor. My name is Lauren St. John and this is Robin Bennett. I am a close friend of Arthur Holmes and the nurse at the desk said I should talk to you about him. Is he okay?"

"I'm Dr. Frankenberry, and no, I can't tell you if he's okay."

The two women looked at each other, perplexed..

"What ever do you mean, doctor?" Lauren asked.

He started walking toward a nearby waiting area when Lauren said again. "Doctor, is he okay?"

The doctor sat and motioned them to sit.

"Let me put it this way. I've never encountered anything like this in my entire career in medicine. Yesterday, I had a patient in a coma, with a concussion, scrapes and bruises. We had yet to determine just how bad he really was."

Lauren interrupted. "Well is he okay?"

"I was coming to that," the doctor said, "this morning the night nurse reported that he all of a sudden jumped out of the bed, removed the I.V. and said something like, 'My God, I've got to talk to Lauren.' I presume that is you?"

"Yes, that's me. Where is he?"

"He left."

Lauren again looked at Robin and then the doctor.

"What do you mean he left? Wasn't he injured or couldn't be moved or whatever?"

"Seemed like all of those things," the doctor replied, "but I guess I was wrong. You know we can't accept responsibility for anything that happens to him."

By this time the nurse that had been talking to the doctor came over and looked at Lauren.

"I don't know if it means anything to you, but the night nurse said that as he was leaving he said something like, 'I have to go back to the car.' I don't know, maybe he meant the car he was in when he had the accident."

Lauren became impatient, taking hold of the nurse's arm. "Do you know where the rental car agency is located?"

The nurse stared at her hand with a frown on her face and Lauren removed her hand.

"No, but the police would probably have the car anyway. I think the state police brought it in. That would mean that it's probably just up the road about 10 or 12 miles. Going west that is."

Robin interrupted, "Thank you, but have you any idea how he would get to the station from here?"

"Don't know, maybe a taxi." The nurse answered.

As they exited the front door of the hospital and started toward the car both Lauren and Robin stopped in their tracks, staring across the street.

"Robin, do you see what I see?"

"You mean the Handy Dandy Car Rental?"

"Right, let's check it out. Might as well drive so we don't have to walk back here."

The rental office was about 10 foot square with a small counter and two chrome- handled chairs for customers. A cheap looking silk tree stood in the corner, and there was a rack with tourist information on it in the other corner. The clerk appeared to be in his early 20s, was on the plump side, wore horn-rimmed glasses and had a crew cut. When Lauren and Robin walked in the door he gasped and dropped the paper work he was holding.

To Lauren he appeared extremely nervous, perhaps at the sight of the two of them.

He stuttered, "Ca-ca-ca-can I hel-help you?"

"Yes, you can." Robin said and stepped forward, resting her elbows on the counter and leaning forward so she was within a foot or so of the clerk's face, "what is your name?"

The clerk blushed. Then said, "m-m-my name i-i-is Elroy."

Robin looked at Lauren with a smile on her face.

"We think perhaps a man named Arthur Holmes recently rented a car here and we were wondering if you could tell us if that's true and if so, where he was going? He is a very good friend of my friend here. Oh, this is Lauren and I am Robin."

He again stuttered, nervously moving his weight first from one side then the other before answering.

"Oh, I-I-I'm sorry. We can-can't give out confi-fi-dential information like that."

Several beads of sweat slid down his face and his complexion turned several shades of red as he continued swaying from side to side.

Lauren looked at Robin out of the corner of her eye before raising her leg and putting her foot on one of the chairs. She slid her skirt up about six inches.

"Robin, look here, I went and got a run in my panty hose."

Robin turned toward her trying to hide the grin on her face as the clerk quickly leaned over the counter almost hitting Robin's head as he did. Robin leaned over even further and almost as if by design, one of the buttons on her blouse popped open, revealing much more cleavage than she usually showed.

"Couldn't you make just one little exception for us?" Robin asked. "You can't imagine how much we would appreciate it."

She knew he was hopelessly hooked as he picked up a clip board then looked at her.

"He r-r-r-rented a 2006 Frid."

"A Frid?" Robin asked with a questioning look on

her face.

"Oh ex-ex-excuse me, ma'am, I mean it was a F-F-Ford that he rented from us. And he headed for P-P-Portersville."

"Thank you so much, Elroy." As she thanked him she leaned over the counter and kissed him on the forehead.

"Oh, ma'am, it, it, it was nothing. And don't worry, I didn't tell the other g-g-guy nothin'.""

Robin spun around looking at Lauren as they simultaneously asked, "What guy?

"A g-g-guy came in and he, he, he was asking about your fr-fr-friend."

"What did he look like?" Lauren asked after taking her foot off the chair and straightening her skirt.

"Well, he w-w-was maybe forty ye-years old. L-l-light brown hair and kinda on the thin s-s-side. He, he already ha-had a car. I th-think it was a blue Chevy."

"Thanks again, Elroy. We owe you one," Lauren said as she turned to leave.

"Yeah, Elroy." Robin added, "if we need anything else, she'll show you the other leg."

"You're impossible, Robin. Get in the car," Lauren quipped as they got back in their rental.

As Robin slid in the passenger side of the car, she began giggling and looked at Lauren, "A bit out of character for you, English Teacher. Do you suppose that Cameo made you pull your dress half way up your thigh?"

"Not more than six inches, smart ass, and no, I did it on my own because it was taking you forever to let your tits hang out. One of us had to take the initiative."

After traveling west on the highway for about 15 minutes, they spotted the state police station, exiting the highway and pulling in to the parking lot. There were half a dozen squad cars in front of a brown brick building and a few people standing in front talking.

"What's the plan, Lauren?"

"I don't know. Let's just hope they'll tell us if Arthur was here."

Once inside the station, Lauren approached the desk. She looked at a piece of paper she had taken out of her purse. It had the name of the officer Brian had spoken to on it.

"My name is Lauren St. John. Is there an officer named Martin Crenshaw here? I would like to speak with him."

Without looking up, the officer at the desk pointed down the hall to the left and indicated that his office was the second door. Lauren could see him sitting at his desk and opened the door after knocking once.

"Hi, I'm Lauren St John and this is my friend, Robin Bennett. May we come in?"

He stood and motioned them to have a seat. "How can I help?"

Lauren took out a picture of Arthur that the college had given her and handed it to him.

"This is Arthur Holmes. I think my husband called you about him and the crash he was in. I came up here to see him in the hospital and find that he left this morning and without a release from the doctor. I'm concerned that he may not be all right. We know he rented a car across from the hospital, and I think he was headed up to Portersville. I was wondering if you have seen him?"

"Why yes, he was in here this morning," the officer offered. "He came for his belongings. He explained that the crash was an accident, and we had no reason to hold them, so I gave them to him. Is there a problem?"

"No," Lauren responded, "only I don't know if he was ready to leave the hospital yet. Do you know where he went?"

"He indicated that he was in fact going to Portersville," the officer said. "One thing however, that seemed a bit strange however.

"What's that?" Lauren asked.

"Well," the officer responded, "when I gave him the envelope with his belongings in it, he immediately took out some sort of paper work and examined it. Then, without even looking at the rest, he simply put the papers back in the envelope, said something like 'I have to go back', then thanked me and left."

After they left the station, the women sat in their rental looking at each other until Robin finally spoke.

"This is it, kiddo. On to Portersville and let's pray he's okay."

JOHN S. RICHARDSON

CHAPTER TWENTY ONE

"This is quite a surprise. You're the last person I would expect to see here. How can I help you?" Brian extended his hand to Greg Allsop and motioned him to take a seat. After sitting back behind his desk he leaned back and stared at Greg, waiting for his answer.

"Brian, this may come as a big shock to you, but I am a Federal agent and Lisa Cantrell is my partner."

Brian sat up in his chair with a look of disbelief on his face. "You mean my partner is your partner? Lisa is a Federal agent?" Brian asked.

"That's right, Brian, and we are investigating a case that may involve Lauren and yourself. Yourself, perhaps indirectly, but not so in the case of Lauren. That's why I took the job at the college."

"I'm listening," Brian said..

"You seem surprised, Brian."

"Frankly, Greg, I am quite surprised about you and especially about Lisa, although I never took her at face value. But as for the investigation, let me guess, you suspect that there is a serial killer on the loose."

"I'm impressed." Greg said. "Have you been investigating some of the related cases?"

Brian stood up and walked around his desk never taking his eyes off Greg.

"You know, Greg; this may sound a bit paranoid, but just for the record, why don't you show me some I.D?"

Greg took out his Federal ID and handed it to Brian.

"I would expect no less, my friend," Greg said. "You can also call the regional office in Atlanta if you need to. Maybe this was long overdue, but I had to be sure I knew who all the players were and who I could trust."

"And you trust me now?" Brian asked, "what changed from a few days ago?"

"I just got a report back from headquarters. You're as straight as an arrow and above reproach."

Brian had returned to the seat behind his desk.

"Nice to know, Greg, but since Lisa is my partner as well as yours, did she pass the same background check?"

Greg's mouth twisted as though in deep thought.

"Funny you should mention it," he said, "but since she is an agent, I should be able to assume that she is clean, too. This is something that I shouldn't be talking to you about but since you asked, do you know something I don't?"

"Not specifically, Greg, but I have this gnawing feeling in my gut. Something in me says that there is more to her than meets the eye. It seems like she came out of no where and all of a sudden, I am sitting here with a partner who was brought in from out of state to work with me. All this mind you, when I wasn't actually working on any blockbuster cases. Further, I could never get any satisfactory answers when I asked about her background. What do you know about her?"

"Frankly, Brian, I had a similar feeling, so I called in some favors and did some checking. As I said, I'm not really supposed to talk about it with anyone outside the department."

"So what'll it be?" Brian asked, "do we try to help each other get to the bottom of this, or do we stand on protocol?"

Greg got up and closed the door to Brian's office then sat back down before speaking.

"Everything from here on is off the record. Agreed?"

"Agreed," Brian said and leaned forward to extend his hand. Greg reached out and shook it. Brian continued.

"You came here to talk with me, so why don't you go first."

Greg leaned back in the chair and propped his hands behind his head.

"I've been investigating what we are positive is a serial killer. The murders date back about 20 years although I've only been on the case about a year. The murders have taken place all over the country, and we have matched the DNA in over 28 cases, including three here in Florida. You were involved in the initial investigation in one of them."

"Yes, I remember it," Brian said. "Go on."

"Well, it seems that all of the victims have been about Lauren's age. I don't mean her age right now, but whatever age Lauren was at the time of the respective murders. When Lauren was 30, a girl 30 was murdered in California and so on. The first one that we can connect to this killer happened when Lauren was 24 and had just finished her Masters Degree. A young teacher was murdered near the university."

Brian interrupted him.

"I remember that one. I was also just finishing my degree and there was a lot of conversation about it in class. You know that Lauren and I went to college together?"

"Believe me, Brian; I know almost everything there is to know about you. Anyway, the coincidence as to the ages would never have connected Lauren to anything until her father was murdered."

Brian quickly rose out of his seat with a shocked look on his face.

"Murdered? I thought he hung himself."

"That's what the local police thought, but some unidentified person sent the agency a key bit of information."

"What was it?" Brian asked.

"A receipt," Greg answered, "for the purchase of several feet of nylon rope with Lauren's father's name and address on it. The sender included a small piece of the rope. After checking with the local police we obtained the piece of the rope that was found at the death scene and it was an identical match."

"How do you know the father didn't send it before he died?" Brian asked.

"The envelope was post marked 10 days after the date on the death certificate. We checked his next of kin and of course, found only Lauren. However, at that point it wasn't a federal case, so we gave the information to the local police and didn't think anything of it until we got the second envelope, a while later. We traced her here after the second envelope was received and a connection was made with the murdered girl at the university and then the ones murdered here in Florida. You know, age physical characteristics and so on. The computer even picked up several women that lived in the state of Maine. The ages and other factors were compared with Lauren and they matched. So while the investigation was an ongoing one for years, we only just connected it here with the death of her father."

"What was in the second envelope?" Brian asked.

"Two pictures," Greg responded. "One of Lauren taken while in college and the other was a clipping of the dead girl from the newspaper. We matched Lauren's picture through a yearbook. And, we were able to match the DNA from the flap on the second envelope with the DNA from all of the other murders we were investigating."

"Were you able to trace the receipt from the first envelope to a particular store?" Brian asked.

"No, the receipt was rather generic with no store name on it and the rope is sold in five or six hundred different locations."

"How about finger prints or DNA from the crime scene?" Brian asked.

"The locals didn't take anything from the crime scene other than the rope that he was hung by because they ruled it a suicide. Get this, they then had a woman come in and clean things up. Smart huh? Brian, I've been doing all the talking. What can you add to the mix?" Greg had taken out a small notebook to write in.

"You're going to find this a bit bizarre," Brian said, "but here goes."

He went on to relate the story about his trip to California and the pictures in Robin's home. Then, the call to Manny about the murder in Chicago and the incident at the condo when Lauren thought it was him outside. Finally, he told him about the alleged accident that Arthur Holmes was involved in after snooping around in Lauren's home town. He paused for a moment then added, "Greg, you mentioned that the computer showed that several of the murder victims lived in Maine. If you take it one step further, you might find that all the victims were either from Maine or had some connection to the state of Maine. At least the ones that I looked at did."

Greg looked at him with a perplexed look.

"Brian, while that does come as a bit of a surprise it fit's the pattern. The thing however that miffs me now is why someone would go to all the trouble of staging the death of Robin Bennett when he could have easily killed her? Makes no sense. And how do you think the killer made the connection between Lauren and Robin?"

"Can only guess why someone would do that Greg. First, I figure that he thought that I would find out about it before Lauren would. He would have had to know when I was going to California, but I guess that's not out of the realm of possibility. I suspect that's when he planted the pictures, and as I said, Robin was off shooting in the mountains somewhere so she wouldn't have known he put them there. They were there for me to find. And if that's the case, then he's playing a game of cat and mouse. As I'm sure you're aware, these types often like to play games.

"As for knowing about Robin, the killer could have found out about her in a number of ways. What about the picture of Lauren you received? You said it was taken when she was in college. Lauren and Robin were inseparable back then. There was even a picture of the two of them in the year book together, some club they were in."

"I guess you're right, but back to the pictures. I don't suppose you have a copy of them do you?" Greg asked.

Yes, I have a copy, but they're not here. I'll show them to you the next time we meet, that is if you can wait that long."

"I would be looking only from the angle as it pertains to a crime." Greg said as he chuckled, "but don't wait to long Brian; I'm dying to see them. Anything else?"

"Matter of fact there is," Brian said. "It's the clues that the killer is leaving. The one in Robin's place, as I said was Electra."

"Was he referring to Robin?" Greg asked.

"I don't think so. I think it was meant for Lauren," Brian responded.

"As I recall, Electra was the female counterpart of Oedipus who unwittingly married his mother and killed his father," Greg said. "If I remember my Greek mythology, Electra had strong feelings for her father, and she and her brother plotted to kill her mother's lover and her mother to avenge the infidelity she committed when her father was off to war. But that wouldn't make much sense, would it? I mean Lauren had nothing to do with her mother's death, did she?"

"No, of course not, and you're right, it doesn't make any sense. The other clues are as vague as that one if you take them individually. In the Chicago case, the word 'Vodu' was written on the car window of the victim."

Greg's face took on a questioning look.

"That's one I'm not familiar with."

"I wasn't either, Greg, but turns out that it is another form for the word Voodoo. Don't ask, I can't answer that one. A clue in one of the other cases was a short strand of nylon cord. I now assume it's the one that you received from the local police in her father's case. I, of course, made no connection to the death of Lauren's father and that clue, but now with what you told me, maybe there is a connection. But in retrospect, I think it may mean something else. For some reason it was laid on the stomach right next to the victim's naval, which was cut out with the precision of a surgeon."

"You think it's a doctor or medical type we're looking for?" Greg asked.

"Not necessarily," Brian answered, "but someone who may have had some training in that area. Then yet another clue was an alphabet printed on a piece of paper like we used in first grade. The odd thing about this was that it had the letter Y repeated. It was like XYY at the end of the alphabet."

"That one I can answer, Brian. I would assume that it means the XYY chromosome makeup."

"I think I know where you're going, but continue," Brian said.

"Everyone has 23 pairs of chromosomes in their body," Greg said. "They determine things like the color of the eyes, the hair and so on. One pair determines the sex of the person. A female has an XX chromosome makeup and a male an XY. Occasionally a male will have an XYY makeup. In some circles it has been theorized that a man with an XYY makeup is some sort of super male that is innately predisposed to violence. Some studies indicate that in the general prison population there is a significantly higher percent of males with XYY than there is in the general public. They were not able, however, to make the same correlation with regard to hard core criminals like killers or rapists."

"So, what do you think, Greg? Do we have a serial killer that thinks he's some sort of superman?"

"Could be Brian, could be. Why don't you refresh my memory. What were the other clues?"

Brian leaned forward, put his elbow on the desk, then rested his chin in his hand and said.

"Well, one of the files contained the word Pollux which was written conspicuously on the victim's forehead."

"You mean Pollux, like in Castor and Pollux? Don't tell me, Brian, Lauren is a Gemini?"

"No, she's a Cancer, Greg, but only by two minutes. She was born two minutes past midnight into the sign of Cancer. Tell me Greg, how'd you make a connection there?"

"Well, Castor and Pollux are the two bright stars located in a constellation that are associated with the Gemini astrological sign. But tell me something, a bit ago you said that all the cases you looked at had a connection to the state of Maine. How did you determine that?"

"Old-fashioned police work, Greg. You know, even

the ones who lived in Florida had connections to Maine. One was remote, in that she went to school in a town just inside the Maine state line. I mean literally a stone's throw from the New Hampshire state line, where she lived. One victim was born here in Florida, but I determined that the mother, who was from Maine, was pregnant when she moved here with her husband meaning that she was conceived in Maine. It was at that point that I was sure that who ever killed these women was connected in some way to Lauren. Guess what else, my friend?"

"What's that, Brian?"

"In all of the cases I looked at, the bodies were dumped in one of three places: In or around a log cabin, in or around a church or in or around a nursing home. The only exception to that is the last murder in Chicago and that victim was discovered in her own car near the lakefront. I am thinking that the killer simply didn't have time to move the body on that one. Tell you what, let's put some of the details on paper."

Brian picked up a black marker and went to the far side of his office to an easel with large sheets of paper on it. Greg stood and spoke as he walked toward Brian.

"Right, how about clues he left, where the bodies were disposed of and so on."

They both began to feel a tinge of excitement at their discovery of what they felt was some sort of pattern developing. They wrote out the clues:

#1- Electra

-*Robin Bennett = Lauren's age but different profession / not from Maine.*

-*Life spared, appears to be cat and mouse ploy*

-*Word Electra written on mirror in lipstick*

#2 – Vodu

-Victim = Lauren's age & similar appearance

-Murdered in Chicago **(Check profession & birthplace)**

-Body left in car with word Vodu written in blood on window; perhaps the victim's

-Killer didn't have time to move the body???

-Need further info to check pattern

#3 - XYY Alphabet Written on paper

-Victim = Lauren's age & similar in appearance – ELEMENTARY TEACHER

-Connection to school in Maine

-Maybe chromosome makeup / super male prone to violence

-Body dumped near abandon log cabin

#4 - Nautical cord found near naval / Naval surgically cut out

-Victim = 40 year old (3 years older than Lauren)

-Teacher from Coastal Maine

-Body dumped in bushes near nursing home

#5 - Pollux written on forehead
-Victim=Lauren's age & same profession

-Lived in New Hampshire / Schooled in Maine

-Body dumped near church

-Pollux and Castor = Gemini / written on victims head in blood

They both sat staring at the written comments in front of them for a moment, when Greg finally spoke.

"So when can you come to work for the agency? I guess we just didn't take it far enough yet, but then I picked it up when it was basically a cold case. Tell you what, I think I need to go back to my apartment and re-look at the files. With the information you have just given me, maybe between the two of us we can get closer to solving this thing. Thanks, Brian; I'll be in touch."

Before rising, he looked at Brian with a strange look on his face.

"By the way, have you seen Lisa Cantrell lately?"

"Strange that you mention it, Greg," he replied, "I haven't, and she didn't show up for the last roll call day before yesterday."

"Well, Brian," he responded, "it's not likely you'll see her again."

"What is that suppose to mean, Greg?"

"You're going to love this, Brian. She was sent to Montana on a new assignment. Seems as though she had an affair with a married judge in L.A. and that's why they shipped her out here. She was attached to your office to do some undercover work. However," he paused, "she was still harassing the judge, and the agency had to get her out of the mainstream."

Greg rose and opened the door. Brian cleared his throat and looked at him.

"That's a very nice apartment complex you live in."

Greg stopped and turned looking questioningly at Brian.

"How is it that you know where I live?" He asked.

"Old-fashioned police work, my friend, old-fashioned police work."

"Have you been following me, Brian?"

A half smile spread across Brian's face.

"Isn't it ironic that we know so much about each other? No, Greg, I've not been following you, didn't need to follow you to find out where you live. Lauren sufficed."

After Greg left, Brian decided that he would Google the word Vodu again to see what he could come up with. After getting on-line and again inputting the word Vodu, he started reading. As he did, his face changed from no expression at all, to curiosity, then to intensity. He looked at the notes on the easel, looked back at his computer screen then back at the notes. He put his hand on his forehead.

"My God, that's it," he said aloud, "I have to get to Lauren, she is in grave danger."

ﭏ ﭏ ﭏ ﭏ ﭏ ﭏ ﭏ ﭏ ﭏ ﭏ ﭏ ﭏ ﭏ

Arthur pulled his rental off to the side of the road and removed the last bandages from his head and neck. He had arrived at the outskirts of Portersville still feeling a bit dizzy, but he knew that he had to keep going. In his heart he felt that the answer was either here in Portersville or up at the log cabin where the reverend had died. He decided to start at the local newspaper.

Once inside, he introduced himself to a thin, aging man sitting behind the only desk in the room.

"Hello, my name is Arthur Holmes. I am a professor at a college in Florida. I'm here doing some research on the death of a reverend who lived here locally, at least for awhile before he died. I think he hung himself."

The man peered over a pair of old-fashioned spectacles, looked at Arthur, then spoke with an accent unique to this part of the country.

"How'd ya do, Arthah?, Name's George Raft. Yaah, I remember the man. Never met him, mind ya. Yer right tho, did hang himself. Story goes that he had somethin' to do with the death of one of his parishioners. I heard the church sent him off by himself to spend his last days in a log cabin."

"Is there anything else you can tell me about him?" Arthur asked.

"Well, anythin' I could tell ya would be pure guessin', but as I understand it there was somethin' to do with a curse. Seems that he convinced a lady parishioner that if she had a son, he'd end up murderin' his fathah. Don't that get all? He talked 'bout a guy called Orepus and a lady named Electric."

Arthur interjected. "You mean Oedipus and Electra."

"Ya, that's right, Oediprus an Lectra."

"But as I understand it, only a girl was born"," Arthur said. Is that what you understand?".

"Well, that was, my understandings too Arthah, but there was all kinda rumors flyin' round at the time. First, there was something 'bout a boyfriend and such. Some say that the father wasn't really the father, if ya know what I mean. Don't rightly know the truth, but there sure enough was some kinda scandal going on."

Arthur was caught by surprise as a voice behind him spoke and when he turned he saw a large woman that appeared to be in her 60s wearing a smock type dress and her hair up in a bun.

"He don't know nothin'. Pay no 'tention to anything he says."

Arthur turned and looked back at the man behind the desk.

"Your wife, I assume?" The man nodded and bowed his head. "Well then, perhaps you can enlighten me as to what really happened?" He asked the woman.

"Twins," She replied.

"You mean Lauren had a twin sister?" Arthur wrinkled his brow.

The woman rolled her eyes and folded her arms in front of her.

"No, a brothah. The boy died at birth and the girl lived. The baby's grandma took on the blame so's the mothah wouldn't have to and that's why she hung herself. Then the reverend took the blame for her death and he ended up hanging himself, too. It was a real mess mind ya, but the girl seemed to end up okay. Young Lauren, that is. Don't think their life was ever normal after that. I mean with Lauren's fathah and mothah. Heard they eventually got divorced. Then the fathah hung himself two or three years ago. Hell, everybody was hangin' themselves." She turned and left.

That's right." The man said adding to Arthur's confusion. "There was that ruma too. Think there's more rumahs than hangin's."

"My God," Arthur responded, "I don't know what to believe. But if there had been a boy, who do you think would know for sure?"

312

"Ya might try the folks that live up off Dundee Road. That is if they're still alive," the old man said.

"You're not referring to the little store a few miles west on Dundee?" Arthur remembered the old lady in the small grocery store near the cabin.

"Yup, that's the one," the old man replied. "Another rumor was that they knew the whole truth, but never would talk bout it. I tried to get the story out of 'em for the paypaah, but they was close mouthed."

The drive back to the little store took considerably less time than the first trip and as he pulled up in front he had to slam on his brakes to avoid hitting the old gas pump in front of the store. When he entered the store he saw that the same old lady still behind the counter reading her bible.

"Hello, again."

Arthur put on his charming face in hopes of winning her confidence. "I was wondering if you could help me. I neglected to introduce myself the first time we chatted, my name is Arthur Holmes and I am a college professor from Florida. I am in Maine for a convention and a friend of mine asked me to look the Reverend up, you know the one I came to see earlier. Well anyway, I talked to the man that runs the newspaper in Portersville and his wife and they told me the strangest story."

The woman remained silent, just staring at Arthur.

"Well, it seems that my friend who was born in Maine thought for all of her life that she was an only child. She's also a professor at the college where I teach by the way. Anyway, the wife of the man at the newspaper said that the rumor was that there was a twin; a boy born that died at birth when the girl was born. I was hoping that you could shed some light on the situation."

The old lady put her hand under her chin, resting her elbow in the other hand, then spoke.

"Don't reckon it's any of yer business, but hell it's been in the closet too long. Part of the rumor is true, the part bout there bein' a boy born. Didn't die though. Me and my late husband agreed to raise the boy as our own for a monthly allowance from the church. They took him at birth so's no one would know. Only the Reverend, the mother and the midwife knew until they came to us with their plan. Don't quite agree with their reason - the curse and all -but we was in hard times and the money came in handy. That's how we could open the store. Been quite a chore since my husband passed. You know the store an' all."

Arthur watched as a tear trickled down her face.

"Ma'am, I surely do sympathize with your past, and wish you well, but I was hoping that perhaps you could tell me where the boy that you raised, that is the man, might be now."

"Well, don't quite know that, but one thing ya should know is that when he became of age, well, we told him."

"So he knows that he was a twin and that he was taken from his mother because of the curse and all?"

The old lady paused to wipe a tear from her cheek.

"Yup, he knows all of that. Once we told him, his whole personality changed. He became nasty and said he'd get revenge. Then, he packed up his belongin's and took off. Think he blamed his sister and the reverend more than his mom. After the reverend moved up to the cabin, ya know when he quit the church, him and Damien, that's the boy, became the best of friends. That was before we told the boy the truth, then after we told Damien the truth, he tried to kill the reverend. The reverend didn't press no charges mind ya, but I could tell that Satan himself was in the boy; no doubt he would end up hurtin' someone. That's when he left."

Arthur thought for a second then asked, "How old was he when he left?"

"He was 22. Heard he headed west, maybe California, though he'd talked bout goin' to college in New York."

At this point, Arthur's worst suspicions appeared to becoming true thinking that perhaps Damien had finally located Lauren and that, in fact, he could be Cameo. He looked at the old woman and asked, "Is there anything else that you can tell me that might be of help in finding him?"

"Can't see how's it would help ya find the boy, but one thing ya should know is that he's special."

Arthur leaned forward, putting his hands on the counter and with a strange look on his face he asked, "What do you mean by special?"

"Well," the old lady leaned forward to within a foot of Arthur's face and continued, "means that he had some kinda special powah. You know the kind that let him get in yer mind. From the day he was old enough to walk he'd just sit there starin' at ya. As though he was lookin' in yer mind. Many a times when he wanted something an I didn't wanna give it to him, he'd stare at me until I would give in an get it for him. Like he had some sorta control over me. My husband hated it. He fought him tooth and nail, but most the time he'd lose."

"Let me ask you something that is very important." He paused. "Did you ever see him move something, say an object, without touching it?"

The old lady thought for a moment. Then she looked at Arthur.

"Ya know, wasn't till he was almost 22, I think. One

day he was in a particeler bad mood and I guess there was somethin' he didn't wanna do. Well, seems like he was buildin' up steam inside him, holdin' his breath and all, 'til he nearly exploded. Cans went flyin' off the shelf and a couple of bottles broke in that cooler back there." She pointed to the back of the store. "It seemed to fit," she added, "was just before he left for whereever he went. He had sent in for a pamphlet on somthin' to do with controlin' yer mind."

"Can you remember anything about it?" Arthur asked.

"Yup, it was some place in California. A college or somethin' that did studies in that sorta thing."

"And where? Do you remember where it was?" Arthur asked.

"Just gimme a minute an I'll think of it. It was called San something." She put her hand to her mouth and closed her eyes.

Arthur impatiently asked, "San Diego, San Francisco, Santa Barbara?"

She stopped him. "I got it, San Josy."

"San Jose?"

"Right, San Jose."

"Thanks a million," Arthur said, "you've been a great deal of help." He took a wad of rolled up bills out of his pocket and put fifty dollars in her hand. "Please accept this as a token of my thanks. You earned it. Here's my card, if you can think of anything else, please call me. Call collect."

Arthur sat in his rental car in the front of the store for several minutes, shaking his head at the bizarre sequence of events before it started to dawn on him just how much danger Lauren was in. After dialing her cell number, he realized that he wasn't going to get any good reception up here, so he wrote a note in his journal.

Lauren, it appears that you may have had a twin brother that was removed from your mother at birth because of a fear of some sort of a curse. Further, it also appears that he was raised by another couple. I met with the old lady that claims to have raised him. Evidently the pastor who was part of the conspiracy hung himself because of an overwhelming feeling of guilt and shame, just as your grandmother had apparently done. Your brother was evidently told of the dastardly deed when he was about 22 and became violent according to the old woman. He tried to kill the reverend, but didn't succeed then left for either California or New York. No one has heard from him since and no one knows what happened to him. I will give you your mother's diary when I get back, it's very revealing. In summary Lauren, I feel certain that you have a twin brother and that your twin has located you and is stalking you perhaps under the name Cameo. You are in a great deal of danger. Oh, and one other thing. The old lady that raised him feels like he had some sort of psychic abilities and further, he may have gone to California to a college that offered a curriculum in that area. It's located in San Jose. Isn't that near where you told me that your friend Robin lives?

When he finished writing, Arthur put the journal in the inside pocket of his overcoat where he had put the diaries then got ready to leave. Pausing momentarily, his curiosity got the best of him and he decided he would go back up to the log cabin on the hill. It had started to rain again and the dirt road that led up to the cabin was awash with mud. He became concerned that he might not be able to drive the car up safely, so he set out on foot grabbing his umbrella, but leaving his overcoat in the car.

The footing on the road was very slippery and he fell to his knees several times before finally arriving at the top, a few hundred feet from the cabin. The rain had intensified, turning the skies to a mass of gray and visibility was at best difficult. As he glanced at the cabin, he noticed that the door was wide open. He doubted that anyone else would have been up here. He searched his mind, but couldn't remember if he had left the door open when he was last here.

Brushing the mud off his knees, he moved slowly toward the open door. Given his condition, the walk up the hill had been very difficult for him and despite the cool air, perspiration was now dripping from his face and into his eyes causing him to squint. He suddenly felt dizzy so he bent down, putting his hand on the ground to prop himself up. He thought he heard a noise coming from inside the cabin. His head began to swirl and a weakness overtook him so he knelt on the ground. As he refocused on the door through blurry, rain-soaked eyes, he felt as though a bolt of electricity had run through his body and the hair on his arms stood up straight. In the distance he could see the silhouetted figure of a person standing in the doorway.

מ מ מ מ מ מ מ מ מ מ מ מ מ

"Is this where you were raised?" Robin asked, shaking her head. "You poor thing, I wouldn't wish this on...."

Lauren stopped her short. "Just because I wasn't raised in a California hot tub, doesn't mean it wasn't a nice place to grow up." Lauren pulled the rental car off to the side of the road near the center of town.

"Hey, look over there," she said, "that's the little park I use to play in, and there's the drugstore where I had my first date." A wide grin spread across her face.

"Your first date was in a drugstore?" Robin asked.

"Yes, Miss bikini-clad, Beach Boy-loving surfer or

whatever you were. My sixth grade crush bought me a chocolate soda in that drugstore. It was my first official date."

Robin shook her head. "Well in any event, we made it to Portersville, now what?"

"I have the location of the bungalow where my father died," Lauren said. "We go to the edge of town and turn onto a road called Mystic Drive."

"Wow," Robin said, "how fitting is that?"

After turning on Mystic Drive, Lauren counted until reaching the seventh house on the right. "This is it, Robin, turn in."

From the outward condition of the bungalow it appeared that no one had lived in it since the death of Lauren's father. The trees that dotted the area around the bungalow were leafless and completely still and there was a quieting calm about. From the outside, it appeared to be no bigger than one room with an outhouse that leaned noticeably to one side sitting in the back. A trellis that went over the sidewalk was broken and dead weeds protruded from a myriad of cracks in the sidewalk.. The front door was weather worn and faded and one of the windows on the side of the door was broken. After walking slowly up the sidewalk, glancing from side to side as she did, Lauren tried the front door and found it unlocked.

"Robin, would you mind if I went in alone for a bit?"

"Of course not, Lauren, but holler if you need me."

Once inside, Lauren looked around the single room that encompassed the entire bungalow. There was a kitchenette off to one side with a desk next to it and a cot in the corner with a small table beside it. Everything was covered in dust. When she looked up, she felt an eerie sense overtake her, seeing the rafter where her father must have hung himself. After walking over to the cot, she gasped then knelt beside it for she wasn't ready for what she saw next. Kneeling beside the small bed, sobbing, she gasped.

"Bofus." It was the teddy bear that her father had given her on her first birthday.

Robin, who had heard her sobs, was now standing at the front door. "Lauren, are you okay?"

Lauren turned toward her, tears now in her eyes.

"It's Bofus, my teddy bear. Daddy gave it to me when I was a year old. Bofus meant 'both of us', him and I." She clutched the teddy bear to her breasts and looked upward. All of a sudden she felt a warm tingling throughout her whole body and she started to shake, breathing deeply to catch her breath. She looked at Robin with eyes opened wide.

"My God, Robin, I just felt something pass through me. It was warm and gentle, Robin," she exclaimed. "It's daddy's spirit. I felt it. I think he must have waited for me before he was able to pass."

She stood, wiping the tears from her eyes and scanned the rest of the room and as she did, a cold breeze swirled from the still outside air and blew through the open door. The sudden rush of air caused the pages of an open book that was sitting on the small table to rustle. She saw that it was sitting next to a cross that was propped up against a plate that had a knife and fork beside it. Walking over to the table, she looked curiously at the book and to her surprise saw that it was a Bible. The page was open to the 23rd Psalm. She leaned over and began reading, 'The Lord is my Shepherd, I shall not want.' One line had been circled in pencil. She read it. 'Thou preparest a table in the presence of mine enemies'.

Picking up the bible she walked toward Robin. "Look Robin, my father is giving me a message." She showed the passage to Robin.

"My God, Lauren, what do you think he's telling you?"

"Look at the plate and silverware on the table. He is saying that his enemies were here, Robin, and he wasn't afraid to die." She tucked the Bible under her arm and added, "we better get back to town and see if we can find out if Arthur has been there."

As they drove down the main street of the town, Lauren glanced back and forth, then looked at Robin.

"There aren't all that many stores here, let's see if anyone has seen Arthur."

After visiting three stores without success, Robin looked across the main street and spotted the office of the local newspaper so they crossed the street. Upon entering, they were greeted by aging man sitting behind a desk.

"Hi, my name is Lauren St. John."

He stopped her in mid-sentence. "Hot dang, if it isn't Lauren Borden, I haven't seen you in a coon's age," the man said.

Lauren stared at the man for a moment with a perplexed look on her face then as though the clouds had cleared and something had hit her on the head she realized who it was.

"My Lord, you're Mr. Raft, aren't you?" Without waiting for an answer she turned to Robin. "Mr. Raft here was my eighth grade teacher." She went around his desk and put her arms around his neck. "It's so good to see you, how have you been?"

"As good as could be spected for an old codger. Didn't you turn out to be a hot toddy."

"Mr. Raft, as I recall, you always had an eye for the ladies, even the young ones," Lauren responded.

"Now don't go spreadin' no rumors 'bout me, but I guess when you was a senior in high school I did some lookin'., You was sure a good looker then an' still are," he said.

"Thanks, Mr. Raft."

Before she could continue he interrupted her.

"Guess you're here lookin' for that Arthah guy? You know he didn't look to be in very good condition. Had some lumps and scrapes and such on his head?"

Lauren looked at Robin.

"So he was here?" Lauren said, "yes, he's a good friend of mine and I think he may be in some sort of danger. When did he leave and do you know where he went?"

"He was here coupla hours ago. We talked for a bit. Woulda talked longah, but my wife butted in. Told him 'bout ya brothah."

Lauren looked at Robin then at the Mr. Raft, "My what?" She asked.

"Ya twin brothah, but don't go g'tting' all up in arms, it's just a rumah and the other part of the rumah accordin' to my wife is that the boy died at birth. So ya see, ain't nothing to be worried 'bout." Lauren was dumfounded, shaking her head in disbelief before he added, "Oh and by the way, I didn't tell the other guy nothin'."

Robin stepped forward leaning against his desk and asked, "What other guy?"

"Well, there was...." Robin interrupted him.

"Don't tell me, a slightly built man with sandy brown hair about 40 or so?"

"That's him, ma'am, and by the way I sent him, Artha that is, up to see the lady that owns the little grocery store on Dundee Road. She's the one that knows most bout this whole thing."

Robin took a pen and paper from her purse.

"How do we get there?"

After receiving directions, Lauren hugged Mr. Raft goodbye then joined Robin who was already in the driver's seat and ready to go.

"Step on it, Bennett, we've got a life to save."

A misty rain was still falling, making visibility difficult, and it was all Robin could do to keep the car in the middle of the road as they searched the countryside for the little store. Lauren was peering intently out of her side window when she suddenly spotted a small store off to the right side of the road.

"That must be it Robin, pull over."

Robin came to a stop near the gas pump and they got out of the car and headed for the store, trying as best they could to cover their heads from the rain.

Before getting to the store, Robin grabbed Lauren's arm stopping her.

"Lauren, look at that car sitting by the road that goes up that hill. Isn't it like the one that Arthur rented from the car rental place?"

"I think so," Lauren responded, "but let's worry about it when we get out of this rain."

By the time they got in the store they were both dripping wet and the old lady was still behind the counter reading her Bible.

"Guess ya bettah grab one of those towels ovah there and dry off."

She pointed to a coat rack that had several towels hanging from it.

"Thanks, I'm Lauren St. John," she said wiping her face, "and this is my friend Robin Bennett. We are here from Florida and are looking for a friend of ours. He's an elderly gentleman...."

The old lady stopped her in mid-sentence.

"I know who ya are. Guess it was only a matter of time fore ya came up here and I guess yer referrin' to Arthah? The old man, I mean." Lauren nodded with a surprised look on her face. "He was here bout an hour ago. We talked a bit then he left."

Lauren looked at Robin then the old lady.

"But there is a car parked over by that road that leads up the hill and it looks like the one he was driving? And how do you know about me?"

"Don't know nothin' 'bout no car. But I'd be mighty careful if you were thinking 'bout goin' up the hill," she answered, "and no need to talk bout how I know ya, just do."

"Why, what's up at the top of the hill?" Robin asked.

"Just an old log cabin," the old lady answered.

"You've been so kind, Robin said, "if I may ask one more favor." "Could we borrow the umbrella in the corner there? We'll bring it back."

The woman nodded her consent before answering.

"Probably somethin' ya should know 'bout the cabin and such." But before she could finish her sentence, both Robin and Lauren were out the door and on the way toward the other car.

Before heading up the hill, Lauren looked in the window of the car and recognized Arthur's overcoat sitting on the front seat.

As she turned toward the dirt road, she wiped her face dry then looked at Robin through the misting rain.

"Robin, it's Arthur's coat, he must be up on the hill. And look over there. There is another set of tire tracks. They lead around the back of the store, but let's not worry about that now; let's get up the hill."

Streamlets of rain cascaded down the hill as they huddled under the umbrella, slowly making their way up the steep incline. Already cold and wet, it was all they could do to keep the rain from distorting their vision. Robin stopped and looked at Lauren.

"Lauren, I can't walk in these shoes, I'm taking them off."

Balancing herself with one hand on Lauren's shoulder, Robin raised her skirt in order to bend her leg enough to slip off the first shoe, then lost her balance and fell on her side in the mud pulling Lauren down with her.

"God, Robin!" Lauren exclaimed trying to stand back up on the slippery surface.

"Sorry, Lauren, I can't. walk in these. I slipped."

"Yeah, but you took me down with you."

"I said sorry," Robin quipped, wiping the mud out of her eyes. "I was just trying to...," Robin slipped again grabbing hold of Lauren for support as she fell.

"Ugh." The impact made Lauren expelled what little air she had left in her lungs as she once again hit the ground, this time covering her other side in mud.

"Damn it, Robin!"

Robin looked at her sheepishly.

"Sorry, again. I couldn't see you because of the mud in my eyes."

After regaining their footing, now completely covered in mud and soaking wet, they made their way to the top of the hill.

Once there, Lauren stared at the ground before motioning toward Robin to look down.

"Look, two sets of footprints leading toward the cabin. The rain must have washed the footprints away on the hill, but the ground here is flat, so they are still here. Do you know what that means?"

"Of course," Robin responded, "Arthur and the other man have both been here or maybe still are." She glanced across the road, "but wait a second, look at that." She said, pointing toward the other side of the road.

"There is only one set of footprints leading away from the cabin and down the hill. One of them left, but the other may still be up here."

Robin reached in her purse, took the pistol out and handed it to Lauren as they moved slowly toward the cabin from the front. Robin stooped to pick up a loose branch that was lying on the ground and gripped it like a club, holding it in front of herself. Stepping carefully onto to the front porch, they could feel the boards give slightly under their weight and they could hear the creaking sound made by the rotting boards with each step they took. Now sheltered from the rain by the porch overhang, they were better able to see better focusing on the door in front of them.

Lauren stood on one side of the door and Robin the other purposely avoiding being in direct line of the closed door.

"Robin,." Lauren whispered, "the lock on the door is broke, stay to the side and use your stick to open it."

The rusty hinges gave off a high-pitched creaking sound as Robin slowly eased the faded wooden door open. Creeping toward the opening, she was able to peek inside, but saw nothing. Shaking her head and shrugging her shoulders, she let Lauren know there was nothing to see from her vantage point.

Lauren looked in from the opposite angle and saw nothing either. She held the pistol in front of her and whispered softly to Robin that she was going in. With one hand holding the pistol and other against the open door, she took a deep breath.

"Dear Lord, don't let Arthur be dead" and lunged in looking behind the door as she did.

"It's okay Robin, there's nothing in here." Under her breath she said, "thank you, Lord."

Robin followed her in and both of them turned completely around as their eyes searched the inside of the small cabin for any signs that Arthur might have been there.

As Lauren's eyes came to rest on the small table next to the only chair in the room she gasped.

"My Lord, Robin, look at the pen on the table. It has a monogram from our college on it. There's no doubt that Arthur has been here."

Robin came over to her and rested her hands on Lauren's shoulder.

"Best friend, you do know what this may mean don't you?"

"I don't even want to think about it," Lauren responded, "there are two sets of footprints coming up and only one going down and Arthur's rental is still parked there. If he had gone back down, he would have driven his car away. It doesn't have to mean that he is dead, Robin. It doesn't." Lauren began to sob, so Robin put her arms around her.

"Come on, Lauren. Now's the time to be strong. I'm going to search the grounds just outside the cabin."

Lauren quickly composed herself and grabbed Robin's hand.

"Wait, don't go out there alone, I'll go with you. There's nothing else in here."

Lauren held the umbrella as they huddled together and walked outside, making their way around the cabin.

The woods on the back side were very dense and they couldn't see much beyond the immediate area. Nothing seemed unusual. Nothing, that is, until Robin caught her ankle on a protruding branch. She looked down and saw what appeared to be blood in an area that was shielded from the rain. A number of branches near the blood appeared to have been snapped, as though someone may have fallen on them. She said nothing.

Lauren motioned to Robin to head back down the hill toward the rental car then put the pistol back in her purse. The trip down was much easier, and they both managed not to fall.

After arriving at the bottom of the hill, Lauren handed Robin the keys to their car.

"I'm going to see if I can get Arthur's belongings out of his rental. Why don't you return the umbrella to the old lady then start the car. Oh, see if you can get a couple of towels as well."

Lauren was relieved that the door to Arthur's rental was unlocked. She removed his overcoat and briefcase, noticing that the keys were still in the ignition. As she opened the door and put his items in the back seat of their rental, she heard a scream come from inside the store. Within seconds Robin came running out, tripped on the stairs and fell to her knees, all the time looking at Lauren.

"What happened, Robin?" Lauren said as she ran toward her, stooping to help her up.

Robin was gasping for breath and it appeared to Lauren that she was trying to talk, but couldn't. She was pointing toward the store.

"What's the matter, Robin?" Lauren asked as she reached to help her up.

Robin regained control of herself.

"She's dead," she gasped. "The old lady is dead. Her throat has been cut."

Lauren stood and quickly went inside the store. There behind the counter was the old lady, blood splattered and pooled all around her and her throat slit from ear to ear. Careful not to step in any of the blood, Lauren knelt beside her and lifted the old lady's hand feeling for a pulse but found none. She looked toward a small doorway with a curtain across it which appeared to go into the back of the store. She removed the pistol from her purse.

By this time Robin had reentered the store.

"Lauren, what are you doing?"

Lauren put a finger to her lips in a motion that told Robin to keep quiet.

"Be careful, he may be in there," Robin whispered.

Lauren walked to the door then eased the curtain open and pointed the gun in the entrance to the room, but there was no one there. It was a small room with a refrigerator, a sink and a small table and chair with a mirror in back of it.

Robin had followed her in and glanced over Lauren's shoulder soon noticing that there was a piece of paper taped to the mirror.

"What's that?" She pointed to the mirror.

Lauren removed the paper and read what was written on it.

"My God, Robin, it's a receipt from the gun range where Mandy and I took the course, and it has Mandy's name on it."

Robin leaned over her shoulder and looked at the receipt.

"What is that written on the bottom?"

"Good Lord, Robin. He wrote 'she's next' on the receipt. He's going to kill Mandy. We have to warn her, but I can't get a signal on my cell," she said, looking at the screen on her phone, "Let's use the phone in the store."

Walking quickly to the phone on the wall, Lauren picked it up and saw the cord hanging lose.

"He's cut the phone cord; we have to get back to Portersville. We can tell the police about this when we get there."

After leaving the store, Robin slid into the driver's seat and started the car. She leaned over, opened the passenger door and shouted, "Lauren, come on, let's go."

As she floored the accelerator and spun the wheels, gravel spewed against the store. Robin straightened the car out and quickly glanced at Lauren then back to the road.

"You know, Lauren, that if we tell the police about this, they are going to keep us here until they sort things out. Even if we aren't delayed, we'll never make the late afternoon flight that connects to Tampa through Boston; we may be able to get on the early evening one, it's a direct flight but it stops once. We have to get back to Tampa in time to stop him from killing Mandy. If we just keep going, we can be in Tampa in the late evening. It's your call."

Lauren put her head in her hands and sighed, then looked at Robin.

"We have to tell the police, but we can't afford to be detained. We have to get back to Tampa as soon as possible. On the other hand, leaving the scene of a crime, particularly in the case of murder, may be a crime in itself. Maybe if we get on the plane then call the police and explain the circumstances they'll understand and won't prosecute us. After all, it's not like we've committed a crime."

She thought for a moment then added, "No, they might have the police waiting for us at the airport. We'll call after we land."

"You're right, Lauren, but did it occur to you that this person, Cameo is only a short time ahead of us? Remember, he must have killed that old woman while we were up by the cabin, so even if he killed her right after we started up the hill, he is at best 45 minutes ahead of us and you know what that means?"

"No, Robin, what?"

"It means there is every chance that he may make the early flight in which case he'll be in Tampa a couple of hours ahead of us. But if he doesn't, he could be on the plane with us. "

Lauren didn't hesitate, responding, "We're going home, can't you drive any faster?"

After driving for about 20 minutes, Lauren looked at her cell phone.

"Robin, I've got three bars on the phone, I'm going to try and get through to Mandy." After dialing her number, she waited nervously as the phone rang for the sixth time. Finally, Mandy answered.

"Mandy, it's Lauren; you're in a great deal of danger. Robin and I are in Maine and Cameo has just murdered an old woman. He's coming after you. He killed her when we were here and left ahead of us. We think he may be able to get a flight that puts him in Tampa before us."

Mandy interrupted her asking nervously, "Why do you think he is coming after me now?"

Lauren cleared her throat.

"After he murdered the old woman, he left a copy of the receipt you must have gotten when we took the gun class." Mandy stopped her short.

"I knew someone was in my room, there were things left on the floor. It happened right after we met last time, but how do you know he's coming after me now?"

Lauren could hear her gasping for breath.

"Mandy, listen good. After I answer you, I am going to give you my husband's cell phone; you need to get a hold of him as soon as possible. Mandy this may terrify you, but I have to tell you. He wrote on the receipt, 'she's next' and taped it to a mirror where we were sure to find it." She could hear Mandy sobbing on the other end of the phone.

"Oh my God, Lauren, he's going to kill me. What am I going to do?"

"Mandy, settle down and get a pen."

Mandy continued sobbing. "Okay, Lauren, give me the number." As she relayed it, Lauren could hear her again gasping for breath.

"Oh, Lauren, please come back. Please help me. I don't want to die. I don't want to die."

"Mandy." She waited. "Mandy, listen to me. I will be back late this evening and will find you as soon as I can, be sure and keep your cell on. After I hang up, wait five minutes, then call my husband. I am going to call him right now and tell him what's going on and that he needs to help you."

She snapped her cell phone closed and then opened it again, dialing Brian's cell phone. After five rings, his recording came on. She left a message.

"Brian, it's Lauren. What I am about to tell you is a life and death situation. I don't have time to tell you everything, but you have to believe me when I say this is critical. There has been a murder up here of an old lady and we can't find Arthur and don't know if he is even alive. A woman named Mandy is going to call you. We think that the same person that killed the old lady is coming back on a plane and plans to kill Mandy. She has your number and will explain what is going on. Better yet, if you can call me back, I'll tell you everything first-hand. Please help her. She is terrified. The man is around 40, with sandy brown hair and on the slight side. That's all we know about him."

She left the same message at her home phone then called the main station number, leaving an urgent message for Brian to call her. As she closed her cell phone, she looked at Robin, who was shaking her head.

"What's that suppose to mean?"

Robin glanced at her then responded. "Why didn't you tell him about Damian, the professor in Chicago? Doesn't he fit the description perfectly?" She paused, waiting for Lauren's reply.

"Robin, I just can't believe it's him. I know the physical description fits him, but I just don't believe it's him. He was too sincere, and think about it. I've known him for over two years and all of these strange happenings only just started a month ago. How do you explain that?

"I guess I can't, Lauren. But come to think of it, how long have you been having those nightmares?"

CHAPTER TWENTY TWO

It was late afternoon and after listening to the message from Lauren, Brian figured that she and Robin would already be on a plane back to Tampa. He tried unsuccessfully to get a hold of Lauren, so he went to the station in order to make himself more accessible. Just as he entered his office, his cell phone rang so he closed the door and sat at his desk, then answered the call.

"This is Detective St. John, how can I help you?"

"Detective St. John, I don't know if Lauren called you yet, but my name is Mandy, and I am in a great deal of danger."

Brian could sense that she was deeply alarmed by the tone of her voice. He took a pen from his shirt pocket and a pad from his top drawer then answered.

"Yes she did Mandy, although I didn't talk to her. She left a message that you would be calling. Please try and remain calm and tell me where you are right now?"

"I'm in the motel room where I have been staying, but I'm sure that he knows where it is. I think he's broken in here before, and I know he's coming back for me." Her voice cracked and he could hear her begin to sob.

"Mandy, please get a hold of yourself and tell me where you are. I am going to come and get you and take you to a safe place, but first I need to know what is going on and what's the name of the motel?"

"It's a Best Western, near I-4, but I have a car. I can come to where ever you say. I don't want to wait here another moment. I'll tell you what I know, but then tell me where you want me to go and give me directions."

"Okay Mandy, please go ahead." Brian toyed with the idea of having her come to the station, as she started relating her story to him.

"I met your wife at the gun class we took together."

Brian stopped her in mid sentence.

"Gun class? What gun class?"

"Oh, didn't she tell you, we took one of those courses you have to take in order to carry a weapon legally."

"Go on." Brian said as he shook his head.

"Well anyway, we became friends and said we would call each other. I didn't actually call Lauren until I knew I had a problem. This man that I met in California, that's where I'm from, anyway he was very nice at first. Then, after a while he became violent. He beat me and raped me when I tried to break off our relationship. I feared for my life, so I set out for Florida to look up a family member when I met Lauren. He somehow found me and followed me here and learned that I had taken the course. One night, he called and told me that if I bought a gun, he would use it on me to kill me. When I met Lauren and her friend Robin...."

" You know Robin?" Brian said, interrupting her.

"Yes," she replied, "the three of us had breakfast one day and exchanged stories. You know, how Robin was being stalked by someone in California and how Lauren had all these strange things happen to her and that they were both worried for their safety. When we put it all together, we figured that it might be the same person that has been stalking all of us. I knew that Lauren was going to see her friend in Maine and all, and I pretty much stayed in my room most of the time waiting for her to get back. She told me that her friend, I think his name is Arthur, could help me. Then, when I got a call from her today, and she told me that Cameo was on the way here to kill me, that's when I called you."

"Cameo?" Brian asked. "Who's that?"

"Oh," she replied, "he's the one that is stalking me and probably Robin and maybe even Lauren."

After she finished he could hear her sobbing openly.

"Mandy, try to get hold of yourself. I have an idea. I don't think it would be a good idea for you to come to the station. I think it makes more sense to meet you somewhere more secluded where the stalker won't be able to find you."

"Wouldn't it be safer at the station Brian?" she asked.

"Just trust me. I want you to come to where I tell you." He replied.

"Anywhere," she said, "just tell me how to get there, and I'll be on my way." She waited for his response.

"I was thinking that when Lauren and Robin get back, they'll immediately come home. I mean to where we live. It might be the safest place I can bring you to, and then we can try and sort out just what's going on. I have to finish up here, so let's say in a couple of hours. Do you know where Carrollwood is?"

"No, but I know where the street called Dale Mabry is. That's how I went when I met Lauren and had the gun class." She had stopped sobbing.

"Good," Brian replied, "just go straight north on Dale Mabry until you come to a street called Lake Carroll. Turn right and go...." He directed her to the condo. "When you get there, if I'm not there yet, park your car on the side of the road just outside the complex. You can't get in without a remote gate opener. Many of the people in our building are on vacation and the street is a dead end with only three other houses on it, so you shouldn't be bothered by anyone if you have to wait. And Mandy, be sure you aren't followed."

卍 卍 卍 卍 卍 卍 卍 卍 卍 卍 卍 卍

Lauren grabbed Arthur's briefcase and overcoat, leaving the keys in their rental and shouted at Robin who was several steps behind her.

"Leave the luggage or we'll never make the flight. We can call the rental company and tell them to pick up our bags."

Robin closed the distance and looked at Lauren.

"Hey, if we can climb that hill in heels while it's raining, we can make that plane. Do you think they'll let us on the plane looking like this?"

Lauren chuckled and responded.

"You look like a mud pie. It seems like everyone is staring at us. Robin look, the mud is starting to fall off me."

As they passed the next to last ticket counter a ticket agent who saw them coming held out a paper towel which Lauren grabbed wiping her face off before handing it to Robin who screamed at the airline attendant as she saw the door closing on the ramp to their plane.

"Wait, we're here. Thank you so much for waiting." She said, looking back at the trail of mud behind her.

Once on the plane, both women went to the lavatory to clean up before returning to their seats. Lauren opened Arthur's briefcase and took out the contents, looking at everything before turning to Robin.

"There's nothing here that tells me anything about what's going on. It's all about the conference and such."

"What about the overcoat is there anything in it?"

338

Robin asked.

Lauren checked the outside pockets and found nothing, then felt something in the inside pocket.

"Look Robin, there's an envelope in here." Opening the envelope, she took out several pieces of paper and stared at them for a moment. Robin peeked over her shoulder.

"What is it?"

Lauren's mouth dropped open and her eyes widened when she took out the papers, then turned and looked at Robin.

"My God," she said, "it's my mother's diary. I can't believe it. How do you suppose Arthur got a hold of it?" Then as she glanced at each page, she again looked at Robin, "Look, it's my diary. One that mother wrote for me."

Robin tugged slightly on Lauren's arm and said, "Put it in the middle so we can both read it."

For the next several minutes both women read the diary, often stopping to look at the other in amazement.

****

DIARY OF ANGELA BORDON

Date: August 9, 1962 - I have been married to Joseph but a month and the pressure from my Father to give him a grandson is already intense. I resist him, but he relents. Joseph says it should be up to us, we have a life of our own, but all my life I have put father first. It is a curse, this thing that I have inherited.

Date: August 29, 1962 -My Father has again told me that I must bring him a grandson. The family line must go on in name. I feel I cannot deny his wishes, but somehow I must, for the consequences are dire. Church is our lives and I must ask for guidance from God for it is not within my power.

Date: September 7, 1962 - All my life my mother has told me that I cannot bear a son. That it would be a tragedy. My reverend has now told me the same. He has seen it and he knows, yet my father wants me to bear the son he never had. Joseph says he will do whatever I want, but is this what I want? I fear not.

Date: September 16, 1962 - It is my 18th birthday and we begin trying to conceive a child. It is very difficult living under my father's roof and trying to conceive a child. I feel he is listening, it is very difficult. Had my father not pushed me into marrying at such a young age, I could have perhaps gone on to college. As it is, I never saw my high school graduation. It wasn't as important as starting a family according to Father.

Date: September 20, 1962 - We continue trying and for some strange reason, I feel that this is the night. My father has been quiet of late; he must know we are trying.

Date: October 18, 1962 - My Father has a look of contentment. He knows. Now the dreadful thought comes into my mind, what if I have a son, what will the consequences be? I love my husband and couldn't bear to be the cause of his demise.

Date: October 31, 1962 - I visited the church today. The reverent has again counseled me about the dangers of having a son. He has seen the curse before and knows that it is in my blood, but only God controls what my baby will be.

Date: November 1, 1962 - I now have the knowledge that I will bear a child, the doctor has confirmed it. I prayed tonight that it will be a girl and that I won't be faced with the decision that I fear to make.

Date: December 24, 1962 - It is Christmas Eve and we have all gathered at the church. People are in good spirit's, but I am reminded of the child in my body. I fear a bit more each day that I will be faced with the choice of husband or Father. I love Joseph, it is not fair to him, and I must make the right choice.

Date: February 12, 1963 - Mother knit's clothes for the baby. They are of the color that a girl would wear. It riles my Father who has demanded that she make clothing for a boy. He says that his daughter will not fail him, that she will give birth to a boy. It is as though he will be the one raising it or that he conceived it. He doesn't even talk to Joseph about what he would like. He has made his mind up.

Date: March 30, 1963 - Father keeps Joseph working 14 hours a day. When he comes home, he is too tired to spend time with me. If only I had the courage to leave. Joseph has told me that we could make it on our own, but I fear that I would not be able to stand the guilt I would have. Leaving home is not an option.

Date: April 23, 1963 - Mother has been crying most of the day. I walked to the church with her so she could talk with the reverend. We all three agreed, that if the baby is a boy, we must do what needs to be done. The baby is due in about two months and I feel like my stomach is huge, bigger than I thought it would be.

Date: May 15, 1963 - The baby is so big now, I feel it will be born early, so it will no doubt be born under the sign of Gemini like both mother and I. I pray now every morning and evening that it will be a girl. If only I could tell. Joseph is very nervous of late, but Father is calm. He seems very confident that he will have his grandson. Both mother and the reverend have told him of the dangers and he scoffs at them. He calls the reverend a superstitious fool. Father is a deeply religious man, but doesn't believe in the curse.

Date: June 20, 1963 - I feel like the baby is about to come. Father is gone off to buy equipment, but Joseph can drive the truck. He will take me to the home. The reverend has arranged for the baby to be born in the home of a midwife. He says that I will receive better care there than in the hospital. The pain increases and is more often now. I must go to call Joseph, I am ready.

Date: June 21, 1963 - I am writing this while the baby is being bathed. She is beautiful, only five pounds ten ounces with red hair and healthy. She was born two minutes after midnight on the 21st of June. I was so relived when the nurse handed me a little girl. Father will be very upset when he finds out, but at least I won't be faced with the choice. I feel relieved for the moment.

Date: June 24, 1963 - I am home now. Father has seen the baby, but won't hold her. He hasn't spoken to me since I got home. I cry myself to sleep, for I have failed my father, but spared my husband. The curse of Oedipus, which lives in my blood will have to wait for now. It has claimed three fathers in our family's history, but not this time. I, like my mother before me, have been burdened by the curse, and so my son would have been born to kill his father, Joseph, just as Oedipus slew his father. It is in the blood and cannot be removed. This I have been shown through the many tragedies in our family. My church has confirmed this fact.

In honor of bearing my first child, I shall give her what my mother gave me and her mother gave to her. The small broach that is the only family heirloom will be hers. It carries with it, the tradition of the family going back generations. She will wear it with pride. She will be the surviving member and will carry on the tradition.

This is the end of this diary; I shall begin another and call it the book of Lauren. She will inherit my memories so that she can pass them on to the next generation just as Mother wanted.

****

"MY DIARY" THE BOOK OF LAUREN

Date: July 24, 1963 - The baby is healthy and will be christened soon, with the name Lauren Ashley. Mother seems to be very nervous lately. She tries to keep away from father as much as she can. I don't understand this and she won't tell me what is wrong. Mother is very sick. The doctor says he can't find anything wrong with her, but that if she doesn't come out of her depression, I feel that she might kill herself. Father shows no mercy. He is very critical of her. He tells her that she isn't taking care of his house the way she should, that it is her duty

Date: August 8, F963 - Mother has gotten worse. She visit's the reverend most every day, I guess to help her cope with whatever is wrong. She won't tell Father what is wrong either, so he has stopped talking to her. It is a very sad house we live in. My only joy is Joseph and the baby. He is secretly looking to find another job. If Father knew, he would be furious and he would probably make us leave. I don't know where we would go.

Date: September 20, 1963 - It is one year from the time when Lauren was conceived and the day of christening. Father won't go, he is still very bitter that I didn't have a son. He blames me and everyone else. I have told him that I don't wish to have another baby for at least two years. He didn't care; he said I would only fail him again,

344

just as mother failed to give him a son. The reverend performed the christening and said things that I didn't understand. He asked that God forgive them, for they have sinned. He looked at mother. I could see tears on her cheek. She wouldn't look at me.

Date: November 23, 1963 - It is Thanksgiving and what once was a very happy day for all of us, was no different than the other days. Mother has gotten worse, but is doing a wife's duty to make sure the husband is taken care of. I try to take care of her, but it is hard with Joseph, Father and the baby. I feel sometimes that my life isn't worth living, but I must go on.

Date: January 5, 1964 - They are taking mother to a hospital for severe depression. The Church is paying for it, or we couldn't afford to send her. The reverend has been sent to another church in another part of the state. They wouldn't tell us where. I guess the hospital is the best thing; there she will have real nurses to look after her. I still don't know what has happened to her. Father just reads his bible at night. He doesn't talk to Joseph or me. The baby is healthy and has a full head of red hair. She is the only thing that keeps me going.

Date: February 20, 1964 - We received word that mother has hung herself in the bathroom of her room at the hospital. Joseph and I have both been weeping for hours. Father says that mother has sinned, that it is a sin to take your own life. He shows no remorse and still sit's reading his bible. For the first time in my life, I don't like my father. He is an evil man with no feeling for anyone.

Date: April 15, 1964 - Joseph has found a new job and we have moved to a small house that we are renting from the church. Our spirit's have improved a lot, but I still have trouble coping. I am now finding it very difficult to show my emotion to Joseph. He has done nothing wrong, but I feel like I will never be close to any man again. Father has done this to me.

Date: May 23, 1964 - I feel incomplete, not knowing why mother took her life. I have tried to find out where the reverend went, but the church won't tell me. They say he has retired and they don't know where he is either.

Date: June 17, 1964 - I will never rest until I find out why mother took her life. Father won't talk to either of us any more, no one at the church knows anything and I now have no other link left to my mother. Perhaps I will never know. Perhaps something happened at the home where Lauren was born, but who is left to tell me, even the midwife has left the area with no trace.

ೞೞೞೞೞೞೞೞೞೞೞೞ

As Lauren finished reading both the diaries and the note from Arthur, she lowered her head and several tears trickled down her face. She turned and looked at Robin.

"My lord Robin, how sad. I feel like I have done something to cause all these people all these problems. No wonder my father committed suicide."

Robin took a firm grasp of her arm and looked straight in her eye.

"Hold on lady, you were an innocent baby and had nothing to do with any of this. These people were living in the dark ages thinking that there was a curse and all and anyway….." Lauren stopped her in mid sentence.

"Robin, that's what all this is about."

Robin let go of her arm and looked at her with a frown on her face.

"What ever do you mean?"

She held the diaries up shaking them.

"This confirms to me that I did have a twin brother just like Arthur wrote in his journal and just like my old teacher said, only he's alive and he's Cameo. Why else would my grandmother and minister both commit suicide? In order to avoid the curse they thought they were under, they sent my brother off to be raised by someone else, so he wouldn't kill my father. Then the guilt was too much and they both hung themselves. He must have found out about it, maybe from the old lady in the store, maybe she raised him, maybe that's why Arthur was headed to the store in the first place. Anyway, he probably blames me for what happened to him and wants to kill me."

Robin looked at her curiously.

"That doesn't explain why he went after me? And what about Mandy? And why did he wait so long to do all this?"

"You're my best friend Robin. If he found me, he surely could find out about you. As for Mandy, I'm not sure, but maybe he thought we were taking that class together and were better friends than we really are. Maybe he's trying to torture me by threatening my friends. Think about it. He could easily have killed me when he was in the condo or any time for that matter. He could have killed you when you let him take those pictures, he could have killed Mandy when he knew her in California. He's playing a game of cat and mouse extending the agony of the victims to savor the final kill."

Robin sat back in her seat and took a deep breath.

"Lauren, I once read a book about twins. Some people maintain that they have some sort of bond that other siblings don't have. You know that allows them to communicate with each other, non-verbally?"

Lauren sat upright and cocked her head to one side as though in thought.

"Robin, do you realize what you just said?"

"It was just a book Lauren." Lauren put her hand on Robin's hand.

"What about all the things that have been happening to me? All the weird things may be because Cameo is controlling me with some sort of thought control. Remember when I thought I had another dream, but you said I must have been outside? Remember in the bar in Boston and the person that no one else saw? The way I dressed to go to Greg's apartment? The guy on the plane that I never noticed and the way the luggage flew out of the chute? These are all things that I had no control over. Do you suppose that he has some sort of ability to control my mind?"

After the third glass of wine, they were both able to relax and even dozed off as the plane took off again after the stopping in Cincinnati, Ohio for 45 minutes.

CHAPTER TWENTY THREE

It was evening as Brian approached the entrance to the condo, and he could see another car sitting off to the side on the grass. Slowing down, he pressed the button down for the passenger side window and peered into the open window of the other car as he stopped.

"Are you Mandy?" he asked.

"Yes, are you Detective St. John?" Mandy awaited his answer.

"Yes Mandy. Follow me in after I open the gate." As he did, he pointed out the window toward a visitors section, where Mandy parked, got out and walked toward him.

When she extended her hand, Brian could feel she was shaking so he put his arm around her.

"You're safe now. We'll go inside and have a drink to steady your nerves while we wait for Lauren and Robin to get home. You can tell me all about yourself and what's going on."

As they entered the foyer, he could see her well for the first time and could she had been crying.

"Lauren didn't tell me anything about you." He said.

She was dressed in a short leather skirt and high heels with a white silk pullover blouse that covered her neck. Her long straight hair swung from one side to the other as she walked and the necklace she was wearing sat down between her breasts. Brian couldn't help but notice the necklace which brought his attention to her breasts which were rising and falling with each deep breath she took. After disarming the alarm on the condo door, they went in and he motioned for her to sit on the couch.

"White wine, okay? Lauren always keeps some on hand."

She nodded her head and crossed her legs then smiled at him nervously. The combination of the forced smile and her seeming innocence's gave Brian the feeling that she was totally vulnerable and completely relying on him for her safety. He thought to himself that he must protect this poor woman at all cost. She was depending on him for her very life.

As she took a sip of wine, he watched her soft lips on the crystal glass and wondered to himself what terrible things she must have been put through by this demented maniac that was stalking her.

"Doesn't that blouse make your neck hot? He asked, "I mean, it's quite warm in here?"

She leaned forward and propped her elbow on her knee then supported her chin in her hand before answering.

"He gave me scars when he raped me, and I don't want anyone to see them."

"Oh, I'm sorry Mandy. I didn't mean to pry. I was just, well," he stammered, "I just want you to know that there is nothing to worry about, I'll take care of you." He could see her face become flush; she bowed her head.

"Thank you so much. You don't know what it means to me to be here with you and to soon see Lauren again. I think my life is about to be," she stopped in mid sentence, "anyway, thank you." She rose up off the couch and walked toward Brian, stopping but a few feet from him, then looking up at him she asked, "Can you tell me what you know about what is going on here? I guess I don't know as much as everyone else."

Brian felt a nervous surge, being here with this woman alone and so close. He took her hand and guided her back to the couch. Sitting next to her, he leaned back and began talking.

"At first I couldn't figure what if anything was going on with my wife. We haven't had the best relationship over the past couple of years. I guess I started to have some concerns when she tried to get in touch with Robin who is her best friend and couldn't reach her. So after trying for several days, I finally contacted a friend of mine in a police department near where Robin lives and asked him to look in on her. He didn't find anything wrong, but I had this sort of hunch." She stopped him.

"Like a gnawing in the pit of your stomach?"

"Yes," he said, "I guess you could call it that. Anyway, I decided to go to California to see what I could find out. I found out more than I had bargained for. I had the key to Robin's place that Lauren kept, so the other cop and I went in and looked around. There was almost nothing out of place, but I found an envelope with some very revealing pictures in it. It started us wondering, so the other cop and I have been doing a little investigating on our own."

While he felt extremely sorry for Mandy, he was reluctant to tell her all he knew at this point.

"Anyway, what really got me going was that my associate in San Jose got a call recently from the man that we think is the killer. He told us about killing a woman about Lauren's age in Chicago. I delved deeper into the situation and found that there has been a series of murders over the last 20 years. None of which have been solved." He could see Mandy's face becoming flush and several tears trickled down her cheek. She looked at him.

"I guess it's the same man that's after me isn't it?"

"It could very well be Mandy, but don't worry, you are safe here with me. Anyway, I put together a string of clues and came to the conclusion that we had a serial killer on our hands."

"What were the clues?" she asked as she put her hand on Brian's hand. The softness of her touch sent a warm chill through him.

"Well," he responded, "I looked at things that were either left at the scene of the crime or written somewhere at the crime scene and began putting them together. The first was at Robin's home where the word 'Electra' was written on her bathroom mirror in lipstick."

"That's odd." She said.

"At first, we thought that the reference was made to Robin," he said, "but I ultimately figured out that it was for Lauren. I looked at the files of the murders in Florida; there were three of them and I found that in one case, the killer left a small piece of nylon cord next to the victims naval that had been cut out." Mandy put her hand to her mouth to muffle a loud gasp.

"Oh my lord, how horrible."

Brian continued.

"In another case, the killer left a piece of paper commonly used by children in the early years of school. On it was the alphabet written in crayon. What was different about it was that at the end the letter Y was repeated. It formed an XYY."

"I don't understand." She said.

Brian squeezed her hand then went on.

"You will. In the case in Chicago only days ago, the word Vodu was written on the driver's side of the vehicle in blood."

Mandy leaned closer to Brian and again put her other hand on his before asking, "What does all this mean?"

He could smell the delicate aroma of her perfume

and sensed that she was feeding off his strength, becoming emotionally stronger with each word he spoke.

I'll tell you what it means Mandy, but first I have to ask you an important question."

"Ask me anything Brian." She said in a somewhat sensuous manner. This was the first time she had called him by his first name and his face became flushed.

"Mandy, where were you born?"

"In Maine. Is that important?" she questioned.

ꙴꙴꙴꙴꙴꙴꙴꙴꙴꙴꙴꙴꙴꙴ

When the plane came to a halt at the gate Lauren and Robin both hurried to the front of the plane and were the first ones off. As they exited the tram from the gate area to the main terminal Robin took the lead.

"Forget the car it will take too long to find it. Let's take a cab."

Once inside the cab, Lauren dialed Brian's cell phone but got no answer. She then dialed her home number and to her surprise, Mandy answered.

"Mandy? Are you okay? Is Brian there with you?"

"Lauren, I'm so glad it's you. I'm okay right now, but Brian heard a noise outside and went to see what it was. Please hurry and oh, is Robin okay?"

"Yes Mandy, we're both fine. We'll be there in about 25 minutes." With that, Lauren prodded the cab driver, "There's an extra 50 bucks in it for you if you can get us to Carrollwood in 20 minutes."

The cab sped off, getting on the Veterans Toll Road, eventually getting off at the Ehrlich exit. At 20 minutes on the dot, the cab pulled up to the big iron gate in front of the condo. Lauren handed the driver $75 and reached in her purse for the gate opener. "Damn it Robin, I must have left the gate opener in the condo, we'll have to climb the wall."

Robin stood staring up at the wall then looked at Lauren.

"Just how the hell do you propose getting up there. That wall is at least eight feet high." She threw her hands in the air then turned as she heard the cab driver speak.

"Lady, for another 20 bucks, I'll back the cab up to the wall and you can get on top then over."

Lauren handed him a 20 dollar bill then motioned him to back the cab up to the wall sideways so they could get on the roof.

As Robin scaled the cab, Lauren again called her home number and Mandy answered again. She could hear Mandy sobbing.

"Mandy, are you okay. What's happening?"

Mandy answered.

"I think Brian is hurt, the man just hit him in the head with a wine bottle, please hurry. I'm hiding out on the patio." The phone went dead and by now both Robin and Lauren had gotten to the top of the wall.

Lauren hung on to a post at the back of a carport then looked at Robin.

"Grab the other pole on the back of the carport and see if you can ease yourself down." Robin took off her shoes and grabbed the post.

"Look Lauren, there's a grassy area in back of the carport. To hell with it, I'm jumping." After hearing a loud thump and Robin moaning, Lauren followed.

"Lauren, I think I sprained my ankle." Lauren took her hand.

"Here, hold on to me. We'll help each other." As they made their way up the steps of the condo to the second floor Lauren instinctively reached in her purse for the pistol before remembering that they couldn't bring it on the plane, so they had left it in their rental car.

Stopping briefly at the front door to the condo to catch their breath Lauren spoke.

"When we go inside, get a knife from the kitchen."

They climbed the stairs to the second floor and Lauren eased the door open which to her surprise was not locked. She saw that the lights had been turned off then stepped slowly in the door followed closely by Robin.

"Over there on the counter, get me one too." Lauren said in a whisper.

Beads of sweat dripped from their faces and they could each hear the other breathing as they started toward the hall. Just as they did, they heard a sobbing sound coming from the balcony. Lauren looked at Robin then walked over and peeked out the open door. She looked down and saw Mandy cowering in the corner her hands covering her head. Lauren reached down, took one of her hands and guided her into a standing position. As she did, Mandy embraced her then whispered to her while gasping for breath.

"I can't be sure but I think he's in the bedroom, and I think Brian is in there too. I don't know how badly Brian is hurt. Please help me. I am terrified."

Lauren took hold of Mandy's shoulders, looked straight in her eye and in a very soft yet confident voice spoke to her.

"If it's the last thing I do on earth Mandy. I am going to stop him. This will be the end of one of us. Please be strong, I need all the help I can get."

Robin stepped ahead of Lauren, but before she could go down the hall Lauren grabbed her arm and pulled her back.

"No Robin, I am going to do this. You wait here and protect Mandy and yourself. Whatever you do, if he tries to get out of here, stop him. Stab him if you have to, but don't let him get away."

Lauren edged her way down the dark hall with her back to the far wall, the knife held in her right hand pointed upward and toward the bedroom door. Not knowing if Cameo had gone into the den or guest bedroom, she swung her head from side to side watching each of the other doors until she was finally in front of the door to the master bedroom. Before entering, she looked back down the hall and saw Robin standing at the far end near the family room with her knife held in front of her. Mandy stood in a half crouch behind Robin.

As Lauren entered the darkened bedroom she let out a scream and as she did Robin turned to Mandy.

"Let's go, she needs…," but before she could get the last word out, Mandy's fist came crashing against her jaw, knocking her back into the kitchen and against the cabinets. The rack of knives and several dishes tumbled down on her, and Robin lost consciousness.

Lauren stooped at Brian's side as he lay on the floor, blood seeping from a gash on his temple. Barely able to speak, he raised his hand and pointed toward the door. Lauren turned and saw Mandy standing at the open door with a hideous look on her face and a knife in her right hand. In one swift motion, she grabbed the hair on her head and pulled a wig off throwing it in Lauren's face all the time laughing.

"Now my sister, my twin sister," she paused. "It's time for payback." As Mandy spoke, she ripped off the blouse she was wearing. "Look my sister, an Adams Apple."

"Damien?" she exclaimed. Lauren felt her world come crashing down around her, as her mind raced with images of the Shakespeare conference, dinner with him, the emails they exchanged and Robin's comment about the possibility of Damien being Cameo. The thoughts dizzied her and her body wretched in indescribable emotion before she regained her composure. "My God I thought you were my friend. All that time in Chicago, you knew even then? How could I not see that it was you?"

"We see what we want to see or in your case what I wanted you to see," Damien replied. "Yes Electra, I'm your twin brother, Damien, sent away at birth to be raised in squalor by strangers that hated me and all because of you and that curse. But I sense that you already know about that, after all you talked to the old woman and read the diary. Isn't it amazing what colored contact lenses, a wig and some makeup will do? But now it's my turn. You will die just as all the rest of them died, and I will place this cameo on your heart." He held the broach that Lauren's mother had given her in his free hand.

"Where did you get that broach?" she cried.

When mother suspected that she was going to have twins, she had another made. I guess she thought you would have a sister. In all your Sherlock Holmesing, didn't it ever occur to you that your broach was a Cameo and that a Cameo is also a brief visit from another person? I visited your life for One Brief Shinning Moment; when we were born. Then I left, never able to avenge your sins until now. I left the police all those clues and yet not one of them, not even the feds could figure out who I was. Not until that man on the floor put it all together, but how could he tell that sweet innocent little Mandy was really a notorious serial killer. I actually think he was infatuated with me.

Doesn't that beat all?"

Lauren started to get up but he pushed her back down. She had laid the knife she was holding by Brian's side and he had rolled over slightly covering it.

"Why did you kill all those innocent women? They had nothing to do with this." As she spoke, she slid her hand under Brian's side until her finger tips touched the handle of the knife.

Still grinning, Damien stood in front of her, his chest protruding in what Lauren thought was surely his ultimate glory. He couldn't resist telling her about his 20 year siege.

"I thought we should catch up, sister mine. I know what you have been doing since I found you, so it's only fair that you know what I have been up to. I started in my early 20s when I found out about you and our grandmother. I was angry all my life and didn't know why until I found out about how they had protected you with not a concern for me. It set off an explosion in my brain. I wanted to kill you, but couldn't find you, so I did the next best thing. All the women I killed were about your age when I killed them; all of them were in some way connected to Maine. You know our beloved birthplace. I tried to make them as close to you as I could, some were even teachers. I searched for you for a very long time and now my search is finally over."

"But if you knew about me two years ago in Chicago, why did you wait until now?" she asked, her voice trembling.

"I needed time to ruin your life first. I tried, but in vain it would appear, to wreck your marriage and drive you to the brink of insanity, just as I was by the misfits that raised me," he responded. "And how long have you been having those terrible nightmares? Two years, isn't it?

Besides, I wanted to wallow in your misery for awhile before my final moment, but never mind that now." She interrupted him.

"Each time you killed a woman; you were killing a symbol of me, weren't you?"

"That's right my precious twin, and I put their bodies in places that reeked of symbolism. First, a nursing home for where we were born, then a church in memory of our church going mother, who didn't hesitate to give me up and for the wonderful way the reverend acted the willing accomplice. Finally, near a log cabin for where that bastard reverend lived, and where I killed him. They thought he hung himself. And weren't those clues I left bizarre?"

"I don't know about any clues?" She sobbed as she spoke feeling like this was all too surreal.

"You don't know, but your husband does. He's a pretty smart guy." Walking in a circle around them he kept the knife against her head the whole time then when he again faced her he brought the tip firmly down her cheek causing blood to start dripping from a small cut. Lauren didn't cringe staring intensely into his eyes.

"First clue was the name I wrote on Robin's mirror in lipstick, Electra. It was for you my sister who devoutly adored her father while I had an alcoholic druggy of a father figure to raise me. But then you didn't know about the lipstick and neither did Robin. I cleaned it off after your husband and the other cop paid her a visit."

Lauren's mouth opened wide as she turned and stared at Brian.

"You went out there?" He didn't answer.

"Pay attention," he said guiding her face back toward him with the blade of the knife pressing against her skin. "I guess Robin told you about the pictures I took? I sent her a copy, but then she didn't see the one with her head cut off." Lauren gasped.

"But he did," Damien said, pointing to Brian. "I'll bet that sent a jolt through his brain. Pretty good looker your friend, I'm going to kill her when I finish with you. Then there was the small piece of nylon cord I left on the stomach of one of my victims. Brian figured out that it was for the umbilical cord and he was right, the cord that we both gave up at birth. That's why I cut her naval out."

Lauren felt a rush of nausea overtake her as he continued talking.

"Then there was the alphabet. I think the cops thought the alphabet killer was back, but I guess Brian figured out that the extra Y at the end spelled XYY. That's for the chromosome makeup of a super male; one predisposed to violence and he hit on the nature vs. nurture thing. I was born with the nature and my foster father took care of the nurturing. He beat me relentlessly. And how about Mandy's last name? Romulus, like in the twins, Romulus and Remus. And the word Pollux like in the Gemini twins that I wrote on the forehead of one of my victims. I guess the Gemini thing was a bit too subtle for your brain. You're a Cancer, but only by two minutes. I was born before you by three minutes and that makes me a Gemini."

Lauren watched him intently feeling the cool steel of the blade against the oozing of hot blood on her face.

"All that smart police work and he still didn't have a clue as to who I was. He even asked me, excuse me, asked Mandy, why I had a turtle neck on. Remember, you even wondered. Then there was my necklace with the recessed etching, the opposite of the cameo. There were plenty of clues that reeked of symbolism and while I was interrupted during the last one in Chicago and had to leave the victim in her car, it was nevertheless my, what do you call it? Oh yes, My Swann Song...." Lauren interrupted him.

"You killed that old lady didn't you? Where was the symbolism there?"

"Wasn't any, she just got in the way. That was the bitch that raised me until I left over twenty years ago. She and her husband don't count. I also tried to off that fortune teller you went to see, but she somehow got away. I think she sensed I was coming after her. I take no credit for the dove and the raven; I think Satan was on my side on that one."

"You could only know all of this if you were somehow in control of my mind," Lauren said, stalling for time as she pushed her hand further under Brian's body trying desperately to fully grasp the handle of the knife.

"Correct little sister. I guess I was born with this gift and when I realized what I could do with it, I went to a special school to develop it further. And you know what they say about us twins having a special ability for non-verbal communications. How do you think I was able to create all those dreams you had?"

"They weren't dreams were they?" Lauren said, her breathing intensifying.

"Seemed real didn't they?" he said, "well it doesn't really matter now. Oh by the way, I thought you were really going to ball that idiot Federal guy in his apartment. Came close didn't you? And you felt so special."

Lauren eyes immediately found Brian's, but his face showed no expression. She looked back at Damien, her body shaking, tears and blood now streaming down her cheeks and said in a trembling voice, "You killed Arthur didn't you?"

Damien edged closer to her and stood looking down then put the blade of his knife against the side of her neck.

"I didn't need to, but he did put up a valiant fight. I thought I killed him when I destroyed the brake line in his car, but he lived through that one. Then at the cabin, I cut him before he ran off into the woods in the rain. Looked pretty bad, bleeding all over himself. He never came back, and I didn't have time to go after him but in his condition, I doubt he ever will."

As he talked, he slid the blade of his knife back and forth across Lauren's face all the while still grinning.

"But back to my Swan Song," he said. "it took the cop a while longer to figure that one out and I had to help him a bit, but I wrote the word Vodu in the woman's blood on her car window, on the one I just killed in Chicago. I learned a lot about the religion while studying for a year in Haiti. Vodu is another spelling for Voodoo. Did you know my sister, my twin sister, that in the Voodoo religion it is believed that when twins are born they are so close that they only possess one soul? One spirit?" Lauren pushed the knife away.

"If that's true, that we share one spirit and one soul, then if you kill me, you will have no spirit and no soul."

The pupils in his eyes dilated and appeared to take on an almost iridescent red glow. His brow furrowed, his nostrils flared and the muscles in his entire body strained with the tension of his most extreme emotion when he began shaking as though convulsing. He let out a hideous laugh.

"Not so sister mine, for you have committed The Eighth Deadly Sin! You have abandoned your spirit and your soul. You abandoned it when you abandoned me at birth, so I must kill you so that you can never claim it back. Then I will finally own it all to myself and you will live in the bowels of purgatory forever."

Still holding the knife, he took off the rest of his cloths until he was completely naked then raised his hands into a praying position. Looking back down at her, he put the knife to her throat.

"Take off your cloths my sister, that you may go to your death as you came in to this world."

Moving the knife to her blouse with the flick of his wrist, he cut each button off, then grabbed it and in one single motion ripped it completely off.

"Please spare Brian and Robin," she began sobbing as she spoke, "they had nothing to do with this."

"How right you are my sister, but they have borne witness to your sins, so they must die as well. Now take your cloths off," he screamed pushing the knife harder against her neck until a new trickle of blood caromed down between her breasts.

Trembling and sobbing, she removed her hand from under Brian then took her bra off. She could see his eyes fixated on her bare breasts. She removed her skirt, shoes and pantyhose; sitting completely naked beside her husband.

"I don't sob for myself or for you, I sob for all those innocent people you killed and for my husband and best friend." He scoffed at her.

"Before you join the others, there is something you should know sweet twin of mine, and it is so fitting that you find this out at the time of your death."

Lauren looked at him through tear stained eyes, blood dripping from the several cuts on her face and neck.

"There is nothing else that you can say to me that would matter."

Damien clutched the cameo in his hand putting it against his heart and brought the dagger up over his head as to ready himself for the final act.

"How fitting it is that I could fulfill the curse of

Oedipus who killed his father." He laughed with a sinister snarl.

Lauren's head snapped back and her eyes glared at him with an intensity she had never felt before. She could feel a sudden fire burning in her brain, and an uncontrolled hatred overtook her.

"Yes, I killed our father," Damien said. "I killed your daddy. I hung him and watched him squirm until he died and now you will join him in hell,"

She shook her head to clear the blood and sweat from her face then stared straight into his eyes. Forcing her hand under Brian's back, she grasped the knife and as Damien's hand readied for the final downward stroke that would give his demented mind final vindication; she pulled the knife out from under Brian and came up into a kneeling position all in motion. In a split second and with a strength she had never known before, she swung the knife directly at her brother's hand; the hand that held the cameo against his heart. The point of the knife went through his hand and split the cameo dead center and the blade went deep into Damien's heart. Blood spewed onto Lauren's hand and arm and across her face in an almost ritualistic baptismal of the blood they shared. He stood erect for a fleeting moment gasping for breath; blood raining down from his chest before he fell to the floor in front of Lauren. The sound of Lauren dropping the knife and of Damien's body falling to the floor broke the almost reverent silence. She wiped the blood off her face in a final gesture that would free her from the man that had tormented her; the man that shared her soul.

Shaking and sobbing, she sat back down then reached over and lifted Brian's head. The blood from her hands and the blood from his head became one and as she kissed him on the forehead.

"I think it's time we had that talk."

He smiled and winced from the pain it caused as he spoke.

"Remember I once told you that one day I would say something romantic to you?"

A curious look crossed her face and she nodded.

"Well," he said, "you sure look good in red. How's that for romantic?"

Hearing a noise, she turned toward the door and saw Robin standing there holding a cloth on her mouth to stop her bleeding.

"Wow, that little Mandy sure packs a wallop," Robin said, holding her jaw, "why did she hit...my Lord, who is that and why are you naked?" Lauren stood and shook her head.

"Meet my twin brother Damien. Sorry he can't get up to greet you, he's dead, and Mandy went with him."

Robin looked at Lauren then Brian then Lauren again and spoke in a soft whisper so that Brian couldn't hear her.

"Is that Damien from Chicago?"

Lauren put her finger to her lips in a gesture that said hush, nodded her head and replied.

"I guess you told me so."

In all the confusion of the moment, they had forgotten about Arthur. The phone rang and Robin was standing next to the night table so she answered it. She immediately looked at Lauren as she listened, then spoke.

"Yes, this is the St. John residence," she paused, "yes we know Arthur Holmes." Lauren's face froze.

"Yes, I'll tell her." She hung the phone up and looked into Lauren's eyes.

"He's gonna be okay. He's back in the same hospital up in Maine, but he's gonna be okay."

Lauren bowed her head and wept; tears of happiness; tears that would relieve her of all the anguish of the past years. She finally understood the deep secret she had harbored in her subconscious all her life and was free of it forever.

ℼ ℼ ℼ ℼ ℼ ℼ ℼ ℼ ℼ ℼ ℼ ℼ

Several days had passed and the wounds and scars were still horrible memories of the bizarre events of the past months as Lauren and Brian hugged Robin goodbye at the terminal at TIA. Lauren had been able to talk with Arthur who had been released from the hospital and was on his way home.

That night, Lauren took out a bottle of the wine that Robin had brought her and poured Brian and herself a glass.

"Here's to the rest of our lives."

As Brian took her in his arms in an embrace that would give them final peace, the phone rang.

"Should we answer it, Lauren?"

"Yes, I told Robin to call when she got home to make sure she was okay." She could see by the display on the phone that it was Robin, so she swirled her long auburn hair to one side and removed the earring from her left ear. With the receiver to her ear she spoke.

"Robin, are you okay?"

"Hey roomie, as promised, I'm here and checking in. I'm better than okay."

"Robin I'll bet you're about ready to crash and sleep for a week." Lauren could hear the muffled sound of another voice in the background.

"Robin, are you okay?" She held her breath.

"Oh, I'm sorry," Robin replied, "we were just trying to figure our where to go for dinner."

"Huh?" Lauren said.

"Oh, Lauren will you put Brian on."

With a perplexed look on her face, she handed the phone to Brian, "she wants to talk to you."

He took the phone still looking at Lauren with an equally perplexed look on his face.

"Brian," Robin said, "just a second, there is someone here that wants to talk to you." He waited until a familiar voice came on.

"Hey amigo, que pasa? I can't thank you enough for the introduction and by the way, dinners on you."

"Manny, you…."

CLICK.

BIBLIOGRAPHY

Innes, Brian. *Profiles of a Criminal Mind.* 2003. Readers Digest Association: Amber Books Limited.

Ramsland, Katherine. *The Criminal Mind.* 2002. Writers Digest Books.

Stout, Martha. *The Sociopath Next Door.* 2005. Broadway Books.

"The Sins*." Seven Deadly Sins. http://*en.wikipedia.or/wiki/Seven_deadly_sins. Wikipedia The Free Encyclopedia. October 2007.

"Violent Criminal Apprehension Program." *Investigative Programs Critical Incident Response Group.* http://www.fbi.gov/hq/isd/cirg/ncavc.htm#vicap. Federal Bureau of Investigation. July 2007.

JOHN S. RICHARDSON

www.ingramcontent.com/pod-product-compliance
Lightning Source LLC
Chambersburg PA
CBHW061302170626
46817CB00001B/20